SERAPH ON THE SUWANEE

SERAPH ON THE SUWANEE

A NOVEL

ZORA NEALE HURSTON

WITH A NEW FOREWORD BY HAZEL V. CARBY
SERIES EDITOR: HENRY LOUIS GATES, JR.

HARPER**PERENNIAL** **MODERN**CLASSICS

NEW YORK • LONDON • TORONTO • SYDNEY • NEW DELHI • AUCKLAND

HARPER**PERENNIAL** ● MODERN**CLASSICS**

HarperCollins books may be purchased for educational, business, or sales promotional use. For information please write: Special Markets Department, HarperCollins Publishers, 10 East 53rd Street, New York, NY 10022.

FIRST HARPER PERENNIAL EDITION PUBLISHED 1991.
FIRST HARPER PERENNIAL MODERN CLASSICS EDITION PUBLISHED 2008.

Designed by Cassandra J. Pappas

The Library of Congress has catalogued the previous edition as follows:

Hurston, Zora Neale.
    Seraph on the Suwanee / by Zora Neale Hurston.—1st Harper
Perennial ed.
        p. cm.
    Reprint. Originally published : New York : Scribner's Sons, 1948.
Includes bibliographical references.

    ISBN 0-06-097359-5 (paper)
    I. Title.
PS3515.U789S47 1991   90-55503
813'.52—dc20

ISBN 978-0-06-165111-3 (pbk.)

08 09 10 11 12   RRD   10 9 8 7 6 5 4 3 2 1

To
Marjorie Kinnan Rawlings
and
Mrs. Spessard L. Holland
With Loving Admiration

CHAPTER 1

S awley, the town, is in west Florida, on the famous Suwanee River. It is flanked on the south by the curving course of the river which Stephen Foster made famous without ever having looked upon its waters, running swift and deep through the primitive forests, and reddened by the chemicals leeched out of drinking roots. On the north, the town is flanked by cultivated fields planted to corn, cane potatoes, tobacco and small patches of cotton.

However, few of these fields were intensively cultivated. For the most part they were scratchy plantings, the people being mostly occupied in the production of turpentine and lumber. The life of Sawley streamed out from the sawmill and the "teppentime 'still." Then too, there was ignorance and poverty, and the ever-present hookworm. The farms and the scanty flowers in front yards and in tin cans and buckets looked like the people. Trees and plants always look like the people they live with, somehow.

This was in the first decade of the new century, when the automobile was known as the horseless carriage, and had not exerted its tremendous influence on the roads of the nation. There was then no U.S. 90, the legendary Old Spanish Trail, stretching straight broad concrete from Jacksonville on the Atlantic to San Diego on the Pacific. There was the sandy pike,

1

deeply rutted by wagon wheels over which the folks of Sawley hauled their tobacco to market at Live Oak; or fresh-killed hogmeat, corn and peanuts to Madison or Monticello on the west. Few ever dreamed of venturing any farther east nor west.

Few were concerned with the past. They had heard that the stubbornly resisting Indians had been there where they now lived, but they were dead and gone. Osceola, Miccanope, Billy Bow-Legs were nothing more than names that had even lost their bitter flavor. The conquering Spaniards had done their murdering, robbing, and raping and had long ago withdrawn from the Floridas. Few knew and nobody cared that the Hidalgos under De Sota had moved westward along this very route. The people thought no more of them than they did the magnolias and bay and other ornamental trees which grew so plentifully in the swamps along the river, nor the fame of the stream. They knew that there were plenty of black bass, locally known as trout, in the Suwanee, and bream and perch and cat-fish. There were soft-shell turtles that made a mighty nice dish when stewed down to a low gravy, or the "chicken meat" of those same turtles fried crisp and brown. Fresh water turtles were a mighty fine article of food anyway you looked at it. It was commonly said that a turtle had every kind of meat on him. The white "chicken meat," the dark "beef" and the in-between "pork." You could stew, boil and fry, and none of it cost you a cent. All you needed was a strip of white side-meat on the hook, and you had you some turtle meat.

But the people also knew that while the Suwanee furnished free meat, it furnished plenty of mosquitoes and malaria too. If you wanted to stay on your feet, you bought your quinine every Saturday along with your groceries. Work was hard, pleasures few, and malaria and hookworm plentiful. However, the live oaks set along the streets and in many yards grew splendidly and gave good shade. The Spanish moss hung down everywhere and seemed to interest travellers from the North, though these were few and far between. Nobody gave these Yankees any particular encouragement to settle around

2

Sawley. The Reconstruction was little more than a generation behind. Men still living had moved into west Florida after Sherman had burned Atlanta and made his triumphant march to the sea. A dozen or more men who had worn the gray of the confederacy were local residents. Damn Yankees were suspect of foraging around still looking for loot; and if not that, gloating over the downfall of The Cause.

This was a Sunday and the sawmill and the 'still were silent. No Yankees passing through. The Negroes were about their own doings in their own part of town, and white Sawley was either in church or on the way. Less than a thousand persons inhabited the town, and more than half the white population belonged to Day Spring Baptist Church. The menfolks, as everywhere, were not too good on attendance, but they paid their dues more or less, and the women and children went.

On this particular Sunday, though, there was a large turn-out. Not that there was any revival meeting going on, which always brought everybody out, nor were they hurrying to the church because it was believed that the pastor, Reverend Carl Middleton, had anything new to say, or any new way of saying what he always said.

Sawley was boiling like a big red ants' nest that had been ploughed up. It was rumored that Arvay, the younger of the two Henson girls was a'courting at last. To be exact, Arvay was not a'courting so much as she was being courted, and what with Arvay's past record and everything, this was something that people had to see.

In the first place, Arvay was all of twenty-one, and according to local custom, should have been married at least five years ago. But at sixteen, shortly after the marriage of her older sister Larraine, commonly known as "'Raine," to the Reverend Carl Middleton, Arvay had turned from the world. Such religious fervor was not unknown among white people, but it certainly was uncommon. During "protracted meeting," another name for the two weeks of revival that came around every summertime, most anybody was liable to get full of the spirit and shout in church and sing and pray. Back-sliders and "sinner-folks" crowded the mourner's-bench and got religion over and over again. But it seldom lasted more than a month after the meetings closed. Nobody heard any more about it until the next time. A local wit put it this way: Sawley wore out the knees of its britches crawling to the Cross and wore out the seat of its pants back-sliding. Excessive ceremonies were things that the Negroes went in for. White folks just didn't go on like that.

So it was something when Arvay Henson, now, took her stand. Arvay could have done so different. In the first place, Arvay was still mighty young to take on self-denying. And then again, Arvay was pretty if you liked delicate-made girls. Her shape was not exactly in style in those parts, but that could easily be overlooked. She had breasts to her bosom, but elsewhere Arvay was lean-made in every way. No heavy-hipped girl below that extremely small waist, and her legs were long and slim-made instead of the much-admired "whiskey-keg" look to her legs that was common. She had plenty of long light yellow hair with a low wave to it with Gulf-blue eyes. Arvay had a fine-made kind of a nose and mouth and a face shaped like an egg laid by a Leghorn pullet, with a faint spread of pink around her upper cheeks. True, she was said to be so slim that a man would have to shake the sheets to find her in bed, but there were many around Sawley who were willing to put themselves to the trouble of making a thorough search of the bed every night. Many a man felt that given the chance, he could put plenty of meat on Arvay's bones. So there was a feeling of shock and loss when Arvay gave up the world. It brought on plenty of talk.

Arvay, young and white, and teasing to the fancy of many men, had got up in church on First Sunday, Communion Day, and announced that she was through with the world and its sinful and deceitful ways. She solemnly said that she had given her whole heart and her life to the work of God. She planned to be a missionary and craved to be sent away off somewhere to take the Word to the heathens. Tell them of Christ and Him crucified, and warn them of the dangers in which they stood

4

in their ignorance, of a burning and everlasting Hell. Also make them know that they had to die, and of the horrors of dying in their ignorance and sin.

Arvay's tearful speech followed the usual pattern, and everybody said it was just fine. There had been nothing about the heathens of China, India and Africa wallowing around on the heavenly chairs, nor ankling up and down the golden streets. None of her hearers could have imagined such a thing. Fancy meeting a Hindu, with his middle tied up in a dhoti and with white head-rag on, around the Throne, or singing in the Choir! It was too much, and nobody tried to imagine any such thing. He ought to consider himself pretty lucky to get saved from Hell. What became of him after that was [just not] talked about. The job of the missionaries was to save. So all of the women and a few of the older men cried tears of joy at the renunciation of the girl. She had to be full of The Spirit to talk that way, and so young, and therefore apt to be deviled and pestered by the flesh. It would be a mighty fine thing, the harried older women thought, if more girls felt as Arvay did. Therefore, on that day of Arvay's renunciation, when the girl had finished off by asking the prayers of the congregation, their earnest prayers that she might hold out and never, never turn back but go on and on to greater grace, "Amens" burst out all over the church. The pastor himself had gotten to his feet and paid his young sister-in-law a great tribute.

"This young girl's devotion to the cause of Christ makes me feel ashamed," Reverend Middleton had said. "Here she is, too young to be sent into the field as yet, but ready and willing to go. Ready to go wherever the Spirit might send her. Her stand ought to make me and all of us grown folks feel ashamed. And if you, my flock feel that you can spare me, I will declare myself ready and willing to go."

The flock had cried some more at the thought of the pastor's offer to sacrifice himself, but it was felt that he could not be spared. Anyway, it would take a lot of money to send him. To compensate for this denial, the parsonage was re-painted, and

5

five dollars a month was added to his salary, bringing the total to an even seventy dollars a month.

Five years had passed since Arvay had turned her back on the world and all its sins and snares. Arvay still played the organ for the Sunday School, and she took an active part in church work. Otherwise, she kept strictly to herself. It was not too difficult for her, because the community soon put Arvay Henson down as queer, if not a little "tetched." Nothing like her sister 'Raine at all, who was robust, not to say a trifle lusty, and pretty in the ways that the rural community favored. 'Raine had a full head of curly reddish hair, big legs and a busty chest. 'Raine was lively and full of chat. 'Raine took after her father's side of the family, while Arvay looked like her mother's folks, and even had her mother's ways to an extent. Maria Henson was overly religious, not given to laughter, and was considered meek and mild. The old heads recalled that Maria Henson had been given to fits and spasms in her girlhood the same way that Arvay was right now. No one thought too much about the seizures. Fits were things that happened to some young girls, but they grew out of them sooner or later. It was usually taken as a sign of a girl being "highstrung." Marriage would straighten her out.

For the last three years, Arvay had been having hysterical seizures, classified in the local language as "having fits." Sometimes they came upon her in church right after the sermon, but more often she was took down right after she got home from the service, and usually when some extra brash young gallant had forced himself upon her to the extent of seeing her home. It called for lots of persistence and a thick hide to "scorch" Arvay Henson home, but her looks and her unattainability nerved various young bucks to try it now and then. After the long walk in almost complete silence on Arvay's part, the venture invariably ended in an hysterical display as soon as the young man got inside the Henson parlor. Hardly did she get her hat off before she was sprawled out on the horse-hair sofa clenching hands and teeth and bobbling around and up and down, and with her mother running in with a small vial of spirits of turpentine and the sugar dish with a teaspoon in it to administer the dose of three "draps" of "teppentime on sugar" forced between the teeth of Arvay to bring her to. The embarrassed would-be suitor stumbled out, and that was the end of his hopes. One by one the more brash were discouraged, and the timid never tried.

But now, the rumor had flashed around that Arvay Henson had met her match. Arvay Henson was being courted in spite of all she could do and say and so the town and outlying country and districts, all were good and stirred up. And the news was so exciting that nobody wanted to be told about it. Everybody wanted to go to church and to be there and see for themselves.

And there were three prongs to stir up interest. The first was that Arvay was taking company at all. The second was who it was who was sparking Arvay; but the most hooking horn of all was the way it was being done.

The man was Jim Meserve, whose ancestors had held plantations upon the Alabama River before the War. In that respect, Jim Meserve differed from the rest of the inhabitants of Sawley, who had always been of the poor whites who had scratched out some kind of an existence in the scrub oaks and pines, far removed from the ease of the big estates.

Not that Jim Meserve had come among the people of Sawley with anything. He had brought little more than the suit he had on, the high laced boots, and the broad-brimmed felt hat, which he wore so rakishly on his curly head. The fortunes of the War had wiped Jim's grand-father clean. His own father had had no chance to even inherit. Jim had come to town three months ago with only a small bundle, containing his changing clothes. But Jim had a flavor about him. He was like a hamstring. He was not meat any longer, but he smelled of what he had once been associated with.

Jim Meserve was very handsome too, and had stirred the hearts of practically every single girl in town. Caps were set to catch the laughing stranger. He was obviously Black Irish in his ancestry somewhere. He had the thick head of curly

7

black hair, deep blue eyes with long black lashes, so that they were what the Irish called "set in with a sooty finger," dimples in his lean cheeks, white strong teeth set in a chaffing mouth.

Jim had the gift of gab, no doubt about it. Within a week of his arrival in Sawley, he had talked himself into a job as woodsman on a turpentine camp. That was a miracle in itself, for "teppentime" folks are born, not made, and certainly not over-night. They are born in teppentime, live all their lives in it, and die and go to their graves smelling of teppentime. And Brock Henson, Arvay's father, who was an over-rider for the firm, and known to be a hard man to handle, had interceded for Jim and got him the job. A man had to go some to out-talk Brock Henson on anything. Brock Henson was a Cracker from way back. Life had not been easy for him, and he had cutting edges on his spirit, in spite of his love of jokes. Working that job out of the squat-shouldered, tobacco-chewing, rusty-haired Brock was a feather in Jim's cap, and gave him a standing.

Jim had the nerve of a brass monkey, everybody agreed. But then, he made no bones about the fact that he was really stuck on Arvay Henson. She just suited him, he said, and was worth the trouble of breaking in. Too, Jim laughed off the notion that Arvay was through with the world and had no use for love. So it looked like the brash devil was a'courting Arvay anyhow in spite of the well-known obstacles.

The Sunday before, Jim Meserve had rushed up to the Henson home and had escorted Arvay to *and* from church and people nearly split their sides at Jim walking along the road holding Arvay's arm with every kind of politeness in spite of all she could do and say. What would come off next? That was what they all wanted to see and to know. The doings were something like a well-trained hound dog tackling a bob-cat, and everybody wanted to be in on the fun. So they were all on the way to church that Sunday morning, walking, in buggies, riding horse-back and some even straddling grass-gut mules or in double wagons pulled by mules.

Brock Henson had never made as much as a hundred dollars in any month in his life. The family lived in a clapboard house more than two miles east of the heart of Sawley, and nearly a mile from the Baptist church. The house had been a dark ugly red when Brock Henson, promoted to over-rider, had moved in ten years before. It had not been repainted since, and was now a rusty, splotchy gray-brown. Only one room in the house, the parlor, was ceilinged overhead. In the two bedrooms and the kitchen, the rafters were bare and skinny. Water for the household came from a well out back, and the privyhouse leaned a little to one side less than fifty feet from the kitchen door. A fig tree, two pear trees which bore pears that were only good for preserving, were scattered far apart in the field back of the house. There was a huge mulberry tree that redeemed the very back of the unkempt garden space.

The Sawley people, eager to be amused at Arvay's expense, had no idea who or what Arvay Henson was. They had no way of knowing that Arvay was timid from feeling unsafe inside. Nor had anyone, not even her parents, the answer to Arvay's reactions to people. They did not suspect that the general preference for Larraine, Arvay's more robust and aggressive sister, had done something to Arvay's soul across the years. They could not know, because Arvay had never told anyone how she felt and why.

Arvay had one comforting advantage over Larraine. Arvay could play music and Larraine just couldn't learn it. Arvay had been asked to spend a summer with her mother's sister in Madison one time, and this aunt could play on the organ some. Arvay had shown great interest and a quick ability and had surprised the family on her return to Sawley in the fall, by being able to pick out melodies, and to play a few songs with full harmony all the way through. The Henson parlor organ, which had been bought years ago for style and had seldom been sounded, began to be used. Arvay was in there nearly every day practicing and practicing. She showed herself very apt with music.

But even this talent and comfort had laid a'road to ambush the timid Arvay. It had brought down upon her her most crushing blow so far, and this hurt had convinced Arvay Henson that happiness, love and normal relationships were not meant for her. Somehow, God had denied her the fate of sharing in the common happiness and joys of the world. Only she knew that her renunciation had been an acknowledgement of this conviction.

It had come about this way. Arvay was not quite sixteen when Carl Middleton, twenty-six, and newly ordained to the ministry, was called to Sawley to pastor Day Spring Baptist church. Middleton was five-feet-ten, deep-chested and husky, so that the godless Brock Henson snurled behind his back that Middleton ought to be mortally ashamed of himself to be dodging honest work like he was doing. Carl Middleton up in a pulpit beating on a Bible and hollering was nothing but a first class teppentime-still hand going to waste.

The female Hensons disagreed with Brock. Maria and Larraine shouted and hollered Brock down that the new pastor was just wonderful. Brock laughed it off by saying that they would naturally say that because the new preacher was a bachelor and 'Raine and her mother were up to baiting a hook for the puzzle-gutted slob. Arvay said nothing in Middleton's favor or against him because she considered him too wonderful for her to ever have a chance with him. She listened to Larraine and the older girls rave over the way one lock of his brown hair dangled over his forehead when he got really active in the pulpit. How his gray eyes blazed and his face got all tied up with rage when he was giving general sin and sinners in general the very devil.

Arvay was secretly glorified then when the new pastor seemed to single her out. He made two or three attempts to talk with the shy and almost wordless girl. Then happening to hear that she could play the organ, he made her organist for the Sunday School out of hand. Then he suggested that he call at the Henson home on Friday afternoons to go over the songs with her for the following Sunday. There was not much talk in the countrified parlor, but Arvay shone inside at Middleton's very presence. She fell in love, and began to live a sweet and secret life inside herself. The pastor leaning over her shoulder while she sat at the organ, little touches of his hand seemingly by accident, softness in his voice, and telling her that she was an exceptional young girl.

This went on for months, with Middleton paying Larraine and none of the older girls any attention. Then, all of a sudden, Larraine developed great interest in church affairs and in the program for the Children's Day exercises in particular. She was always on hand in the parlor or at the church. And Larraine was seventeen and had on long dresses and could take company. The Sunday after Children's Day, Middleton scorched Larraine home from the night service and the next day Larraine announced to Arvay that she and the pastor were engaged to be married.

Even with 'Raine married to Middleton, Arvay could not bring herself to feel that her instincts had deceived her. Ah, no! There had been a mistake somewhere. Maybe even at the bottom of Carl's sudden marriage with Larraine.

It was twice as hard for Arvay because she had no one to whom she could open her feelings. Not to her parents who were bragging over 'Raine catching the new pastor. And certainly not to her only sister whom Arvay felt had somehow toled her true love away from her.

Believing in her heart that she was secretly loved by Carl, it gradually came to Arvay that the next move was up to her. The best plan would be to get herself sent far off to some foreign land. Some day, and without doubt pretty soon, Carl would follow her there. She would be standing in a flower yard, and she would see Carl coming a long way off, tired and worn out and sad. He would kneel down on his knees, kiss the hem of her garment, tell her how it all happened and beg her to forgive and to forget. Larraine would be dead—of a broken heart because Carl had found her out and told her to her face that she had parted him from his true love by her double-tongued lies and deceitfulness.

11

Outside of her dreams Arvay could detect no weakening in Carl except for a kind of a look he gave her sometimes from the pulpit. Otherwise, Larraine seemed to have her husband fetching and toting at her commands. But Arvay comforted herself that right was bound to win some old day, and dreamed and waited. The waiting was mighty hard, for Arvay found that it caused her to dream dreams that made her body plague her in miserable strange ways. For instance, what got the matter with her every time that Larraine got pregnant? It was something beyond Arvay's understanding. Some imp of Satan seemed to grab hold of her and drag her right into the darkened bedroom where Carl and 'Raine were, and made her look and see and hear from beginning to the end. It was after 'Raine's second announcement that Arvay felt her spasms coming on.

Not a soul in Sawley suspected this secret life of Arvay's. Most of them would have laughed at her if they had known about it. Carl Middleton had soon shot his bolt in Sawley. The new wore off him mighty quick. He never did say anything that had not been already said, and his repetitions were not very dramatic. His church members allowed that he would do, and that was the best that they could give him. He stayed home with his wife and had no loud kind of vices. Some complained that he couldn't lead a song worth talking about. Some wag went so far as to say that Reverend Middleton couldn't even raise a tune if you put a wagon-load of good compost under him and ten sacks of commercial fertilizer. They would have thought that a pretty young girl like Arvay was clean out of her head to be making so much out of nothing. But Arvay had felt wanted and warm and secure and important to someone for awhile, and it was hard for her to forget.

CHAPTER 2

That Sunday morning Arvay had no idea of the extent of interest in her affairs, but she did know how she felt. She fooled around and lingered over the breakfast table.

"Don't you reckon that you ought to be getting yourself fixed for Sunday School, Arvay?" Brock Henson asked sharply. "It's nearly nine o'clock."

Arvay jumped visibly and quivered. "That is, if I was going. I don't reckon I'll be going this morning."

"How come?" Brock demanded. "Before now, look like you couldn't get there soon enough. Why ain't you going this morning?"

"Oh, I just don't feel to be bothered, I reckon. Somebody else can preside at the organ one time, I reckon. I won't be so much missed."

"Call yourself trying to cold-shoulder Jim Meserve, I take it. If you had the sense that God give a june bug you'd feel glad that he feels to scorch you to and from. Ain't you never going to have sense enough to get yourself a husband? You intend to lay round here on me for the rest of your days and moan and pray?"

"I help you to say," Maria Henson agreed. "Arvay ain't acting with no sense at all. Here all these gals around here 'bout to bust they guts trying to git to him, and Arvay, that

13

seems like she got the preference with him, trying to cut the tom fool."

"You all talk like I ain't got no feelings at all. You reckon I feel like pulling off down the road with him so he can make a fool out of me in front of everybody? Naw! I just ain't a'going."

But in the end she was driven from kitchen to her own room to dress. In sullen anger, she took as long as she could. She was no more than half dressed when she heard her father greeting Jim Meserve out on the porch. She became so nervous that she was useless to herself. It was a good thing that Maria ran in and helped her into the pink lawn dress at last, and put her accessories in her trembling hands. "Aw, good gracious, Arvie! You ain't ready as yet? What in the nation you been doing all this time?" Maria made quick and anxious movements as she grumbled and rushed the dressing of her daughter along. "Got Mister Meserve out there waiting all this time. You don't even act with the sense you do have. Move! I'll button your frock for you. Make haste, Arvie! Don't comb and pull at that hair all day. Mister Meserve sure looks noble in his Sunday clothes. Make haste before he gits tired of waiting on you and leave you."

Arvay in the deeply flounced pink lawn dress, and with her flaxen hair swept up in front into a high pompadour, stood grim and panting before the looking-glass, her eyes stretched wide in fear like a colt that has been saddled for the first time; stood jerking at the body of her dress across her bust.

"You're all ready, now. I'll go tell him that you'll be right out. Naw, no need for you to grab up that Quarterly. Sunday School must be mighty nigh over by now. Here's a clean handkerchief for you pocketbook. Hurry on out to greet the young man."

Arvay heard her mother taking extra spry steps down the hallway and out on the front porch.

She halted with cold trembling hands in the doorway to brace herself. While she was doing this, she glanced around. Just as Arvay had accused him to herself beforehand, Jim

14

Meserve had a face full of grin. He was doing the talking, and her parents were seconding every word with nods and smiles of agreement. Currying favor, Arvay mentally scorned them, and acting two glad dogs in a meat-house!

She stepped out on the porch with a long fast step, made the briefest manners of her lifetime without halting, and was almost loping by the time her feet hit the ground. By not turning her head in the slightest, she could pretend to know nothing about the dismay in the faces of her parents, and to have no notion at all about what Jim Meserve was thinking. She had offered the grand insult, and now maybe she would be left in peace.

Halfway to the gate she felt her elbow being caught by a man's long and strong fingers, and the tall shape of Jim Meserve was walking along beside her.

"Why, Miss Arvay," Jim said in great concern, "you wouldn't run off and leave me, would you?" They came to the shabby gate and he swung it outwards with one hand, while clinging to her arm with the other. "And I already know your answer to that.... 'Not if you can keep up,' is what you mean to tell me, ain't it, Miss Arvay?"

As they turned towards Sawley, Arvay heard a suppressed guffaw from her father and her face flamed. She looked up angrily into the young man's face and said nothing for several steps. Then she could hold in no longer and said from between clenched teeth, "What you grinning all over yourself like a chessy-cat for? You act like you found a mare's nest and can't count the eggs."

Jim Meserve seemed to take enjoyment out of her burst of rage and laughed some more.

"Grinning just like the Devil's doll-baby!" Arvay added as a further insult.

"Wouldn't hurt your face to grin a little, would it, Miss Arvay? You got yours all tied up in a winter-knot, or like you been feasting off of green persimmons."

"That wouldn't be necessary at all, Mister Meserve. You'se doing enough grinning and skinning back your gums for the

15

two of us. I'd give a good whoop and a holler, though, if you was to go on about your business and leave me be."

"Why, Miss Arvay?"

"Why? Well, just because."

"That don't tell me nothing, Miss Arvay. I know that is a woman's reason for most anything, but not being a woman, it don't spell out a thing to me. Go ahead and tell me something that I can understand. I might be sort of chuckle-headed, so don't chunk the whole pan of bread at me; crumble it up fine so I can handle it."

Arvay stopped in her tracks and tried to release her arm by a gentle jerk, but it did not work.

"Why do you want to come a'pestering and a'picking at me for? You know that you just want to make game of me!" There were tears in her voice if not in her eyes. "I never done nothin' to you for you to come taking me for a figure of fun, and making a laughing-stock out of me for folks to poke fun at."

The laughter died off out of Jim Meserve's face, and he stopped and stood looking down into her tortured eyes for a full minute.

"So you got notions like that about me, Miss Arvay?" Jim asked very soberly and kept studying the girl's face.

"You and everybody else," Arvay replied defiantly, but with something child-like and pathetic in her voice.

"But why, Miss Arvay? Why would anybody want to poke fun at you?"

"Because, because you don't, you couldn't mean what you say, that's how come."

"And why wouldn't I mean what I say? Why wouldn't I or most any man want you for your sweet little self?"

"Because you just wouldn't, that's all," Arvay stuttered out, and her face flushed red and she worked her eyelids rapidly to hold back the tears. At the point of failure, she shut her eyes tightly for a second and made a quick quarter turn to hide her face.

Instantly Jim seized her by her shoulders and whirled the

16

slim girl back to face him, and Arvay's hand flew up and slapped Jim's face with all her might and main. "You leave me be!" Arvay tried to release herself and run away, but Jim held her too firmly. "I told you to quit bothering me!"

"No, Miss Arvay, that I can't do at all. You need my help and my protection too bad for that, I see." With a solemn kind of soberness, Jim drew the shrinking Arvay to him. "You have made me see into something that I don't reckon you understand your ownself. I have to stay with you and stand by you and give my good protection to keep you from hurting your ownself too much. No, I can't leave you be, not until you and me both can see further."

"Oh, you don't have to take it on yourself to worry about me, Mister Meserve," Arvay protested weakly.

"Oh, but I do! I have to because you don't understand your ownself, Miss Arvay, and somebody stronger than you, and that can see further than you, and somebody that feels your care, will have to be on hand to look after you. Now we got things all straightened out like. Come on." And Jim let go of Arvay's shoulders and took her companionably by her hand and faced up the road. "You'll get more used to me before long and see into things."

"See into what?" Arvay questioned shortly as she followed Jim along the road.

"Oh, a lot of things, Miss Arvay, that you ain't got the right ideas about as yet. It's bound to come to you in time. I'll be around to look out for you and point out things."

Arvay refused to comment further, and with eyes straight ahead of her, she walked determinedly on the sandy road. After a few paces, Jim shucked off his solemn manner, and returned to his laughing good humor in a marvellous way. He chuckled and squeezed Arvay's arm lightly.

"Didn't take me long to learn just how you're made, Miss Arvay, and now I know how to handle you. You and me are going to have a mighty high old time together."

The straight road waved along over the slight rises. On either side yellow and blue flowers were ornamenting the

17

spring. They passed groves of live oak, scrub oak, scattering pines, and over towards the river, bay and magnolia in exotic white bloom. Deep curtains of gray moss hung from the trees and waved ever so slightly in the breeze. Budding wild grapevines and briars tangled up trees and peeped out from upper branches. Possum persimmons spread their limbs among the rest.

But Arvay took these in through a gray veil of apprehension. Folks would be coming along this road and see her in the company of Jim, and she pictured them grinning slyly and making jokes about her. Her mind imaged up the picture of the future. After Jim had made a public show of her, he would naturally get himself a regular girl, and they would all laugh at her, Arvay, and say how Jim Meserve and whoever his wife might be had made her look like a fool at a funeral. If only nobody came along! Oh, but she was not born for luck. Somebody would be sure and certain to come along. Arvay walked in dread of that moment.

All of Arvay's fears were confirmed, as a shabby old buckboard came abreast of them, with the deep sand pouring from the rim of every wheel. There was no mistaking that one and all were extremely interested in her in company with Jim. Their necks craned out, and their eyes snapped in curiosity. Old Lady Minnie Brawley was so scared that her wrinkled-around old eyes might miss something that she reached up a freckled old claw and flung back the bib part of her floppy calico bonnet the better to gaze and to peer. Grins and giggles broke out among the younger members of the clan. Her oldest son, who was at the reins, had to pull to a halt and scrape up some talk the best way that he could.

"Mawning, Miss Arvie, and Mister Jim. Hit's mighty hot and dusty walking for you all," he said. "You better hop in here with us and ride on to the church."

That grass-gut horse had more on him right then than he ought to have had, but Arvay suddenly saw a way out of her embarrassment.

"Yessuh, I thank you," Arvay said eagerly and made a

18

motion to approach the buckboard. As crowded as it was, it would be almost a miracle if she was able to get in. There would certainly be no room for Jim.

"Mighty much obliged to you all for your kindness." Jim smiled his most charming, and swept off his hat to the Brawley females, while with his other hand, he held Arvay's arm so that she could not advance. "But I can't see room for the two of us, and knowing Miss Arvay as I do, I know that she would disfavor to part with my company, and so as not to disappoint her so much, I think that we'd better just walk."

Arvay could have screamed and fought, especially as she saw how Brawley whipped up his horse and wheeled off. Making haste to get to the church-grounds so they could talk and tell. She tried to disengage her arm, but just then she heard another rig coming up behind them and looked back in unhappy defeat.

"Let go of me!" she hissed. "Making a fool out of me right out here on the Big Road. Acting just like the Devil!"

"Don't know who told you, honey, but you sure got it right. Those who know me well call me by my right name, Peter Rip-Saw, the Devil's high sheriff and son-in-law."

Arvay looked over her shoulder and dwindled down in helpless misery. What could she do? She would die before she let folks see her out there on a public road tussling and scuffling with a man. It would cause all kinds of talk, say she was letting a man get common with her. There was nothing for her to do but to pass the time of day and swap manners with the loaded down carriage and the two double-team wagons that passed them in rapid succession.

But the unusual activity along the Big Road did not sufficiently prepare Arvay for the spectacle when she came in sight of the church-grounds. The place was thronged as she had seldom seen it before. Horses, mules, buggies, wagons, buckboards and carriages were crowded together out under the oak grove where the congregation usually collected and ate from baskets on Big Meeting Day. Many bicycles leaned against the trunks of trees. People were mingling and moving about. It was the social time between the letting out of Sunday School and the taking in of morning service. Arvay looked, and unconsciously clung to Jim's arm.

"Where in the world did all these folks come from?" Jim asked in surprise. "Everybody seems to be present from Joe Cry to Jimmy Giggle."

"Indeed, I sure don't know," Arvay mumbled.

As Jim boldly led her around and talked and joked with folks, Arvay had her ego nourished by the envious looks from single women and courting girls. Her vanity put on a little flesh, and she began to say a word or two herself to people. And besides, right in front of all those jealous girls, Jim was treating her like she was some precious play-pretty that might break in two. Bradford Cary III's wife could not have been handled more up to time than she was being handled. She was being helped over every little stick and root, and he fended so that she was not bumped into and jostled around. It was a soul-satisfying mock-up. If only it could be so!

Arvay saw three girls in a bunch trying to look amused at her, but even Arvay could see that it was hardly big enough to reach across their thin-lipped mouths. It didn't taste near as good as they were trying to make out. They were the three ringleaders in the social set of the poor. The most popular at all the square dances, barbecues and things like that. To make sure and crumple Arvay's feathers, they got themselves in the way so that she could overhear their comments as if by accident.

"That don't mean a thing. Mister Meserve is much too lively and used to things to waste up much time on missionaries."

"And what would he want with a skinny thing like that? He being tall and spare-built hisself, he would naturally want somebody with some meat on they bones. Folks don't go to the butcher-shop to buy bones unless they aim to make lye-soap."

There was a blow of mirthless laughter at this piece of wit, and the chunky girl, giving a switch to her full hips, was encouraged to go on. "Can you imagine them married and in the bed together? I bet they would sound like a big dish-pan of crockery rattling together."

The three tickled themselves out loud at this and looked at Arvay.

"Oh, it won't never come to that," the third announced with assurance. "I got enough meat on my bones to straighten him out and put a stop to this. Don't you worry."

If Jim heard, he gave no notice. He accepted an invitation to a square dance for himself, and his especial company, Miss Henson, ten days later.

"Is that all right with you, Miss Arvay?" Jim asked with great solicitude.

"Most certainly!" Arvay replied and looked the three leaders of the sawmill set dead in the eyes.

But Arvay was sunk again when she and Jim went inside and beheld most of the young folks, married and single, packing into the center aisle pews behind them to comment and to be witnesses to what went on. She sank down into her seat, three rows from the front. Jim did not seem to notice a thing. He came parading like a king down the aisle behind her, stood until she had entered the pew, came in after her, stood and looked out over the fast filling church, hitched up his pants and sat down.

Suddenly Arvay became conscious of Carl's inspection from the back of the pulpit. It was funny, but she had forgotten all about the man she had thought that she had loved so hard and so hopelessly for six long years. But there was no mistaking. Every time that she looked off, when she brought her eyes back to the pulpit, she caught him watching her in a curious way from under the awning of his hand resting on his brows. It made Arvay nervous, and she squirmed.

And there was Jim Meserve brazenly leaning against her, shoulder to shoulder. It gave Arvay some kind of feeling of being caught acting unfaithful by Carl Middleton. Why? Never had a word of love passed between them. Even so, his look seemed now to say that he had seized upon her secret,

21

and he was sadly accusing her of defection. She inched away from Jim as far as she could, which was only a few inches, but Jim promptly closed the gap again. A loud whisper somewhere behind her applauded Jim.

"Go, gator, and muddy the water!"

"I'd give a spot cash one hundred dollars if Jim would up and buss her."

"Oh, he'll do it all right."

"Aw, aw! That Arvay would throw a acre of fits."

Along about the end of the uninspiring sermon, Arvay was startled by a quick but tender pressure on her arm by Jim. She turned her head in surprise and their eyes met head on. He was looking at her in some intense and hungry way. Some common pulse began to pump something from Jim to her. Arvay noticed for the first time that Jim was made out of flesh. It was too intense, and Arvay, flushing deeply, snatched her eyes away. She flung her eyes up to the choir stand, and in doing so, caught her sister's eyes upon her. Larraine must have been looking at her for some time, because the look was set, and it was as plain as day that Larraine was not pleased at what she was looking at. Her face was as naked as a jay-bird in whistling time. Her eyes went from Arvay to Jim and back again.

Arvay knew that look only too well. Just let Arvay get hold of something that gave her particular pleasure, and that look came over Larraine. Only today, there was an out-done look mixed up in Larraine's face, and Arvay knew why. There was no way in the world for 'Raine to handle Jim first and then fling him at Arvay when she was tired or he was damaged and scarred. She had Carl Middleton, and she had three children to boot. Let her pout and crave! Here was something that she could do nothing about. Something that Brock Henson could not snatch away from Arvay and hand over to Larraine. Jim Meserve, placed beside Carl Middleton, was like a slick race-horse beside a grass-gut mule. Was Larraine sitting up there being sorry that she had been in such a haste to grab Carl?

"Excuse me, Miss Arvay," Jim was murmuring as he got up

22

from his seat. Jim was following the local custom. The collection was lifted right after the sermon. It was the habit of the young courting men to go outside immediately after the sermon, stretch their legs for a few minutes, and then just as the collection began, to swagger back in, and ostentatiously hand their lady-love a coin to put in the collection. It was a sure sign of who belonged to whom.

After the young men had bestowed their gifts, the girls arose proudly, and with their fellows swaggering after them, paraded up to the table, and dropped their coin with a ring. One young couple right after the other parading up, and returning simpering to their seats. It was hard on the girl or the fellow whose time had been beaten, but it was a triumph for the winners. Arvay cast her eyes up briefly at Larraine, and trembled as she realized what was about to happen. Never had she marched in the parade before.

The deacons took their places, the pastor made his appeal for money, the organ struck up *Pass Me Not O Gentle Saviour* at a lively pace, and the choir rose and lead the singing. The young men waited until the old fogies had thinned out, then they came back in looking like conquerors, and began to rejoin their ladies, giving the money out before they took their seats. Jim pressed a quarter into Arvay's palm, hitched up his britches arrogantly and sat down. It only waited now until some couple began the parade.

"Come on, honey," Jim whispered to Arvay. "We might as well lead off."

Arvay got to her feet, feeling every eye upon her. They had hardly made the aisle, though, before fifteen to twenty other couples were struggling into the aisles. Arvay went back to her seat feeling an exhilaration that she had never known before. She belonged to something. They nodded and grinned at each other, these couples, as they met and passed going up and down the aisle. She looked up to see how Larraine was taking it. She could hardly sing along with the rest for watching Arvay, and she was not smiling either. Arvay looked and felt glad.

Surrounded by her new associations, Arvay lingered in front of the church with Jim, feeling like she had fed on kings. Out of this feeling came a tremulous desire to take refuge in this man. To be forever warm and included in the atmosphere that he stirred up around him. The feel of his long-fingered hand on her arm, and the look from his eyes tingled her in a way that she had never felt before.

But with the intensity of desire stirred up in her came despair. This was the prettiest man that she had ever laid eyes on. He didn't have any great vast money, but this was no common Cracker boy whatsoever. Why, even the Carys had heard mention of his folks. What in the world did she have to win him with?

Ah, no, this pretty, laughing fellow was too far out of her reach. Things as wonderful as this were never meant for nobody like her. This was first-class, and she was born to take other people's leavings.

He had scorched her to church and back today to make good his bet. It had turned out very nice and happy for her in a way, but then again, it had given her something to wish for which she could never have. Nothing to do but submit herself to her fate.

But submission tazzled you all up inside. To cover up her feelings, Arvay began to try to be quick and care-free with answers, and began to talk at random. She hardly knew what she was saying and doing before she arrived at her gate.

"Oh, no indeed, Mister Meserve, you don't think my hair is the prettiest in the world, no such a thing." And Arvay affected a hollow laugh to show that she was not as simple as he might think. "I know that you just say things [like] that to pass the time. You think country folks like us ain't got no sense, I reckon."

"Why, Miss Arvay! You don't mean to tell me that you disbelieve me what I say?"

Arvay hung her head and refused to meet his eyes, even when he shook her elbow and tried to make her look.

"You do wish to get rid of me, don't you?"

Arvay still stumbled along and said nothing.

"Silence gives consent, Miss Arvay. Look like I hit the nail right on the head."

They were at the gate, and Arvay wanted to rush inside and away, but Jim detained her by holding her arm.

"But you might as well save yourself a whole heap of trouble in that line, Miss Arvay, because I'm going to marry you first and last."

Arvay was half in the gate. In spite of Jim's smiling way, there was something serious-sounding in his voice, and Arvay looked up into his face to see what his words really meant. Something in his eyes sent the blood rushing to her face, and involuntarily Arvay bowed her head and concealed her face on the top of the shaky gate-post.

"Oh, you know that you don't mean that, Mister Meserve." Arvay mumbled and lifted her face the slightest.

"Oh, but I do, Miss Arvay." Jim chuckled a little.

"You act like I, that is, somebody been just waiting around for you to ask 'em that. Supposing that I don't love you, or no other man, enough to marry 'em."

"That would mean that you didn't have all that belongs to you. I'd make a girl like *you* a damned fine husband." And Jim laughed at his own brashness.

"I been laying off to give my life to missionary work, Mr. Meserve. Even if you mean what you say, I'd have to take time to make up my mind."

"Oh, I mean it sure as you're born, and so far as making up your mind is concerned, that matters a difference. Women folks don't have no mind to make up nohow. They wasn't made for that. Lady folks were just made to laugh and act loving and kind and have a good man to do for them all he's able, and have him as many boy-children as he figgers he'd like to have, and make him so happy that he's willing to work and fetch in every dad-blamed thing that his wife thinks she would like to have. That's what women are made for."

"You reckon?"

"No, I know it. Since I been here in Sawley, I done got in

the notion that I'd like to get hold of one of the useless things to keep for a play-pretty. I'm going on twenty-five, been knocking around the country for seven years now, seen a lot of women and places, and seen a lot of things. It's about time I settled down, get me a real pretty wife, and start to raise me a house full of young 'uns."

"Well, you don't have to worry." Arvay smiled with a corner of her mouth. "From all I can learn, plenty of these girls around here would be only too glad to have you. It looks like you can just about take your pick."

Jim grinned. "That being the case, I'm picking you. I'm marrying you because I'm too tough for you to get shed of like you seem to be trying to do."

There it was, straight and simple. But this was like coming through religion, Arvay considered. Like your thoughts while you were out at the praying-ground in the depths of the woods, or being down at the mourners' bench during protracted meeting with the preacher, deacons and all the folks from the Amen corner standing around and over you begging and pleading with you to turn loose your doubting and only believe. Put your whole faith in the mercy of God and believe. Eternal life, Heaven and its immortal glory were yours if you only would believe. The hold-back was that it was not all that easy to believe. That was just the trouble. Bad luck, yes. That was easy to believe in from human experience, but a whole heap of happiness and good luck just didn't come to folks like that. Certainly, things had never turned out that way for her. Now, was she to believe that this very pretty man clothed in all the joys of Heaven and earth was for *her,* and all that she had to do was to part her lips and say "yes" to have him all for herself for life? Oh, no, this was just another hurting joke being played on her.

"You figger that you'se all that tough, Mister Meserve?" Arvay imagined that Jim's hand on her elbow trembled some as he assisted her through the gate. Naturally, she was mistaken. How could this brash man, with everything in the world at his command, be nervous about anything? Knowing

26

his power, he was just funning with her to show to the world that he could do what other boys hadn't been able to do. She glanced up at his face briefly and saw a deep grin beginning to spread out over his face.

"Sure do, Miss Arvay. What I'm about to tell you will give you some kind of idea. One time I was bossing a gang of lumberjacks and we was felling a big stand of cypress when a terrible thunderstorm come up all of a sudden. It was a mighty bad storm, Miss Arvay. Big wind a'blowing, heavy drops of rain, both chain and ball lightning forking from tree-top to tree-top and zig-zagging around something awful. Well, a great big bolt of that lightning, red-hot and gritting its teeth, took off and headed straight at me. It's a habit of mine, Miss Arvay, when I catch a streak of lightning aiming at me, to stand in my tracks and slap it right back where it come from."

Arvay with the front of her skirts lifted slightly was mounting the steps side by side with Jim. She looked up at his face in buck-eyed astonishment.

"Slap lightning, Mister Meserve?"

"Yep, because I don't aim to be imposed on like that by nothing nor nobody. But this here streak of lightning must of been even faster than it's supposed to be, because the next thing I knowed, it had done got past my hand and struck me."

"Struck you, and you ain't dead?"

"That's right, Miss Arvay. I'm shamed to admit it, but it hit me, *kerwhammmmm!* and right in the head at that. All I could do to stay on my feet from that lick the lightning hit me. Man! But was I mad! Just as hot as Tucker when the mule kicked his Mammy. All them colored men that was working under me come running to see if I was killed. Outside of a slight headache, there was nothing wrong with me at all. Told 'em they might as well go on back to work. I wasn't hurt at all, but that sneaking bolt of lightning was done up pretty bad. Yes, Ma'am! Last I seen of it, it was going off through the woods a'limping."

Jim's face brimmed over with laughter like an orange being squeezed, and he stood with one hand resting on the jamb of the door holding back the explosion until Arvay joined him in it.

"Why, Mister Meserve!" Arvay flashed angry eyes up at him. "Telling that big old something-ain't-so, and on the Sabbath Day at that!"

Jim stood in utter amazement as she made to push past him and go inside. "Poking fun at people and taking 'em for dumb fools!" Arvay went on. "Nobody with any sense would put a bit of dependence in anything that you say. Always trying to make light of folks."

With that Arvay flounced angrily inside the house. Jim hesitated outside the door for a second. If he had not been specifically invited to partake of dinner by Brock Henson, warmly seconded by Maria, and had not gladly accepted, he would have turned and left the place. But he followed Arvay. She was flinging her hat on the home-made hat-rack against the wall in the hall, and as Jim came up to her, was about to walk away without even offering to rest his hat. As he removed it, she snatched it out of his hand and hung it on one of the cow-horns without a word.

Maria, with an apron over her Sunday clothes, poked her head in the back door of the hall and beamed.

"Oh, so you all got back from church, did you? Walk right in the parlor, Mister Jim, and make yourself comfortable. Dinner'll be on the table tuhreckly."

"I thank you, Mrs. Henson." Jim replied as cheerfully as he could and walked on into the parlor ahead of Arvay. He sat down on one of the old parlor-rockers near the organ, and Arvay sank down on the horse-hair sofa on the other side of the room. She reached for a palm-leaf fan from the lower shelf of the table and began to fan herself nervously.

"You mean that you didn't see the joke in that tale, Miss Arvay?" Jim asked.

"Oh, so that was supposed to be a joke? I don't favor so many jokes, Mister Meserve. I don't like to be took for a fool. I admire for folks to talk plain and say just what they mean."

Arvay stole a look across the room and saw that something

28

seemed to be troubling the man in his face, and she interpreted it from what she had inside her. Fear flew to her heart. Maybe Larraine knew her old feelings about Carl, and had maliciously said something to Jim about it. She remembered that Larraine had been talking to Jim for a few minutes on the church-grounds while she had been tied up elsewhere. It would be just like 'Raine to do a trick like that.

Jim, for his part, balked and puzzled, was trying to find an easier way with Arvay. While he sought, he entertained himself by taking stock of the room. There was the what-not in one corner loaded down with the usual things: sea-shells, a mustache cup and saucer with a motto on it in gilt letters, a cheap Japanese fan spread open, numerous other bits of cheap crockery with fanciful shapes and colors. There was the inevitable center table with the big family Bible on the under shelf. On top of the table was the parlor kerosene lamp, with a decorated globe, and a strip of red flannel in the oil compartment for decoration. A cheap family album was on one corner of the table under the lamp, and a stereoptican lantern with pictures on the corner cater-cornered across. The remaining corners held fancy cups and saucers.

The four walls were crowded with ill-assorted pictures. All those in frames had nails beneath them so that the frame rested on those nails and leaned out from the wall at the top. The place of honor, over the mantlepiece was held by some artist's concept of General Robert E. Lee at Manassas. In that era, battle scenes were in high favor, and in these scenes, the generals all sat on rearing, fat-rumped horses. Though the enemy was always right up under the feet of the general's horse, he assumed that the men he led could not see them. Generals always pointed either their swords or their fingers to show [their] men the enemy. Lee, astride his famous Traveller, was pointing at the blue-clad Union soldiers and looking furious.

There were lithographs, unframed, depicting Bible scenes tacked plentifully around the walls. Peter was there in his unfortunate attempt to walk the waters like Christ. Acknowledging his lack of faith and his failure, he was pictured as squatting on the surface of the water, looking up guiltily into the face of his Master, who stood there calmly on the waves. It struck Jim that if Peter could squat like that without sinking, he could walk, and he started to comment on it, but remembered and held his peace. The other pictures, with the exception of a gaudy calendar advertising feed, seed, and fertilizers, were family pictures done in the prevalent crayon enlargements in showy frames. Brock Henson in a fierce mustache was on a bamboo easel in the corner by the sofa. There was one, obviously the wedding picture, in which Brock sat cross-legged in a chair with a stiff derby hat on his knees, and a young and pretty Maria standing beside the chair with one hand resting on his shoulder. Maria the mother, was in another frame, seated with a fat blob that must be Arvay on her lap, while another disfigurement that had to mean Larraine in a highly ruffled dress, leaned against her knee. This picture gave him an opening for conversation.

"That's you and your mother and your sister, ain't it?"

"Yes." Arvay answered, and ceased waving her fan for a moment. "That was took in Monticello one time when I wasn't nothing but a baby. A man come long two or three years back making enlargements, so Ma give it to him to get enlarged."

"Oh, I see." Jim pretended an interest that he did not feel, and now that he had an opening, he carried on. "Larraine looks so jolly in the picture, and even when you talk to her, that I'm surprised that she took up with that sorry preacher. How come that to come about, you reckon?"

"Why?" And Arvay's eyes flung wide open in a fright that Jim could not understand. "Why, how come you to ask a thing like that?"

"Oh, it's nothing to take so serious as all that, Miss Arvay. I just had the notion that your sister wasn't so full of religion as all that, and neither your pastor, so far as that is concerned. He looks like nothing but a big old humbug to me, and I

30

wondered how she happened to get took in by something like that."

"Oh," Arvay sort of gasped, and the next thing Jim knew she was sprawled out on the sofa in the grip of a spasm.

"Good God, she's took with that again!" Jim jumped to his feet. "Mrs. Henson! Mrs. Henson!" He called out. "Come quick! Miss Arvay is having another spasm!"

Mrs. Henson came running, and she had the sugar dish with a teaspoon in it in one hand and a small flat bottle of spirits of turpentine in the other. The harshness of spirits of turpentine had earned it a high place as a cure-all.

"Oh, do, Jesus!" Maria Henson panted. "Look like she's took worse than usual. Help me with her, will you, Mister Jim?"

"Be only too glad to, if you'll show me what to do."

All the time, Jim was studying the behavior of the girl very closely.

"Hold her down, will you, whilst I drop three drops of this here teppentime on a spoonful of sugar. That always fetches her around."

Jim obligingly took hold of Arvay's shoulders, while Maria, with shaking hands, fixed the preparation.

"Got to git it to her mighty quick," Maria trembled out. "Git this spoon betwixt her teeth [or] she's liable to bite her tongue off." She stooped and tried to force the spoon between the clenched teeth. Just then, Arvay flailed out with both arms, and the loaded spoon went flying across the room. "Oh, my Gawd, Mister Jim! She's liable to be done bit her tongue in two before I can git anymore fixed for her. Hold her for me tight as you can, please."

"Here, you're nervous your ownself, Mrs. Henson. You better take hold of her shoulders and lemme try to fix the medicine and get it in her mouth."

Jim's tone of authority gave Maria confidence, and she grabbed hold of the struggling girl, while Jim retrieved the spoon, dipped up fresh sugar, and standing directly over

31

Arvay's head, took the little bottle and began to drop the turpentine. He was very deliberate.

"Make haste!" Maria screamed. "Git that spoon in her mouth before she bites her tongue! Do, my Maker!"

"She ever bit it as yet?" Jim asked calmly as he waited for the second drop to fall.

"Naw, but she's liable to. Hurry up!"

But Jim, standing there tall and composed over Arvay, would not be hurried. There were seconds, it seemed to Maria between each drop. Two of the drops were finally deposited on the sugar in the spoon. The mother looked anxiously, tracing the course of each drop. Jim looked from the bottle to the spoon, to Arvay's face and back again to the poised bottle and the spoon. Now for that last third drop. Suddenly his hand gave a nervous twitch, and the third, or maybe third and fourth drop together, missed the spoon entirely, and landed right in the outside corner of Arvay's right eye.

Then a hurricane struck the over-crowded parlor. Arvay gave a yell from the very bottom of her lungs and catapulted her body from that sofa. She was all over the room at one time, seemingly, knocking over and upsetting things. Jim thought that she was going to climb the wall like a cat, and all the time she was gasping out yells. Jim heard Brock's footsteps hurrying up the hall just as Arvay got her directions and split out of the door. She collided with her father, rushed on past the temporary obstruction, and vanished down the hall in a cloud of flying yellow hair and pink skirts. Nothing but scream and screech in her wake as she made it to the back porch.

There was a frantic rattle of metal from the back porch.

"Poor, poor, thing!" Maria moaned. "Trying to git to some water to wash out her eye. I better go help her."

"We can all go help her with her eye," Jim offered as Brock Henson appeared in the parlor door. "Looks like she's sort of over her spasm by now." Jim and Brock Henson stood face to face and looked each other dead in the eye for a long moment. "We'll give what aid we can in washing out her pretty eye." With a dry grin smothering in his face, Jim led the way to the back porch.

Arvay was splashing cold water in her face frantically. Brock went and ranged himself against the wall. Jim took the half empty water pail and went out to the well and drew it full. Maria fluttered around like a hen with ducks for children at the edge of a pond and made little noises of sympathy.

"What took place in there, Arvay?" Brock asked unnecessarily, as Jim mounted the porch with the full bucket of fresh water.

"That varmint! Oooooooooh! He poured teppentime right in my eye! He done it a purpose, too." Arvay splashed and sobbed.

"Oh, I don't reckon he meant it to hurt you," Brock said casually. "Your eye ain't hurt none to mention. That being the case, you sure ought to thank him. Quickest cure for spasm-fits I ever did see. Yessiree!"

Arvay turned on Jim. "You long-legged scoundrel-beast, you! You and your no-count jokes. I got a good notion to take me a gun and kill you!"

"Aw, now, Miss Arvay," Jim drawled in good-humored unconcern. "You wouldn't take and kill you best-goodest would you?"

"Git away from me, sir! Git on away from me! Pouring teppentime in my eye for a joke. Git! Light a shuck often this place!"

"Damn!" Brock breathed deeply impressed. "Jim, you sure done worked a miracle. I never knowed that Arvay had that much life in her."

"It's all right, Mr. Henson, I'll be able to handle all that. A woman knows who her master is all right, and she answers to his commands. We'll make out good enough."

Arvay, egged on to greater rage, ran to the shelf and seized the bucket of water.

"Git from here, Jim Meserve! If you don't hurry up and git from here, I aim to dash this bucket of water on you. Git! And don't you dast to foot this place again."

33

Arvay was further maddened by the evidence that Jim was not sorry for what he had done. Not godly sorry anyway. He put on a sorry look on his face, but his eyes were grinning.

"Go ahead and fling that water on me, if you will and want to, Miss Arvay, but you ought to know that I wouldn't want to do a single thing to hurt *you*, not on purpose, anyhow. I beg your humble pardon for letting that little tetch of teppentime git into your eye. I wouldn't harm a hair on your pretty head. Fact is, I'd rather all the rest of the women in the world to be dead than for you to even have the toothache. That's the way I feel towards you."

Arvay had no more wish to throw water on Jim at all, but she stood there with the bucket in her hand, and not knowing how to get rid of it with dignity, just stood there. Jim helped her out. He stepped up, took the pail and put it back up on the shelf, then turned with an undisguised grin on his face this time.

"It was a good thing, Miss Arvay and you know it. Saved you a lot of spells of sickness, and me a whole lot of doctors bills."

Arvay got that, and right in front of her parents too. It gave her a stirring feeling inside, though she still held her mouth in an angry line.

"Anyhow," Jim went on and actually laughing now, "it got you to your feet long enough for me to talk to you and to tell you how I feel."

Arvay began to believe a little in Jim's sincerity, him talking like that right in the presence of her folks, and all. Then a terrible feeling of guilt came over her. Even if Jim meant it, she was not fitten. Here was the most wonderful man in all the world pomping her all up, and she had been living in mental adultery with her sister's husband for all of those wasted years. She was not fitten for a fine man like Jim. He was worth more than she was able to give him. The Bible said plainly that you could sin inwardly just as much as if you had actually done the thing, and she had sinned. Nothing to do but to turn her back on her happiness and never let on that she had ever wanted

Jim. But now that meant turning from the noonday of joy back into the dark mole holes that she had been living in so long. It was a terrible choice. But to be honest with Jim, there was nothing else for her to do. She acted on the conviction immediately. She brushed past him towards the door into the hall to retire to her room until Jim was gone.

"Where do you think you're going?" Jim demanded and grabbed her by her arm and jerked her backwards. "You can't leave here unlessen you say that I'm forgiven for what I did."

"I, I better go comb my hair, I reckon," Arvay said.

"Yeah, do," Maria urged. "It looks like a whoo-raw's nest. Dinner is all fixed, so don't be all day in there."

"And come ready to say the right thing soon as you get back," Jim ordered. "Shake a leg! The foundations of my patience gives way mighty easy."

Arvay went off meekly enough. She wanted to be by herself to think awhile anyway. She was falling into step with hope and she wanted to pick herself over inside just in case. As she combed out her hair and put it up again, she thought and asked questions of herself. If Jim really wanted her, what about herself?

Now, in the first place, was she really in love? She was beginning to feel that she was, or could be anyway. She might recede from this high point in the future, and retreat to the one of ruthlessness where only those things that count with the neighbors would seem worth fighting for, but right now she was smoking with illusions.

And the way Jim had talked coming along the road made things seem too easy. He had just as good as excused the woman he married from all worry and bother. In so many words he had said, "Love and marry me and sleep with me. That is all I need you for. Your brains are not sufficient to help me with my work; you can't think with me. Let's get this thing straight in the beginning. Putting your head on the same pillow with mine is not the same thing as mingling your brains with mine anymore than crying when I cry is giving you the power to feel my sorrow. You can feel my sympathy but not

35

my sorrow." All in all, that meant that if she married Jim Meserve, her whole duty as a wife was to just love him good, be nice and kind around the house and have children for him. She could do that and be more than happy and satisfied, but it looked too simple. There must be a catch in it somewhere. Being of high family, and having more book learning than she had, and being all that handsome, he could be as choosey as he pleased, and he was bound to be looking for something else. There was bound to come a time when he was going to feel outdone in not finding those other things in her.

Arvay took a long, tremulous breath. Her heart was leading her into the arms of Jim Meserve. The fearful future lying in ambush for her. Well, maybe God would have mercy and help her when it came. She might be able to hold onto Jim, and keep him from quitting her some way or another. Holding her breath in a fearful tenseness, she changed into a fresh dress, pinched her cheeks to make them pink, and slowly went out to join Jim and her father on the back porch.

Jim looked at her with admiration and came and stood in front of her and looked down earnestly into her face.

"All right now," he jollied, "what you got to say?"

"I got to forgive you, I reckon, Mister Meserve."

"You had better. I'm liable to take and frail you good."

Arvay smiled and cast her eyes to the floor. Then she reached out timidly and took his hand. "Come on. I got something pretty to show you before Maw can get dinner on the table. 'Tain't nothing but a mulberry tree, but I think it's fine."

Arvay pulled and they jumped off the porch into the yard. Just then Maria stuck her head out of the kitchen door.

"No time for that now, Arvie. I'm just putting dinner on the table."

"Won't take but a minute, Maw. I want to show him where I used to play doll-house."

"What in the nation for, Arvie? 'Tain't a thing out there for nobody to see at all. You ain't had no play-things out there for the last longest, and Mister Meserve done seen a many mul-

36

berry tree before now, I 'speck. I wants to git out of this hot kitchen over this cook-stove."

Arvay didn't talk back, but she led Jim on off determinedly. She held on to Jim's hand and hurried him along. Her mother had no idea about her at all, she was beginning to believe. Before anything more could be said, she wanted a cleansing of her sacred place. She wanted Carl and all her thoughts about him to be gone from under that mulberry tree. She wanted to feel that the temple was cleansed, and that she herself was clean and worthy of what she was about to receive. Only the strength that Jim radiated could drive out the old things. Jim just had to come here and broom out before she risked sitting down to the table with him and having him say that he cared for her and ask her to marry him. Arvay all but ran across the field, dragging Jim along with her.

They entered the place under the tree and stood there hand in hand, almost hidden from the outside by the low-hanging, supple limbs. It was a cool green temple of peace.

"Oh, but this is nice and pleasant," Jim exclaimed. "I don't fault you for liking it here. Feels like we got the world all to ourselves under here. Just you and me."

Arvay held tight to Jim's hand and said nothing. She led him around the tree in a solemn walk till they came back to the same spot again. She stood looking up through the new green leaves, punctuated by tiny fuzzy things that looked like green, stubby worms. Those were the young mulberries coming on. She was just standing there clinging to Jim's hand and feeling that everything little had been swept away by bigness when she heard her mother bawling for them, sharply and impatiently.

The feeling around the table was tense for a while. Everybody thinking about the same thing and trying to act like they were not. It was obvious that the tale Brock felt impelled to tell about marriage customs in the backwoods of Arkansaw was prompted by his thoughts.

"Girls marry off soon back in Arkansaw where I come from," Brock began by way of ringing in his story, and both

Arvay and Maria jumped at the crudeness of the way Brock was bringing out what they were all thinking about.

"You didn't come from no Arkansaw," Maria snapped by way of heading off what she knew was coming. "You was borned back there in middle Georgia."

"Matters a difference about where I was borned, Maria. I'm talking about what I learned when I was visiting over there in the backwoods of Arkansaw. Now."

"You ain't even been nowhere near there, Brock, so you might as well squat that rabbit right now and jump another one. Anyhow, nobody don't want to hear that old-time lie. You done told it so many times that everybody is sick and tired of hearing it."

That was a way that Brock had for the last year or so. Everything that happened was in Arkansaw, influenced by a paper-backed book that had the rural South by the ears for the last few years and had become a sort of laughing Bible among them, called *A Slow Train Through Arkansas*.

"But I want to hear him tell it," Jim said. "Never been in them parts myself, and I'd favor to get some information on the marrying subject just as quick as I can. I needs any assistance I can get hold of along in here."

Arvay as well as her mother suffered. Act too anxious, and it might drive the man away. And just as things looked kind of hopeful, Brock had to flap his big mouth. Arvay sat stiff with misery. Maria suddenly remembered that she had not brought in the bowl of gravy and the pitcher of lemonade, and mentioning it, gave herself opportunity to not be present when the disaster struck her child.

But Brock, full of his purpose, was not hurried. He wallowed the thing around and waited for Maria to go and come. He watched Maria settle miserably into her seat again and then began:

"Oh, 'tain't much of a story, Jim, it's just the habit they got back there in them Arkansaw mountains. When a fellow sees a girl he figgers he'd love to marry, he goes to her Paw and asks for her. So the girl's Paw, if the fellow is agreeable to him, calls the girl to him, and they stand her up in a barrel. If her head sticks out, they figger that she's old enough to git married, and he turns her over to her new husband."

"Unhunh!" Jim chuckled. "That's a good system, but how about it if she ain't tall enough for her head to stick out the barrel? Do the fellow have to wait till she grows some more?"

"Not in Arkansaw." Brock laughed. "Naw, indeed. If her head don't stick out, they saws the barrel off some."

Both of the men burst out laughing loud at that, but Arvay felt stiff around her lips, and the fork fell from her fingers. Jim was going to think that she was much too old to marry from that. But she saw Jim with a serious face look at her as if he had caught her in some crime.

"Then they don't have no chance to do no missionarying around out there, eh?"

"Not a tap." Brock assured him positively, "And it's a damned good thing too, I figger."

"You got a barrel handy, Mr. Henson?" Jim asked with a serious face.

"Sure have."

Jim pretended to scramble to his feet. "Well, maybe it can wait till after dinner is over. Into the barrel Miss Arvay goes, and if her head sticks out, I'm marrying her just as sure as gun's iron."

"You sound like you got serious notions about courting, Jim."

"Look like none of you all don't understand me quite as yet," Jim replied very seriously. "I talk just like I spit. When I spit, it hits the ground, it never comes back to my mouth, does it?"

"Don't recollect that I ever knowed a thing like that to happen," Brock considered.

"Well then, when my word goes forth, I never rue back on it either. And I mean to say right here that I mean to marry Miss Arvay if she will have me. That's been my whole intention ever since the first time that I laid eyes on her. That's what I stayed here in Sawley for. If she can see her way clear to marry me, I mean to do all within my power to do to make her life comfortable and happy."

"Spoke like a natural man," Brock said quickly. "Nobody couldn't say no more than that. So far as I'm concerned, you have my consent. I couldn't wish her to be in better hands. Now, what you got to say on the subject, baby?"

Arvay took good notice. Her father was not in the habit of using pet names to her. Calling her "baby" now was his way of pleading with her to consent. She had known for a long time that her father wanted her to be married and off his hands, so that was all right with her in a way. It was something different from that that made her fumble and twist the fringe of the tablecloth and drop her eyes while they all waited so anxiously for her answer.

"I thank you for your compliments, Mr. Meserve, and I'll accept if you feel that you really want me. That is, providing you make me a promise not to drop no more teppentime in my eye."

CHAPTER 3

"A rvay, what in the world is got the matter with you?"

"How, Ma?"

"Out and gone nearly every blessed night. We ain't had but a month from the start off to get you ready for your wedding, and you ain't got no time to waste traipsing around with Jim from place to place. If it ain't a cane-grinding, it's a candy-pulling. If it ain't that, it's a peanut-biling. If it ain't a peanut-biling, it's a square dance, and you never used to dance. And you need all that time to get your sewing done. You got no time for all that."

"Jim, Ma. Look like he wants me with him."

Arvay did not choose to elaborate. It was true that Jim liked to attend all those social doings, but Arvay knew that she was not forced to go along with Jim. Her fear would not let her trust Jim off too much alone. Nobody was going to whisper anything to Jim while she was present. Being a preacher's wife, Larraine no longer danced, but she did attend many of the other doings. Arvay felt the need of getting her things ready even more than her mother did, but her unease would not permit her to risk letting Jim run into Larraine when she was not there.

Larraine had been rather nice, though. She had made Arvay a wedding nightgown trimmed with lace, and had bought the white kid slippers to go with the white dotted swiss that Arvay was to stand up in. Brock Henson had provided the money for the goods for the wedding dress and the Alice blue mull dress that Arvay was just finishing off this minute. She was to put it on for the reception. It was cut low in the neck with short puff sleeves.

Arvay was always with Jim in public, but she held away from him when they were alone. She did not feel fitten for him, never realizing how her contradictory behavior worried the man. Jim supposed that she would not go back on her promise, but that was not enough for Jim to marry on. He wanted things complete. His worries on that score followed him everywhere. To bed, at the table, and at his work. It was like a sandspur sticking in his skin. Particularly, he thought about it a great deal as he rode or walked through the "drifts" inspecting faces on the trees and checking generally on the work.

Two weeks of his marriage, Jim was down in the woods checking up for the pay-roll at the end of the week. Jim loved the silent chasms of the drifts. The growths, the birds and the sounds of the wind in the pines. A man could think down in there, and feel.

Jim Meserve was what was known as a woodsman in the turpentine plan of things. That meant that he was the resident head of a camp. He ran the commissary and kept the accounts of the workers and made out the time. It was his job to "ride the woods" before the semi-monthly pay-day and evaluate the work of the chippers and dippers. Their pay depended upon the number of trees streaked or dipped. The number of trees could be reduced by the number improperly worked. The limit of a "drift," a territory of one chipper, is known as the "butting-line or block," so as Jim rode his horse from drift to drift, he could enjoy both the beauty and the solitude of the pine woods. Free from the press of details around the camp, Jim came alive and stretched out his soul. Usually then, he could work out his problems. This day, he felt that he had something to bother over.

Jim was not so sure that that was what he wanted, but he

found that he could not help himself. What was the matter with his engagement? He felt as if he had grabbed hold of a running man by the coat, and the man had run off, leaving Jim holding the empty jacket.

"Hands full of nothing, mouth full of 'much obliged.'" Jim heard somebody singing blues at a distance.

"Nobody but Joe Kelsey," Jim laughed. He ought to know that was Joe. He was in Joe's drift. Only two men working it, the chipper and the dipper, and he knew Joe's voice from Charlie's. He ought to know it anywhere, as he said. He had made a friend out of the Negro, or the Negro had made a friend out of him, one or the other.

"Good time to run up on Joe, too. Maybe Joe might know something that could help me just in here." He hurried back to his horse and mounted. He had spotted a few cups that Joe had not cleaned out well, but he didn't care too much. That was not so good for the company, but he was not going to kick up a fuss with Joe Kelsey about it at all, because somehow, he liked the man tremendously. Joe Kelsey was a reddy brown Negro, ugly as sin, but with the best-looking smile that Jim had ever seen on a man. It always lit him right up. It always made Jim feel like playing and joking. Just seeing Joe put him into a playful mood and he decided at once to slip up on Joe and play some practical joke.

Now Joe had switched to that teppentime song:

"Oh, don't you see dat rider coming?"

The song went on to point out to dippers, chippers, woodcutters and teamsters the perils of being caught fooling around on the job by the over-rider.

Jim got up close to Joe's back and made a sudden howl like an angry bob-cat on the kill. At the same time, he clawed his fingers and stuck them into Joe's broad back.

Joe jumped around, pretending great fright, and for a minute both men went into the act of pretending. Then they both broke into loud laughter.

43

"You *ought* to be skeered, Joe, even if you ain't. You ain't doing a goddamn thing down here in this drift but shamming."

"Why, you, Mister Jim! Why, I'm almost to the butting-line."

"And leaving nigh on to a barrel of gum behind you that you ain't dipped clean, you scoundrel-beast, you."

Joe did not defend himself by claiming perfection. He pointed out his family worries, the slick and tricky way that moonshine likker had a way of slipping up on him, and so on and so forth.

"I know, I know," Jim retorted in mock sternness. "It's Saturday nights that's your trouble, Joe. Saturday pay-night, you spend all you got on likker and women. Before draw-day, you're pestering my life out of me for more money. Pretty nearly every man on the camp is the same way. Saturday night! Saturday night! Look like that's all you colored folks live for on this camp, Saturday night!"

Joe looked very serious while Jim was preaching. When the woodsman had finished, Joe kept on looking serious. Finally he scratched his head and seemed to reach a conclusion.

"I speck youse right about that Saturday night business, Mister Jim. Fact of the matter is, I knows youse dead right. But if you ever was to be a Negro just *one* Saturday night, you'd never want to be white no more."

Jim looked at Joe in astonishment for a moment, then he burst out laughing and turned away.

"You're just all right, Joe. Maybe I could learn something from that."

Jim went on to where his horse was tied and mounted. Nearly a mile farther to the west he came upon another man chipping and dismounted. This was not Joe, so Jim was critical. He got into an argument with the chipper.

"Sink 'em in, there Charlie, sink 'em in! You ain't doing a

44

thing but scratching that tree. Keep on scratching, and you'll be done scraped up kin. Sink 'em in!"

Charlie let his streaking iron rest on the ground for a minute as he turned a surly look on Jim. The known best chipper on the camp to be spoken to like that!

"I'm sinking 'em. What you want me to do, cut the tree down?"

"And looky there." Jim jumped from the depth of the streaks to something else. "You're drawing that face in. Keep on, it'll tossle afterwhile. And I noticed some trees back there where you put on some streaks too deep. You must be figgering on laying by timber instead of making gum. Work like that can kill off trees."

After more fault-finding, and leaving a surly Charlie behind him, Jim rode on off. He knew that he was too finicky with the man, and he knew that it was because he was not just satisfied with Arvay in a way. There seemed to be a hold-back to her love. Did she love some other man whom she could not get, and was just marrying him so as to be able to say that she had a husband of her own? Or was it that damn missionary business? Whichever one it was, it could be a lot of trouble later on. But what to do? He loved the girl too much by now to give her up! So what in hell to do? Whom could he turn to for advice? He could think of no one but Joe Kelsey, and possibly his wife, Dessie, who cooked and did for him around his bachelor quarters on the camp. Joe had plenty experience with women, certainly. Maybe he could help.

But what Joe said that night on the commissary porch, after he had listened intently to Jim about his coming marriage, worried Jim even more.

"If it's like that, Boss, you got something to think about. Because if a woman don't get hold of the man she really wants, God help the man she do get. And if she don't get hold on none at all, God help the surrounding country!"

However, Joe did leave one shine of hope out of the things he said.

"Most women folks will love you plenty if you take and see to it that they do. Make 'em knuckle under. From the very first jump, get the bridle in they mouth and ride 'em hard and stop 'em short. They's all alike, Boss. Take 'em and break 'em."

Jim Meserve went to bed thinking hard.

CHAPTER 4

Arvay and her mother were in the girl's bedroom sewing in a rush the next afternoon when Arvay heard somebody hail at the gate. It was Joe Kelsey astride a sweating horse. Recognizing him as one of Jim's men, Arvay told him to come on in.

He had a note from Jim, and Arvay tore it open and read it while he stood on the steps and waited.

It was a short note. All it said was that Jim would be there the next day right after dinnertime to take Arvay for a buggy-ride. She had better have on her good clothes, for they were going somewhere. Arvay told Joe to wait and took the note inside and handed it to her mother.

"That pesky Jim! Look like he don't intend to give you no chance to get your things ready at all. Might as well sent him word to come ahead. You young folks ain't nothing like we was in my day. You ain't at all responsible. If it wasn't for me doing most of the work, you'd be in a pretty fix, I'm telling you."

Arvay turned on her heels and went on back to the porch and gave Joe the message for Jim.

Over her mother's outraged protests, Arvay put on the blue mull dress the next day. She thought that it was very becoming to her looks. She was ready away ahead of time, but ate no

47

dinner. She was excited and curious about this buggy ride, and besides her corset was laced very tight. She put on the new leghorn-intention hat with the big pink rose on the floppy brim and waited. She could not help from wondering, and even worrying some. Maybe Jim had found out. She looked down at her high-buttoned white shoes and wondered. Two more weeks and she would be safely married. She wished that the time would hurry up and come.

Jim drove up just after one. He was dressed up in his suit of clothes, a new hard felt hat with a wide brim, and he had attempted to lay his thick black curls with water. Arvay watched him through the parlor window as he hitched the rig under the chinaberry tree near the gate.

"There's that Jim of your'n out there at the gate," Mrs. Henson observed unnecessarily. "And dressed up so it 'ud take ten doctors to tell how near he's dressed to death." Mrs. Henson grumbled it out, but there was pride in her manner. "Reckon you better hurry on out and meet him. Don't bring him inside this tore-up house."

"No, you go, Ma. If I bust right on out there it would look like I was dressed and waiting on him. Look like I was too anxious to get him." Arvay was reluctant to find out news if it should happen to be bad.

So Mrs. Henson went to the door, noting as Jim came down the walk that was lined on either side with quart bottles stuck neck-downwards in the ground that Jim Meserve was a well-built man. He made her wish that she was young again. Jim had it all over the square-built, stocky man with the red face that she had married. He had it over Carl Middleton too, so far as that was concerned. They called Arvay slow and poky, but she was doing mighty well for herself.

"Come right in, Jim, and have a chair."

"No, Ma'am, I thank you. Ain't got much time for setting. Got to hurry right along. Where's Arvay, Ma'am?"

"Putting on her last fixings. You know how these young gals is." She turned her head inside the door and called out to her daughter, then turned back to the young man standing

48

impatiently on the porch and gave the opinion that Arvay would be along "tuhreckly." He knew how these courting gals was, she reckoned.

In another minute or so, Arvay stood in the door and smiled at Jim.

"Well, I guess I'm ready. Where you taking me today?"

"Oh, you find out in plenty time. You ready?"

"Much as I ever will be, I reckon."

"Then the two of us is ready and rearing to go. But before we drive off, I favor to see that playhouse you used to play in under that mulberry tree. Oh, hello, there, Mr. Henson! Didn't expect to find you around home this time of day."

"Bear got me and I knocked off. Got my pay-roll all fixed up and ready anyhow." Brock Henson explained as he came to the door and made a place beside his wife where he could see the young couple on the porch.

"The bear is out there all right. Mighty hot for this time of the year. Persimmons won't never get ripe if this kind of weather keeps on."

"Where you and Arvay headed for dressed up like that?" Mrs. Henson asked, but her husband nudged her into silence.

"Oh, just round and about, Ma'am," Jim answered and took Arvay by the arm and headed her off the porch. "First thing, I want Arvay to show me her playhouse. Just favor to see the place today."

Arvay led Jim around the house towards the back, and trembled as she went. Jim held the girl's arm all the way as they went along unevenly over clods that had grass grown over them, through patches of broom-straw and down to the back and bottom of the place where the huge mulberry tree stood in swaying majesty. There was a breeze, and the big leafy growth rolled in the arms of the wind.

"Well, here it is," Arvay said as they stooped under the low-hanging willowly limbs and straightened up in the wide shady area under the tree. It was like a green cave under there, or like being inside a big green tent. Arvay wanted to hear what she would hear.

"Mighty nice place to play house in. You must have had a high old time with your playthings under here."

"Reckon so. But I growed out of things like that long time ago. Don't even know what become of the last ones I used to have."

Jim went and leaned against the great trunk of the tree and fixed his eyes on the girl in blue. He studied her so long that she became embarrassed.

"That would be natural," Jim conceded at last. "But anyhow, you just go along acting like you was playing house again anyhow. I figger that you would look awful pretty at it. Go ahead."

After some embarrassment, Arvay tried to re-live the thing for Jim, wondering what on earth he wanted her to do it for.

"Pa made me and Larraine a playhouse, and it used to be right here. Over there by the tree we had some sea-shells and things. Oh, we about fetched anything under here that we felt to keep to play with. Bottles and jars, and oh, you know things like that."

"Yeah, I know. Something like in a boy's pockets."

"I reckon so. I never even had no brother. What I liked to do when I was under here playing by myself was to catch hold of two low limbs like this and play like I was in a swing, and lean way back and gaze way up into the top of the tree. It looks so cool-like and tender green away up there. And when the wind shakes the leaves some, you can see through to the sky." And Arvay caught hold of two limbs and bracing her heels against the ground, play-acted the thing out for Jim. Her body was stretched out so that she was almost reclining as she trusted her weight to the limbs above her. "And that's when I found out that Heaven was so far off."

"How, Arvay?"

"Well, I looked and I looked as hard as I could through the top of the tree, and I never could make out a thing. No angels moving around or nothing. I never could see a thing, so I knowed that Heaven was further away than folks made out it was."

50

Arvay pulled herself erect, took off her heavy hat, and deposited it on the roots of the tree. Then she returned to her reclining position and peered earnestly up to the very top of the tree. Her skirt slid up slightly, revealing the tops of her shoes, and a glimpse of the ruffled top petticoat beneath.

Looking upwards so intently, Arvay did not see Jim when he sprang away from the trunk of the tree. She only knew that he had moved when she felt his arms suddenly thrust beneath her, and his hands digging into her side.

"Let go!" Jim commanded shortly.

Arvay brought her head up shortly, and for a brief moment their eyes met and held. Arvay's eyes questioned fearfully. Instinct told Arvay something, and she held on to the limbs desperately.

It was no use. Jim took one hand from under her and tore her grip from the swinging limbs. In a fraction of the second she was snatched from the sky to the ground. Her skirts were being roughly jerked upwards, and Jim was fumbling wildly at her thighs.

"Jim! You—"

Jim was gritting his teeth fiercely on encountering the barrier of her tight-legged drawers, seeking an opening. Finding none, Arvay felt one hand reach up and grasp the waistband. There was a "plop" and the girl knew that the button was gone. A tearing sound of starched fabric, and the garment was being dragged ruthlessly down her legs. Arvay opened her mouth to scream, but no sound emerged. Her mouth was closed by Jim's passionate kisses, and in a moment more, despite her struggles, Arvay knew a pain remorseless sweet.

Not until Jim lay limp and motionless upon her body, did Arvay return to herself and begin to think, and with thinking, all her old feelings of defeat and inadequacy came back on her. She was terribly afraid. She had been taken for a fool, and now her condition was worse than before. It was more than she could bear, to have been so lifted up for a few weeks only to be cast down like this. What was to become of her now? Where would she turn for refuge? Not to her folks, certainly.

She would get no sympathy there. Larraine would put on airs, and pity her all the more.

Jim moved slowly and dreamily and began to kiss her on her mouth and all over her face.

"I love you a million times more, darling," Jim whispered and took his hand to brush back the fallen strands of her hair from her forehead, and to kiss her there too.

He got to his feet, modestly bringing her with him so that they both stood erect and covered at the same time. He held her at arms length for a long minute, and tried to look into her downcast eyes. When he released her, he turned his back for a minute, and rearranged his clothes.

"We got to, we better be going now, honey. Come on and let's make haste."

So he had all he wanted of her, and he was ready to go.

Arvay's eyes crept over to her torn garment lying far over to the right where Jim had flung it.

"If you would be so kind as to excuse me for a few minutes, I—"

Jim understood and walked to the edge of the green wall and turned his back.

Arvay went swiftly to her drawers and picked them up. She shook off the little dust and a dry leaf and looked them over. The starchy little ruffle around the legs still stood bravely, but Arvay realized that she could not put them on. The button was gone, and the plaquette was ripped all the way down one leg to the ruffle. But if she did not put them on somehow, what was she to do? Not roll them up and take them into the house under her arm. Her mother's sharp eyes would never miss a thing like that. Come walking into the house after being off with a man with your drawers under your arm would never do with Maria Henson. The drawers would have to stay there under the tree until Arvay got a chance to sneak them into the house and sew them up again. Anyway no one ever came to the mulberry tree nowadays. Not wishing to leave such an intimate and revealing garment lying on the ground, Arvay looked around for a better place, and spied a dead snag of a

52

limb at the level of her head, and she hung her drawers on that. Then she walked over in deep embarrassment and stood beside Jim.

Jim turned and looked her over carefully. He smiled as he picked a dead leaf and bits of trash out of the back of her head. He smiled because he realized that the poor innocent thing knew nothing about secret trysts. She had no idea about leaving tell-tale signs.

"I better get you your hat so we can hurry on," and strode to the trunk of the tree and picked up the hat.

"I had sort of forgot it," Arvay admitted, and Jim smiled again.

"Lemme place it back on your pretty head," Jim murmured, and set it too far back on her head, and studied the effect for a minute. He changed it two or three times, while Arvay stood passively with a faint smile of embarrassment on her face.

"Look like I ain't so good on placing hats," Jim admitted at last with a laugh. "You better hook it on your ownself, I reckon. But hold on a minute, I got to take another kiss before you move."

With that, Jim caught hold of either side of the wide brim and pulled Arvay's face close to his. He kissed her ligntly once or twice, then let go of the hat and began to kiss her passionately and hold her tightly in his arms. Unconsciously, Arvay's own arms went up and were locked around Jim's neck.

"That's right, sugar." Jim murmured. "Hug my neck for me. Hug me tight."

Jim's urging was altogether unnecessary. Some unknown power took hold of Arvay. She pressed her body tightly against his, fitting herself into him as closely as possible. A terrible fear came over her that he might somehow vanish away from her arms, and she sought to hold him by the tightness of her embrace and her flood of kisses. It seemed a great act of mercy when she found herself stretched on the ground again with Jim's body weighing down upon her. Even then she was not satisfied. Somehow, she seemed not to be able to get close enough to him. Never, never, close enough. She must

53

eat him up, and absorb him within herself. Then he could never leave her again.

When she was on her feet again, Arvay kissed Jim voluntarily and without words. Jim returned the kiss then grabbed her hand.

"Now I know we got to go, and we better hurry."

He grabbed her hat off the ground, and seized her hand and together they stooped and came out from under the mulberry tree. Over her shoulder as she stooped, Arvay glanced back at her drawers swinging ever so gently in the breeze. She took it as a kind of sign and symbol. Where this man was hurrying her off to, she had no idea, but she was going, and leaving her old life behind her. Left behind, but not forgotten, to be picked up another time, perhaps.

When they reached the house, Arvay turned her head to the left so that she could not see the back door. Her mother might be standing there and would read her like a book. Arvay held on to Jim's hand and went on around the house. Her parents had evidently seen them when they came out from under the tree, and were following their progress, for as they came abreast of the room where her parents slept, she spied them peeping through the sugar-sack half curtains at the window. Arvay started, and Jim, looking in the same direction to see the reason, saw them too. They were doing their best to see all they could and interpret. They snatched heads back guiltily, but the young couple had caught on to what was going on. Then Brock, to cover up, shoved the curtain aside to hail them through the window.

Jim looked, grabbed Arvay by the hand and began to run towards the gate and the buggy tied there. Their progress was not fast enough for Jim evidently, for he stopped, grabbed up Arvay who was slightly behind him, and ran staggering for the gate. He was growling like a tiger which had just made a kill and was being challenged. With the weight of the girl in his arms, he kicked open the gate, made it to the side of the buggy and thrust Arvay in as Brock Henson reached the front door. He untied the reins in a frenzy and leaped in himself while

Brock walked the width of the porch to the steps, with Mrs. Henson stooped shouldered in the door and her caved-in mouth wide open. Jim grabbed the reins, slapped them smartly on the rump of the horse and yelled, "Git up! Git up, there!" And Arvay found herself flying down the sandy road.

She could not hear Brock exclaim, "Well, I'll be god-damned!" as he gazed down the road after the flying buggy. "What the hell do you reckon is going on?"

Nor could Arvay hear her mother complain, "Something that don't mean us no good, I'll bound you. Could be drag-ging our girl off somewhere to rape her and then leave her here on our hands. A young 'un without no name for us to look after and to feed and raise. All that money, nigh on to forty dollars that we done spent already on things to marry her off in, too. Brock Henson, youse the biggest fool I ever did see in all my born days! If you was any man at all, you'd take that shot-gun and get on your horse and overtake 'em. Make him marry her before the sun go down."

"Aw, I wouldn't be in such a hurry, if I was you, Maria. Arvay wasn't hollering or nothing. We couldn't swear to a thing."

"Arvay not hollering!" Mrs. Henson snorted as she went to the steps and shaded her hands and looked down the road. "Nothing like Larraine. That Arvay ain't got the sense she was born with. According to my notion, you had better go get your gun."

"Better let well enough do," Brock admonished and reached for the back of a rocker turned to the wall, whirled it around and sat down. "Far as I can see, things is coming along just fine as it is. Don't reckon Jim Meserve is the kind to back out now, with the wedding day all set and all. It would take a mighty heap of gall."

"Gall! That Jim ain't nothing else but gall. Tell me!"

Brock sat down, scrooged the chair around so that he did not have to look at his wife, cut himself another chaw, chawed his tobacco and spit his juice. He could send it expertly clear over the bannister and into the yard.

55

Speeding down the road towards Sawley, Arvay was tugging with the same emotions as her mother. Jim was silent there beside her as if nothing much had happened. He kept the horse at a fast trot and paid attention to the road. Arvay kept a fearful silence because she did not know how to begin what she wanted to say in order to find out what she wanted so much to know.

They were passing the last open field before the straggling houses of Sawley began when Jim turned his face upon Arvay and grinned.

"Arvay Henson!" Jim hailed oratorically, "The apostle to the heathens!" Then he chuckled some more.

Arvay looked at him with quickly troubled eyes. Look like Jim was making fun of her. Something closed up inside of her.

Jim laughed again. "No need for you to go proaging clean around the world no more looking for no heathens to save, though."

"Why, Jim? Is they all done saved or died off?"

"Naw, indeed. That is, I reckon there's plenty of 'em still left to save. But their case don't come up in your court no more."

So after what went on under the mulberry tree, Jim figgers that I ain't fitten no more to tote the Word, Arvay thought. No getting away from what had happened. Her drawers hung on the mulberry tree, waving with the wind. Who was she now, to be telling folks how to live?

"Don't be looking so sick over it, and putting on a long face, Arvay. Missionary work is for old maids and preachers. Youse a married woman now. You ain't got no time for that."

"Married?" Jim was cruel to be making game of her at a time like this.

"Why, sure you're married, Arvay. Under that mulberry tree."

"All I know is that I been raped."

"You sure was, and the job was done up brown."

"I could have hollered for Pa."

"And it would not have done you a damn bit of good. Just

56

a trashy waste of good time and breath. Sure you was raped, and that ain't all. You're going to keep on getting raped. You couldn't be hollering for your Pa every day for the rest of your life, could you?"

"Every day?" Arvay looked across and up at Jim in startled bewilderment. "You sure got plenty nerve."

"So I been told. But that's the way the cloth's been cut, and that's the way it's made. No more missionarying around for you. You done caught your heathen, baby. You got one all by yourself. And I'm here to tell you that you done brought him through religion and absolutely converted his soul. He been hanging around the mourner's bench for quite some time, but you done brought him through religion, and saved him from a burning shell. You are a wonderful woman, Arvay."

The elements opened above Arvay and she arose inside of herself. This must mean that she had been forgiven on high. Her secret sin was forgiven and her soul set free! Else why would Jim be talking like she thought he was? She had paid under that mulberry tree.

"You talking about me and you, ain't you, Jim?"

"You know so well that I ain't talking about nobody else."

"But, but, you just got through saying that you meant to keep on raping me. That . . ."

"You got that right, and I mean to tell you, rape in the first degree. We're headed for the courthouse now, just as fast as we can wheel and roll. And the minute we get there, we're going to take out some papers on it."

"Jim!"

"You didn't realize? Good Lord Almighty! Where else would we be headed for? Arvay, I got a letter from love today, and I'll go to Hell but what I answer it. Git up there, you good-for-nothing nag, you! Git along!"

Arvay was back at her father's house before sundown, a married woman. The news of the elopement had spread over town quickly, and by seven o'clock, people began to arrive to wish them well. Her mother, balked of the wedding excitement,

57

was all put out at first, but of necessity made the best of things as they were. Both parents joined in pleading with Jim to stay the night and give people chance to come and make merry. Jim compromised. They were around until nine o'clock, then he drove the six miles out to the camp with his bride.

Jim carried Arvay over the doorsill and kissed her as he set her feet down in the turpentine shack.

"Well, honey, you're home, for two months anyhow."

"Two months?"

"Yep. You know that I ain't no teppentime man when it comes right down to the thing, and then it don't bring in enough now that I got me a wife. Two months is enough I figger to fix us so we can go away from here and hunt up a better-paying job."

Teppentime shacks are not built for beauty. They are temporary shelters. In a few years usually the woods are worked out, and the camp is moved. The houses are torn down and put up again at the new location. But this house with its four crude rooms looked beautiful to Arvay. The rooms were immaculately clean, but the most important thing to her was that it was her own home. "This is ours," Arvay murmured as she went about touching furniture and walls.

"Yep. Your dice, baby, to do just as you damn please. Gimme a kiss now and hug my neck for me. We better go on to bed. Pay-day tomorrow and I'll have a lot to do."

Jim himself began to get ready for bed immediately, and Arvay timidly followed him. She found out the reason for Jim's haste very soon. Less than ten minutes after the lamp had been blown out, there was a gentle rustling outside the bedroom window, and then the full tones of a guitar broke out, playing in the way that only Negroes play that instrument. Clear melody, full-bodied harmony, and added bass that imitated drums.

Arvay leaped out of bed and stood at the window. She could not be seen because of the darkness within aided by the curtains at the window. She stood in her bare feet and wedding nightgown and lived through the serenade. Instrumental pieces, blues sung by men and some by women; spirituals, not sad and forlorn, but sung with a drummy rhythm to them; work songs and ballads.

The music outside did something strange and new to Arvay. The strains induced pictures before her eyes. They conjured up odors and tastes. Streams of colors played across the sky for her, and she tasted exotic fruits. Looking out into the white moonlight of the night, she saw the trees and the woods for the first time from inside. The sky-scraping pines became feeling beings, standing there forever watching, and watching, and whispering with their branches in a rumbling song. They were the tree-men with the many toes probing into the earth. The giants who stood forever on one foot and waited.

The concert came to an end on an old ballad that Arvay had heard often, but had never really learned. It was being led by a female voice, a deep alto, backed up by the other mingled voices and the guitar. Arvay resolved that she would learn that song the very next day. The song was an old, old ballad and it haunted you. Sweet and bitter mixed up in just the right amounts.

> Love, Oh, love, Oh careless love
> Goes right to the head like wine
> Broken the heart of many a poor girl
> But you'll never break this heart of mine.
>
> Love, Oh, love, Oh careless love
> Love, Oh, love, Oh careless love
> You cause me to weep, you cause me to moan
> You cause me to leave my happy home.

The ballad went on for many more verses, and Arvay was all but moved to tears. After a few minutes, she noticed that the serenade was over.

"Oh, that was just too sweet and too wonderful, Jim. Don't expect to ever forget this night, the longest day I live."

"This is some of that damn Joe Kelsey's doings," Jim grumbled to hide his own emotion. "It would be just like that bastard to cut a caper like that."

He stooped over quickly and fetched a five gallon jug from under the bed and hurried to the window.

"Thank you, folks. Me and my wife both thank you for the music of welcome home."

There was great applause at this, and Jim had to wait a long time for it to die down. Then Arvay saw a male figure step nearer the window, strike a pose and begin to deliver an elaborate ramble of welcome to the newly wed couple. After a few sentences, the speaker got lost and scrambled in the jungle of florid syllables, and the crowd outside began to jeer and scream with laughter.

"That'll do, Joe Kelsey," Jim yelled out with mock seriousness. "You done lied enough for one time. Here, take this jug of moonshine and see that everybody gets some. Now, don't go on off and drink it all up your ownself, you buzzard, you! You know I know you, Joe."

There was loud laughter at this back-handed caress, and the crowd hurried off to the Jook to have themselves a time.

"You oughtn't to have spoke to the poor man like that, especially after he got up the serenade for us, Jim."

"Pay that no mind, honey. Joe knows where he stands with me. I would trust Joe Kelsey quicker than any man on earth I know of, and Joe knows it."

"Is he the same one that you been sending in messages by?"

"That's right. He's my right-hand man around this camp. Dessie, the woman who's been doing for me here, is his wife. Two nicest folks it has ever been my pleasure to meet. I made arrangements for Dessie to help you around some. Hope you find her all right too. She's evermore easy to get along with."

Arvay was a daughter of the South. She knew exactly what to think from that.

"Joe is your pet, I'll bound you."

"Kee-reck! Different from every other Negro I ever did see. He's remarkable. Honest as the day is long. Just mighty damn fine, that's all."

60

Arvay sympathized and understood. Every Southern white man has his pet Negro. His Negro is always fine, honest, faithful to him unto death, and most remarkable. Indeed, no other Negro on earth is fitten to hold him a light, and few white people. He never lies, and in fact can do no wrong. If he happens to do what other people might consider wrong, it is never his Negro's fault. He was pushed and shoved into it by some unworthy varmint. If he kills somebody else, the dead varmint took and run into the pet's knife or bullet and practically committed suicide just to put the pet in wrong, the low-life-ted scoundrel-beast! If the white patron has his way, the pet will never serve a day in jail for it. The utmost of his influence will be invoked to balk the law. Turn go *his* Negro from that jail!

Arvay had asked, and Jim had consented for her to help him out around the commissary. He conceded that it would be a help to him and the women on the camp for the store to be open all day.

So from time to time, Arvay could have been seen, if anybody watched her closely enough, weighing up a pound or so extra for Dessie and Joe on everything. She balanced this off by either cutting somebody else light weight, or waiting until she was alone in the store and adding a pound or so to some other account. Side-meat added to one, sugar and coffee to another, snuff and tobacco to still other people, and growing very haughty and mad if anybody complained. She came to be very fond of Dessie, and Joe was her husband's man.

Her married life moved on smoothly and happily for Arvay except for one thing. Larraine and Carl drove out two or three times every week. Larraine came even when Carl did not, and Arvay wished so much that she wouldn't. She couldn't say a thing against it, and that made it very hard. Jim would think it funny if she ordered her own sister off the camp, but that was just what Arvay felt like doing.

Larraine was too bossy, Arvay felt. Dashing in and bossing around, and taking things in charge. It looked as if she could not bear for Arvay to be the head of a single thing.

Arvay objected to Carl, not because he dipped in her business at all, but because he stirred up memories, and kept her feeling of guilt alive and active. She wanted to forget the whole thing. To cast it in the sea of forgetfulness, where it would never rise to shame her in this world, or condemn her in the Judgment.

In this same connection, Larraine gave her a lot of worry. She was always calling Jim aside and giving him advice on how to manage things. Arvay, fearing that Larraine knew of her secret passion of the past, feared that 'Raine might by accident or intention let her tongue slip. Jim would lose his faith in her, and then where would she be? She would be miserable every time that her sister managed to get Jim off to one side. She searched his face for signs after every session. So far, she had seen nothing, but she wished that Larraine would stay off the place. Oh, well, the two months would soon be up, and she and Jim would be off somewhere too far for Larraine to be around. Arvay shook and trembled, and saved her complete happiness for that day.

Then the blow fell. She had been married for only six weeks when she was almost knocked off her feet by Dessie.

They were in the kitchen together. Dessie often helped her out in more ways than she was being paid for. Dessie looked at her very hard and began to chuckle.

"What's wrong, Dessie?"

"I declare! That husband you done married is all parts of a man."

"What do you mean by that, Dessie?"

"Youse knocked up, that's what."

"Knocked up?" Arvay had heard the term too many times to misunderstand what was meant by it. Arvay just did not want to hear it.

"Going to have a young 'un, just as sure as youse born to die."

"No, Dessie. I'm sure that you're mistaken. I, I ain't noticed a thing."

"That's because it's a little early for signs just as yet. You ain't hardly more'n a month gone up right now. But you will. I can see that th'obbing in your neck. Youse up the creek, honey, and they ain't no iffs and ands about it."

"Dessie!" Arvay moaned.

"Oh, 'tain't nothing to be scared about. I done had five, and 'tain't nothing to the thing. You has birth-pains, naturally, but lemme tell you, them is the easiest forgotten pains they is in all the world. Oh, you remembers enough about it later on to tell about it, but that's about all you can do. Don't you worry none."

Arvay had every intention to keep the secret to herself until after Jim had notified the owner that he was leaving, but she had no chance. Larraine drove up that very afternoon behind her little bay mare, and Dessie, not realizing what she did, hurried to tell "Miz' Middleton" the news. Jim came home to get a new hame to take out to the barns and Larraine had to up and blab her mouth to Jim.

Jim was glad and proud enough, but the upshot of it was that Jim said what Arvay had feared. It meant that they could not go away until the child was born. He wouldn't think of dragging his wife around from pillar to post in her condition.

In her nervous turmoil, brought on by disappointment and memories of other frustrations, somehow Arvay found her eyes fixed on Larraine's throat. That night Arvay had a strange dream. She saw 'Raine's white neck. It was huge like the standpipe at the water works, and down its long length blood was running and running from a huge gash near the top. Somehow she was impelled to look at her own hands, and in her right was a long sharp knife. Arvay woke up with a start, and scrouged up just as close to Jim as she could. She was almost afraid to go to sleep again.

Another night Arvay dreamed that she was in a beautiful forest of trees and very happy. Music and singing were coming to her from unseen voices. Suddenly the instruments and voices hushed as if in terrible fear. In the silence, Larraine came walking through the woods. A tiger leaped upon Larraine and tore her throat away. Great streams of blood ran down and some of it clotted between Larraine's breasts. Somehow Avary was not afraid of the tiger. She looked on indifferently as the beast lapped Larraine's blood fiercely, and when he was sated and moved away the music began again. Waking, Arvay shuddered with remorse. She knew then that she had been hating her own sister for years.

Jim himself began to notice how nervous Arvay was getting to be. He thought that the store was too much worry for her, and told her not to bother with it anymore. He would make out all right. But Arvay said no, it was just that she was tired of teppentiming, she guessed, and wanted to make a change.

"Jim, please! Take me on off. I won't care if we don't have much spending change for a while. I just crave to go away from here."

"Can't see my way clear to do that, Little-Bit. It wouldn't be the right thing for me to do. You're nervous on account of your condition. I wouldn't be no kind of a husband at all if I didn't look out for you no better than that. And then, Dessie is an A-number-one mid-wife. I'd ruther for you to be where she could see after you."

"Couldn't we go and take Joe and Dessie with us?"

"That would be a hot come-off when we don't even know where we are going to be our ownselves. You just wait. The minute that you get able to move with the baby, I'll make a move."

"Six more months, maybe, Jim."

"Can't be helped, Arvie. It ought not to seem so long. And then too, you got your folks close around to do for you. Your Mama and Larraine both. Naw, I can't see no sense in pulling out now, and running you into danger."

Arvay developed strange moods and appetites. A great craving for meat, and for clay. Arvay had seen many people in Sawley eat clay, but she had never touched it herself. Now she had a taste for clay, that fine, cream-colored clay which she had seen her mother eating all her life. There was not much clay in Florida, but there was a deposit not too far from Sawley, to the north of town. Many a time Arvay had gone with her mother and seen her eat it hungrily after a rain. She had even seen her mother bake it into little cakes and sigh with satisfaction afterwards. It had tasted so smooth and good!

But Jim exploded with disgust when Arvay asked him to get her some clay from the bank to eat. He pitched into Dessie hot and heavy when he found that Dessie had sent her twelve-year-old son for clay and smuggled it in to Arvay. He had better not find any more of the goddamned filthy, dirty stuff around the place. If he did, he was going around the ham-bone looking for meat! That was the word with the bark on it. Nothing but a notion anyway. No nourishment in the thing.

Arvay hungered and retreated inside of her self with her fears. She came to the place where she wished that Larraine would tell and have it over with. But, no, Larraine was acting cruel. Holding the thing back to keep Arvay in suspense. There was nothing for Arvay to do but huddle with her eternal fear and wait.

The first quarrel arose over something which Jim contended later was trashy, and had nothing to do with them.

Arvay had gone back to reading a chapter in the Bible every night. Like many others, she had the habit of letting the Bible fall open and reading the chapter where it opened as a sort of message.

The night of the quarrel, the Book fell open in Genesis, and at the story of the killing of Abel by Cain. She read for quite a while; then Jim, beside her in the bed, asked her what she was reading, not because he was interested, but so as not to feel lonesome and excluded. Arvay told him.

"And it was an awful crime for Cain to do," Arvay commented. "It wasn't Abel's fault if God didn't accept Cain's sacrifice."

"And I don't blame God neither. I'd turn against a man that didn't have no better sense than to burn a stinking cabbage right under my nose."

"But what else could he have done, Jim? He tilled the fields, didn't he?"

65

"That's what I been told, Arvay. Cain's first crime was not killing his brother Abel, but in not having no sense of humor. The man was so chuckle-headed that he couldn't even take a joke."

"Joke?" Arvay was so outraged that she hurriedly propped herself up on one elbow and frowned down into Jim's face. "You must be crazy or [an] awful wicked one, to be looking for jokes in the Bible."

"Well, if it's about the doings of people, it must be plenty jokes in there."

"Well, I never!" Arvay sighed and sank back on her pillow. "Jokes in the Word of God."

"Sure, Arvie, if you can see 'em like they is. Now, take this same man, Cain, that you been reading about. He never would have got into all that trouble if he could have seen a joke. He never would have up and scorched a stinking, rotten cabbage under God's nose for no sacrifice. Common sense ought to have told him God wouldn't stand for him stinking up Heaven and all like that. How come he couldn't have made God a nice cool salad and took it to Him? That would have been something out of his garden too, wouldn't it? Tell me!"

The battle raged and roiled. The sacred quality of the Bible, sinner-people who could make mock of holy things. Folks given to jokes and the dumbness of those who couldn't see a joke, and on and on. Jim was not really annoyed at first, he just enjoyed teasing Arvay, but Arvay went further than Jim thought necessary, and he stung her somewhat with ridicule. For the first time, Arvay refused Jim's goodnight hug, turned her back on him and got as far away from him as she could.

It was three whole days before the house got warm and intimate again. But fights leave scars on people, no matter how slight, and both had revealed things inside them that they usually concealed. Jim found out that Arvay considered him a sinner and a scoffer. Arvay found out that Jim thought her a trifle dumb.

CHAPTER 5

It was in the heat of summer when Arvay's baby came. With Dessie there giving expert aid, commanding Arvay to "Bear down! Bear down, I tell you!" making the girl get out of bed and kneel at the foot and strain against a sheet twisted into a rope and tied to the bed-post, Arvay came through easily.

After a while, Dessie brought Arvay's baby to her, all attended to and dressed. It had cried briefly when Dessie smacked the breath of life into it, then Arvay had heard no more. It was very quiet when Dessie put it in her arms, and Dessie was quiet too. Arvay was afraid that it might be dead.

Something must be wrong. She could tell from Dessie's kind eyes trying to lie to her and look enthusiastic. "It's a boy, and I know that his daddy will be glad."

Arvay looked at her baby, and then she understood. It was nothing like Jim at all. The hair and eyelashes were perfectly white. It would be a blond. That was disappointing but not serious. What else she saw made Arvay cry out in horror.

"Dessie! Dessie! What is the matter with my child's hands?"

"It would take a God to tell, Miz' Arvay. Them don't look much like fingers, do they?"

"Good gracious! They look more like strings. And his hands, Dessie. Why they look too little for his body."

Arvay passed her hand over the quiet baby's head as if to

comfort it and then gave another cry. There was practically no forehead nor backhead on her child. The head narrowed like an egg on top. Arvay began to cry. Then when she had cried a while, she looked her baby all over and cried some more. The feet were long, and the toes well formed, but they looked too long for a new-born baby to have. And there was no arch to the tiny feet. They were perfectly flat, with a little lump of flesh huddled under what should have been the in-step. Arvay studied the little red bundle of flesh in her arms.

It certainly did not favor Jim. Who did it remind her of? Finally she knew. He looked like her Uncle Chester, her mother's youngest brother. The one that they seldom talked about. The one who was sort of queer in his head. Oh, Jesus! How could she show this child to Jim? In what words could she explain? She handed the bundle off to one side, so as to be sure not to overlay it, and turned away and cried.

When Jim came, he acted like Dessie. He tried to say something nice. Arvay kept up with his face with her eyes. Jim was kind and asked her how she felt over and over again, but he did not enthuse at all. He kissed her and petted her much too much.

"What must we name him?" Arvay asked and prayed.

"Oh, no rush about that at all," Jim said casually. "We got plenty time to figger that out, Little-Bit. You just rest your self up good so we can move off from here."

Arvay was left alone with her child. Jim mentioned details of work. Too bad, but he was in a sort of a slow hurry. Had to look after things. He was a family man now, and had to make support for three.

Arvay could not keep from continually searching over the child. She was made conscious of the mouth at last. It was exceptionally small, and what there was of it was concentrated in the bottom lip. It was a tiny pink pug thrust out at the world. It did not hang loosely at all. Just a tiny half moon no bigger than Arvay's finger nail.

But the size of the mouth was no measure of the appetite of the child. He attacked ferociously when put to the breast.

Arvay had to laugh at his eagerness. It was strange that the child seldom cried out demanding to be fed. Occasionally he made a low whimpering sound and moved his limbs in complaint. But always he seized upon the breast; he did not simply accept it as most children did. Jim, watching one afternoon, looked on with astonishment.

"It's a damn lucky thing that you got plenty of milk, honey. If you didn't have it, I'm mighty scared that young 'un would eat you clean up. Look at him go to it!"

The baby's defects only increased Arvay's love for it. She mooned over it, caressed it with pity added to her love. She spent a long time morning and night bathing it, rubbing it over with sweet oil and massaging and manipulating the narrow head. She was doing her best to shape it into a more agreeable form. Whether it was on account of her labors, or just nature, she was surprised every morning to note a little change. The head gradually ceased to be different enough to attract particular notice, and Arvay rejoiced with tears. Still, the bones of the string-like fingers did not appear to be gaining in size and strength. For a long time, the finger bones felt like limber cartilage to the touch. Arvay wondered if her son would ever be able to use his tiny hands. Nor was there any change in the shape of the baby's feet. It took on weight and grew decidedly better-looking if you did not examine the hands and the feet.

Arvay shut herself in the bedroom with her baby where she could talk aloud to herself for a while every day after Jim had been gotten off to work.

"Poor little thing, you! Mam is going to love you, don't care who else don't care. You couldn't help it. You ain't the blame at all. This is the punishment for the way I used to be. I thought that I had done paid off, but I reckon not. I never thought it would come like this, but it must be the chastisement I been looking for. You're Mama's precious honey, and don't you cry."

This was an unnecessary admonition, for the baby seldom cried. Even when he was several months old and a husky body, the child made few demands. It lay in the crude crib that Joe Kelsey had knocked together, calling on no one until he was picked and fed or attended to. Neither did the child show any recognition or eagerness at the sight of anyone at all. He seized upon his food almost angrily, and when he was full, he could be put down again without a murmur. One thing only Arvay began to notice about him very early. The child seemed to be very much afraid. Any sudden movement, any strange object introduced into his presence brought screams of terror. Otherwise, Arvay's son was a world within himself.

When a week, ten days, and then two weeks went by and Jim had made no mention of a name for the child, Arvay gritted her teeth and put on a brave show of outwitting her husband. She included Dessie.

"Let's we bake a cake, Dessie, for the baby."

"Baby? He ain't near old enough to be eating no cake, Miss Arvie."

"I know, Dessie, but I want you to help me out with a cake for giving him a name."

Then Arvay smiled in a sly way. "I mean to get ahead of Jim and name the baby my ownself. It's natural for a man to want the first boy named after him, but I always loved the name of Earl David, and said that if I ever had a boy-child I was going to name him that. While Jim is laying low to fix up some big preparation to name the baby after him, I mean to get ahead and say it first. Supper tonight, I'll place the cake on the table with the name all wrote on top. You know how men folks are, and we women have to take advantage of 'em now and then."

Dessie agreed and the cake was made. Arvay was by no means sure that Dessie had been taken in, but that part did not matter. It was a case of saving face.

Jim made no objections to the choice of a name at all. Said it was very pretty, and a whole lot better than plain Jim Meserve. He didn't know as he wanted a child named after himself anyway. Let every man have a name all to himself.

That was a nice way of putting it, Arvay reflected at the other end of the table. Jim was putting on to keep from hurt-

70

ing her feelings. Before she went to bed that night, she opened the new family Bible, and on the lined page at the back, wrote *Earl David Meserve, born July 26, 1906.*

Jim was off somewhere in the quarters. Probably at Joe's house, where Arvay suspected Jim found the occasional drink that he took, and was taking more and more often here of late. He probably would not be home for some time.

So Arvay felt free to get on her knees and pray. First, she asked God for the health and welfare of her child, and please, let Earl David never be taken away from her. Then she prayed for Jim. Prayed for the saving of his soul; that he be moved to hurry up and take her away from the vicinity of Sawley and keep on loving her.

CHAPTER 6

Two months after Earl was born, Jim gave notice to the turpentine firm that he was leaving, and that announcement gave Arvay great satisfaction. Where they were going, how and why did not concern her. It did not matter so long as she was going away from Sawley. When they sat in the day coach, with the round-topped metal-bound trunk in the baggage car, and the telescope bag and the shabby old satchel in the rack over their heads, they had all their worldly possessions with them. Jim had around a hundred dollars in his pockets, mostly from the sale of their household goods, and his last paycheck. Her husband was beside her on the seat, and her baby was in her lap. They were headed east and south away from what she used to know and feel and Arvay was asking for nothing more.

They landed in Citrabelle, a bright-looking flowery town on the Florida ridge south of Polk County. By ways that Arvay knew nothing of, Jim had come to a decision to settle there, and had a job as foreman of a crew of fruit-pickers. She knew that she was settled in a light and airy cottage painted a bright yellow and trimmed with white. She did observe that folks down in these parts did seem to be powerful fond of painting houses and planting flowers. It was a very pretty habit, though, and Arvay put out to have herself a flower yard too. Outside of the miles and miles of orange groves, the people raised nothing but vegetables to eat. Not a speck of cotton or tobacco, or the things she was used to seeing growing. Things had a picnicky, pleasury look that, while it was pretty, made Arvay wonder if folks were not taking things too easy down in here. Heaven wasn't going to be any refreshment to folks if they got along with no more trouble than this. As far as she could see, the place was plumb given over to pleasure. Flower-yards looked as if folks had spent as much time fixing and attending them as they did back in west Florida to raise a crop of corn, peanuts, cotton or tobacco. It was the duty of man to suffer in this world, and these people round down here in south Florida were plainly shirking their duty. They were living entirely too easy. There just didn't seem to Arvay to be any kind of honest work that kept folks bowed down from can't-see-in-the-morning till can't-see-at-night. Then too they could get hold of all the oranges, grapefruit and tangerines that they could lay under without spending a cent. What treat would a whole orange or tangerine in a Christmas stocking be to a person down in here? It just didn't seem right for folks to live as loose and as careless as all this. And look at the wages that were paid down in this vicinity! It was hard for her to believe. It worried Arvay so that finally she had to seek some information from Jim.

"When do these folks around here get down to work sure enough, Jim?" Arvay asked one day.

"Get to work, Arvay? Why, that's what they're doing all the time."

"You mean folks round here don't do no more'n this, and make all that money?"

"That's right. Fruit is the main thing, then truck-gardening. Ninety-day crops down in here. Three crops a year. Sell it to the commission houses, put your money in your pocket and put in another crop."

"Well suh! Nothing much to do but just wallow around. I don't know what's to become of folks. They'll be too lazy to draw they breath after while."

"Feel like you're being carried to the skies on flowery beds of ease, eh?" Jim laughed. "You married yourself a man, honey. I told you, like that old hymn says, marriage with me never was designed to make your pleasures less. Rest easy, you ain't seen nothing as yet. I aim to have you living so fine some day that this will look like a teppentime camp beside it. You're such a baby-child, Arvay. Maybe that's why I love you so hard." He kissed the back of her neck. "You don't have to worry about a thing. You got a man who can bring it when he come."

Therefore, Arvay knew nothing about the desperate struggle Jim was going through for their very existence. She did not know about those terrible three weeks when Jim, knowing nothing about citrus-fruit production, had stood around with his hands in his pockets feeling and turning over the little money he had, and casting about for some way to get into the work. How he had finally decided that since the colored men did all of the manual work, they were the ones who actually knew how things were done, and how he had taken up around the jooks and gathering places in Colored Town, and swapped stories, and stood treats, and eased in questions in desperate hope, wondering if his money would hold out until he could get a footing, and how he had finally gotten information which landed him his job.

She did not know that fruit-cutters seldom worked at all from the end of the season early in June until it opened again around the middle of September when they began to cut grapefruit, however short of money they might be. But Jim had made an arrangement to look after the company groves during the summer months, seeing to the pruning, ploughing of the groves, fertilizing and hoeing. His pay envelope would be less, but it would be enough to keep them going, to save them from living on credit and having a big grocery bill facing him when the season opened. He had persuaded at least half of his crew to go along with him, and they worked all summer and opened up in the fall with money ahead.

During those summer months, Jim used his head too. Gain-

74

ing a greater intimacy with his men, he subtly worked up the spirit of rivalry in fruit-cutting. Who was the best, sure enough? There got to be arguments and contests about it. The men took to bringing their bags and clippers along and any left-over fruit in the groves they were tending got cut in a fury of competition. There is always some fruit that gets over-looked and always sour-orange trees in every grove. They make a particularly fine-flavored lemonade. The men never left one with fruit on it now, and when the season opened up, they were rearing to go. They told him of the best cutters in other crews and for other companies, and Jim shifted around until he had nothing but experts under him, and augmented his crew by three men. By Christmas, they were "raising a fog" in any grove that they were thrown in, and the amount of fruit they cut had been duly taken note of at the packing-house. The manager stopped Jim and had a talk with him. He was particularly grateful because Jim had served during the off months when it was so hard to get work done, and his record since the season opened was impressive. It was now arranged for Jim to get the same money all the year round and a bonus for exceeding a certain number of boxes a week. His men got their added money in the number of boxes they cut. They were the highest-paid men in that part of the state and getting known. To foster the spirit, the manager lined Jim and his men up on the loading-platform the day before Christmas, praised them to the highest in front of everybody, and presented each man with a Christmas turkey.

Arvay had the big turkey that Jim had received. She baked it and they ate it, but she never asked for the story behind it, and since the eager Jim, feeling no curiosity in her about his achievement, was that kind of a man, he did not offer her the information. He ate his dinner, and went off somewhere and came home drunk. Arvay was displeased about it and acted sullen, but she never sought the why of that either.

That did not mean that there were no high places in her existence. In spite of her silent resentment over Earl, and in spite of her lack of expression, there were times when they

75

grabbed hands and mounted to Heaven together. They played music on the instrument of life. It was merely that two or three of the keys were out of fix, and there was a break in the tune when they were touched. There was no other child besides Earl, and neither of them dared mention it. Both were torn between longing and fear. A normal child would cancel out to an extent the disappointment over Earl, but then, supposing it came here another Earl? Arvay knew nothing of contraceptives, nor did Jim mention anything like that. She just noted that at certain times Jim found it convenient to stay out late, and come home tired. And he drank more than he used to. Arvay took what happiness she could in looking after Earl. She avenged herself on Jim by spending hours in his absence in teaching the slow-moving Earl to walk and to talk. It was slow and hard work, but by the time he was a year-and-a-half old, he could stay on his feet and take a few steps. A few months later, she was overjoyed to hear him lisp out a word. It was either "eat" or "meat," Arvay could not tell which, but it was a word and she was proud and glad.

She had worked on those feeble hands and feet so hard they had to respond some to the continual manipulations and oilings. Earl didn't look so odd now, and she was proud of her work. He was still scary and showed no particular attachments. Secretly, it hurt Arvay to see that he did not show more preference for her, who gave all her time and energy to him, than he did for Jim, who bought him little toys and candies, but never played with him at all. So Arvay used to make up little fibs to tell Jim when he came home about the cute and loving things Earl said and did when they were there alone. Jim never believed a word of it, she could tell, but he never put himself to the trouble to make her out a liar. He took it for just what it was, her consolation, and let it go at that.

Who shall ascend into the hill of the Lord? And who shall stand in His holy place? Arvay thought that it would be herself when and if she could birth Jim a perfect child and by this means tie him forever to her. Jim felt that he would stand on the mount of transfiguration when Arvay showed some appreciation of his love as expressed by what he was striving to do for her. Thus they fumbled and searched for each other in silent darkness.

Therefore, she was both exalted and torn with anxious fears when she passed her time and knew that she was pregnant. She looked at Earl, and day by day sloped around and could not find tongue to mention her condition to Jim. She had seen his terrible agony at the birth of Earl; he could not bear that again. He might just slip on his travelling-shoes, and she would never know where he made his last tracks. Well, Earl was two years old, and able to get around some, and if push came to the shove, she could go back up home to her parents and get some kind of a work while her mother looked after Earl for her.

While she was bumbling around in this miasma of fear, Jim literally jumped into the house one afternoon, grinning proudly.

"Well, sugar, your husband's done got you a home."

"A home?"

"Yep. I done beat a man out of five acres of good land."

"Naw!"

"Yep. It's not right up in town, though. Out to the west of here, close to the Big Swamp. It's even been cleared, but not having no attention paid to it in seven years, it's growed up some. Don't take long in a climate like this. Better throw on something, and let's go take a look at our land."

Arvay knew the general direction. The Big Swamp was a growth that ran north and south for eight or nine miles, and formed the western barrier of the town. They strolled on out there hand in hand in happiness. Jim led her to the place, and told her that they were now on the east line of their property.

"Why, Jim, this just fine! I bet you had to pay a plenty for all this land."

"Nope. I told you that I beat the fool out of the place. He ain't paid no taxes on it since he's had it, and he was about to lose it for taxes anyhow. So he said if I would give him two hundred cash, he'd make me out a clear deed to the place, then I paid up the taxes and it was mine. Of course he don't have nothing to do with that part no more. That's between me, the State, and County. But it's something less than a hundred all told."

"Naw, Jim!"

"That Cracker could have kept up his taxes, and made a good living out of this land besides, but he was too damn lazy and trifling. One crop of anything one time a year would have taken care of everything, but it was too much work for him. Come telling me that he had been trying to get money enough together to hire a nigger or two to put it in shape for him, but seemed as if he never could make it. When he got it, it was all fresh cleared. I don't know what more he wanted. Well, maybe that was the way it was meant to be so we could get hold of it. I'll bet you anything it'll be clean as a whistle a month from now, and I'll be planting me a grove."

"Oh, Jim! It do place us way up yonder, don't it?"

"Well, it gives us a toe-hold anyhow. My next young 'un is going to be born on his Daddy's place. I never did like the idea of no child of mine being born on borrowed land."

Arvay's heart began to beat very fast. My goodness! You couldn't never fool Jim about a thing. She might as well own up to it.

"You sure got the sharpest eyes, Jim. Here I ain't no more'n two months gone. How did you know it already?"

"Is that so, honey? You're mistaken, and I didn't know it, but I'm ever so glad to get the news. Come on here and hug my neck."

"I'm so glad that you're glad, Jim. I . . ."

"Just give me something more to scuffle for. This one is bound to look like me. That means I'm in the ham-scram and got to hustle like hell to get a house up for him to be born in. I ain't been half doing, but I got to stretch out now and be a man."

They walked over the place hand in hand, Jim pointing out and stepping off and talking. Those two or three scattered palmetto palms, he was going to leave standing. They looked pretty scattered around in a grove. This east end of the place

78

was good and sandy. Just the right kind of ground for a grove. The sandier the land, the thinner the skin and the juicier the orange. He was putting all but a half acre in grove. When it got to bearing good, it would more than take care of the place. The house site with the flower yard, the vegetable garden and barnyard would be that other half an acre. That would face towards the west, and the land began to slide off into muck up that way, which would make it more suitable for vegetables and flowers.

They wandered on up that way to give Arvay a chance to pick out where she wanted the house to be placed. There was a good-sized camphor tree about seventy feet back from the west line, and maybe fifty feet from the north line and Arvay decided that she wanted the house placed so that the tree would shade her kitchen door.

"A woman spends so much time around the back that it would be nice to have it cool and shady."

"You're right, Arvay. In fact, all the family passes more time out back than they do anywhere else, and it don't seem sensible to place everything out front for other folks to look at, and don't have nothing for comfort. We can say, then, ten feet from this tree is your kitchen door."

Everything was nice and agreeable until they faced towards the west, then Arvay stood still in her tracks and gasped.

"Jim! Looka there!" and she pointed dramatically at the swamp.

The swamp was so obvious, that Jim thought she must be pointing at something else.

"What is it, honey?"

"That Big Swamp."

"Ain't it noble? I just wish that I was in shape to take in right up to the edge of it. That's the finest stretch of muck outside the Everglades. And look at that stand of timber! If I just had the cash that five acres of that timber would bring, we wouldn't have to worry about a thing. Don't you fret, honey, some day I'm going to get it for you."

"Get it?" And Arvay's eyes flew open in terror. "I don't

want no parts of that awful place. It's dark and haunted-looking and too big and strong to overcome. It's frightening! Like some big old varmint or something to eat you up."

"Why, honey, that ain't nothing but a lot of big trees and stuff growing together. Nothing to hurt you at all. They grows so thick and big and plentiful because the land is wet and rich. Some underground water breaking to the surface in spots along in there. Ain't never been disturbed and been growing like that for maybe thousands of years. That's what makes that land so rich. Plenty stuff done rotted into it, and none of it been used up for cropping. I sure would love to own it."

"Jim, it don't look safe to even be around. I know it's just full and running over with varmints, bears and pant'ers, and wild-cats and gators and rattlesnakes. . . ."

"Not hardly no rattlesnakes, Arvay. They likes clear high, dry ground. We run upon quite a few around in groves. Of course, there would be plenty of moccasins in a place like that, but since you don't have to go in there for nothing, you don't have to worry about that."

"But my child, Jim. Earl is too little to know how to look out for hisself, and he's liable to stray off in there, like young 'uns will, and get snake-bit, or tore to pieces by some varmint or other."

"Earl?" And Jim laughed harshly. "That scary thing ain't apt to stray nowhere at all. If that's all you got to worry about, you can put your mind at rest. He's scared to death of even a baby chicken, and then he ain't all that active."

"You can laugh, Jim, but that place is frightening and awful. I wish that you wouldn't buy the place."

"You mean you want me to give up a lifetime start for a notion like that? Naw, Arvay, it wouldn't be fair to you and my children to give in to a thing like that. Besides, I done passed my word to the man, and the deal is closed."

"Well, I reckon 'tain't nothing more to be said, Jim, but that swamp is a frightening thing."

"Oh, you'll get used to it after a while and pay no attention to it. Any varmint out of there that I catch trespassing on my property will wish that he had stayed at home. Don't you worry. It's a good half a mile off anyhow, and wild animals are more scared of men than we are of them. They ain't apt to bother around."

Jim went right to work clearing and planting his land, and laying the plans for his new home. He would have loved to tell Arvay how he managed on so little money, and let her laugh with him, but Arvay seemed very listless about it, and kept dwelling on the matter of the swamp every time he brought the matter up.

The cleaning up of the five acres had really cost him only ten gallons of moon-shine at a dollar and a half a gallon, ten pounds of sugar, two ten cent bags of salt, a quart of vinegar and some red pepper. There was a foot-note of a half a box of shotgun shells. All he did was to mention his purchase among his crew and the necessity of getting the thing done, to be called aside by two of the men an hour later and be told that if the above mentioned supplies were furnished, the job could be taken care of the first slack Saturday that came along.

Jim furnished what was suggested, and was extra careful not to ask what would become of the shot-gun shells. Too many Crackers saved hog-feed by letting their hogs run wild in the woods until just before time to butcher for Jim to want to know too much. If a big barbecue was going to be held on his place to get it cleaned up, he knew nothing about where all that meat came from. Having provided what was suggested, he showed no further interest until late Sunday afternoon when he was urged to go take a look at the place.

No less than two hundred grown people could have gotten all that work done over the week-end. From fence-line to fence-line the place was thoroughly cleaned and even the brush piled and burnt. As a gauge to the size of the gathering, Jim found a barrel under some trees that had been full of lemonade, but was empty now. Monday, downtown, the markets which usually got the colored trade were wondering what on earth had become of the colored folks. They had more than four hundred pounds of unsold meat on hand. His crew brought him many compliments and assured him that anytime he needed any further help, why all he needed to do was to let them know. He was a perfect gentleman, and they were only too glad to oblige him. It was the same every way he turned. Negroes whom he had never seen before were saying the same thing. Jim was laughing up his sleeve and wanted to take Arvay into the joke, then decided against it.

Once he was on the inside, he found that he got help in other ways. It seemed to be a sort of underground system in Colored Town that the whites did not know about. Two brothers who were good carpenters and did a good deal of work for the best real estate firm in town sought him out and made him a very reasonable figure to build his house, furnishing all the materials. They had, it seemed, connections with a big lumber company, and they could buy cheaper than he could himself. Jim decided to chance it and was more than satisfied with the results. Never did Jim go out to see how the work was coming along but what he took a jug along with him, and never did he go but what some others were around helping the carpenters work.

When the house and barn were declared finished, he took Arvay out to see her new home, and found all the trash cleaned up and hauled away.

"Jim," Arvay objected after the house was inspected, "it's nice and all, but they done toted off all that scrap lumber. It would of helped us out quite considerable for stove-wood. You ought to go make 'em put the last piece of it right back on this place."

"Then I wouldn't be no gentleman no more, Arvay, and that would cost me something. That's like broken food from the table. The help don't look for ladies and gentlemen to trace up a thing like that. If I act like I don't notice it, I got a lot of willing friends, and nobody will ever steal a thing off this place. I got this house built way under the regular figure anyhow. All of 'em would feel hard towards me if I went around asking about those scraps of wood. Leave it be."

82

Arvay felt a comparison in this, and it hurt. Jim just as good as said that she wasn't used to things, and he had to teach her and tell her. But she had a child on the way, and only the Lord knew whether it would come right or not. If it was deformed, she would need all the good-will that she could get hold of to stay with Jim. So she pressed her teeth together and said no more.

Arvay just had no idea. She had no understanding to what extent she was benefiting from the good will that Jim had been building up ever since he had come to town. She knew nothing of his twisting and turning and conniving to make life pleasant for her sake. Neither had she any knowledge of the little arrangements he had made with the butcher-boys on the through trains to handle small lots of fancy fruit to bring in a little something extra. She never asked anything, and so Jim never volunteered to tell her.

She saw the young trees being set out in the grove, but she did not know that a friend of one of the men on his crew worked at a nursery, and had fixed it so that Jim was getting the benefit of every doubt, and the doubts were numerous. His grove was planted to the very finest and the most money-making trees. Only the oranges like Parson Browns, Pineapples, Temples, Navels and Valencias went into the Meserve grove. The very early and the very late fruits when the prices would be high. The early fruit to one side and the late to the other with a broad band of grapefruit down the middle. The tangerine were set like a border trimming the grove on all sides towards the house. All budded stock so that Jim could look for a crop on the third year. Since he had the usual contract of six years to pay for his trees, he never actually paid a cent out of his own pocket. Before the time was up, the grove had paid for itself over and over.

CHAPTER 7

Arvay had planned the roomy bedroom in the northwest corner of the house for herself and Jim. It was
across the hall from the front room, or parlor. In the
old-fashioned double bed in this room her second child was
born.

To the physical pain of her labor was added her secret worry
as to whether the child would be normal or not. She gave birth
to the squalling infant in an agony of uncertainty.

She kept her eyes closed as long as possible while the doctor
and a woman friend attended to it, pretending to be in a
swoon. But she opened her eyes as soon as she heard the
doctor exclaim, "What a fine baby! Good set of lungs too. Just
listen at her squall!"

"Do lemme see my baby, Doctor." Arvay struggled to one
elbow with her eyes fixed on the fat child that the doctor was
hefting. "I know it's got to be tended to, but lemme see it first,
please."

It was a fine-looking infant, and active. Arvay looked at the
reddy-brown down on its head and sighed. It reminded her of
Larraine. Why couldn't it look more like Jim and been a boy?
She let them take the child from her and sank back on her
pillow. Where was Jim? He had been there before her last

terrible pains. What would he say and do when he saw the little girl?

The bed had been changed, and she had been bathed and changed into a fresh nightgown when she heard Jim's voice outside the room door. Then he came in with the baby in his arms.

"A damn fine baby you had for me, honey."

"She looks a little like Larraine, don't you think?" And Arvay twisted her mouth in an apologetic kind of a way. She hoped that Jim could see his way to forgive her.

"Lorraine!" Jim snorted in scorn. "In the pig's eye! My child don't look like Larraine, nothing of the kind. She takes right after my mother, as you would know if you had ever seen her. She's got that same auburn hair and her mouth and eyes. They're light blue now, but them eyes will be a kind of blue-gray in a little while. Larraine! I'm naming her Angeline, after my mother, too."

Arvay closed her eyes in happiness. She could have asked no more of God than this happiness and enthusiasm out of Jim. She hoped that Jim was right about who the child took after. She didn't want any child of hers taking after Larraine. Jim came and sat down on the side of the bed with the little bundle in one arm. With the other hand, he caught hold of hers and stroked up and down her arm tenderly.

"You better let me have the baby then while you go write in the Bible."

Jim reluctantly placed the bundle in her arms and crossed the hall to the living room and wrote: *"Angeline Meserve, Sunday morning, January 7, 1909, at 4:45. A pretty and healthy daughter."*

While Jim was writing, and in his enthusiasm wondering if he ought to add something more, Arvay was examining her new daughter from head to foot. The child was perfect. Not even a birthmark to mar the tender white skin. When Jim returned, she had the child at her breast.

From that hour on, Arvay found out what Jim was like as

a father. He was hanging over the baby's crib practically all the time that he was in the house. He had to look at the child and touch it before he could leave for work in the morning. He came bolting in from work and made for wherever the baby was. It made her laugh to see him changing the baby's diapers, if the child happened to wet herself while Arvay was busy. He was afraid that her skin would get chafed if she had to wait a minute. Arvay kept to her bed a week, and the last day of her confinement, she had to smile at Jim's childishness. He came in with a little white box and hurried to the crib. Propping herself up on one elbow, Arvay could see him trying to put a little gold finger-ring on Angeline's finger. His disappointment was great when he found that the finger was too small as yet, and the ring kept slipping off.

"You ain't supposed to place that on until the child is older, Jim. What is that else you got?"

It was a little gold locket with Angeline's name carved on it. A tiny gold heart hung from a fine gold chain. Jim was dangling it in front of the baby's eyes and trying to delight it.

"Look like I got three babies on my hands," Arvay smiled. "It would be better if you laid it away, Jim, until she gets about three months old. That'll be time enough to start to ornamenting her up."

Then Arvay turned her face away. There had been no little ring nor anything for poor Earl. Already, she could see the pattern opening out. Her own childhood all over again, with Angeline favored like 'Raine always had been, and she made ready to resist. The lines were drawn, and she had become a partisan.

She was hardly up and around before she detected a new drive of energy in Jim. He began to make new plans. He turned and twisted every way to bring in more money, and to place it so it would grow. He bought a Jersey cow so that there could be plenty of milk and butter around the house. He came home one evening with two hundred strawberry plants and set them.

"By the time that big woman of mine gets so she can eat,

86

I want her to have strawberries with cream all over 'em. The little rascal!"

Jim bragged on Angeline excessively, but even Arvay could see that the child was quick to catch on to things, and further, that the baby had a decided preference for her father. By the time that Angie was three months old, she could distinguish Jim by sight, and knew the sound of his voice, which puffed Jim up enormously. Arvay could be nursing her, with Jim across the room. The moment he spoke, Angeline would release the breast long enough to turn her little head quickly and show her toothless gums in a smile at Jim. She would go to him at any time from Arvay's arms. One afternoon, Arvay was changing Angie into clean things so that she would be nice and fresh when Jim got there. She had bathed and powdered the baby, and was folding a diaper to pin on her, when Jim arrived and began to call out. Immediately the little thing began to move her limbs about eagerly, and even tried to pull herself up to go to him. As Arvay kept on with the dressing and Jim did not appear, Angie first began to fret and then to scream in angry impatience.

"Shut up!" Arvay scolded as she jerked the baby into her clothes. "I'm the one that's doing for you, and you squalling after Jim. Hush!"

Jim overheard her and flew into the room and snatched Angeline up in his arms. The little devil immediately behaved as if she had just been rescued from mortal danger. She snuggled her head up under Jim's chin and looked out at her mother in a most accusing way.

"You need that little rump of yourn blistered good for you, that's all," Arvay commented. "Give her back here, Jim, and lemme fling her dress over her head. That ain't nothing but a petticoat."

But the instant Arvay reached up her hands, Angeline scrambled and clung to Jim and pretended utter terror. Jim fended Arvay off and ran out of the backdoor laughing.

"You may think that's funny, Jim, but I sure don't. That child has got to be taught to mind. That very young'un is

87

going to cause you to suck sorrow some of these days."

"Aw, naw she won't, because she loves her Daddy, and she's always going to do what her Daddy tells her to do." Then he laughed. "If she don't do like I tell her, then I'll do like she tells me and we'll be bound to get along. You ain't to hit her, well no more'n to slap her little hands. Please don't have me to come in and find no whelps on this child, Arvay. If I ever do, it's going to make a lot of difference between us. I mean that from my heart."

"Well, people!" Arvay gasped in amazement as she saw the serious look on Jim's face. "This is my first time to see a man cut the crazy over a child to that extent. Look like I done borned somebody to be over me in my own house. I don't count for nothing no more around here, I see. Angeline is the boss."

"Naw, honey, naw. You got the wrong understanding. Yes, I love the child with all that I'm able, but don't you see it's because she's yours that I love her so? I'm loving you through her and her through you."

Arvay was mollified to an extent, but still she wondered. She hated to be low enough to feel jealous of her own child.

Then Jim took to going off from home nearly every night. Once the baby was asleep, he found some excuse to go out nearly every night, and he usually came in with liquor on his breath. That gave Arvay to wonder if the bonds between them were not slackening off.

What was more disturbing, Jim, usually so good-natured, began to get into fights. Arvay wondered what had got into the man. It was more puzzling because the fights were never serious. No pistol-whippings, no cutting-scrapes nor things like that. Just fist-fights that even left no marks on Jim worth mentioning. Furthermore, they always ended up in complete making-up with his opponent. Jim and his opponents were thicker after the battles than before. What was it all about? Oh, Arvay just knew that one of these nights, some desperado was going to kill her husband dead. She fretted and worried and begged Jim to desist. Jim took her solicitude for him with a pleased smiled.

They had kept up a correspondence with Joe and Dessie Kelsey. Three or four letters a year each way, and now in her worry, Arvay called them to mind. Jim always liked having Joe around, and maybe if Joe was here, Jim could be broken of these new habits. She knew that Joe wanted to come, but had never been able to get enough money together to bring his family. Without giving her reason, Arvay broached the matter to Jim one evening.

"Damn, Arvay! I'm sure glad you mentioned Joe. Wonder why I didn't think of him before now? He's the very man I need. I can easily throw up a house back there in the grove for him, and have him right here. I'm going to send for him. You drop him a line and tell him to be ready to leave from there in a week. I'm sending his train-fare Monday week."

Arvay was very pleased at the way Jim had taken her suggestion. She felt that she could look forward and see her happiness ahead. It was as if she had been walking in the dark and come to a house where a light leaned out of the window and smiled.

But before Joe and his family could get there, Jim got into another fight that was a fight. It was to go down in local history as the Battle of the Horse's Behind.

Jim left home early that night, telling Arvay that he was going over into Colored Town to see about getting the house put up in the grove. She never did know if he reached his destination. She forgot to ask in the excitement afterwards.

The fight was with Hawley Pitts. The two men were not enemies, but certainly they were not exactly friends.

Hawley Pitts had the reputation of being the ugliest white man in the county, and probably that had something to do with his social outlook. He was tall on a broad-built frame, with a very red neck and ears. But it was Hawley's mouth that had made him his great reputation. His lips were unusually thick—thick at the corners of the mouth. He must have felt shy about his looks, for he had taken occasion to throw off on Jim

Meserve's "pretty looks" more than once around the bar-rooms when he was sure that Jim could hear him.

Jim, seeing several of his cronies in the bar as he passed, hailed and decided to halt for a few minutes for a drink and an exchange of pleasantries. A score or more were lined up along the bar, and Jim made a place for himself and ordered.

Hawley Pitts had the floor. He was bearing down on Pearly Snead this time. Pearly was a harmless fellow, something under middle height, and slight of build. His wife had run off from him the week before with another man, and was said to be over to Lakeland living with him as man and wife. Some friend had seen her, and told Pearly where she was, and Pearly was so much in love that he had taken out over there and humbled himself enough to beg her to come back to him regardless. What made it bad, Pearly's wife had not only refused with scorn, but meeting someone from Citrabelle on the street in Lakeland, she had laughed and repeated Pearly's tearful plea and her answer. It was soon all over Citrabelle, and now Hawley was having himself a time ragging Pearly about it.

Hawley was too big for Pearly to fight to any advantage, and so he tried to make a laugh and leave the place, like he was humoring the joke.

"Where you trying to sneak off to?" Hawley demanded, and grabbing Pearly by the back of his shirt, hauled him back again. "I ain't had my proper amount of fun out of you yet. You stay right here till I tell you that you can go."

Pearly wanted to fight. Anybody could see that. His fists balled up and he eyed Hawley's face in a hungry way. But he decided that it would not pay, and tried to turn it off in a grin. Hawley saw the same thing that Jim and the others did, and he laughed, and jerked Pearly's shirt out of his pants all the way around.

"You got a willing mind, Pearly, but too light behind. You're just as hot as little sister but scared to fight, eh?"

Jim moved in next to Pearly, and looked Hawley hard in the

eye across Pearly's head. He looked so hard and so long that everybody got quiet.

"Hawley," Jim said finally, and with great deliberation, "I could object to a big, over-built man like you picking on a runt like Pearly. I could get mad because you was born a fool and tell you about it. But I pass all that up, and just take exception to your face." Jim spoke in a nasty quiet way that made his voice carry all over the place.

"What the hell you mean?" Hawley asked. "Taking exception to my face?"

"Yeah, your damn ugly face! I'm bound to take exception, Hawley Pitts. No scoundrel-beast can disrespect *my* wife without giving a strict account to me."

This was certainly exciting, and everybody drew in close.

"Your wife, Jim Meserve? What the hell *is* you talking about sure enough? Why, I ain't hardly ever even broke a breath with her on the streets. Accusing me of insulting your wife!"

"Naw, you ain't been talking to her, Hawley, and I give you full credit for having *that* much sense. But you been committing something worse than that."

"All right! All right! Now what can you claim that I ever done to your wife?"

"You been offering Mrs. Meserve the dirtiest kind of a disrespect. You been proaging out here in the public streets where she could come along and see you with a face like that."

"My face?" Hawley felt his face suspiciously. "I must say that I can't catch on to what you mean." Hawley kept looking from one man to another.

"Yeah, your natural goddamned face! Why, I'd just as soon for her to see you without your pants on as that face. It's a damn lie. It ain't no face at all. I can't consider that thing no face. And that mouth of yours just won't do at all. It's a horse's behind, and a female horse at that."

Spontaneous and raucous laughter broke out instantly. Even Pearly could take a part.

"You, you, say a thing like that to *me?* That's fighting talk."

"I mean it that way, Hawley. No man can insult my wife without giving me some satisfaction. If I allow you to get away with exposing a face like that on the public streets, next thing I know, you'll be out in broad daylight without your damn pants on. The only way you can get out of fighting me here and now is for you to hurry on home and ask your wife for a pair of her drawers and put 'em on that face of yours before you brazen out in public anymore. Git for home!"

The two men went together like lightning. The infuriated Pitts charged, and Jim met him halfway and straightened his head up with a powerful drive to his neck. Men scattered in every direction to be out of the way but at the same time be where they could take in all the battle.

There was no under-dog in this fight. The men were about the same height. Hawley had several pounds of advantage, but Jim was five years younger. It was hard blow for hard blow and neither man dodging away. Fists drumming against chests, and heads and teeth bared back in the frenzy of the battle. Take a blow and give as many as possible in return. So good a man, so good a man! Knock down and drag out, with the men on the side lines jumping up and down and cheering action. Up and down the room in rough and tumble; from the off wall to the bar and back again, panting, gasping, scuffling and smiting and being smitten. It was a close fight, and if Jim got more applause, it was due to his more nimble foot-work, and greater popularity around town. Hawley went down at last and stayed down, but Jim Meserve knew that he had been in a battle and that he had fought a man.

"Got enough?" Jim panted standing over Hawley. "You going to quit being so brazen and put some drawers on that face?"

Hawley did not have to answer, for just then the town marshal, who had been at the door for the greater part of the fight, ran in officially as if he had just arrived.

"What the hell is going on in here?" the law demanded and glared all around him.

"Jim Meserve picked a fight with me and jumped me," Hawley mumbled, getting slowly to his feet.

"He did?" The marshal glowered at Jim then looked around at everybody in the place. "Who saw what went on?" the officer evaded.

Nobody had seen a thing, it developed. Pitts appealed to first one and the other but not a soul would go as far as to witness to a thing. Oh, some kind of a scuffling had gone on, but not a man there could rightly swear to a thing. Who had started it, who had hit who was more than they could say.

"Hell! It was a fair fight wasn't it?" one irritated citizen blurted out at last. "What more can a man ask for than that? If Pitts had of won he would of felt that Jim was a sorry sport to have swore out a warrant against him, wouldn't he? I wouldn't go a step to testify for nothing."

Feeling mistreated and imposed upon, Hawley, with slumped-down shoulders, turned and started to leave the place. It was Jim who hurried forward and caught him and brought him back. Hawley jerked away angrily at first, then Jim charmed him with his eyes, and took his arm and drew him back to the bar.

"Set 'em up," Jim said to the bartender. "Me and my friend Hawley are having a drink together. What's yours, Hawley? It's on me. Come on all you jar-heads! This is to Hawley Pitts, a fair fighter and a true friend."

There was a moment of bewilderment, then every man in the place crowded up to the bar and began to lay down money and order and yell for Jim and Hawley to wait until they got theirs. Pearly tucked in his shirt-tail and joined the rest. A half hour later, no one who was not present would have known that there had been a fight. Jim led them to make over Hawley and to feed his ego. Jim slipped in something about Hawley's swell build and his loaded muscles, and Hawley swelled like a pouter pigeon. He swelled so that he had room inside for a big gesture. So he reached and got Pearly and placed his big arm around the little man's shoulder.

"Say, Pearly, you being luckier than the rest of us, not

having no old hen to bother with, how about us all going over to your house and finishing off this thing?"

Pearly was so tickled that he almost split wide open, so they all went over there and caroused for a couple of hours. Jim could see that they had done a good thing, for after an hour or so of the kind of stories men tell when they are off to themselves and a few more drinks, Pearly stood up and announced, "What the heck am I worrying about *his* hard luck for? What business I got feeling any sympathy for *him?* He got her on his hands, let him keep her."

Having secured himself some more partisans, Jim went on home in high fettle, but Arvay all but fainted when she saw his face and knuckles. She made a great demonstration of her sentiments, and Jim felt highly paid. He kept on being brusque and telling her not to fuss over him, but all the time he was leaning right into it. But Arvay did not understand.

"Jim, you got ways that I don't believe that I'm ever to understand. What you want to get into a fight for is more than I can see."

"Just put it down to me being a man and part Irish and let it go at that. You get so at times that you got to give vent to your muscles. Don't bother too much about understanding right now. Just hug my neck for me and call it square."

CHAPTER 8

The arrival of the Kelseys made life exactly right for Arvay. For some time Jim was kept close around the place getting Joe and them settled down and the work laid out. Joe and his three big boys were to look after the grove and the place. Dessie was to take care of the family washing. Arvay did not know enough about groves right then to realize that the grove would need no particular care for a year or more. She did not notice that because Jim had Joe and his boys broadcast black-eye peas over the entire grove. That crop served a three-fold purpose. It provided an enormous amount of additional food for the added mouths. The cows could eat the pea-vines for hay. It was a cover crop that added nitrate to the soil. That was all for the grove, and Arvay did not notice that Jim and Joe were off in a huddle a great deal, and that more often than not, Joe was not even on the place. His big boys did the milking, looked after the barn, the chicken-yard and the garden.

Arvay was not to pay too much attention because Dessie was up around the house most of the time. It was just as good as a visit to west Florida to hear Dessie talk. Arvay was brought up to date on everything that had happened since she left. Whose babies Dessie had caught, and who were supposed to be the fathers, but who they really favored, and so on and on as they set hens, being careful to put all the eggs but two of a setting in with the right hand to hatch out pullets and only two roosters to a batch. They took hens off the nests with their broods, housed them in coops and kept going over Sawley, Jim and Joe.

Dessie caught on to the signs right away, and Arvay saw them confirmed in her body. She was going to have another child. But thinking things over, she waited nearly a month more to speak of her condition to Jim.

The day, or to be more exact the night, that Arvay chose for the revelation was unfortunate for her.

Jim, eager to accumulate and prosper as well as to help Joe out, had set Joe up in a whiskey still. It was located about three miles to the south in the very edge of the hammock. Joe could pay back the money that Jim had put out as he went along. All over a certain profit was to go to Jim after that. Both men considered that fair as Jim was to furnish the customers while Joe ran the still.

Joe had made his first run that night, with Jim and most of the important men of the community present. Everything had gone off swell, and a very good time had been had by all. They could look forward to good likker, because Joe really knew how to make it, charred barrels and all. There was no need for him to get rid of it in a hurry, so it could age. No law was going to touch that still. The law was present at the run. Moonshine likker was an old southern custom. Nothing wrong with it at all. So Jim had come home feeling fine.

As soon as Jim began to undress, Arvay stirred in bed and told Jim of her condition.

Jim was in a mood for wit and laughter, and Arvay's solemn eyes provoked him more. And when her eyes and her tone of voice plead with Jim to excuse her for what had happened, Jim just could not resist pulling Arvay's leg a bit. So he stood straddled legged, put on a stern face and pontificated.

"Now, as to that matter you just mentioned, Arvay, I'm agreeable, providing you promise me one thing."

"What is it, Jim?"

"You can have that baby, providing that you swear and promise me to bring it here a boy."

"Why, Jim! What a thing for you to make me swear to! How on earth can I tell what the child will be?"

"Easy enough. Just make up your mind to do as I tell you, and have that child a boy. I never did want no girls around the house."

Arvay stretched her eyes, and looked at Jim a long time before she could say a word.

"That's a mighty funny thing for you to say, Jim. The way you makes over Angie nobody would think you didn't want no girl."

"Oh, I'm just putting on when I carry on like that, Arvay. I don't really want no girl, and don't you dare to have me no other one."

"Jim." Arvay gulped and swallowed. "That's no way to talk to me at all, and me in my condition too. It's cruel and mean, that's what it is. Cruel."

"Cruel? Why, what do you mean? If I got a cruel bone in me, this is my first of hearing about it. Why, I'm a mighty good-natured man, according to all that I can hear. Look how nice I acted when you up and had Angie on me. If I had of been cruel, I could of made you tie her up in a sack and chunk her into the lake, but I didn't do it. Or made you take her out in the swamp and lose her, but I never done that neither. I seen you was fond of the little thing, so I let you keep her for a pet. I'm a mighty good-natured man. Tell me!"

The stricken Arvay turned her face to the wall and said no more. Jim got into bed and blew out the light. After probably half an hour, Arvay murmured, "Jim."

"What is it, Arvay?"

"Supposing, supposing the child was to be born a girl."

"No use in supposing, Arvay. I know that you wouldn't have no girl after I done told you specifically to bring it here a boy." Then Jim went on off to sleep.

Arvay did not get to sleep until nearly morning, lying awake and supposing what could happen if the child happened to be a girl. And as she conjectured, she trembled.

Jim had evidently forgotten the teasing that he had given Arvay the night before, for he kissed her tenderly on waking and fondled her hair.

"You ain't to take no chances and run no risks, Arvay, in your condition. No lifting and stretching at all. Earl is big and old enough to keep you in wood and water. See to it that he keeps that bucket full in the kitchen, and keeps plenty of stove wood in the box."

"He ain't but seven, Jim."

"I could tote in wood and water long before that, Arvay. You let that boy do something and get manly. Naw, I don't want none of Dessie's young'uns doing it for Earl. I'll fill up the bucket and the box every morning before I go. Earl is to look after it for the rest of the day, you hear?"

"Yeah, Jim. He can't . . ."

"It's all cut and stacked, ain't it? More'n two strands of good dry oak and pine out there for you to burn. All he got to do is tote in two or three pieces at a time and fill up that box before you start to cook supper. You understand?"

"Yes, Jim."

"In your condition, I want you to have every care. You ain't to worry about a thing. And don't look so sad and solemn, Arvie. You never got with this young'un out in no palmetto scrubs. You got it right here in the bed with Jim Meserve. You got full protection."

Arvay almost spoke and reminded Jim of what he had said the night before. But she could not bring herself to do so.

Jim went to work planning to make things better for Arvay in every way. With any luck at all with the still, by the time the child was born, he would have that carpet for the parlor and hall that Arvay wanted, and he would surprise her with a piano. Arvay played much better than she did when he married her, but that old second-hand organ was no help. He was going to deck her out with a brand new piano if things turned out as he hoped.

In her fear and desperation, Arvay fled back to her old time

98

religion. Again and again she considered calling to Jim's mind his promise to love and protect her, but each time she failed of the courage to take her fate into her own hands and bring the matter to a head. Arvay could feel no faith in her own power over Jim, so she began again to take great stock in miracles. Arvay crept into the Bible and pulled down the lid. She made herself into parables and identified herself with Hannah before the conception of Samuel, and with Hagar, driven out into the desert by Abraham, and other sorrowful women. All day long during the hours that Jim was absent, Arvay went around muttering prayers for deliverance from her fancied danger.

Along with the habit of talking to herself, Arvay acquired the subconscious habit of keeping one hand on her abdomen. Any hand that was not busy at any time that she was awake went to her body. Round and round went the hand, round and round and round and round, as if she caressed the child inside her, and sought to placate it and persuade it to be a boy. In fact, she besought it aloud when she was sure that she would not be overheard.

"Be nice, honey. Be nice, now, and come here a boy-child for your Mama. You see the fix I'm in. Jim is liable to leave me if you ain't a boy. Me with three little hungry mouths to feed and to do for. I wouldn't have nowhere at all to go. Except to go pile up on Larraine, and I'd rather be dead and in my grave than to have to do a thing like that."

Arvay mentioned the same thing to the Lord several times a day.

Then, when she was seven months gone in pregnancy, Arvay discovered that Jim's demand had been only a joke. The day she found that out had been a trying one for her.

Angie was a great favorite with Bubber, Dessie's oldest boy, who was twenty, and working as yard man on the estate of a wealthy Yankee. Thoughtlessly, Bubber had brought home a mango for Angie and none for Earl, the night before. Arvay had put it away until morning. In mid-morning, Arvay had given it to Angie, and told her to divide with Earl. The children were out in the yard, and Arvay went on with her sewing.

Soon there were inhuman screams from the frontyard. Arvay's instant thought was that some wild beast had crept in from the swamp and was attacking Earl. The terrible snarly howls kept up as Arvay raced through the house to the front, grabbing the breech-loader from the head of the bed as she ran. She knew little about handling guns, but this did not occur to her as she ran.

The sight that met her eyes was far worse than if she had found a wild beast attacking her son.

Earl had the mango clutched in one hand as he lay drawn up in a knot on the ground. Angie was standing over him, hitting at the boy with a tiny branch of verbena, with the flowers still on it. Angie was striking at Earl with the spike of verbena, and Earl was on the ground clutching the mango and emitting those animal howls.

What had happened was obvious to Arvay on the porch. Earl had snatched the mango and attempted to flee to some safe place and eat it. He had run towards the corner of the yard and come up against a tangle of alaman bushes overrun by a Cherokee rose growing along the fence. There the little girl had overtaken him, and he had dropped to the ground. The verbena bed was at hand, and Angie had broken off a branch no more than a foot long and was menacing her brother with it.

The scene told Arvay more than she wanted to know. The twig could not have hurt very much even in the hands of a grown man, and certainly three-year-old Angie could do him no harm with the thing. And the sounds! There was nothing human in them. She would never forget them the longest day that she lived. Earl had never made sounds like that before. Not in her hearing anyway.

Arvay leaned the gun against the porch with a shaking hand. A terrible anger took hold of her. For a confused minute, she did not know whether she was angry with Earl for his coward-ice, or with Angie for teasing the poor child. Then she knew who was to blame. Bubber had no business to bring that mango on the place. She got off the porch and bent over the howling Earl and wrenched it from his hand and flung it over the fence.

"Hush up! Hush up, I tell you!" she cried as she hauled her son to his feet and shook him violently. She felt that if those sounds kept up another minute that she would lose her mind.

But while Arvay sought to cut off the sounds, Angie ran out of the gate and recovered her fruit, and was eating it. Earl saw her, and began to howl again. He kept it up until Arvay had dragged him clear around the house. Arvay had no time to take the mango from Angie again. She was too occupied with Earl. Those sounds had to cease at any cost. No doubt Dessie had heard them already. She must never learn that they had come from Earl's throat.

Arvay was shaken as she had never been before in all her life. Even the sight of the child at birth had not been as shocking as this.

"Oh, God, is my child going to be marked from this?"

After the noon dinner, the children were out in the yard, each amusing him and herself in their own way. Earl wandered on down to Dessie's and Arvay was glad. After a while, Angie lay down on the front porch and went to sleep.

It was time for Arvay to start the supper finally. She went out in the kitchen and put on the stew, washed some yams and put them in the oven, and a pot of snap-peas and okra. While they were cooking, Arvay suffered as she washed the rice the regulation five waters and left it to soak. It would cook very quickly when she got to it.

There was no more wood in the box. She had no wish to call Earl to get the wood for her. If only some of Dessie's children would happen up.

Then a great anger and revolt seized upon her.

"I'm a'going out there and get me a turn of wood! Let Jim Meserve just try to help himself. If I overstrain and this child come here too soon, I don't care. It could be a blessing. I won't have to worry anymore. It's got to come here a boy, is it? I'll fix him! Let him worry like I been worried all this time."

Arvay went out into the yard, but she did not reach the wood-pile. Halfway there, she got to the pump and halted. No reason to it, her mind just wandered, and she halted. There was no water bucket on the broad shelf that Jim had built around the pump for Arvay's convenience, but Arvay took hold of the handle of the pump and started to pump. The pump had a strong suction, and the round handle went up in the air at the first stroke. Arvay let it stay there with her hand attached. She stood there for several minutes, her right hand hanging to the up-tilted pump handle, and her left hand going round and round over her abdomen. She hung there like a rag-doll and mumbled and suffered.

Then her eyes saw the sun in the west. It was just over the tops of the swamp trees. Some atavistic impulse arose in her, and suddenly the sun took on divine significance. She looked at it for several minutes, then slowly left the pump and advanced to a clear space facing the west and lifted her arms to pray.

"O, evening sun! You go where God is every night. Please take Him a message from me. Tell Him to take this child from me right now, or let me know that it's coming here a boy. Give me a sign by you. And, O evening sun, when you get on the other side, tell my Lord that I'm here praying. Tell Him . . ."

Arvay started violently, for just at that moment a shadow came between her and the sun. After a second she got it straight and knew what it was. Jim had come around the corner of the house from the front.

"Oh!" Arvay let her arms come slowly to her sides.

"What's the matter, Little-Bits? Sending up a prayer for rain? I hope you get an answer, because the grove could certainly stand it along in here."

Arvay retreated before Jim for several steps. Backing back towards the pump but keeping her eyes fixed on Jim who had been smiling at first but was standing looking at her now with a worried look on his face.

"Naw! Naw, Jim Meserve, I wasn't praying for no rain. Know what I was praying for?" And now Arvay began to come forward again. "I was praying for God to take this child from me right now."

"My God, Arvay! What for? You know what that would mean, don't you?"

"I sure do. And that's exactly what I was praying for."

Jim was able to calm Arvay down after awhile, and find out what was the trouble. But not for long. When with difficulty Jim recalled the incident and told Arvay that it was a joke, she was not comforted at all.

"A joke! A joke and here I been suffering all this time! Jim, I'm never going to forget you for this thing."

Jim did not laugh it off as he had been inclined to do at first. He was quite serious, and apologized to Arvay most humbly. But when the only response he got was an indicting stare then a shamefaced hanging of her head, Jim dug deeper.

"But, Arvay, I thought that anybody at all would see through a joke like that. Anybody with even a teaspoonful of sense knows that you can't tell what a child'll turn out to be until it gets born. And furthermore, you know so well that I'd go to Hell for my daughter, and wade through solid rock up to my hips to do it. And then again, I'd be bound to love any child that you had for me."

Somehow, one of Arvay's braids had worked aloose, and Jim looked at her standing there with her head bowed and the yellow braid dangling over her shoulder and she looked pitiful and helpless to him. He did not want to talk about the thing any longer, nor to remember anything at all against her.

"You didn't act like it, Jim," Arvay accused sullenly. Then the corners of her mouth went down and her voice trembled. "Looked to me like you just aimed to quit me, and was just fixing up any old kind of a shabby, sorry excuse to do it on." Arvay choked back a sob. "And me with three little bitty chillun on my hands to look after and do for. I was hurt-ed, Jim. Hurt-ed to my very heart, and felt like I was throwed clean away."

103

"Goddammit, why?" The sight of Arvay's drooping figure, the piteous tone of her voice made Jim see the months of pain and fear that Arvay had lived through in silence and so needlessly, and it was almost more than he could bear. It made him angry that Arvay should have suffered so uselessly, and through her belated revelation, make him agonize so. "What cause have you ever had to doubt me, Arvay? Have I ever mistreated you in any way whatsoever? Have I ever neglected to do my utmost for you and for my children?"

"Can't say as you have," Arvay murmured with her eyes still lowered.

"Then why would you put such an utmost application upon a silly thing like that? Where is your common, ordinary sense? Why did you want to twist a joke around like that?"

Jim whirled and loped off without waiting for an answer. He fled down into the peace and green calm of the grove to be alone in his anguish of feelings.

There was not sufficient understanding in his marriage, Jim said inside himself. It could not keep on like this. He was panging and paining far too much. What help for it except by parting from Arvay?

Minutes and possibly an hour passed with Jim controversing inside his mind. His thoughts and feelings made living pictures thrown against the white sand of the grove and the dark glossy foliage of the orange trees. He wouldn't be coming home anymore from work of evenings and finding Arvay doing around in the kitchen fixing him the kind of a supper that she figured he might choose and fancy. He wouldn't be grabbing up that sassy, impudent little piece of girl called Angeline. That bossy little chunk of prettiness that had the spunk to tussle and squall for what she wanted until she got it. And even poor helpless Earl. Who on earth would look after and protect him if his father was not around? And this place, who would love it as he did and push it on to the beauty and helpfulness that he saw in it? What would poor helpless Arvay do with a place like this on her hands and nobody to tell her and show her what to do about it? And Arvay herself, what would become of the poor weak thing without the proper person to give her the right care? She needed and required the best that the world could afford. No one understood that but himself. Some other dumb fool might come along, find her forlorn and take the advantage and brutalize her in some way or other.

With that thought, Jim leaped up from where he was seated under a grapefruit tree as if he had found himself in striking distance of a rattler, and headed back towards the house. My God! What had got into him? Had he really been wallowing around under that tree thinking about quitting his wife? Arvay had acted dumb, but what more could you expect? She was a woman and women folks were not given to thinking nohow. It was not in their make-up to do much thinking. That was what men were made for. Women were made to hover and to feel. He had gotten used to the comforts of a home through Arvay, and her tender and loving care. He could not do without a woman now after that, and what other woman on earth was he willing to suffer with and do for? Why, she wasn't even born yet and her mama was already dead. Arvay was his woman, and it was his privilege to do for her. It was his part to put in the thinking. He had no business pushing off nothing like that on her. He had played the fool, not Arvay. As Jim neared the house the thing came to him that had been dodging around in his mind for years. There was something about Arvay that put him in mind of his mother. They didn't favor each other in the face, but there was something there that was the same. Maybe that was what had caught his attention the first time that he had laid eyes on Arvay. Maybe that was why he had never missed his family since he had married her. All the agony of his lost mother was gone when he could rest his head on Arvay's bosom and go to sleep of nights.

That was just part of it, Jim went on, as he strode on through the thriving young grove. There was something about Arvay besides her good looks. Something like a vapor, which reached to him and delivered him into her hands tied and bound. Now, supposing some other man should find out what

105

he knew about Arvay, and be soothing his trashy head on Arvay's soft and comforting bosom, and breathing his breath in her face? Oh, but Jim would kill him dead wherever found.

In the kitchen Jim found Arvay switching around as fast as she could to finish his supper. And right away he became the loving and protecting husband, the ardent lover. He seized Arvay midway in a passage from the table to the stove and held her tight and kissed her and murmured sweet soothing things until that mysterious green light appeared in Arvay's blue eyes. Arvay's eyes had some strange power to change like that when she was stirred for him. Each time that she succumbed to his love making, Arvay's eyes gradually changed from that placid blue to a misty greenish-blue like the waters of the sea at times and at places. It warmed him, it burned him and bound him. But Jim did not consider himself weak in being overcome like that. He placed Arvay as having powers that few women on earth had. The strange thing was that she did not know her own strength. Maybe it was just as well. Knowing more, she might not have been so contented where she was. Twenty to twenty-five years later on, he could afford to let her know. No sense in crowding his luck.

Gradually, as the days went by, Arvay regained her composure, but she retained a residue of resentment. She felt like a fool for having suffered all those months so needlessly, and she stubbornly blamed Jim for making a fool of her.

And to add to that, the child was a boy, and as Dessie exclaimed, the spitting image of Jim. Couldn't have been anymore like Jim if Jim had spit him out of his mouth. Jim promptly named him James Kenneth Meserve, and he came to be called Kenny.

When Arvay was able to be up and around, she found a new carpet in the parlor and the hall, and there was a piano sitting where the old wheezy organ used to be. Next thing to be done, Jim said, was to have running water in the house. He aimed to put in electric lights some of these days.

The still that Arvay knew nothing about was doing well

indeed. Jim added another room to Joe's house and sunk a pump down that end of the grove. Dessie was going to have another baby herself, so Arvay thought that Jim was very good-hearted to get another woman to come in and take care of the washing so Dessie wouldn't have to strain. Arvay had to smile when Jim began to talk about buying an automobile. That back-gap was going to be widened into a driveway.

"Jim sure has got big notions," Arvay confided to Dessie. "It's nice to have all them big notions, but getting hold of the money is another thing."

"Oh, he's born lucky, you might say," Dessie answered mysteriously. "He's liable to stumble up on it. You never can tell."

Arvay had no idea about anything. But all the new improvements around the place lifted her up. From what she heard from west Florida, she was far and ahead of Larraine. Carl was still pastoring small charges. He had shifted twice since Arvay and Jim had married, and the changes were always for the worse. His youth was no longer a selling point.

What in the world had been the matter with her, Arvay wondered, wanting a man like Carl? Well, she had been young and ignorant then. Maybe she should tell Jim all about it now. But no, that would give him a stick to crack her over the head with. Better let sleeping dogs lie. Anyway, she'd never be able to feel resentment toward Larraine from now on.

CHAPTER 9

Kenny Meserve was a very lively child; everybody made over him. Arvay noticed that he would hang around the piano just as soon as he could walk. He was bold, and even more self-assured than Angie, but he had a cute smile to go with it.

Kenny got no public notice, and deserved none, until he was eight years old.

His favorite playmate and faithful follower was Belinda, three months younger than he was. Belinda was Dessie's baby.

Kenny was bossy like his father, and he preferred Belinda to all the other children he knew because Belinda was persuaded that he was very smart and showered admiration in various ways upon him. Then too, Belinda was right there on the place and handy. But Belinda's greatest charm for Kenny was her artistry. Belinda could stand on her head. Stand on her head with a better balance than Kenny had ever seen in any one. It was perfection, and Kenny admired her no end for it. He would even have been jealous, but he had taught it to her. Even though the pupil now surpassed her master, Kenneth was not jealous. She was a product of his skill.

Belinda contended that Kenny turned the best cart-wheels of anybody in the world. Kenny could always think up some scrape for them to get into, too. She could always help carry things through. It was a solid friendship.

It was through this friendship that Kenny came to public notice, and Arvay came to tears.

Kenny had led his expedition into town and wound up at the railroad station. The train came in, and Kenny particularly liked trains. It was the rhythm of movement and sound that entranced him, but he did not know that then. All he knew was that he loved trains. He got to see them seldom too, living out of town like that.

The train was a crack Pullman and parlor car affair—New York to Palm Beach and the Florida east coast in general. As the train blew for Citrabelle, Kenny with Belinda beside him, lined up beside the track to enjoy the sight. Kenny was so overcome that he felt to worship. He wanted to do something in worship of the train. But what? A portly looking tourist came out on the platform between the coaches as the train slowed to a stop. He looked at the children and smiled. It was a nice smile, and that decided Kenny.

"Mister! Mister!" And as he finished shouting Kenny threw a perfect cartwheel. As he came up, he had another idea. He would offer the most perfect thing on earth to this train and the man who smiled on the platform. "Want to see Linda stand on her head?"

The smile got broader. The man misunderstood. He thought that Kenny was after making himself a little change. He tossed Kenny a quarter with an indulgent smile and said, "Sure thing. Let Belinda stand on her head."

Belinda needed no more than a flourish of the hand from Kenny. She made the proper approach, and in an instant, was standing on her head. Kenny looked raptly first at Belinda, and then at the man on the step.

"Ain't she wonderful? Nobody can't stand on their head that good. Nobody but Belinda. I showed her how myself."

Belinda's performance was attracting enormous interest among the passengers on the train. Kenny was about to burst his shirt with pride at the excitement Belinda created. He did not understand the reason. Belinda was innocent of underwear. She was there on her head, with her short percale skirt hanging over her face, with her shining little black behind glinting in the sun. Kenny was innocent, and besides he had seen it so often as he put his pupil through her paces that he paid no attention. As yet the two had no idea of nakedness.

Therefore, Kenny was outraged when he was heckled by a gray-haired chesty woman from the car ahead.

"Boy! You! You shameless little rascal, you! Turn that child down!"

Kenny was surprised and evermore hurt at such lack of appreciation of art. Here was the greatest artist of her time, and some fool hollering to turn her down. Kenny gave the outraged matron a snurling look, and ignored her after that. The excitement on the train was increased rather than diminished by the protest. Passengers from the off side of the cars crowded over to see the show. There were smothered chuckles, and some unsmothered, running the whole length of the train.

"Turn her down, I say!" the woman screamed again.

Kenny had not thought of gaining money by the show. It was intended as a tribute. But the nice man had given him a quarter to turn Belinda up. Two-bits was a heap of money when you came right down to it. If it was worth all that much to see Belinda stand on her head, it was worth double the money to stop seeing it.

"Fifty cents to turn her down!" Kenny shouted, clothed in innocence and arrogance.

The audience roared with laughter at this turn of affairs. The heckler became more furious at being opposed, and then made the butt of laughter by the dirty-faced little imp on the ground with his frayed palmetto hat shoved far back on his head.

"Fifty cents indeed!" The woman screamed. "You turn that child down, I say!"

Kenny turned to Belinda like an impresario and directed:

110

"Wiggle your toes, Belinda!"

Belinda knew what was meant. She was to show that she could move her lower extremities and still keep her balance. That was the most technical part of the thing. Few could accomplish that. So the wrongside-up child proudly waved her fat legs and wiggled her toes. Kenny flung his eyes up at his audience. "What did I tell you? You have seen the most wonderfullest thing on earth."

The train was about to pull off, but the woman, who was evidently accustomed to being obeyed, gave another angry and impatient command to turn Belinda down.

"You heard what I said. Fifty cents." And Kenny braced his legs far apart and eye-balled his heckler belligerently.

The audience howled.

"Attaboy!" The smiling man who had donated the quarter tossed another at Belinda. Somebody else flipped a coin, a big round silver dollar.

"Hooray for Belinda!"

Silver money began to spout from every window and platform.

The train began to move, and Kenny signified that Belinda could end the performance. She came down gracefully as the train pulled out of the station to more cheers. The last the passengers saw of the two children, they were standing and smiling and waving after the train.

When it had rounded the long curve to the south, and was no longer visible, the children searched around and collected the coins in Belinda's skirt. It was too much for them to count exactly, so they went across the street to the general store and Carl Galloway, the son of the proprietor, who waited on the people, counted it for them. Nine dollars and some odd cents.

"Whoo-eee! Belinda, we're rich as we can be!" Kenny gloated and bought a dozen bananas for them to eat on as they walked homeward in clouds of triumph. Neither of them could make out what was wrong with that crazy woman.

"Tetched in the head," Kenny diagnosed.

"Tetched in her head," Belinda repeated as always.

The two children sankled on home eating bananas and feeling happy, never dreaming that the story of the performance was being told and laughed at all over town. That Kenny Meserve! He took after his Pappy all right. Nobody but a Meserve would have thought up such a thing.

Jim heard about it as he came through town after work. He was joshed and teased, and he laughed and replied in kind. He was rather proud of Kenny. A chip off the old block, all right.

So Jim was put out when he got home and found Arvay all upset over the incident. Kenny and Belinda had been whipped and were in deep disgrace. Jim took exception right away.

"What is it to be lawing and jawing about, Arvie? It was nothing but children's doings. They ain't got the least idea about nothing unless you done put [it] into their heads. Let it be."

"I won't let it be, Jim! The way the twig is bent, the tree is bound to be inclined. I try to raise my children clean and right. I don't intend to have nobody around here toling a young'un of mine off and leading him astray. I don't intend to put up with it at all."

"Ha! Belinda leading Kenny! That's a joke. Nobody ain't apt to do no leading around Kenny Meserve. He's too much like his old man for that. I take it as a grand insult for you to even say such a thing. That was Kenny's own idea from stem to stern. Anyhow, what can be done about it now? It's done and over with."

Arvay looked up into Jim's positive eyes and gave a pained gasp. She slumped in silence for awhile before she spoke.

"Belinda being that no-count Joe's young'un, I reckon any caper that she might up and cut just have to be put up with. Look like Joe is the boss on this place."

"Now just what do you mean by that, Honey?" Jim asked in surprise and irritation. He made an impatient gesture, then comprehension came to him. He gave a big, clapping laugh and picked Arvay up and sat down with her in his lap.

"This baby-wife I got can't stand for her husband to think well of nobody but her." Jim caressed Arvay under her chin

112

and cajoled her along. "Look, Little-Bits, I think as much of you as God does of Gabriel, and you know that's His pet angel. But . . ."

"But what?" Arvay pouted.

"But Joe is my helper. Sort of standing at my right hand. You don't know what a lot of help Joe has been to me, off and on. You're my wife, the most precious thing that I got, and nobody don't compare with you. What's between me and Joe is something different altogether and I wouldn't want you to take a pick at him. Just try to feel and believe that every move I make is in your interest, baby. Will you try to feel that without me always having to tell you so?"

Arvay nodded, then under Jim's kisses slipped one arm about his neck.

"Long as Joe ain't got more influence over you than I have, Jim, I ain't got a thing against him. I don't aim to make out that I like the notion of them young'uns being up around the depot naked and all, though. It ain't Christian. It's more like little heathens that ain't got nobody to teach 'em right from wrong. And Kenny . . ."

Jim realized what was before him. No amount of reasoning was going to do any good. Arvay lived by her feelings and not by conscious reasoning, so he fondled her and cajoled and teased her and thus got her mind off the subject and left her feeling assured.

The lifeless scare-crow that Arvay had set up herself had been knocked down and trampled under foot, and Arvay had a great feeling of power and victory. As much as Jim thought of Joe, she had more power of her husband than Joe had. It made her feel very good. So uplifted that she was extra nice to Dessie and her children next day. She so far forgave Belinda's little bare body that right after breakfast she dug out all of Angeline's clothes that her daughter had outgrown and gave them to Dessie for Belinda. The feeling of guilt drove her to town to buy enough white lawn to make Belinda a dress for Sunday School and a ribbon bow for her hair.

Something more than remorse was moving inside Arvay.

113

She found that it was a kind of gratitude for the happening. Out of it had come her first glimmering of really being Jim Meserve's wife, and while it was not anything like a full realization, a hope, a possibility that it could be so. She might come to win this great and perfect man some day. That being the case, it was worth all the world to be right there in the house with Jim and to have the privilege to do for him the best that she knew how. It was a good thing having Joe and his family on the place. They had brought her luck.

So reconciled was Arvay, that she surprised herself by the way she reacted to a small incident that happened a few days later.

Jim had ordered some cement for the front walk, and the white man who delivered it drove up with it under the camphor tree in the back yard. Kenny and Belinda were playing out around there, and came running up to see what was arriving. The driver saw the children as he jumped down from his seat, and to make talk with them, pretended that he did not know who they were. His face was all ready to smile at his own teasing as he looked at Kenny first and asked, "Whose little boy are you?"

Kenny gave him a look from under his long lashes that called the man a dumb fool and retorted, "You know so well that I'm Kenny, Jim Meserve's son."

The man looked at Arvay, who had come to the door and winked his eye and chuckled. "And mighty proud about it, I see."

"Sure." Kenny braced himself and challenged the man with his eyes. "My Daddy can lick any man in the world."

"You don't tell me!" The truck-driver affected to be mightily impressed, and making no fun out of Kenny, turned to Belinda and asked her, "And whose little girl are you?"

Belinda wanted to come off as well as Kenny had, and was obviously stumped for an answer for a moment. She shuffled her bare feet in the sand, then flung up her head and said, "I'm Miss Arvay's little girl, that's who."

Both the truck-driver and Arvay had their mouths wide

114

open for a minute and couldn't close them. Then the driver gave a great guffaw. He had gotten his laugh at last.

"Aw, gwan! Miss Arvay ain't your mother, nothing of the kind!" He rocked and rolled with laughter. He slapped his thigh, and looked to Arvay to join him in the joke.

"Yes I is Miss Arvay's little girl too," contended Belinda about to cry. "Yes I is, too. She gived me a pretty white dress for Sunday School," and Belinda spread her skirts to illustrate, "and a *pretty* pink ribbon for my head. Yes I is her little girl so!"

Arvay saw Belinda about to cry and understood. Belinda valued her and counted on her care and wanted to be loved by her. Arvay knew that feeling.

"Yes indeed, Belinda is my little girl," Arvay said with conviction as she came slowly down the steps to direct the delivery of the cement. "Born right here on the place, and I wouldn't take a play-pretty for her either, I'm a'telling you!"

It was worth something to Arvay to see Belinda's happy and triumphant look. With her head away up, Belinda marched around in a small circle with her soiled little skirt spread out on both sides.

"That *is* right," the driver agreed and fell in with the play. "Excuse me, Belinda. I just forgot." With that, Arvay pointed him to the wash-shed, and he began unloading the sacks of cement under there, while the two children looked on importantly.

Arvay felt very light-hearted for the rest of the afternoon, and told Jim about it as soon as they were alone in the bedroom.

"Knew from the very first time that I saw you, Little-Bits, that you was all heart," Jim remarked feelingly.

"You reckon?" Arvay blushed under Jim's approval.

"Naw, I know, honey, and that makes up for a lot of things. I can read your writing. Know you a lot better than you know your ownself, Arvay, and always have."

"I try to do what's right, Jim. Always did, to the best that I know how."

"And I believe you," Jim remarked after a pause. "You do the very best that you know how." Jim kissed her then and let it go at that. He went to bed feeling very encouraged. It looked as if Arvay was finding her way. The only snag was, could he make her understand that there was a way and that it was necessary for her to find it? How was he to bring a thing like that about? He had tried every way that he knew how and had only temporary results. Maybe it would just come all of a sudden some day. Then life would be perfect indeed.

Things went on very comfortably, Arvay thought, for two whole years. Many improvements of living took place around the house. Jim sank a deep well with a motor pump and there was running water in the house and a bathroom. The house was thoroughly screened and had a fresh coat of paint. Then came electric lights. Everything on the place reflected a greater degree of prosperity, and Arvay felt fine, but that was because she had no idea of the major source of Jim's income. Whenever she thanked Jim for some new comfort and inquired about possible raises in his salary, Jim always answered her in a parable, using a gambler's phrase, "Good dice are bringing the money!" As Arvay did little visiting around and encouraged few visitors, she knew nothing about the still.

Time and again when Jim made a big sale, he longed to run to Arvay and show her his pockets loaded down with money, but he knew his wife too well for that. Having anything to do with alcohol in any way whatsoever would outrage her religious principles. Jim was down in the grove talking over the work with Joe, or off somewhere on business, was all that she ever knew.

Then one day a dash of gossip fell in her ear while she was downtown on the streets, and Jim found a crying, outraged woman when he got home. Arvay was still too unsure of herself to lay down any ultimatums to her husband, so she took it out on Joe. He was leading her husband astray, and on top of that, she had a half-grown son, and he too was in danger of being ruined by Joe and his likkery ways.

116

Jim gritted his teeth and told Arvay that it was not Joe at all. He was the one who was responsible for the whole thing, and that she was not to tackle Joe on the subject at all. It was his still, and Joe was just running it for him. Let Joe right alone. Furthermore, it all had been done for her furtherance; she had and was enjoying the benefits from it. He had not meant for her to know, but now that she did, she was not to say a word to Joe about it. Joe had been careful to protect Jim, capable and ever so honest and faithful. Joe had run the risk of the chain-gang being faithful to him. It would be a very shabby return to place the blame on Joe.

With her hands tied like that, Arvay could not blaze out on Joe as she burned to do, but she showed her feelings by short-talking Joe everytime that she had occasion to speak to him. There were no more of those pleasant little exchanges of talk. It was a short "yes" or "no" or "what" and no more.

Arvay was throwing the rabbit in the briar patch without knowing it, and she would not have cared if she did. Under Jim's pressure, Joe had put some of his likker money into two lots in Colored Town. He had never admired working the grove, and now he felt that he had a sufficient accumulation of money to knock off. Only his feeling of loyalty had held Joe on the job for years. So now, under Arvay's short-talking, Joe claimed that his feelings were hurt-ed. He never liked to be around where he wasn't wanted. Miz' Arvay seemed like she would rather have his space than his company. It would be much more better if he took his family and got off the place. Which he did in a kind of a slow hurry. He had the shell of a six-room house thrown up on his lots and moved into the unfinished structure. That was as far as the house ever got. Joe bought himself a car and announced that he had got to be people in Citrabelle. Doing things on a high-toned scale. Heavy-set Daddy. If a woman asked him for a nickel, he gave her a ten-dollar bill. Ask him for a drink of likker, and he bought her a whiskey-still. Joe Kelsey was really some trouble. Money coming in from the still and not too much work to do, Joe said that he was getting more like the rich folks every day.

117

Living on premises and tending to groves was in the past.

Arvay was secretly joyful when Joe moved, but not for long. When the little house in the grove was empty, Arvay found that its silence left a vacancy in her days. Joe and Dessie and their children were a part of the pattern of her life. She was too proud to own it to Jim, but Arvay missed them, and wanted them back very much. It was denied her the simple way of just going to Dessie and telling her to move on back. Jim could do a thing like that, and would have done so but he believed that it would be against his wife's wishes. Therefore both of them glummed around and snapped at each other for other reasons.

Keeping her remorse to herself, Arvay could not know how Dessie wanted to return. With Joe cutting the tom-fool like he was, Dessie had small pleasure in being the mistress of her own home. A word of welcome from Arvay would have brought her and her children back. Joe would have been along in time.

The house in the grove was empty and Arvay was sorry and Jim was glum about it.

CHAPTER 10

Arvay could see Jim walking over the place and looking around, his thoughts reflected in his face. Things were getting to look shabby. Barn and chicken-yard not looked after, and fence-rows growing up in weeds. Arvay used to sit out under the camphor tree of afternoons and sympathize with the scenery, but now she avoided being caught out there. It might give Jim a chance to comment on the state of things, and the very thought of that put a squinge in her. She could see that Jim was aggravated and fretted about the way things were looking, because he was different from her father. Everything had to be neat and well-cared for around Jim.

He took to going off on fishing trips with men friends of Saturdays, coming back late of Sunday afternoons. Some of his men friends had cars, and he went off with them.

After months of days, Jim came back off of one of these trips and said to Arvay, "I've got somebody for the house in the grove."

"I'm mighty proud and glad about that, Jim. Who is it?"

"A white family."

"Would I know who they is?"

"Not hardly. He's a fisherman from over on the coast. That is, he was till he got a bad case of fish-poisoning and had to quit it for a while. He needs something to do to take care of his family till he can get well enough to go back to fishing."

"How many young'uns is he got?"

"Two. Girls. One is a little chap around seven or eight years old. The other one is almost a grown young lady. Around Earl's age, I reckon."

"Mighty far apart, I would say. How come that?"

"I ain't responsible, so I really wouldn't know. Didn't even feel that it was my business to ask."

A few days later the new family drove up in a truck. It was homemade from an old Ford car.

Arvay was annoyed because she felt that Jim had held things back from her. Jim had said that they were white folks, but the man turned out to be a Portuguese, and his name was Corregio. That made them foreigners, and no foreigners were ever quite white to Arvay. Real white people talked English and without any funny sounds to it. The fact that his wife was a Georgia-born girl that he had married up around Savannah did not help the case one bit, so far as Arvay could see. The woman had gone back on her kind and fallen from grace.

But the sins of the parents certainly had not fallen [on] the children's looks. The older girl had dark brown hair and eyes, and the hair was lit up with golden glints. That would come from her mother's light brown hair. She was more American looking like her mother, but there was a sort of Latin overlay that made her exotic. She was already ripe-looking, and all in all, a very pretty girl. It seemed strange to Arvay for her to be named plain Lucy Ann with those looks. The younger girl was named Felicia, and her name fitted her. Great, soft mellow eyes with lashes so long that Arvay said that you could almost plait them. High arching eyebrows in a shiny black curve, that almost met over the bridge of her nose. Her hair was so thick and rich that Arvay thought with wonder that she must have ten hairs to every one of Angeline's and she had always considered that Angie had an extra thick head of hair. Young as she was, already it went curling to her waist. Her lips were red, red, and rosy.

Jim could have told her all these things at the start, but he had not done so, and Arvay couldn't say that she liked it at all. It was as if he called himself slipping something over on her. Come to think of it, what did this Gee know about tending a grove? And this Georgia Cracker woman who had lowered herself to marrying a foreigner, was not going to be one bit of service to her around the house. This was no laughing, obliging Dessie. There were two separate families now on the place.

Angeline and Kenny stood and gazed as the Corregios unloaded their things and toted them in the house. They too were disappointed. Lucy Ann was too old to interest them, and Angeline scorned Felicia off as much too young for her company. Kenny sidled around to Felicia to see if she was any use to him. When he found that she could neither skin the cat, throw cartwheels, stand on her head, walk on her hands, nor use a pop-gun, he was through. Anyway, he had arrived at the stage where he was scornful of girls. The weakly things couldn't play ball, run or fight worth a cent. Just a waste of good material.

Earl was not at home when the new tenants arrived. Optimistically, and because she had no one else to send, Arvay had sent him after the clothes. He had been gone for two hours, and she did not expect him back for some time as yet. The distance to Colored Town was not great, but Earl always took a long time to go any place and return. His movements were so undecided and slow. It was around sundown when Earl came stumbling through the gate. The clothes were beginning to hang out of the bundle. Arvay was on the watch for him, and ran out to catch the dangling clean things. No use in scolding him. He couldn't do any better than that. She simply took the basket from him, and let him stumble on after her into the house. Arvay told him that he must be all tired out, and sent him on into his room, that he shared with Kenny, to lie down for a while before supper.

Arvay had the supper nearly ready, and hurried back to the kitchen to finish off things. In that way, she forgot to mention

121

to Earl that they had folks down in the small house now. It didn't make any difference she thought, as she went about preparing the supper. He would know it soon anyway. She was making out a pan of biscuits when her attention was gradually caught by a peculiar kind of noise. A whimpering, whining, that broke into a kind of a yelp now and then as it grew more insistent. Something like a dog penned up in a strange place, or when a hunting dog sees its master take down the gun and is impatient to be off on the chase.

It seemed to Arvay to come from the vicinity of the boys' room. The thing was so puzzling that Arvay tipped through the hall to the door and listened.

It was coming from in there all right. She wondered if that devilish Kenny had toled somebody's dog off and got it shut up in there. Arvay was vexed with Kenny. He knew how scared Earl was of animals. So scared that he would not even go near a live chicken. Kenny was always pestering her for a dog, but no pets had ever been allowed on the place on account of Earl. Now, look like that Kenny had stolen a march on her, and slipped a puppy in there to frighten poor Earl to death. She wanted to turn the door-knob and see, but her hands were in the biscuit dough and she couldn't. Then the sounds ceased, and Arvay turned away with relief.

"Maybe I was mistaken. Somebody could of passed along by the place with a dog."

She was shoving the big pan of biscuits into the bake-oven when she heard the sounds again. She could not be mistaken this time. She ran to the door of the boys' room and listened. Along with the whimpering yelps, there was a sound of running feet around inside the room. That would be poor Earl, too frightened of that puppy to even scream. Kenny was going to catch it, and catch it good for this. She took hold, and flung the door wide open.

Her eyes flung around angrily, but there was no dog in the room. Earl, with unseeing eyes, was doing the trampling and running around. She stood and he couldn't help seeing her there, but there was no recognition in his eyes. She became frightened and called his name, but it made no difference at all. He was bent over with his head and nose thrust forward and running and turning back on his course and running like a hound dog hunting for the scent. He found it, lost it again, and turned fast and hunted to pick it up again. Whining and whimpering and making growly noises in his throat from time to time. At last, he seemed to fix on it as coming through the window, and with a sound of triumph he flung himself against the screen. It was nailed around the window and didn't give, and the horrified Arvay saw him fling himself against it time and time again, and then begin to scratch and claw at it furiously. Arvay screamed at him to bring him to his senses. The only way she knew that her cries were heard was that he looked, and thereby his attention was directed to the open door. He didn't see his mother. He only saw the opening, and dashed and sprung for it, knocking Arvay down as he leaped past and over her, and by the time she could look, he was leaping out through the kitchen door.

Arvay jumped to her feet and ran after him calling him to halt. By the time she reached the kitchen door, though, she could spy him running down through the grove like a hunting dog on the trail. He turned and twisted frantically, but finally headed dead for the house in the grove. Arvay sprang from the door and raced after him.

"Oh, my God! He'll go there in that condition, and I can't bear for them folks to see my boy that a'ways."

Arvay was in a good way to lose the race, but she was saved by seeing Jim, who she did not know had come home, coming from the direction of the house in the grove. He saw that something was wrong with Earl right away, and planted himself in the path of Earl's loping advance. When the boy was in reach, Jim tackled the slender frame and bore it easily to the ground. When he had subdued the thrashing and struggling to an extent, he slung Earl over his shoulder and hurried with him to the house, carried him back into the room and locked the door on him.

"What in the world's come over the boy, you reckon, Jim?"

123

Arvay panted out, when Jim returned to the kitchen.

Jim dropped down into a chair at the table, and rested his forehead in his hands.

"It would take a God to tell, Arvay. Anyhow, now we know that we got to keep a sharp eye on him after this. No telling what might happen. Don't leave him out of your sight when I'm not on the place."

Arvay could see that Jim was mightily shaken. He had a grayish film over the skin of his face, and his eyes looked scared. His shoulders sagged and sagged, and he didn't feel to talk anymore, not even when they all sat down to eat.

Arvay was stirred up too, and agreed with Jim that he was right. But as the days passed by, she decided that she couldn't keep up with Earl all the time and get her housework attended to. Two weeks later, when Jim went off right after supper, she missed Earl around dusk-dark, and went all over the place in frantic search of him. She found him at last with his eyes glued to the kitchen window of the little house, hungrily watching the Corregio family gathered around the supper table. They were eating and laughing and talking mightily, and perhaps that was why none of them as yet had noticed the face pressed against the window. Arvay approached as quietly as she could, collared Earl, and clapped her hand over his mouth to prevent any betraying sounds, and dragged him away. The only way Earl resisted her was to bite the hand that she had placed over his mouth. Otherwise, he let her lead him away.

Jim demanded to know how Arvay's hand got hurt like that, and she had to tell him. Two of her fingers were bitten too badly for her to hide.

Jim sat on the side of their bed and thought some time before he spoke. Then, taking Arvay's bloody hand in his own, he said, "Arvay, this can't go on. Earl has got to be put away."

Arvay's eyes flew wide open in terror.

"Why, why, what do you mean by that, Jim?"

"Just what I said. Chattahoochee, Arvay. Earl ain't in no condition to be aloose."

124

"Why you say a thing like that, Jim?"

"Now, don't ask me no dumb questions like that, honey. He's liable to hurt himself." And he stroked the wrist of her injured hand. "He'll do harm to other folks. We ought not to risk it. No later than sunrise in the morning, we ought to take steps to put the boy away."

"You set there and think that I'm a'going to agree to a thing like that?" And Arvay took her hand away angrily. "Putting my child in some crazy house? Nothing much wrong with Earl. He was all right, and you know it, until you fetched them furriners here on the place. They must have some different scent from regular folks and it maked Earl sick in some way or another. All you got to do is to get rid of 'em; and Earl will be all right."

"No, Arvay, you're ever so wrong about that. Something about one or the other of those girls has woke up something in the boy. They didn't put it there, though. It's been there all along. You see the boy can't control himself, and we had better take things in time."

"Jim, as I have said time and time again, there's things about you that I'm never to understand. Would you rather to place your own son in a crazy house than to do away with them people?"

"Those folks ain't got a thing to do with it, Arvay, I keep on trying to tell you and to show you," Jim snapped angrily. "Why can't we look at this thing in a sensible way and take steps to head off trouble? Why do we have to duck and dodge and whip the Devil around the stump and lay ourselves open to sorrow and trouble? Why can't we just quietly put the boy away and provide for him, and let it go at that? I don't hold *you* responsible for his condition. It come through your father's folks, but you didn't have nothing to do with that. I'm trying to be fair about it all I know how, but look like you won't try to meet me at all."

"That's right, throw it up in my face!" Arvay blazed. "I know that you been had it in you to say all the time. I been looking for you to puke it up long time ago. What you stay

125

with me for, I don't know, because I know so well that you don't think I got no sense, and my folks don't amount to a hill of beans in your sight. You come from some big high muck-de-mucks, and we ain't nothing but piney-woods Crackers and poor white trash. Even niggers is better than we is, according to your kind. Joe Kelsey's word stands higher than mine any old day. You can say it don't, but actions speak louder than words. You give him more credit for sense than you do me. All I'm good for is to lay up in the bed with you and satisfy your feelings and do around here for you. Naw, I'll never give my consent for Earl to be put away. Never so long as my head is warm. Earl is always wrong because he's like my folks. 'Tain't never nothing wrong with Angeline and Kenny because they take after your side. But I'm here to tell you that I'll wade in blood to my knees for him. He's not going to be put away."

"Well," Jim said quietly after a wait, "you've had your say, and I know a whole lot more than I used to. I reckon it wouldn't be no use for me to call to your attention that there was no compellment about us getting married, Arvay. I didn't have it to do. I knew what your folks were like before we got married, so I must have wanted to marry you."

"So you decided to put up with [it] even so, eh? But you can't stand nothing that looks like my folks around the house. Since you hate the sight of Earl so bad, why don't you just quit me and lemme go on back where you got me from?"

"Because you're my wife, and I put in to spend the rest of my days with you. All right, Arvay, I won't be the one to break up our home. Henceforward, I got no more to say on the subject of Earl. I submit to your determination. One thing you got to understand, and that thoroughly. I'm not telling Alfredo Corregio to move out. I have a reason for wanting him around, and here he stays till I see further. Suit your ownself about Earl. But bear in mind that anything bad that happens will be laid at your door."

"Satisfaction to me," Arvay snapped. "I know so well that Earl wouldn't hurt a living soul."

Jim looked at Arvay's injured hand significantly, then began to take off his shoes.

"I only wish that I was as sure about that as you seem to be, Arvay. I love Earl too, but I'm a man that's given to facts. And what makes it worse, I know, and you know too, that Earl's got some great craving after guns. Only thing I ever noticed that he wanted to play with. Goes hog wild just at the very sight of one. You know so well that I've had to keep my shot-gun, rifle and pistol hid away for the last three years, and daresent leave 'em loaded, just in case he might run upon one of 'em."

"Oh, I know what you're hinting at, Jim. Earl did aim that rifle at Kenny one time, but he was just playing, and you know it."

"Naw, I don't, Arvay. I do know that he pulled the trigger several times, but the gun just wasn't loaded. Kenny might have been blown to pieces. Naw, I don't know no such a god-damn thing that Earl was joking. I wouldn't swear to no lie like that, and I don't aim to take no chances."

"Things *is* come to a pretty place when you done got so you call me a liar to my face." Arvay began to cry. "And all because I try to take up for my child. The poor, pitiful thing ain't got nobody to care for him but me."

Jim sank wearily into bed and kept his mouth.

CHAPTER 11

Mrs. Corregio was a handsome woman, a year or so older than Arvay. Bright-eyed, a trifle full-bodied and full of laughs and jokes. And hardly was she settled on the place than she took to a habit that offended Arvay mortally. Finding that Jim was fond of sea-food, she was forever—or so it seemed to Arvay—cooking up batches of fried shrimp, devilled crabs, fish in Savannah kinds of ways, and sending one of her family up to invite the Meserves down to eat with them. Arvay stood steadfast in her tracks and refused to go or even to touch a mouthful of what she called "Geechy messes," but Jim accepted with pleasure and came back telling how good it was. Jim even offered the grand insult of urging Arvay to get the recipes from Alfredo's wife and fixing some of those dishes her ownself. Jim had had no experience in being a woman and he didn't understand. It kept Arvay worried and hurt. She put the worst interpretation on it; that Corregio woman was "fly" and doing her level best to bait Jim Meserve in.

And if it was not the mother, then it could be that Lucy Ann. Unfortunate as it was, you had to admit that the girl was really pretty and ever so young and fresh, and Jim was too much around that house in the grove. He claimed to be making some kind of plans and talking things over with Alfredo, but you never could tell. Arvay wanted to be fair about the thing, and often and again she reminded herself that Jim was old enough to be Lucy Ann's father. She called to mind the girl's instant popularity on coming to Citrabelle. All the grass was worn down on that little back road from the cars and the feet of eager young local fellows. Jim laughed over it, so he couldn't be thinking of the girl for himself. Jim was not that kind of a man to take a back seat or ring a backing-bell for any man. So she ought to feel satisfied, only she wasn't. No matter how you twisted things around, Jim was spending too much time down in there. Arvay felt double-teened and over-powered by those Gees. So she contended about Earl. Her aim was to hit a straight lick with a crooked stick. Jim, however, was acting mighty stubborn about it. He reminded her that the Corregios never would have been there if she had let Joe alone.

Instead of getting rid of them as she wished, Arvay was truly alarmed when Jim announced that he was closing down his still. He was selling out right away to a couple of men who had been trying to buy in with him for some time. Arvay's interpretation of the sale went like this: The Corregios had gotten such a hold over Jim that he had turned against Joe Kelsey. Any day now they might turn him against his own wife. If they could run off Joe Kelsey, God from glory! Anything was apt to come off next. They could run the hog over anything.

The truth of the matter was that Jim was getting out because an election was coming up and the man most likely to win the nomination for sheriff was doing a lot of speaking before women's clubs and church groups and swearing that he would enforce Prohibition even if he had to ring the entire county with deputies as close together as pickets on a fence. No use in playing the hog, Jim concluded. He had done mighty well. Better be satisfied with his profits and knock off. He had, in addition, put away enough to give him a start in another business. He sold out. The last run was celebrated hilariously by most of the prominent men in the county, and Jim gave Joe a lump sum, and the still went into the hands of its new owners. That last run had been the rooster, the boar, the bull, the stud and stallion of all stag parties. Jim had abdicated like a king.

Some time back, Jim had bought a strongbox and kept it in the closet. Arvay noted now that he was careful to keep it locked and the key on his ring. She had no idea how much was in there. That made her feel shut out. She accused the Corregios of being behind that too. Jim was so careful for fear that Earl would prowl upon it and get hold of weapons. The tension over Earl kept them from talking things out, and neither knew too much about what the other had in mind. The very air of the home was charged with opposition.

Arvay did a lot of communing with herself. Now, she thought, Jim's real feelings were exposed. He had never taken her for his equal. He was that same James Kenneth Meserve of the great plantations, and looked down on her as the backwoods Cracker, the piney-woods rooter, and thought that he could just run the hog over her in anyway that he pleased. He could tell her to her face that those Gees were there to stay and she couldn't help herself. He could snatch her son from her, to accommodate those Gees, and stick her child in a crazyhouse. Well, she might not come from no high muck-de-mucks, but she would show him a thing or two. She was Little David to his mighty Goliath. He might go for a big cigar, but she would smoke him!

Jim went around feeling down-hearted. He could not understand why Arvay was acting so bull-headed and contrary about Earl. She had seen the signs just as plain as day. Why did she want to chance what could happen most any hour. What the hell was the matter with her nohow? Here he had got hold of Alfredo and was doing his level best to get into shrimping, a legal and profitable business to bring her more comforts and pleasures and she looked like she was pulling against him. She had reared and pitched against the still, yet she acted like it made her mad when he sold it. He didn't make her out at all. Didn't she want him anymore? He couldn't make heads nor tails out of that part either. She came to his embraces eagerly enough, but the very next day she was pouting around as usual. As much as it would hurt him, if she wanted to get shed of him, he would grant it. But she fended off any hint along that line too. What on earth was he to do? It all fumed up from Earl somehow, and Jim began to resent the boy. Then he would catch himself and reason over it. Earl was a pitiful thing and not responsible. If he could only make Arvay see things in the right way about the boy, they could be happy again.

All unconsciously, Jim was giving Arvay more cause for worry every day. Jim was fond of children and petted and played with Felicia too when he came upon her playing with Angeline and Kenny in the grove. Arvay noted with displeasure that within a week of the coming of the Corregios, her two younger children had made friends with Felicia and included her in everything, even begging her to eat with them when they were called to supper if she happened to be up around the house at the time. Arvay looked and listened, and felt that she was losing ground all up and down the line. She blamed Jim for it all. He just would insist on having that family around. So everytime that she saw Felicia romping with her children; everytime that she heard blow-outs of laughter from the house in the grove of nights, and knew that Jim was down there taking part, and thought about Earl being in that room under watch-care, she boiled. She felt that she and Earl were shut off in loneliness by themselves. So from one thing to another, Arvay began to entertain a strange thought. She began to consider quitting Jim. She could not hold up her end against what she had to contend with. The great river plantations were too powerful for the piney woods, but never would she bow and buckle herself down and acknowledge it. She would march away from Jim and go back with her own kind.

First, she wrote a letter to her mother saying that she was coming to pay her a visit. She was bringing Earl along so her mother could see how he had grown. Two years before she had paid a short visit and carried all of her children, but this time, she was only bringing Earl.

As for support, Arvay figured that she could give music lessons, take in some plain sewing, and make enough to feed and clothe them anyway. She would be satisfied, for she would be where nobody looked down on her, and nobody would be talking about putting poor Earl away.

Still, Arvay wavered back and forth until she told Jim that she wanted to go see her mother, and take Earl along, and he handed her two hundred dollars, and did not question her about when she would be back. That decided her. In a cold fury she packed all of her best clothes and those of Earl's and went off to Sawley.

Arvay's ardent championship of her background and her family got a set-back as soon as she stepped off the train. Sawley looked poor and shabby and mean. Nothing like the bright flourishing look of Citrabelle. Things dragged around and houses looked like shacks and had no paint on them. Even the bank seemed narrow-contracted and silly. Beside the winter homes of the Yankees around Citrabelle, Bradford Cary's home no longer appeared so rich. Everything seemed to have shrunk up since she moved away.

Beside her own home and carefully tended grove, the Henson house and place looked just too awful for words. Inside and out, the place galled her. Before she was in the house two hours she found herself criticizing things.

"Mama, why don't you put on one of those housedresses that I sent you? Why you want to go around in them old raggedy things?"

She had not eaten out of cracked dishes in so long that her gorge rose at doing so now, and she hated to put the bent and rusty old cheap forks to her mouth.

But she braced herself to glory in her folks and keep up the fight. She spent the next day cleaning piles of old junk and mess out of the house and burning it over her mother's protest. It was no use at all that Arvay could see. Just junk for junk's sake. She had fallen over an old horse-collar as she came in the front door the first time. Then too, Arvay wanted things nice and clean for Earl. Rats, roaches and flies were simply

132

taking the place. He could get hold of any kind of sickness at all from things like that. Why, her barn at home was better than this. Jim had bins lined with tin to keep out the rats and had screen wire on the doors and windows to keep biting flies away from his horse and cows. It had been so long that she had clean forgotten that some folks had flies and roaches and bed-bugs in their houses.

In her second day of dragging out junk and burning and scalding and scrubbing, Carl and Larraine and their five children jolted up in an old Ford and lit down. Arvay could not see that they were any improvement on the scenery at all. Some changes had been made. Either they had changed or she had.

"What awful gang of Crackers is that?" she asked herself as the car pulled up in the yard, and before she recognized who they were. True, Carl had been turned off from Day Spring for some years now, but they didn't have to look as poor and as common as all that. Common in the flesh and common in what they had on. It was all right seeing them here in Sawley, but Arvay was not sure that she would have liked to own them in Citrabelle. They were too poor for anybody to like them too much, and to have many friends. So common-cladded, and their poor-looking skins, and unbred feet and legs, and the whole make of them. She was indeed glad that Jim was not standing beside her now and seeing her folks as she saw them. She wouldn't have a thing to rear back on. They made Arvay angry, letting her down like that. It made her feel to be cruel, and she let Larraine see all of her things. It did her good to see Larraine letting her eyes get narrow at the style and cut of her clothes, and see her fingering the materials on the sly. Off-hand-like, she handed Earl five dollars to go into town with his cousins and treat them to ice cream and things. It did her good to see the look of gloating pride on her mother's face. Maria gave Larraine a cut-eye look as much as to say, "Now, how do [you] like that come stepping up to you?" Arvay was not bringing up the tail end of things any more.

Arvay could not make the house very comfortable or pretty,

133

but she did get it fairly clean and orderly. She went into town and got some stuff for curtains, and fixed up what had been her and Larraine's old room for Earl, and settled him down in there. She herself slept in with her mother. She laid in a good supply of staple groceries, and began to consider ways and means.

If she was to give music lessons, she would need a piano. Where was the money coming from for that? Then it was a considerable distance for children to walk to take lessons. She would need a new sewing machine to take in sewing, but the same thing was in the way. How many folks would walk that far to fit and try on a cheap dress? Ready-made things were getting to be the style in Sawley like everywhere else. Arvay decided to go out under the mulberry tree and think things over.

The problems of making a living were immediately swamped by her emotions when she got under the tree. There was an old wooden box under there, probably left by some children picking mulberries. Arvay sat down on it, dazed by the feelings that swept over her. A memory inexpressibly sweet. No injury that she could conjure up could stand up beside the ecstasy that she had felt here. God, please have mercy on her poor soul, but she was a slave to that man! How? Why? Those were answers that were hidden away from her poor knowledge. All that she knew was that it was so.

Far, far up in the leafy haven of the tree, she spied a small gray body nestling close to the trunk of the tree. It was a screech owl sleeping during the daylight hours.

The screech owl was a lonesome creature, crying and shivering from housetops and nearby trees during the darkness for something or someone to come and drive away the lonesome feeling from its heart. Nobody that she ever knew of liked to hear that cry. They said that it meant the approach of death. Maybe they thought about death when they heard it because death was such a lonesome thing.

Sitting there, Arvay asked herself, would she have ever escaped from this ugly and lonesome place if Jim had not come

134

along and just seized upon her and carried her off to the light? She doubted it. She could have spent all her days in that awful old house, her heart sleeping in the daylight of men, and crying lonesome in the night. Crying pitiful and lonesome like the screech owl.

Then what had got into her? Was she fighting Jim to get back to this?

Arvay went back to the house and wrote Jim a letter. It was the first one that she had written in the five days since she had been in Sawley. She would not, however, let on that she was backing water. What she wrote was that her father being dead now, and her mother getting old, would he mind if she left Earl up there with her mother for a while to keep her company? Maria really ought not to be there in the house all by herself. Please answer right away and let her know what he thought about it. His ever-loving wife, Arvay Meserve.

Jim answered by Special Delivery. He too thought that her mother was too old to be there alone. If she felt that she could spare Earl, why not let him stay there with his grandmother for a while? He could send five dollars a week for Earl's support as long as he stayed there, and anyway, he thought that they ought to look after Maria, now that Brock Henson was dead. He planned to send Maria ten dollars every month to take care of her groceries as long as she lived. Arvay was to find out about the taxes on the place and let him know. That was to make sure that Maria had some place to stay and take any worry off her mind. Let her last days be her best ones. He wanted Arvay to know that he missed her presence, and hoped that she would not be away from him too long. Her ever devoted husband, Jim.

Out of the money she had on hand, Arvay paid up the taxes, and left word at the office that the tax bills from now on were to be sent to her husband in Citrabelle. Carl said that he didn't have the time, so Arvay paid a man to plough and harrow the place and put in a vegetable garden, so Earl could have plenty of fresh things to eat. Like he was used to at home.

The sacrifice of parting from Earl was almost more than she

135

could bear, but the call of Jim could no more be resisted than the sun-flower can help turning its face to the sun. Her heart, her body, everything about her cried for the presence of that man. How in the world had she ever thought that she could stay away?

CHAPTER 12

Arvay's hackles got up just as soon as she reached home. She had been compelled and overpersuaded by her attachment to Jim to the compromise on Earl, and she resented her enslavement.

She observed that nobody bowed down, and not one soul repented because Earl was away from there. There was an air of triumph, and a sort of freedom-feeling that gave a big Amen to Earl's absence. Moving around in this atmosphere, Arvay got fiery mad.

"Earl's got just as much right to be here as anybody else, and a heap more than some that's flourishing around here so much," she told herself.

But Arvay was able to hold her feelings in for two whole weeks. After that, she began to wonder out loud if poor Earl was getting a sufficient to eat.

"Of course he is, honey. I sent the money ahead, and on top of that I sent a crate of fruit, and made arrangements to keep a good supply on hand up there. You know that your mother wouldn't neglect and mistreat Earl. From the way she wrote me, she's ever so glad to have him with her."

"Yeah, but I know, Jim. I feel and believe that Mama do love the boy, but she's getting old and apt to be careless about fixing regular meals."

Jim blunted that off and put the conversation to death by motioning to Angeline to pass him the dish of lima beans. From Arvay's point of view, he acted hateful that way every time she brought the subject up.

"Earl is liable to get to proaging around down there in the field and get hisself snake-bit," Arvay began to worry a week later.

"Didn't I understand you to say that you had the place ploughed up and put under cultivation?" Jim asked in an off-hand way.

"Yeah, but a snake could happen to be crossing the place to get to the woods and Earl could get bit and die like a dog up there with nobody to see after him right."

Jim let that lay right where Arvay had flung it and went on about something else. He encouraged Kenny to tell him all about a new tune that he had just learned from Joe, and how he had got it down perfect how to tune the box from the key of C into *Sebastopol,* called "Vasterpool" by Joe, and back again. Kenny asked for a quart whiskey bottle so he could break off the neck and keep it. Joe was going to start teaching him how to bottle-neck.

Arvay came to the breakfast table one morning relating a dream that she had had. That Suwanee river was no distance from the house at all. It was ever so deep and treacherous. In her dream she had seen poor Earl following some boys down to the river and being over-persuaded to go in swimming, and getting drowned. Arvay told how she saw his poor body go down and get hung on a snag way under the water and wasn't even found until it was much too late.

"That comes from that big mess of pig-tails that you had yesterday," Jim chuckled. "I tell you about eating all that heavy kind of stuff. You're liable to dream anything with something like that laying heavy on your stomach."

Nor, as weeks went by, could Jim be persuaded to sit down and worry over a dozen more gruesome possibilities. Every week, as Jim had requested, Maria dropped them a card saying how well Earl was getting along. Pretty occasionally, a boy who lived down the road a piece stopped by, and took Earl into Sawley with him to see the movies. Earl had a good appetite and was doing well. Didn't act homesick at all.

It was going into the sixth month since Arvay had left Earl up at Sawley that she decided she had been baffled around enough about her son. Without even bothering to pack a bag, she just caught the eleven o'clock train and went to Sawley, took the indifferent Earl from her protesting mother and brought him on back home. She had not even bothered to tell Jim that she was going. The next afternoon she was back and slamming things around in the kitchen defiantly.

Angie, beginning to pout out under her blouses and getting boy-conscious, merely said, "Oh, hello, Earl. I see you got back" and wetting her finger, tried to lay a fish-hook curl just in front of her ear. Kenny poured out on the indifferent Earl all about how he was learning to make that weeping sound on the guitar with his bottle-neck. Gosh, but he was getting good! He had frammed *John Henry* behind Joe all the way. With Joe bottle-necking and carrying the tune, and him framming out a mean bass, it was something.

Jim got home an hour or so later, and without even giving him the time of day, Arvay whirled on him with, "You see that Earl is back home I reckon. I know you don't like it, but you can't help yourself."

"Why, good evening, Arvay. Did you hear me say a word against it? You come home with your behind stuck up your back like a black ant."

"Well, I just want to let you know in front that Earl is home, and he's here to stay. If he have to be drove away from his home, I'll go along with him."

"Aw, what the hell!" Jim exploded and went out and took pains to slam the door as he went.

Out on the front porch Jim halted and began to reason more than to feel.

"Now why the goddamn hell Arvay want to act so contrary for?" He walked out to the top step and took a stand. "But Arvay is a true mother, bless her heart! I can't fault her too

139

much for what she's done, crazy as it is. Mother-meat never gives over, I reckon. They'll die and go to hell for their young."

With that conclusion, Jim simmered down. He was not blind, and shuddered at what might be ahead of him. Then his manhood and the obligation of it took hold of him.

"I'll have to throw my strong arm of protection around her the best that I can. Nothing else left for me to do."

CHAPTER 13

Arvay looked at the clock. It was just before nine o'clock in the evening. She looked because she hoped that it was late enough to tell Kenny to leave that piano alone and go to bed. Kenny had somehow transferred what he learned on the guitar to the piano and could drum out quite a few pieces. But it was all what Arvay called rag-time stuff and reels. Now he was in there, stomping and drumming out that tune on the piano called *Charleston!* and he and Angie were chanting it and dancing it off. "Hey, hey! Charles-ton! Charles-ton!" How Arvay had come to hate that tune. No matter which way she turned, she couldn't hear nothing else, unless it was *Shake That Thing.* Some Ethel Waters, who Kenny and Angeline thought was great. So Arvay was watching the clock. At nine-thirty, she was going to make them stop that racket.

It was on a Thursday night. Arvay had a little low rocking chair in her room and she took up two shirts of Jim's and began to sew the buttons back on. This wash-woman she had didn't care how she wrung the buttons off of things. The wash came home with buttons missing, and rips and tears in clothes. Dessie wouldn't have let things like that happen. She would give a play-pretty to have Dessie back right now. Jim was off somewhere. Could be down there in the grove running off his mouth with Alfredo as usual for all she knew. Earl was in his room by his lonesome self. He had gone in soon after supper to go to bed. He had been home for over a month now, and went off by himself a lot. Just vanished off. Arvay always took for granted that he was around the place somewhere to himself, and never bothered. He seemed to have forgotten all about the house down in the grove since his return, and Arvay felt vindicated and glad.

"Now, just look at this shirt, will you?" Arvay broke out in anger. "That trifling woman's done shoved all the buttons off this shirt with the smoothening-iron. Dessie always took more care than that. Dessie is a good woman, don't care which way you take her. Wonder if I was to—"

A short shriek, full of terror, ripped the air. Then a long, long cry, and then more short screams as if somebody was suffering awful and mortal pains of danger. Arvay sprang to her feet and stood with her eyes flaring and the shirt dangling from her hand.

More shrieks, then a short howl kind of a sound and yelps mixed in with the screams. It sounded from the grove, and Arvay ran head-long towards the back door. From there she heard mingled voices yelling in excitement from down at the bottom of the grove. There were no more shrieks of pain, and no more yelps and growls.

"Gee whizz!" Kenny breathed back of Arvay's shoulder. "Sounds like Earl."

"Couldn't be," Arvay said shortly. "Earl's been gone to bed too long to talk about."

"It sounded like him to me too," Angeline insisted, and the three of them pitched out of the door into the darkness and went hurrying towards the source of excitement. The children ran faster than Arvay could.

Arvay was going fast, though, when she suddenly whirled and ran back to the house. She ran to the boys' room and flung open the door. Her fingers flew to the switch and drenched the room in light so as to make sure. Earl's bed was empty. He had never been in it at all.

142

"Do, my Jesus! Something has done hurt my boy!"

Arvay fled the room and the house and headed down through the grove. She was panting with fear and crying. That swamp! She had always known that some beast bred in there was going to hurt her child.

She turned back once again to grab the axe from the wood-pile, slung it over her shoulder and ran again. Be it a hundred panthers and bears, she would slay them all this night.

There was a small group gathered tight together, and somebody was holding a lantern and shedding light down on the ground, and they stood still and looked. She could make out Mrs. Corregio, Felicia, her own two children, and a man. She could hear more voices close at hand and running towards them.

"Where is he at?" Arvay screamed out of her fear as she rushed up.

Mrs. Corregio pointed in the general direction of south with her arm and hand, but never lifted her face from weeping to see who it was that asked.

Arvay was close enough now to see what they were looking at. It was Lucy Ann Corregio lying on the ground. Her heavy, glinty hair was spread out far beyond her head, and tangled like. Her eyes were closed and her mouth was open loosely. Blood was running down from a mangly spot on the side of her neck. The fingers of the white hand that lay limply across her body were chewed and bloody. The tubular maroon-colored skirt that she had on was up almost around her waist and there was a bleeding wound on one thigh. She was lying so quietly that for a long minute Arvay could not tell whether she was alive or dead.

Three men, seeing the light, came scrambling over the fence in their haste and joined the group.

"What's the matter? We heard screaming. Who's hurt?" Then they shoved their way into the circle and looked down, and the veins began to swell out in their necks. Arvay could hear running and shouting off to the south and the west in the grove.

143

"Help!" A shout came to her ears. "Head him off. He's gone thataway. Help!"

Arvay burned and turned to dry ashes inside as she heard a short series of triumphant yelps from the distance.

"That's Earl!" Kenny shouted. Arvay wheeled to the side and struck him hard on the side of his head.

"Shut up! Get on back to that house, the two of you. Git!"

Arvay turned with the axe still over her shoulder and headed her children before her. They were cowed by her manner and ran ahead after a few steps homeward in the dark. They bolted inside ahead of her and disappeared. Arvay leaned the axe against the steps and went on in to seclude herself and think what steps to take. Then she realized how her coming off like that would look in case they were trying to make out that it was Earl, and went slowly but deliberately back down into the grove.

By that time many men had gathered. Lucy Ann was not there on the ground any more. She had been lifted and carried inside the house and her mother and sister were in there with her. From the babble of talk Arvay learned that the girl was not dead. Somebody had gone to fetch a doctor. Somebody else had gone to notify the police.

"Aw, to hell with that!" Arvay heard one man say. "We know who did it. What we need is a posse to run the so-and-so down and string him up. Can't a clean-living, pretty white girl like Lucy Ann get no more protection than that? Don't need no damn Sheriff. Let's go, men!"

There was a muttering and a motion of a head, and the men quieted down to a grumble. They saw then that Arvay was present. They shifted around and said nothing to her at all. But their eyes and their ways made Arvay's flesh crawl all over her. She melted out and went on back to her house.

She found that she could walk the distance, but her feet were on the drag. The horizon to the south flashed intermittently with lightning, playing for some distant rainstorm that way. The faint echo of rumbling thunder sank way down in the west.

As she approached the steps, she found something for her mind to handle, to drive off the madness of fear. She must be sure to put the axe back at the wood-pile. Jim was extra particular about everything being where it was supposed to be. When he went to split kindling-wood in the morning, he would be mighty mad if that axe was not to his hand.

But the axe was not leaning against the steps as she had left it. Naturally. Jim had come along, and put it back where it belonged. That meant that he was back from town, and she was glad. Just to use up time, Arvay walked over to the wood-pile and looked. The axe was not stuck up in the chopping-block as Jim invariably left it. It was not leaning against the block as Kenny sometimes left it. Arvay looked all around the wood-pile, but the axe was nowhere around. That was very funny. Then the weak trembles ran all over Arvay. Maybe some man, thirsting for her son's blood, had passed there and picked it up. She rushed fearfully into the kitchen, and closed and bolted the door behind her. She was very glad that the children had neglected to turn off the light as they went through. Darkness held unspeakable terror for her this night.

She headed on across the room to get to her bedroom and wait there for Jim. She was almost at the door leading into the hall-way, when she felt, more than heard, some movement under the table. The table cover that hung down on all sides made it shadowy under there. She flung her hands up to her breast, and gapped out a sound from her throat. Her eyes were compelled to the floor, and she saw the head of the axe being snatched under the table farther, and she heard a kind of a snarl.

Something rose up so suddenly under the table that it tilted and sent the salt celler, pepper sauce bottle and vinegar crashing to the floor. A form began to spring away from the overturned table as Arvay leaped for the door, grabbed desperately for the light switch, and plunged the room in darkness so that she could not be so easily seen and make her escape.

The tall slight form of Earl fell on her back and tried to grab at her throat. Arvay fought the weak hands off after a short

145

struggle and held them powerless to harm her there in the dark. Holding to the limp fingers for dear life, she shoved his head back violently twice to keep him from biting her hands.

"Don't lose no time, son, like this. Run! They aim to kill you just as quick as they can lay hands on you. Run! I don't aim to hurt you. Run, and run fast and get somewhere and hide. Now, run!"

She released the hands, and heard Earl's steps breaking for the back door, and his fumbling with the lock. Arvay flew over there and drew it back for him quickly.

"You ain't got no time to lose. Run just as fast as you can."

"Yes, Ma'am," Earl muttered. In a moment more, the form faded from the door, and Arvay heard fast steps padding around the south side of the house and away through the front. Arvay bolted the door again and hurried to her room at the front.

She had hardly reached it when men surged all around the house and grim and angry voices sounded outside of every window.

They wanted Earl. They wanted him, and they meant to have him. He might as well come on out peaceable, because if he didn't, they'd get him even if they had to burn the house down on him to get him.

Arvay tipped across the hall to peep out of the parlor windows, but found her two children in there, their faces charged with terror. So Arvay, seeing her young, found the strength to stiffen herself and walk to the side window and speak to the men outside.

"Earl is not here," she told them. "I don't know no more where he's at than you do."

There was a sullen silence, then a muttered conference. Arvay knew that there could be few strangers out there. Most of them had to be men that she knew. They hated to face her and break right into the house. After a long while, the same voice spoke, a voice that was unknown to her.

"We'd like to talk to Jim if he is there."

146

"Jim ain't here neither. He went off right after supper. Said that he was going to step downtown."

There was another period of low mumbles. Then Arvay heard somebody say, "I saw him passing some time ago. I think I know where to find him."

But just at that minute, Jim came urgently through the front gate. Arvay saw the dark mass move to meet him, and close in around him near the gate. There was talk and talk, though Arvay could not distinguish a word. Both Kenny and Angeline wanted to run out there where Jim was, but Arvay made them keep quiet where they were. Finally, Jim walked down the path alone and mounted the steps.

"I'm going along with the men, honey," Jim said quietly, and took pains to place his arms around her waist and keep them there while he talked. "We're going to try to locate Earl. That is, if he's not hid around the house somewhere."

"No, he ain't here, Jim, and I don't know where he went to."

"Well, I certainly am sorry to my heart that he up and ran off. It makes things look mighty bad, and harder for me to handle. I hate worse than anything in the world that he did what he did."

"Oh, they done already persuaded you that Earl is guilty, eh?"

"Aw, honey, please don't. Them others don't need to know, but you and I know how he acted before he was took off to west Florida. Then tonight, there can't be a shadow of a doubt about the thing."

"Why can't there be, Jim?"

"Because, honey, the girl has come to now, and she says that she started out to the outhouse with a lighted lantern in her hand. She saw Earl when he jumped out from behind the corner of the house after her. She tried to run, but he was on her before she could get a start. She saw him, honey. Alfredo and them heard her hollering, and Alfredo leaped out of the door. Lucy Ann had dropped the lantern, but it's one of them ship lanterns, and it didn't go out. Alfredo could see Earl and recognize him. He had the girl down by then, and was biting at her legs. He never let go until Alfredo was almost on him, then he sprung up and took off through the grove with Alfredo after him, but he lost him. No, honey, no doubt about the thing. Alfredo and all of 'em realize that the boy is not just right in his head, and with me taking care of all doctors' bills and everything, Alfredo won't press the charges if Earl can just be found and give himself up."

"What good will that do, Jim?"

"What good will it do? Arvay, practically every man out there has got a wife, a sister or a daughter, and some all three. You ought to be able to see how they wouldn't want nobody like Earl loose on the community. You got a daughter. You know just how you would feel if it was somebody else, now don't you?"

"Yeah, but if I just thought that Earl was guilty."

"Aw, honey, please don't hurt me no more by giving me the idea that you feel I want to be unjust to my own son. Did you know that the screen wire is all tore loose from his window except at the top? That means that when he made out that he was so sleepy right after supper, he was being cunning enough to fool us and give himself time to tear loose that screen so he could get out without anybody missing him. For all we know, it might have been done before dark. Before I go off, I got to go and see that it's nailed down again good and tight. I don't want him doubling back and sneaking in through that window and maybe hurting you or Angeline or Kenny, or maybe all of you."

Arvay let him go without saying another word. She remembered that scene in the kitchen no more than an hour ago. The weak fingers feeling for her throat and the axe. The intent was here, only the strength was lacking. But then, Arvay comforted herself quickly, poor Earl thought that she was somebody else.

Arvay heard men's voices and the pounding of the hammer as the screen wire was firmly nailed back in place. Two men whom she knew well came shamefaced through the house

148

with Jim and spoke softly to her as they tramped around helping secure all the windows and doors. Jim cautioned Arvay and the children not to open them on any account until he returned. Then he went outside, placed himself in the midst of the posse of around a hundred men and they tramped off to search for her son.

As the hours stumbled past on rusty ankles and she heard nothing, Arvay began to hope that Earl had gotten clean away. Towards daylight, what was left of the mob came back to the house with Jim. They had a new lead. Jim thought that Earl might have taken refuge at Joe Kelsey's house, and they had been there just a short while ago. Earl was not there, and had not been there, Joe swore. But the Sheriff and some others thought that Joe was acting funny and guilty. Joe was holding back something that he knew, the Sheriff charged.

Joe was naturally terrified, and looked and looked at Jim with pleading eyes. Jim knew that Joe was hiding something, so he told Joe that it was all right. He must tell them anything that he might know.

"I don't know for sure, Mister Jim, but Earl could be down in the Big Swamp somewhere."

"Naw, Joe. You must be mistaken. Not Earl. Scary as he was, I can't see him rashing around in that swamp."

"But I have seen him going in there, Mister Jim, often and on." Joe looked at the Sheriff with a sly grin and continued. "When I used to have business down in there, I have seen him ducking and dodging down in there. I never hailed him because he never acted like he was slipping and I thought he called hisself playing sort of hide and seek and I would just ruin up the play by letting on that I seen him. Oh, yeah, I have seen him going in and coming out too many times."

They got the general directions from Joe of where Earl had been seen. Bloodhounds had been sent for. They were back at the house to get something of Earl's for the hounds to take his scent from. Then they veered to the south and streamed off towards the swamp. The bell-toned dogs sang out on the trail before long, and the men marched forward to that.

149

The search went on and on. Now and then, Arvay could hear the distant baying. The day died behind the deep dark swamp, and still Jim did not come home. Hawley Pitts brought word about three o'clock the next afternoon that Earl had been located. They had trailed him to a place deep in the swamp that was almost opposite this house. Jim wanted her to know. He was staying to try and handle things. He wanted some hot coffee and something that he could eat.

Arvay rose up right away. She made Hawley eat, then she packed up a big mess of meat and bread and a dinner-bucket full of hot coffee all sweetened and with cream in it, and sent it back by Hawley.

"Tell Earl I say to come on home with you all, Hawley. Tell him I say so, please."

"Oh, I tell him, Mrs. Meserve, and don't you fret nor worry. Nobody don't want to hurt the boy."

Two hours later, Jim sent word by somebody else that Earl was surrounded and he would be home just as soon as he could persuade Earl to give himself up to the Sheriff. They were close enough to the boy to make themselves heard, but Earl, so far, acted as if he didn't hear them. He was in a spot that was hard for them to get to. They could see him as plain as day, but he was hard to rush, and they found out that he had a gun. A Winchester rifle, and just as soon as anybody tried to get near him, he levelled the gun and dared them to come on.

No sooner had the second messenger left than Arvay went to the parlor and peeped behind the piano. Yes, Jim's rifle was really gone.

Now when and how had Earl got that rifle out of the house? He certainly did not have it when he fled the house that night—and Arvay trembled as she remembered—or he would not have seized that axe. Arvay went back in her mind and recalled that Earl had often disappeared from around the house for long periods since his return from Sawley. He could have sneaked that gun out on any of those days. Well, it certainly was a lucky thing that the gun was not loaded. Then

150

a frightening thought came to Arvay. If he had searched around until he found the gun, maybe he had found the ammunition too. Arvay whirled and ran across the hall into the bedroom and to the pair of old boots in the back of the closet. Jim had had two boxes of long cartridges for that repeating rifle. Squatting on her heels, Arvay searched deep in the boots and found that both boxes were missing. With her face white and hands trembling, she was able to find comfort for a moment in the assumption that even if Earl did have the gun and the ammunition, he still did not know how to handle any kind of a gun, let alone that repeating rifle. But how could she swear to a thing like that? Off from her mother up there in Sawley, Earl might have asked and been taught something about handling guns by the boy who had been chumming around with him. All country boys knew something about guns. One hand fluttered to her breast, and still squatting on her heels, Arvay collapsed against the closet wall.

"My God, my God! It's a wonder somebody ain't been killed!"

Jim did not return to Arvay all that night. The word came that the posse were in a tight fix because the men dared not show themselves too plainly for fear of getting shot. Every time anybody showed himself, Earl upped with that rifle and levelled down. Coming at him from the rear meant cutting a way through two miles of dense swamp.

Jim staggered in home with a haggard face and told Arvay how it was. He saw the suffering in her own eyes and was very gentle with her.

"I know how you feel, Little-Bits, and I'm doing all I can to make things come off peaceable and right."

"Oh Jim, Jim! Why can't you holler out to Earl and let him know that you're there to help him and . . ."

"I haven't been doing a thing but begging and pleading with him, honey. I have told him and told him that nobody wanted to hurt him, and nobody was going to harm him if he would only come on out and give himself up. But, Arvay, Earl

151

acts like he don't know me from nobody else." Jim hushed and bowed his head on his arms for a minute.

"He draws that gun on me every time I try to get near him, and the men are all getting wore out from fooling with him. Nobody's said so in my hearing, but I know so well that if it wasn't for my presence, they would have killed Earl long time ago."

Arvay looked at the drooping figure of the man there at the table and a tender feeling went over her. But for too many years Arvay had thought of her husband as a being stronger than all others on earth. What God neglected, Jim Meserve took care of. Between the two, God and Jim, all things came to pass. They had charge of things. She had been praying ever since she had found out that Earl was surrounded in that swamp. So far, God had not made a move so it was up to Jim. So now, Arvay went to her husband and hung by her arms around his neck as she sank to her knees beside his chair.

"Jim! Jim! Don't let them men kill my boy. Just get him back safe one more time, please, Jim, so we can put him away." Arvay pressed her wet face tight against Jim's chest and whispered, "Please, Jim."

Jim hugged Arvay tenderly and tried to make her see the difficulties of the situation. To get to where Earl was, you had to watch your step mighty careful. Big roots humped up, and a slip of the foot, and over you would go into that deep spring that was running swiftly underground. Even a good swimmer would have all that he could do to keep from being carried away underground by that water. And there was no doubt that Earl would shoot while the man was struggling in the water. You had to creep along slow, and expose yourself to be shot at. The men were getting pretty tired, but he would do the best he could.

Jim went on back and joined the men. He had a promise that nothing would be done until he returned. He thanked them on his return for being so considerate of his feelings. He realized that this thing could not keep on forever.

So, calling soothingly to Earl, Jim started from the south

border of the sink hole and began to pick along to where Earl stood braced between two great cypress trees. Earl's face was cold and unrecognizing. Jim caught hold to vines and shrubs to keep from slipping off the precarious footing into the water, and said nice things to Earl and kept going. He was a good half way along the dangerous route when Earl stepped forth and levelled the rifle and took aim.

Jim's Stetson leaped in the air and fell into the pool. A tiny trickle of blood started down his forehead as he fell on his face and tried to shield himself behind the bole of a tree. Earl, seeing his father where he had no chance of escape, advanced to get Jim exactly under his gun-sight again. Jim was helpless before him.

There was a shout of fury from the watching men. One gun, two guns, then two or three more blazed. The slight body jumped and fell forward with the rifle under it.

CHAPTER 14

Arvay saw some men coming late that Saturday afternoon—just a few men, with Jim, his hat in his hand, walking slowly in the lead. The rest of them followed Jim, and leaned together, carrying something between them. Arvay fled into the bedroom and slammed the door.

The men stopped out there in the yard at the foot of the steps, and stood there with their heads uncovered. Jim came into the bedroom and found Arvay leaning against the wall near the foot of the bed. The pain was showing in his face so that Arvay almost overlooked the little spot of dried blood above his right forehead. His broad shoulders hung down like a cape. He placed his arm about Arvay's waist and without speaking, led her to the front door.

The silent bareheaded men looked at Arvay, then looked down at what was at their feet.

"I'll go and have the bell tolled," Hawley Pitts offered, and all the others nodded solemn agreement. It was a relief that they could do something kind for Arvay and Jim.

"I'll thank you kindly, Hawley," Jim said. This was indeed a great kindness. The body of his son was not going to be handled like a criminal. Friends were going to accord it the ritual of a good Christian who had died in his sick-bed, with the pastor and the family and friends standing around the bedside. Jim tucked his head a brief moment on Arvay's shoulder, then lifted it. "Yes, I'll thank you to toll the bell."

Hawley nodded, and turned his big frame towards the gate.

"Stop!" Arvay screamed, and tried to tear herself from Jim's embrace. "No you don't. Don't go tolling no bell for my boy. Earl ain't dead."

Hawley stopped dead in his tracks, and all the men looked from one to the other, then down at what was lying at the bottom of the steps.

"You needn't to look, and try to make out that's my boy dead there on the ground. It's somebody else. Oh, please don't toll the bell."

Jim took Arvay in his arms, and putting one hand firmly under her chin, lifted her face and made her eyes meet his.

"Look at me, darling. Look your Jim in the face. Our Earl is dead, honey. The poor thing was not sufficient for the world he was forced to live in. He has come to his peace at last. But the world ain't finished for you, honey. You've got me beside you. We got our two children and a world of loving friends. Our child, born out of our deep sweet love, is dead, honey, and laying out there on the ground. He's out there waiting for you to bid him in. You have always give him your love, haven't you? Well, out of that, go, darling, and give him the look of peace."

Arvay felt the power of Jim coming over her. She rested her head on his shoulders for a moment, then left the shelter of his arms and moved forward. She went down the five steps and stood over the body. She saw the many wounds in the chest. Slowly, she lifted the veil of Spanish moss that covered the face and gazed. Somehow, none of the bullets had struck Earl above his shoulders. The weak but handsome face was unmarred and was inhabited at last by a peace and a calm. Arvay passed her hand over it slowly as if to probe

155

the mystery of the vanished life as well as to caress. Slowly now she stood erect and looked at Jim. She felt his arm beneath her shoulder just as plain as if he had been standing beside her. Arvay bowed her head and said softly, "Yes, now you can toll the bell. Toll the bell for my boy, somebody, please."

CHAPTER 15

"Hug my neck for me, honey," Jim drew near in the bed and pulled Arvay closer to him. "You haven't been sweet with me for a whole month now."

"Jim! And poor Earl dead and covered up in a four-sided grave!"

"But I'm still here, honey-pie, and still your husband."

"But I'm grieving so, Jim. I . . ."

"Naw, Arvay, you ain't grieving as much as you let on. You're mourning all right, but that ain't grief."

Arvay tensed herself to return a shocked and outraged answer, but just then Jim began to rub her shoulder as he talked, and then to slide his hand gently down towards her breasts in little circular motions.

"You just hate to own to yourself that a great burden done fell off your shoulders."

"Naw, Jim, I'm never to get over losing my boy, and losing him the way I did."

And at that moment, Arvay hated herself, because for the life of her, she could not move away from Jim, nor could she fling his hand away. She found herself softening, relaxing, and then throbbing under Jim's hand. She hated the man violently, and she hated him because he had so much power over her.

"Don't, Jim," Arvay murmured drowsily. "How in the

world can I mourn for my boy with you feeling and hauling over me like that? Stop!''

But Jim did not stop, and Arvay did not resist him. Her body got warm and she seemed to be sinking, sinking, down through the mattress, through the floor and through the world on some soft cloudy material, and drifting off through the rim-bones of space. Passive, passive, receptive and dream-like, until she felt Jim's first kiss on her lips. It came as a great mercy and a blessing, and Arvay departed from herself and knew nothing until she came to earth again and found herself in the familiar bed.

Jim turned on his side, laid his head on her breast and went right off to sleep with Arvay's fingers running through his hair, and she went to sleep herself with her hands tangled in his curls.

When morning came, Arvay knew that she must come back to her family somehow. She would have died rather than admit that Jim was telling the truth, but she knew it for herself. She acknowledged to herself that she had put on the greatest show of grief when she caught herself feeling relieved. A great, great burden *had* been wrenched off her shoulders, something that stood between her and Jim, and she hated to admit that anything that did that was worrisome. She had worn a shield and buckler for eighteen long years, and it had been very hard on her heart at times, but she had taken her stand, and stubbornly held it, because she had seen no way to retreat. Something must be wrong with her, for she knew that she could part with anything, even principles, before she could give up this man.

It was a Saturday, and the children were around the house and they worried her. She wanted to be alone to herself to feel and to think. They were so alive, and romped and played so noisily. Even at their Saturday tasks of helping out with a thorough cleaning, they found the energy and the occasion to chase each other back and forth through the house and around in the yard and yell and scream.

"What kind of a Devil am I?" Arvay asked herself, as with

158

her head tied up in a towel, she swept down the cob-webs over the house. "I ain't got time to put up with my own young'uns while I think about Jim. Here I want 'em out of my way so I can give all my attention to what went on last night. That man's got me so that I'm just about as near nothing as anybody could be. Well, I just got to fight against it. I'll show him. When he comes home, I'm going to be mourning harder than I ever was, that's what I am."

Dinner was the mid-day meal. Jim got off early on Saturdays, but he was never home that early. By the time he knocked his men off and they got back to the packing-house and got paid off and all, it was always mid-afternoon. The whole house was clean, and her own room was just a little bit garnished. That vase full of pink oleander blooms on the small table by the head of the bed was not put there to tempt Jim of course. It just made the room look more cheerful like. They had been through a lot of grief, and a few flowers made things look more brighter.

"Mama, we're through with the dinner dishes, and please can I go over to Joe's and practice some?" Kenny asked, and gave a pleading look up in her face. "You ought to let me go this time, Mama. I haven't been for a long time now. Maybe I'll be done forgot all I used to know on the box."

"Gwan, then, and stop bothering me, Kenny. But you better be back in this house before dark, else I'll attend to you, suh." Then an inspiration came to Arvay. "Angie better go 'long with you to see to it that you come home on time."

The two children screamed in joy and tore out. They went running and tussling out of the gate and away. Arvay took a long breath of relief and went about her thinking.

It led her to the boys' room. She went inside and looked around. In spite of her dedicated air, she knew exactly what she meant to do. She gathered up all of Earl's clothes and folded things one by one on the bed. She was going to put them somewhere out of sight. She was through going in there and sitting when the children were not at home and fingering Earl's things. Yes, Earl was dead. Nothing she could do would bring him back. She would store his things away out in the barn for a keep-sake. She could creep out there at times unbeknowings to Jim and handle them when she felt to. Arvay bundled everything up and tied the large package up neatly. She placed it on the floor by the door, then took time to place everything so that the room belonged to Kenny in full. It had taken her quite some time because she would not move hurriedly. It did not seem right to move like that. She looked at the package as she left the room. It could stay there until Jim or the children came home, and took it upstairs in the barn for her.

"I ain't giving in to Jim at all," Arvay told herself. "But it'll make a little more room for Kenny, him being so active and all."

Arvay came out and walked into the kitchen. She wanted to look over what she had to fix for supper. She might decide on something that took a long time. She felt for a good nice meal.

There was food in the house, but nothing that her taste called for in particular. Jim and the children might not care for what she had either. A nice bait of stew beef, browned down low with good gravy and rice and string beans out of the garden with that ham hock, with new potatoes dropped on top of the beans to steam, and maybe stir up a pan of ginger bread to eat with the buttermilk afterwards. That ought to be kind of nice for Saturday night. A baked chicken and sweet potatoes could be the main things for Sunday dinner. She would slip on something and go pick out the meat herself, instead of using the telephone, which Jim had fixed to save her steps. It was Saturday anyhow, and quite a few things had to be bought for the coming week. Jim favored his stomach.

Therefore Arvay was not at home when Jim arrived. She took the shortcut across the back of the place on her return, but saw nothing of her husband. So she went in by the back door, laid the package of meat on the table, and went on to the front of the house to take off her things before starting to cook the supper. Arvay halted long enough, though, to chunk up the dying fire with a piece of fat pine and two pieces of

160

good dry oak. Then she decided that it might be better to get the stew on to simmer while she changed and rested awhile.

Jim bragged on Arvay's beef stews. He said that he had never liked beef stew before he had married. It was really something wonderful the way his wife fixed it. So Arvay browned the chunks of red meat carefully, added salt and whole pepper corns with a little flour, added her water, then clamped down the pot lid and went on up front to change.

No sooner did she enter the bedroom than she heard Jim's voice out around the front gate. With her hands uplifted to take off her hat, Arvay went to the front window to look and see who it was that Jim was talking with.

She gave a great gasp. It was Fast Mary, a young woman whom folks made lots of jokes about.

Fast Mary had been crying, Arvay could see from the way her shoulders moved when she snuffled, and the way she wiped her eyes with her sleeve. The window was open, so Arvay stood in the shadow of the curtains and listened.

"You say that Kenny insulted you, Mary?"

"He sure did, and hurt me to my very heart, too, now." Some more sniffles. "I wasn't bothering him at all. I was sitting on the steps at the Long House, that's where I live, and he and his sister come along, and looked at me and begin to giggle and poke fun at me."

"That Kenny is a little limb of Satan. You musn't pay no attention to him. But just what did he do and say?"

"Stopped and looked up under my clothes and pointed, Mister Jim. It's kind of hot today, and I was kind of thin-cladded like, and . . ."

Arvay saw Jim pass his hand over his mouth for a moment, and she knew exactly why. According to the folklore of the town, the weather had nothing to do with the way Fast Mary dressed. She was well known, without having a real friend in the town. She had the misfortune to be too good-looking and too available for women to take to her, but not pretty enough for any man to excuse her generosity and want to protect her. Nor had she the avarice nor the hardness to turn her position

161

to profit. Mary had an accumulation of poverties that worked against her. So Fast Mary had a room at what was known as "The Long House" because it was a one-story structure of about fifteen rooms, side by side, all facing on a common porch. A cheap homely unpainted building inhabited by such as Mary.

"So while I was setting up there on the top step of my house, trying to catch myself a sort of cool breeze off the gutter and looking around, your two children come along, and Kenny, he had to stop and point. He said that it looked like a mulberry pie. I wasn't bothering him nor nobody else."

Arvay saw Jim choking down a laugh while Mary buried her head in the crook of her arm and cried. Jim got his face fixed for sympathy and a serious consideration of the case just as Mary raised her eyes.

What do Jim mean by listening to all that rigmarole from that fan-foot, that street-walker, that brick-bat for? Arvay thought from her hiding place behind the curtain. They say any man can have her for a fish sandwich and a drink of gin. They claims that she takes men right up on the court-house lawn on dark nights, asks 'em for a dime apiece, lays down, grabs hold of the grass and tells 'em, "Let's go!"

"Well, Mary," Jim was saying with a half-hidden grin on his face, "you realize that Kenny ain't hardly twelve years old as yet. He couldn't be expected to know what he was talking about. It would take a man with experience to give you a sound opinion."

Mary's head and eyes came up quickly, and even from where Arvay stood she could see a different look in Mary's face.

"That's right, Mister Jim. Take for instance a man like you. You wouldn't say a thing like that about me, would you?"

"I couldn't say nothing one way or another, Mary, not unless I got hold of more information than I have. You could maybe give me a full description, and then I would know whether Kenny was lying or not."

Arvay almost forgot herself and hollered out through the

window on hearing that and watching Jim's sly grin and Mary beginning to wring and twist herself. For a second, Arvay felt to burst right out there and jump on her. But Jim would say that she had lowered herself. But she had to let it be known that she was home somehow and get that woman away from her gate and that soon. Suddenly she knew what she was going to do. She flew back to the kitchen, grabbed her scrubbing-bucket, got some hot water, dumped some Gold Dust in it, grabbed her scrub-rag and brush and broke for the front porch. She remembered to halt at the door, and come out on the porch just as if she had no idea that anybody was around.

Mary, facing towards the house, saw her first, and Arvay could see the bad surprise in her face. Then that made Jim look around.

"Why, hello there, honey!" Jim looked and sounded as if he didn't care. "I didn't know that you had got back home as yet."

"Well, I'm here." Arvay stated most positively.

There was a bodied silence, then Jim said, "Mary here's been telling me that Kenny's been up to devilling her some way. Poking fun at her, and she come out to let us know about it."

"Kenny and Angie left here to go to Joe's house. Where would they come in contact with Mary?"

"She says that it was at her house, that is The Long House."

"What in the world would Kenny be doing at The Long House?" Arvay asked in a bruising way.

"Oh, they wasn't there, exactly, Miz' Arvay," Mary hurried to say, as ingratiatingly as possible. "They was just passing by and Kenny had to stop and meddle at me."

"Don't you worry, Mary, I'll really tend to him for meddling with *you.*" Arvay snatched a rocking chair viciously and began to look it over for dust. "I'll mighty nigh beat him to death."

Mary didn't go for no weather prophet at all, but she knew when the climate got too cold for her clothes. Mary turned and went away, and went away so hurriedly that she took the wrong direction. Instead of turning north towards town, she turned south where there was nowhere to go except along the Meserve fence line. Jim decided not to use the front door just then, but went clear around the house, and Arvay heard him come in the back door and fool around for a minute or so before he came up the hall. Arvay was too mad to look right then. And now that she had come out there with that outfit under false pretense, she had to do something with it to fool Jim.

"That Kenny!" Arvay exclaimed out loud. "He won't do a single thing like you tell him to do. Sent him out here to scrub this porch, and these steps ain't seen a drop of water. Then had to sankle around that Long House. I aim to take me a bunch of peach hickories and use him up."

From back in the house, Jim chuckled amiably. "No more than to be expected, honey. You know how boys are about doing anything useful around a house. You just have to stand right over 'em to get anything done at all. Kenny had business to clean that porch and them steps for you," Jim hurried to be agreeable. "You ought to tan his hide for him when he gets back."

"Without a doubt," Arvay declared, though she knew very well she had no such intention. She was wondering about Jim, and as mad as fire with Mary. Jim was going to have to sense her into something about Mary and that quick. Maybe all this month past while she had been mourning, Jim had been fooling around that Mary. She was just wondering how to tackle the subject when she saw Mary retracing her steps. Arvay had no intention of speaking to Mary, so she attacked the top step with a great flourish of soap-suds and scrubbing brush. To be sure not to look around she put plenty of muscle into the job.

"Humph!" Arvay heard behind her from the region of the gate. "Some of these old nice-nasty folks make me sick of my stomach. Putting on all them holy airs, and trying to slur at me."

Arvay raised up and look over her shoulder at Mary, who was not passing the gate, but standing there, face all broken up with anger, and her arms akimbo. Arvay stood and looked with the brush in one hand and the cloth in the other and scorned the cheaply clad young woman with her eyes. She washed the face, the thin body, the cheap dress and the run-over high-heeled shoes with a look that was as good as hurling a bucket of solid sewage over the girl. Mary took it all in and reacted accordingly.

"Don't you be looking at me with your scorn like that!" Mary bellowed. "Making out I ain't nothing. With your cold-acting ways, nobody in town can't tell whether you're a man or a woman."

Jim had retreated somewhere inside. Arvay favored Mary with another scornful look, dropped the brush in the bucket, dipped her cloth, wrung it out with great deliberation, then said coolly, "That ain't *your* trouble, honey. They all know about *you* . . . exactly."

Arvay heard a smothered chuckle from Jim. He was in the bedroom.

"You, you!" Mary, in wild rage, floundered for an answer to that. "I, I, well, never mind. That's all right for you, Madam. I won't do nothing to you. I'll place you in the hands of the Lord. I'll pray for you, Miss Arvay. I'll get down on my knees for you! And when I get down on *my* knees and talk to God . . ."

Fast Mary kimboed herself again, wagged her head positively and angrily, and left the rest to Arvay's imagination. Anything was liable to happen from that. Arvay could even look for another Flood.

Arvay stroked her with her eyes again and slimed her over like a million snails. She dried the top steps with the big rag, then dropped it in the bucket and took the brush in her hands.

"*You* praying to God against anybody? Humph! That's a pretty come off. I'll bet you when you get down on them rusty knees and get to worrying God, He goes in His privy-house and slams the door. That's what He thinks about *you* and *your* prayers."

Maybe it was not what Arvay said and the way she said it

165

that hurt Mary so much. It could have been that loud cackle that came out through the bedroom window. Jim was in there roaring with laughter. So Mary flirted her skirts and began to move off.

"That's all right for you, picking at me when I ain't done nothing to you." Mary halted for a moment and called back: "Just because I ain't got no whole heap of money like you, you think that you got a call to take and hurt my feelings. Treat me just like I was some old dog. I got feelings just like anybody else."

"You keep 'em away from my husband then, and you'll get along all right," Arvay yelled back. "Just let me catch you a'wringing and a'twisting your narrow self and grinning up in his face one more time if you dare, and I'll take me something and do my level best to salivate you! Rack on away from here!"

In her rage, Arvay did not bother to fake at the steps anymore. She dashed the bucket of water in the yard and went storming back through the house.

"You sure did give poor Mary a reading, honey." Jim was still chuckling as Arvay passed the bedroom door. "Come here."

"What do you want?" Arvay asked as she stood stiffly before him.

"You, as usual, but right now I want to know if you feel mad at me?"

"What I got to feel mad with you about, Jim? I don't reckon you told that heifer to come racking up here to grin up in your face. I don't believe that Kenny and Angie said or done a living thing to that fan-foot. Anyhow, it shows how low she is to be setting in public with her no-count, trashy legs gapped open, knowing that she wasn't dressed for that. If they did even look at the slouchy wretch, she grabbed at the occasion to run to you hoping to get a trade out of the thing before it was over, the hungry-gut sow!"

"You reckon that was her idea?" Jim shied off.

"What else? But you wouldn't stoop to nothing like that,

that is I don't reckon you would." And Arvay questioned Jim
with her eyes.

"Well, I'd have to be pretty hard up and starved out to come
to it, I reckon, Arvay. It would be tough titty at that."

"I help you to say!" Arvay encouraged the idea. "Now I
reckon I better go fix you some supper." She looked at Jim
hard, lying there across the bed, then slowly turned to go.

Arvay went into her kitchen. She took good pains about
everything and fixed things well. The ginger bread was full of
raisins and spices, and the crust glittered from plenty of butter,
eggs and milk when she drew it out of the oven. Around the
supper table neither Arvay nor Jim mentioned a thing about
passing The Long House to the children. Let them keep their
little secret, while their parents kept theirs.

Arvay took the supper things off the table, went to the big
earthenware churn and filled first all the glasses, then an earthenware pitcher of fresh buttermilk and set it convenient to
Jim's hand. He was very fond of fresh-churned buttermilk. She
made generous squares of the thick hot ginger bread and piled
up a plate of it on the table. Then she sat back down, accepted
Jim's compliments on it and the children's cries of delight and
arranged herself inside.

"You going to town I reckon after supper, Jim."

"Bound to. Saturday night, you know. You want to come
along?"

"Not in particular, Jim."

"Something you forgot to get while you were downtown
this evening and want me to bring it for you?"

"No, I reckon I about got everything. I just wanted to ask
you if you run into Joe to mention to him to step here. I got
a little few things that Dessie could make use of with that
houseful of young'uns she's got. Tell Joe to step by here and
get 'em."

"Saturday night, and Joe is bound to be downtown somewhere, and I'll tell him sure. But if it ain't too heavy, I could
just as easy take it along and hand it to him. What is it you plan
on sending Dessie?"

167

"Earl's things. I got 'em all fixed up into a bundle and tied."
Arvay bit into her ginger bread, chewed, swallowed, then
fumbled with her fork before she lifted her eyes. "They
wouldn't be fitten for nothing by the time Kenny growed up
big enough to wear 'em. They's bound to fit somebody in
Dessie's house. No need in letting 'em lay round here and rot
when somebody could be getting some good out of 'em. They
ain't a bit of use around here."

Arvay saw Jim's head come up and felt his searching gaze.
The blood of her body began to climb to her head. She felt
her ears getting hot and knew that her face was flushed. She
lowered her face and began to poke at the tiny fragment of
ginger bread on her plate like a maiden. Passionate pictures
formed on her eyelids and faded and were instantly replaced
by others. Earl lying dead there at the front steps. That first
time that she had seen Jim Meserve, his broad felt hat shoved
back from his tumbling curls and his white teeth flashing in a
laugh as he talked with two other young men in Sawley. Their
first visit to the mulberry tree. Earl as a new-born infant and
her pangs of pain at the sight of him. Coming down the court-
house steps the day of her marriage. The moment that she
knew that she was pregnant for her Jim. Wrapped in a glory
cloud, she had walked to the window and looked out at the
tall pines around the camp and heard them singing in the
wind. The joyous moment when Jim had come running into
the room with the newborn Kenny in his arms. Earl in his
coffin. The pictures stopped and a bell was tolling, and tolling
and tolling.

She looked up suddenly at Jim for help and he was there at
the head of the table and the tolling ceased in her head. The
same way that her agony had been bearable that day when she
had looked from the dead face of Earl to Jim up on the porch
by the door. Yes, Jim Meserve in his flesh was really there at
the table with her. This was a miracle right out of the Bible.
For some reason, still and as yet not revealed to Arvay, this
miracle of a man had married her. She had been blessed
beyond all other women of this world. How on earth had she

ever risked losing his presence? Jim was there, but at any moment he might vanish from her sight, never to be seen again.

"You, you won't let them men keep you off from home too late tonight, will you please, Jim?" Arvay murmured without looking at Jim directly.

"No chance of that," Jim answered heartily. "I can attend to what little I got to do in no time, then I'll rattle my hocks on home."

Jim got up at once and hurried off. Arvay sat wrapped in a glory cloud of feeling while the children chattered on without her paying them the least attention. Arvay was off in a far country until she was recalled by Angie and Kenny contesting over the ginger bread. Both claimed the right to the still uncut other end of the dessert. Arvay came to herself with a jolt.

"Don't you!" she shouted as she sprang to her feet and snatched the pan from both of them. "I just dare you to touch that other end. You know that your Papa likes them corner pieces! Touch 'em if you dare and I'll salivate you!"

CHAPTER 16

Angeline Meserve was in her bedroom all by herself. It was a comfortable room, and fixed up with the oddities and little fripperies that a girl of seventeen would be apt to think attractive. Pennants of different high schools, souvenirs of school parties and dances.

The warm May sunshine came in through the two windows that faced the south this Sunday morning. Angeline had shoved back the curtains so that the room was brightly lighted. She herself was utterly without clothing, planted before the long mirror in her dresser, admiring herself. Her thick, curly hair was loose and fell well below her shoulders and in the light looked like a flood of ribbon-cane syrup in a clear glass bottle with the sun shining through it. Angeline had the comb in her hand and was combing it with slow movements, and posing her hair first one way, then another: over her right shoulder, straight back from her face and down her back, then over her left shoulder, as she posed and smiled at herself.

"Wonder how Hatton would like to see me like this?" And Angeline smiled and smiled. "Or maybe he would rather see me like this," and she changed her hair and her position. She stood with both arms flung out languidly, her head far back, and her hair tumbling away from the back of her head as if it had been poured. Her feet were close together and her pubic hairs reflected back from the mirror like a triangle of bronzy gold pointed downward in the heart-shaped area of her pelvis. "But maybe he don't care about seeing me in no way at all." The smile fled away from her face. "Some of those older girls can beat my time with him." The girl looked sad and solemn. She stared at the creamy perfection of her body through smoky eyes. The stiff, out-thrust breasts with the old-rose nipples, the perfection of line down to her bare toes.

"Why? Why will Hatton turn me down for them? My shape is all right, and I'm not ugly in my face neither." Angeline's lips began to tremble. "It's just because I'm too young for him, and they won't let me take company."

Angeline went and flung her despised perfection across the bed and began to cry.

"What chance have *I* got against all those old grown girls that's after Hatton? I wish that I was dead."

Angeline had been crying and glooming for some time when she heard her mother calling her.

"Ma'am," she muttered through her pillow finally.

"With Jim and Kenny out the way, even though it's Sunday, I can work some on your graduating things. I can fit and try on this dress anyhow, and be ready to run it up and whip on the ruffles tomorrow. Get into that new white slip and I'll be right in there to try on this dress."

"Yessum." And Angeline got up sullenly, took the new slip out of the dresser drawer and snatched it angrily over her head.

Arvay crossed the hall and came into Angie's room with her arms full of billowy white, and her pin-cushion pinned to her bosom. Businesslike, she flung the unfinished dress over Angie's head and began to size up and pin here and there.

"My, goodness, Angie! This dress come near being too tight across in here." Arvay was too nice to mention breasts. It was just across in here. Her eyes popped, and she looked hard in her daughter's face. It was startling and shocking too. While she wasn't looking, her girl had taken on the shape of a woman. As she fitted on down, she took note that Angie had

171

shaped out round her hips too. She worked on in silence, turning Angeline this way and that. Things went on very well until she got to the hem.

"Better step up on that chair, Angie. My knees gets too tired squatting down so long. Get up there so I can level this hem."

Angie got up on a wooden-bottomed chair. Now she could see only the lower half of herself in the glass. She could see her mother pinning a deep hem in the dress that let it hang just below her knees.

"Mama! Stop putting all that hem in my dress, making me look like I was some little old girl! No, Mama, no!"

The pitch and intensity of Angie's voice made Arvay jump.

"Why, Angie!" Arvay looked her surprise. "What in the world is done got into you?"

Angie was jumping up and down on the chair in a frenzy like she used to do when she was a little girl and determined to have her way. She was jumping, stomping her feet and screaming "No!" over and over like a chant.

"I'm not going to wear no short dress! I'm seventeen, and I'm not no little girl, and I'm not going to wear no short dress. I'm not going out there on that platform in no short dress like I was some little girl. I'm not going to . . ."

"Why, Angie, you act like you done gone clean crazy through your head. Look like you would feel proud for folks to think that you was schooling out so young. Plenty time for you to look like some full-grown woman. When you school out of college up there in Tallahassee later on, then you can be fixed up more like a woman. I . . ."

"I don't care if I don't never get to no Tallahassee!" Angeline grabbed her hands full of the dress and started to rip and tear. Arvay was just in time to prevent any damage being done by grabbing Angie's hands. "I don't care if I don't never go to no college at all. I'm not going out there to that exercise where folks can see me looking like no little child of a girl. I'm old enough to take company like other girls do, and I'm not going to be made out to be no child. Beat me if you want to,

172

you can't kill me, and if you kill me, you sure Lord can't eat me. I'm not going to wear no short dress."

Arvay stood back and looked at the raging girl up on the chair for a long time before she could bring out what was in her mind.

"Oh, so you looks upon yourself as a grown woman now, I see." She said it very quietly and tightened her lips.

"Well, I am, ain't I?" Angeline retorted defiantly. "Some folks my age are married, and even got children."

"Call yourself hitting a straight lick with a crooked stick, I take it." Arvay murmured this equally quietly, while she looked up at the stranger standing on the chair. "The main idea you want understood is that you smell yourself and wants to take company. Boys and books don't mix, Angie, and I ever hoped that you would school out before you got a notion like that in your head."

"Think I aim to be some old maid sitting around teaching school or something?"

"Well, you said a while back, around Thanksgiving, that you wanted to go off to that college for girls up there in Tallahassee and school out, didn't you? Nobody didn't ask you for that. You said it your ownself. I ain't never had much schooling; never had the chance to rub the hair off of my head against no college walls, and I thought that it would be mighty nice for you to get hold of the advantage that I missed. All I know is my a b c's. Read some and figger a little. I thought that it would be nice, after you mentioned it, to have my girl come home with papers to hang on the wall."

"It would be nice too, Mama." Angeline spoke without heat in her voice now. "But, but, if I got to stay little for four more long years for that, Mama, I'd rather not. Fact is, I don't think I could live that long."

"Just what would rush you to a four-sided grave so soon, Angie? I wish that you would let me know."

"Because I want to take company, and . . ."

"Is it somebody particular that you so anxious to be with?" Arvay asked and trembled down her limbs.

"Yes, Ma'am. It's Hatton Howland, Mama."

"Hatton Howland? Ain't that that Yankee boy that drives that blue Chivvylay and works at the filling station?"

"That's right."

"But he's a Yankee, Angie, and you're born and raised up in the South, and to mingle up like that ain't—"

"I don't care!" Angie shouted passionately. "I don't care if he even come from Diddy-Wah-Diddy! I don't care nothing at all about no old Civil War. I don't care nothing about Jeff Davis nor Abraham Lincoln nor Lee nor nobody else if it's got to come between me and Hatton Howland. Compared with him, it comes before me just like a gnat in a whirlwind."

"You and this Hatton must of been seeing mighty much of one another to be feeling that a'way," Arvay remarked. "Though to my rest, I can't see when it could of been."

Angeline jumped down from the chair and sat on the bed.

"Mama, I been loving Hatton since way before Christmas, but he never noticed me at all. Treated me just like I was some little bitty girl. Flourishing around with all those twenty and so on years old women, and wouldn't do no more than pass the time of day with me." Then an intense glow came from behind Angie's eyes. "But, Mama, all the boys around school are crazy about Hatton, and so they asked him to the Easter dance. And what you reckon? I asked him to dance with me, and he did, Mama! Hatton Howland danced with *me!* Then while we were dancing sort over in a corner around the potted palms, I kissed him, Mama, and then he asked me to dance with him next time. And ever since then, he's been noticing me a lot."

"I see," Arvay mumbled off. "But I never thought a girl of mine would put herself in the way of a man like that. I thought that she would look upon herself more than that. I'm hurt to my heart to hear it."

"But, Mama! You just don't catch on so good. You see, I knew that poor Hatton would love me if he only knew me, so I had to let the poor thing know, so he could come to be happy some day."

174

Then Angie was not a grown girl anymore. She rushed to her mother and began to cry with sobs.

"But you wouldn't let me take company when I asked you to, and you keep me looking like some little old twelve-year-old girl, and all them grown old girls are taking the advantage of me. Riding around in Hatton's car, and going to the show and to parties with him, and I can't go nowhere and can't do a thing, and they're going to take him away from me."

Arvay held the sobbing girl a long time and let her cry. She had felt so warm and surrounded these last three years. Now the thing she had feared but refused to look at openly had come upon her. Her children were growing up. The little family circle could be broken up. A tall, loose-jointed, rusty-headed boy with gray eyes could make her daughter carry on like this. Angeline didn't need her. She was willing to give up all the care that she had given her, all the plans that she had made and had been made for her for that freckled boy from somewhere up in Michigan, who worked at a filling station to help support his widowed mother. Trying to keep Angie a child had done her no good. It was as if a crack had opened in the wall of her home and a cold damp draft was blowing through.

"Move, Angie. I got to get what I'm going to do on your dress for today off my hands and see about fixing dinner. Get back up on the chair one more time."

Angeline got back up on the chair with swollen eyes. With dead-feeling fingers, Arvay dropped the hem of the stiff organdy dress to Angie's ankles and pinned it all the way around.

CHAPTER 17

"S o I reckon we better leave her take company, you think, Jim?" Arvay asked in the privacy of their bedroom late that Sunday afternoon when she and Jim were both lying down, sluggish from the heavy meal.

"You know that I don't mind, honey. You was the one that was against it. I thought that it would have been all right the day she turned sixteen."

"Well, then, I can tell her that if she gets her di-plooma all right, we can let her have company a couple of nights a week. Maybe after the new wears off, she won't be so hog-wild over that Hatton Howland and all. You reckon?"

"How do I know, honey? It could be Angie just thinks she loves him because he's older than she is. Young girls are apt to feel that way. Or because she wants to have it that she took him away from those older girls. And then again, she might really care, for a while anyhow. Love is a funny thing, Little-Bits. Seems like that one person gets next to your heart, and you can't shake 'em loose no matter which way you twist and turn. You just got to go on serving 'em all your born days."

For a space, Arvay traveled the road that she had come for the last twenty years. Her love had mounted her to the tops of peaky mountains. It had dragged her in the dust. She had been in Hell's kitchen and licked out all the pots. She had stood for moments on the right hand side of God.

"I hope my child don't fall such a slave to nobody that they can just handle her anyway they will or may, and she be so under the influence that she can't help herself. I don't never want her to know the feeling of that."

Jim looked at Arvay very hard for a minute, then he let his head sink back down on the pillow and smiled a secret smile.

"I differ from you on that, Arvay. I want her to feel just like that. That is the only way to be in love. It ain't really love when you gamble with your stuff out the window. Leave all your best things outside and come in and get in the game, and soon as you win a little something, jump and run."

"But it's so compellment, Jim. When you'se so that anything a person puts on you, you'se willing to take and swallow just so you can still be there."

"Love ain't nothing else *but* compellment, honey. 'Tain't love when you can help yourself. When you can chew but you can't swallow, you're just filling out an arrangement. I don't say that I'm rearing for my girl to jump in love so soon like this, and with Hatton neither, but when it do hit her, I want it to be the real thing."

Now, just what was real love? Arvay asked herself and sat in silence searching experience for the answer. She could find no one word to express what she felt was love. Maybe these high-bred, book-learnt kind of folks had been taught and told what it was, but nobody had taught her things like that. Arvay did come to a kernel of what she felt that love ought to be and to do. Love to her meant to possess as she was possessed. To be wrapped around and held in an embrace so warm and so tight that the Booger Man, the raw-head-and-bloody-bones of lonesomeness, could never come nigh her. An eternal refuge and everlasting welcome of heart to rest and rely on. Never had she been sure that she possessed anyone, though Jim had told her time and again that she owned him through and through. It was too wonderful to be so for her, but she hoped for that miracle for her daughter, and she was not too ready to believe that Angeline had found it in Hatton. How could

177

it come to pass between a Yankee and her daughter? It might be, but Arvay felt to wait a long, long time and see.

Arvay was determined, and held onto to her own construction of things even after she saw that the moment the permission was given for Angeline to take company, Hatton Howland seemed to fairly infest the house. The Friday and Sunday nights arrangements didn't hold water, because other times he was there supposedly to talk about music with Kenny. Hatton just took up around the place, that was all. He came with a saxophone and pretended to practice with Kenny at the piano. But the graduating exercises the last Friday night in May, and getting ready and all, kept Arvay so busy that she could take comfort in that. Kenny was conducting the school band for the exercises, and what with seeing to a new suit for him and Angie's clothes, and rehearsals, things were not too obvious for her.

But Angie's infatuation was as plain as day after that. She laid her diploma on top of the piano and seemed to forget that she had it, but she took the bouquet that Hatton sent her for graduation into the bedroom clasped in her arms and gave those flowers every care. They were the new Talisman roses, and the way she found new things to exclaim about them every hour or so hurt Arvay to her heart.

The tocsin sounded for Arvay the Sunday night following Angie's graduation. Jim had climbed into his Buick sedan that morning with Alfredo and gone over to the coast. He had not returned at nine o'clock that night, and Arvay was in her bedroom with the door stretched wide open so she could hear what went on in the parlor across the hall. She had quietly worked her little rocker as near to the door as possible, and sat there pretending to devote herself to a Wine of Cardui almanac. She glanced at all the pictures of the women who wrote that it had done them so much good. Women who had yearned for children for years, but none came to bless their homes. This one had taken only ten bottles when a lovely child came to gladden her home. She recommended [it] to all women in her same fix.

Arvay's ears caught a long silence, then some sort of quick and sudden movement, then Hatton's voice, husky and drugged like.

"Angie! Do that again, and so help me, I'll rape you!"

"So rape me, and I'll help you!" came just as fervently from her daughter's lips.

Arvay was on her feet in an instant, with the intention of rushing across the hall, denouncing Hatton as a low-down scamp and a scoundrel-beast, and no gentleman whatsoever, and driving him off the place. Hatton being gutted and shot with tacks, Angeline would be attended to for lowering herself to that extent. But with her feet at the bedroom door, she became confused as to just what to say when she got into the parlor.

"I don't mean to say a mumbling word! I'll kill him dead and then stomp his head, the Yankee scamp, the dirty Carpetbagger! Done burnt out and robbed and murdered all over the South, and now come back to take the under-currents of my child! I'll get me a gun and go in there and shoot him dead."

Arvay ran on tip-toes to the closet, flung it open and laid her hand on the Winchester repeating rifle, and instantly, its association with Earl made it burn her hand. She snatched her hand away, fled to the dresser and fumbled desperately under Jim's handkerchiefs, ties and collars until she laid her hand on the revolver. Her fingers trembled so that she had trouble breaking the gun and shoving in the cartridges. She loaded it fully, then whirled and walked to the door.

At that moment the front door flew open and Jim came stalking in. Arvay was surprised. Her agitation was so great that she had not noticed the sound of the car entering the yard. Jim, with a good-natured look on his face, stood in the hall between the two doors and looked first into the parlor and then at Arvay with the gun gripped in her hand in the bedroom door. He started, then wordlessly shoved her back before him as he entered the bedroom and closed the door.

179

In hot, jerky phrases, Arvay told him the story. To her surprise, Jim chuckled.

"Nothing to laugh over, Jim Meserve. While you set here sniggling and giggling, that scamp is liable to be over there raping our child."

"You mean our child is liable to be over there raping Hatton, don't you?" He laughed some more. "If I know my daughter, this is one battle that the Yankees will never win."

Then Jim got very sober in the face. Fiddling with the revolver in his hand, he sat on the side of the bed and considered.

"I think I had better spend some time tomorrow looking up Hatton and finding out all I can about him. So far, I don't know nothing excepting that his Papa and Mama come down here from somewhere in Michigan eight or nine years back and settled. Since his old man died, his Mama's been renting rooms to tourists in the winter time. I reckon what little Hatton brings in since he got out of school helps along. I don't know a thing against his character, so far as I have heard. He does seem to be mighty popular with the young folks. Could be because he's got that nice-looking car. But anyhow, I'll look into things without delay."

"Look into things, Jim? What for? 'Tain't nothing to be looked into as I can see. His case don't need to come up in our court at all. Just run him off the place and double-dog dare him to foot this place again. That's all that you need to do. Shoot him down like a mangy dog if he dast to shove his toe-nails across this doorway another time."

"Don't look like you're taking Angie into account. Her feelings have got to be considered. Unless I'm mighty mistaken, Angie's got her mind set on having the poor boy, and I'm mighty afraid that he's going to be had. If he don't want her, and is determined not to have her, if he got good sense he better grab the first thing smoking and make his left-here now. If he don't, and that mighty quick, he's a gone ginny."

"Well! If this don't take the rag clean off the bush! You

mean to set there on your honkers and don't do nothing at all?"

"Nothing for me to do till I see more into things, Arvay. You know so well that Angie is my heart-string. I can't bring myself to take no steps that might hurt her feelings. Lemme search up this Hatton Howland and see if he will in any way do. If he won't, I'll have to try and seek some way to make her see that he won't do for her. Now, come on and let's go cross there and act nice with 'em and see can't we get some idea how the land is laying."

Arvay's experiences of love and passion told her things the moment that she stood in the parlor door. Angie and Hatton, being warned of their approach, were seated on either end of the sofa. Arvay stood and took in the situation with her experienced eye. Indeed, things had come to a critical fix. Angeline, drooping in her corner of the sofa looked to be under a heavy dose of laudanum. The long lashes of her eyes drooped to almost closing. Hatton, flushed in the face, was fidgeting like he had a hot stove lid in the seat of his pants. To Arvay's knowing eye, Hatton further betrayed his condition by throwing one arm about a pillow and patting and petting it with the fingers of his long, strong hand. Arvay smiled inwardly with a feeling of morbid triumph, and crossed the room slowly and took a seat opposite. This romance was unwelcome to her at this time, but it was not all one-sided, anyhow. Angeline was giving this long tall boy just as good as he sent. Angie had put Hatton on the linger, all right. Yes indeed!

Arvay was seated in a big chair close to the piano. She was so interested in watching and learning that she just sat and had nothing to say. Through her preoccupation she heard Jim, with the aid of a lot of jokes and sayings, skillfully lead Hatton to talk about himself and his plans.

Hatton made eighteen dollars a week at the filling-station regularly. Of course he picked up some tips, eight to ten dollars in the run of a week on an average. The Chevrolet, a little over a year old now, was paid for. The Howland home place was clean and clear. It had been about half paid for when

181

his father died, and since then, he had managed to pay the debt off and the place was clear. His mother had nothing at all to worry her mind. She picked up a good deal on her rooms and meals during the season, and he could carry things over the summer months with ease.

"You Yankees can really find a dollar," Jim laughed. "I have to hand it to you. You really know how to hustle."

Hatton laughed with Jim. "Well, you know what they say about us Damnyankees down here. Come down with a dirty shirt and five dollars and never change either one and still manage to end up rich."

"So you intend to follow that example too, do you?"

"Well, I'll give in to the extent of changing my shirt, but I really am determined to get hold of something."

Neither Arvay nor Jim missed the sly glance at Angeline as Hatton talked. It was a prod for the girl to take notice.

"I want a wife and a home some day, and I don't want it to be too long off, either. A man ought to have something to give a wife after he takes her away from her home. If it costs me every drop of blood I own, I mean for *my* wife to have something."

"That's a nice thing to say, you child," Arvay stepped in, "but have you got anything besides yourself?"

Hatton, instead of being crushed, gave a mysterious smile. He cut one quick look at Angie, then at Jim and then put on a casual look.

"Oh, I'm not in any danger of starving to death right away. I think that I can say that I can get along. But the money that I handle now is not a drop in the bucket to what I intend to have a little later on. When and if I marry, I want it so that my wife can toss a ten dollar bill in the penny collection in church, and if the usher looks surprised at her and frowns, take her finger and beckon him back and fling in a hundred and tell him to go with that. If she catches him frowning any more, she'll call him back and fling in a thousand."

When the laughter died down, Jim worked his hips out

182

eagerly to the edge of his chair and leaned forward towards Hatton.

"Spoken like a man, Howland. I don't favor nobody marrying for nothing but pure love, and when he comes to that, he ought to be able and willing to do the last thing on earth to look after his woman and the children they might have. That oath he took before God and man when he stood on the floor ought to come in front of everything else on earth. No excuses granted nor accepted. Come pay-day, leave your pretty wife sit on her front porch and look down the road and say with a smile, 'Well here come my husband and them.' "

"Them what?" Arvay asked.

"Them dollars, fool. Let him be man enough to bring it when he comes. It might be so that you have to make your own rules, and ignore all the ready-made ones that folks already know about, but bring it when you come."

Jim at least did not miss the quick, bright and hopeful look that Hatton flashed him for a second.

"You look at things the same way I do, Mr. Meserve. When I get a wife, I mean to bring it or die in the attempt. Being a Damnyankee, I can't let business get away. Why don't you let us have your business, Mr. Meserve? I don't remember ever having the pleasure of servicing your car."

"You goddamned hustler," Jim chuckled. "All right, Hatton. You got a right to pull in all the business you can. I need a good grease job right now. I go to work pretty early, so it will have to be after I knock off tomorrow evening."

"It doesn't have to be that way, Mr. Meserve. If you stop by the station, I could drive you to work, bring the car back and service it, and pick you up any hour and any place that you say."

"You sound like somebody who means to get ahead. That's the ticket! I'll be there at seven o'clock sharp tomorrow morning."

The two men had made a date to talk, but the inning went over Arvay's head. She wondered why Angeline gave such a rustle and began to pick over herself. With a nervous gesture,

183

the girl grabbed up a pillow and began pulling at the threads in the seams, and ripping them open without knowing what she was doing. Arvay reached over and took the pillow out of her hand and dropped it on the floor beside the piano.

Hatton arose abruptly. "Think that I better hit the hay. Be waiting for you at seven o'clock in the morning, sir. Goodnight, Mrs. Meserve."

Angeline stood up with determination and went with Hatton to the door. While she lingered out on the dark porch for a few minutes in low conversation with Hatton, Arvay too saw a chance to speak.

"Well, what do [you] make out of it, Jim?"

"But he sounds mighty promising, for a fellow as young as he is."

"Promising! Shucks! I like to see some of those things *done.* I'd rather *see* a promise than to hear about it any day."

Jim said nothing to that, and they sat awhile, both concerned with the unseen matter on the porch.

Arvay was on the lookout for Jim when he came home late the next afternoon, but Angeline was looking even harder. She had crept out to the front gate, and was there to run and jump on the runningboard when Jim slowed for the turn in.

"Daddy! The car's been washed and polished!"

"Yep, your Yankee put about the best servicing job on her that I've ever seen."

Angeline flung her arms around Jim's neck and practically choked him to a stop in the yard.

"Did I hear you say, *my* Yankee, Daddy?"

"Did I hear *you* say that?" Jim countered.

"Did you hear *Hatton* say that, Daddy?"

"Well, something to that effect."

Arvay, looking out of the kitchen window, heard it all, and saw her daughter fling the car door open in a frenzy, leap in Jim's lap and almost strangle him while she covered him with kisses.

184

"You got him for me, Daddy? You made him promise? Oh, Daddy, Daddy, Daddy, Daddy!"

"Hold on here, baby. I didn't make him promise me nothing. I thought that my girl could handle a thing like that herself."

Angeline got very quiet. Jim hugged her shoulder and laughed.

"I didn't need to, Angie. It didn't take but a minute or so for me to see that you had already laid poor Hatton under conviction. All I could do to keep him from crawling down my throat. From what I could learn, he's been holding off for fear that I wouldn't let him have you."

Angeline went into another frenzy of hugging and kissing her father and uttering senseless sounds.

"So I didn't need to bother about that end," Jim went on. "We just talked business together."

Jim shoved Angie out of the way and got out of the car and came on inside the house. Angie and Kenny had their usual tussle for the wheel to drive the car into the garage. Kenny beat Angie to the seat that time, she flirted her skirt at him, then ran on into the kitchen behind Jim.

Jim came in extra nice to Arvay. He had brought her a large bag of Japanese plums and forbade the children to touch a one unless their mother gave them permission.

"I know how you love the things, and there were three big trees on the place where we cut fruit today, so I made a couple of the men pick you some since they were so handy. I hope that our two trees will bear next year. Then you can have all that you want to eat."

They fooled around with off-hand talk and comments until they were around the supper table, then Jim got around to what he meant to say.

"That Hatton Howland is quite some hustler in this world." He cut into a baked yam and looked across at Arvay with a brightness in his face.

"I don't see where working at a filling station is nothing to brag over," Arvay said.

"And it ain't. It seems that he just holds onto that for a stall so he can't be picked up for vagrancy and have to tell where he really makes his living from."

"Well, how do he make his living?" Arvay asked wearily.

"He's no slough. He got that job as soon as he got out of school, but he seen that he would never get independent working like that. So he worked around and got in with the Boleta man, and started out to selling tickets for the Numbers. He made so good till a couple of years back, the head of the Big House up in Orlando sent for him, and put all the business in this county in Hatton's hands. He's really been making the money since then. On the quiet, naturally. No wonder he could pay for that car spot cash, pay off what was owed on his mother's house, wear the kind of clothes he wears, and to cap it all off, he's got some two to three thousand dollars stuck away. That ain't bad for a lad of twenty-two."

"Except that he's liable to be placed under arrest at any time and work it out on the chain-gang."

"Aw, naw. The Big House up in Orlando has seen to that. He's got all the protection from the law that he needs. Not only that, he don't have to run no risks in turning in his collections. They got a man with guards to come around and pick it up."

"I see, Jim. That Yankee is smarter than I give him credit for."

"Just what do you mean by that?"

"You done let him out-talk you, that's what, and you goes for smart. But he's took you right on in."

Arvay kept a close watch on the ardent courtship, but still the runaway marriage in mid-June was something that she was not prepared for. Kenny, who had gone along with Angie and Hatton called her around sundown that day and told her. Arvay turned from the telephone with slumping shoulders.

"Jim, my girl is married to Hatton." Arvay leaned against the jamb of the door and her lips trembled. "I, I just can't get it into me that my baby girl is old enough for nothing like that.

186

And then, and then the way it was done, Jim. I, I . . ." Arvay twisted her mouth to keep from crying. "Her shoulders ain't old enough for a responsibility as heavy as that. Oh, Jesus!"

Arvay advanced into the kitchen making fumbling motions with her hands. "They're over to Hatton's Mama's house."

"Well, why don't you call 'em up and tell 'em to come on home, honey. That's all they're waiting for."

Arvay stood for a space in heavy silence, then she seemed to come alive again. She looked to Jim hopefully and touched him on his arm.

"You go call 'em, Jim. It's better for you to talk to 'em and tell 'em to come on home. Whilst you'se doing that I can fling some egg-nog together for 'em to drink. Go ahead and make 'em come on home."

Arvay was in a feverish frenzy as she switched around getting ready to receive the young couple. Rinsing out and polishing up the cut-glass punch bowl and cups that went with it. Jim had to run out and help her along.

"Run out to the hen-nests for me, Jim, please, and fetch me all the fresh eggs you can find . . . . Oh, I hope and pray that I got enough cow-cream to go in the egg-nog. I ever vomi-nates poor-made egg-nog . . . . Hand me that bottle of whiskey here . . . . Now where in the world did I lay that nutmeg grater? Now I had that nutmeg in my hand just a while ago. Lord, I can't tell my head from my feet. . . . Dip me up another cup of sugar, there, Jim. . . . Thing like this just would have to come off when I ain't got nothing fitten to eat in the house. . . . You reckon that Angie's room could be fixed up good enough for 'em to stay in till they can do better, Jim? Hatton would be ever so welcome if he thinks the place is good enough for him. . . . Here take this egg-beater and whisk up them whites for me whilst I get down my cake plate and slice what's left over from that white pound cake I made for last Sunday. . . . Just lift up that punch-bowl for a second whilst I slide this Sunday tablecloth on the table. Things will look nice and clean. . . ."

The table was arranged with the brimming bowl of egg-nog

so rich that it poured slowly, so yellow with egg yolks that it was a dark gold. The cake was sliced and arranged in a swirl on the fluted plate when they heard Hatton's car slowing down in the yard. Arvay put out her best napkins, and stacked her best plates to eat cake from.

Then Arvay stood trembling and with a fixed smile on her face looking towards the front door.

"Drag it on in here and get your whipping!" Jim yelled out as they heard the shuffling feet of the three on the front porch. "Come in with your britches down!"

Angeline flung open the door and led the others in with a laugh.

Jim grabbed Hatton and wrestled him around boisterously and hollered over his shoulder to Arvay. "I got this one, you grab the other one and frail her good! We'll show 'em how to run off and marry on us."

Arvay did catch hold of her daughter, hugged her first lest the fiery temper of Angeline prompt her to say the things that Arvay feared, then slapped her two or three times playfully across her buttocks.

"Now, Madam, get in that kitchen and taste that egg-nog I fixed for you. Git!"

Angeline looked at Arvay in astonishment for a minute, then ran for the kitchen pretending to cry loudly into the crook of her elbow. Arvay followed as if in pursuit.

In a minute or two everybody was around the table. Hatton pulled up a chair and sat as close as he could to Angie and placed his arm about her waist. Angie turned a look of such utter happiness upon him that a pain ripped up and down Arvay's body. She was presiding at the punch-bowl, and the hand with the ladle shook a little.

"Things sure can change in a hurry," Arvay said as cheerfully as she could as she dipped up egg-nog and filled cups. "This morning, Angie, you wasn't nothing but my little girl, and now this evening you're a married woman."

"That's right, Mama," Angie murmured with lowered eyes. "But I'm still your little girl, ain't I?"

Arvay dropped the ladle and rushed around and flung her arms about Angie's shoulders and buried her face in the back of the girl's neck. "To be sure and naturally, baby. Only I feel another gap, a kind of a vacant place in my arms. I . . ." Arvay choked back a sob and looked pitifully at Jim.

Hatton stood up and looked pleadingly at Arvay and spoke with emotion.

"Mrs. Meserve, I know that you feel hard towards me for stealing your daughter like I did, but I love her so much, and when she said that she would have me, I was scared to wait. Scared she might change her mind, so I rushed off and got papers for her while she was still in the notion. I intend to be good to her till the day I die, and I hope that some day you can forgive me, and look upon me as a son."

Neither Jim nor any of the family was ever to know what it cost Arvay to say what she did next. She took her seat again and spoke slowly.

"Time changes folks, Hatton, as they go along the road. Some things a person one time wouldn't do for big money, they get so they'll do 'em for nothing. If you love Angie like that, and feel to be my son along with it, I'm only too proud and happy to have you."

Hatton got up without a word and completed the conquest. He bent over Arvay's chair and kissed her respectfully. Tears began to run down her cheeks.

"What makes females cry so much?" Kenny looked from his father to Hatton in genuine bewilderment. "We just left Mrs. Howland crying, and come home and find Mama doing the same."

"Because we born children, take pains to raise 'em, and then they leave us for somebody else, Kenny." Arvay was sobbing full force now.

"Look like you would be glad to get rid of 'em some day or other and take some rest," Kenny pursued. "When I get grown and marry and have children, I don't intend to let mine lay around me but so long. I'm going to run mine off by the time they get half grown and let 'em go scuffle for themselves. I'll be sick and tired of 'em by that time.''

They laughed a long time at that.

"Oh, you hush up, Kenny," Arvay chided. "Your last diapers ain't hardly dry yet, and you come telling grown folks what to do. Ain't you something?"

"But I think that's a darned good plan, Mama."

"Yeah, Kenny, but supposing they never come back to you? You would be hurting your ownself maybe more than them. A mother feels to keep in quotation with her child and don't care what it takes to do it."

"Table that!" Jim bellowed, "and let's open up the house for new business. Now that I got me a grown son, we got to make some arrangements."

"If you mean some place for Angie and Hatton to stay till they can see further, I don't see no reason why they can't stay right on in Angie's room. We could maybe get hold of a bigger bed."

Angeline and Hatton exchanged quick and embarrassed looks.

"Mother Howland is fixing us up a room over there," Angie said.

"Oh, that don't need to call for any long discussion," Hatton said. "Until we can build, which we intend to do just as soon as we can locate a lot that Angie likes, we got two homes, and we can stay at first one and then the other. We are in a shape where we don't need to be no burden on nobody, and soon as we can build, we'll get into a house of our own."

"Take your behind down off your shoulders, Hatton. You said that you wanted me to look upon you as a son, didn't you?"

"Yes sir, and I do."

"Well, you're at home here just as much as anywhere else, and if you listen to the advice I give you, you won't be building for quite some time as yet, and you won't be buying no lot right up in town. You willing for me to lead you and guide you?"

190

"In every way—Dad."

"Well then, let me place my wisdom tooth in your head, and put you on the road to something big. Don't never be afraid to try big things, Hatton. The time to get scared is when you mess with something little. That's where you get your whipping. Ready for the question?"

"Let her rip!"

"You have told me about your Number business and the money you got put away. There'll be another county election in a couple of years, and things might not be the same. Before that time, if you're as smart as I think you are, you'll put your money into something where no cheap and hungry politicians can't bleed it out of you in one way or another. Too many politicians look on their offices as a means of receiving what they call stolen goods. Let some smart man make a pile in some illegal way, then bleed him for it. You take all the risk and they take all the money. Get me?"

"I guess I do."

"Well, before the next election comes around, I want you to hide all that money you make on Numbers in land. Then you can't be touched. Land is highly legal. You will be a realtor by then."

"I'm willing, that is, if you will show me how."

"It's something mighty big and hard that I got for you to do, but if you're willing to tackle it, it will give you a lifetime start so you don't never need to be in the ham-scram again. You and Angie can go right on from there to something really big."

"Gee, that sounds like something. Lead me to it is all I ask you to do."

"Okay, if you got guts in you, this is where it'll show. I want you to clear that swamp."

"Swamp?" Some kind of sound burst out of everybody. Jim was the only calm person in the room. He reached over, laid his hand on top of Arvay's and began to stroke it in a gentle and affectionate way.

"That's what I said, son, that swamp. There's a great big

191

fortune hid in that dark old swamp. All it needs is the brains and the nerve to get it out. I been wanting to tackle it for nearly twenty years. Ever since I bought this place, but I wasn't in no position to handle it then, and anyhow the time wasn't right. The machinery necessary wasn't on hand in those days. Now it is, you're young and smart, and you can do the job that I been saving up for my sons to do. When you see daylight through that place from here, you're going to be a mighty well-off young man. Are you game?"

"You bet your bottom dollar if there's anything can be made out of it, and you show me how to go about it."

"It's so damn easy and soft that I hate to tell it. All these smart real estate operators done slept a good bet, and I don't want 'em woke up until you get things tied up so that they got to come in by you to get a smell."

"Keep on, Dad, my pockets are already crying for that money."

"Well, the truth is, that's all state land. The State of Florida and nobody else wants to be bothered with it in the fix it's in. Like Miami Beach before that guy from Indianapolis come along and filled it in and made it worth plenty millions. Then they were willing to pay a fortune for a home site on it."

"But my few thousands wouldn't be a drop in the bucket, Dad."

"That's where you're wrong. If you bite big enough, you can get a whale of a lot of cash right out of that swamp without hardly moving a muscle. If you take in two miles north to south on this side, then run a line straight through the swamp far enough to take in that lake back there in the woods about two miles from the swamp and square it all off into a rectangle, you get enough timber to bust a bank when you sell it off. Putnam, or any of those big fellows will buy a fine stand like that, and after you sign the contract, nothing more for you to do but to sit back while they go in there and take the lumber out and hand you the check. In fact, just as soon as they estimate the footage in there, you get your check in front. Then you can lay it aside until they get through, and have it

192

on hand to develop your real estate with. You got to fill in the lowest part, and then you are ready to develop a new addition to this town. That swamp has held the town from growing west long enough."

To Arvay's astonishment, and somewhat to her dismay, Hatton took the proposition under consideration. A week later, Hatton said that he was willing to try it. She could not make herself believe that the thing was really going to be tackled, until Jim and Hatton drove up to Tallahassee for two days, secured the huge tract for a few cents an acre, and she saw the surveyors at work.

"What on earth did you want to sic that poor boy on that nasty old swamp for, Jim?" Arvay asked that night as they were getting ready to go to bed. "He could of made a living some other easier way."

Jim was unbuttoning his shirt, and he paused and looked at Arvay combing out her long hair in front of the dresser.

"Don't you have no idea, Arvay?"

"Why, no I don't, Jim. You done bought that boat for fishing and all, and got Alfredo working on it for you. I don't see how come you couldn't take him in with you on that."

Jim dropped down and began to unlace his shoes. He got more quiet and took a long time before he looked up at Arvay again.

"So you really ain't got no notion why I wanted that swamp cleaned off, have you, honey?"

"Naw I told you. None at all."

Jim jerked off first one heavy shoe and then the other.

"Well, maybe it'll come to you some day."

They didn't talk about it anymore and went on to bed.

CHAPTER 18

The year that followed Angie's marriage was to Arvay faintly melancholy, like twilight. Many things came to make her happy and proud, but the old familiar things in her life were fading away.

Arvay was alone much more than she used to be. Jim's shrimping business was on a safe enough basis now for Alfredo to move his family over to the coast with him so that there was no one living on the place now but Jim and Arvay, and Jim drove to the coast as often as possible these days. Kenny was up at the University of Florida at Gainesville. He wrote frequent and enthusiastic letters home, mostly about his activities in the University band, but that was not like his familiar presence around the house. Angeline was sweet and dutiful, but Angie was Hatton's wife first before she was anything else.

Arvay had ceased to worry about the success of the marriage. Angie and Hatton got along beautifully together, and neither he nor his mother did or said anything that Arvay could put down as a dirty Yankee trick. In fact, Arvay admitted to herself that she was jealous of that woman. By degrees Angie was becoming a Howland, being influenced by both Hatton and his mother. Arvay could see Angie's brisk new ways. Getting vigorous and thrifty increasingly, and proud about it. Putting up jams and jellies and running up house-dresses for herself. This in spite of Hatton's fond indulgence of Angie to everything that she wanted. And financially, Hatton was doing remarkably well. Under Jim's tutelage many wealthy and able business men had been induced to buy into the project, and things were being done on a very big scale.

With a melancholy pride in the astonishing rise of her daughter's husband, Arvay watched the progress of things from the coming of the surveyors to the completion of the sumptuous club house of the country club in the new Howland Development.

As Jim had predicted, modern machinery and methods had cleared that swamp in an amazingly short time. Arvay, from her seat on the front porch, watched the gangs of husky black roustabouts rumbling past in truck loads, singing, chanting, laughing as they went to the swamp and moved about in their high boots, and swinging shining axes to rhythm, felling the giant trees. Gnawing at the feet of the forest to make way for the setting sun.

Arvay was surprised at finding herself feeling a sympathy with the swamp. She was used to certain outlines against the sky and now it seemed a pity and a shame for those trees to be destroyed. She had hated and feared the swamp, but long association had changed her without her realizing it. She and the swamp had a generation of life together and memories to keep. She hated to see it go. But the horde of black men sang and chanted and swarmed and hacked, machinery rumbled and rattled, huge trucks grumbled and rolled until one day Arvay saw the sun setting behind the horizon of the world. The opening spread north and north before her eyes. The swamp monster retreated before the magic of man.

Arvay watched the conquest of her old enemy with the utmost fascination. It was very personal to her, though she never said so to anyone. She followed the progress of the men day by day. Now they were nearing the place of Earl's death. Who knew how many times Earl had been there before that fatal day! What had he done and felt there? Another day and they were about at the place. Arvay was so excited that she could scarcely sleep that night. The next morning she was in her rocking chair on the porch very early, as soon as Jim had gotten off to work. This morning, perhaps at this minute, those men must be felling those three big trees by the pool, and those others that surrounded the glade. Oh, do, Jesus!

Did that swarm of black men see or hear anything mysterious, or feel any strange presence? Were they halting, looking puzzled over some small something that she had failed to find on her secret visit to the place? Was there another place in there that she knew nothing about? Something that might reveal the unknown inner life of the son that she had borne. Arvay burned to halt the trucks loaded down with the miry, sweaty men as they rolled past her door at sundown, but then again, how could she ask them anything? She could watch and feel and forever wonder, but she must keep such things to herself.

Where the loggers had been one day, the bulldozers followed the next, and right behind the big machines came the long train of dump-trucks pouring dry sand into the narrow, muddy gully that had been the lowest part of the swamp. Raw, dark gashes made by the bulldozers were streets stretching across the new fill and would soon be paved. Sewers, water-mains and electric lines rushed across to take the comforts of civilization to those who would make their homes over there. Influence had brought prompt action on the part of the county, and no sooner had the area opposite the Meserve place been filled in than Arvay saw the engineers laying out the ornate stone causeway that was to arch the low part of the land for the main highway. Tons of cement and steel were delivered and piled not too far from Arvay's front door, and she could watch the approaches of the causeway being laid. It began no more than a hundred feet from her front gate.

As Jim had predicted, the giving of the tract for the links and the club house had been a smart move for Hatton. The right people bought sites in the new development and it bloomed. The Howland Development exerted a tremendous

196

effect on Citrabelle and the surrounding country. It came along and stratified the town. The original line of the swamp gave accent like a railroad track. Those who belonged moved west.

Hatton and Angie had one of the choicest sites on the big lake that was now known as Lake Charm, and Arvay felt pride in that. She saw her daughter friending with people whom she herself had never dreamed of associating with. The sons and daughters of first and second degree Yankees and wealthy southerners. Angie and Hatton played tennis and golf, went in swimming, canoed and motor-boated with the rest, and talked about getting sun-tanned.

Arvay took pride in all this, but underneath, it created a kind of lonesomeness in her. It made her wonder if she was needed anymore. She felt outside of this new life of her daughter. Kenny never seemed homesick either. What went on up there at the University seemed to fill his life. Jim was carried away with his shrimping and ran back and forth to the coast. Arvay considered that she had only her hands to offer service with, and since nothing was required of her in that way anymore, she felt unnecessary most of the time. Her house was silent now, and her arms felt empty and useless. This Howland Development seemed infinitely more threatening to her than the dark gloom of the swamp had been. It was ever so personal to her, so she kept up her vigil on the porch, keeping track of every new change out there.

Jim watched it too, and with great satisfaction. When he did not prowl around over there of a Sunday, he took his newspaper and they sat on the porch and watched.

They sat there one Sunday and watched the cars glitter south from Citrabelle, swing around the huge half circle and sweep across the causeway.

"Just look at that!" Jim beamed at Arvay. "Hatton and the company are really selling and making money, but quiet as it's kept, we haven't been hurt a tap by the deal. This place is worth a whole lot more than it used to be on account of that development."

Jim was looking at her and beaming so that Arvay sensed that Jim was looking for her to say something, but for the life of her, she could not make out what was expected of her. She thrashed around for a while in her mind, then did the best that she could.

"I'll bound you," Arvay nodded and agreed. Then an alarming thought came to her. "But you don't aim to sell our home, do you, Jim?"

"Hell, no, Arvay! Not till Kenny gets through college anyhow. This place will be worth a whale of a lot more by then. You don't seem to realize how big this development is and what a change it has made in things around here."

Again Arvay could feel that Jim expected something of her but she still had no idea what he wanted her to say.

"Yeah, it's mighty nice, all right. But from the sums and amounts of money that folks have been spending over there it sure ought to be, Jim."

"Hatton's done mighty fine," Jim persisted. "Angie married her cup off when she landed that boy. Sensible, honest and with plenty push to him. I would of hated for her to miss a chap like that."

Arvay sat up and took a long look at Jim. Certain things were stirring in her mind.

"Well, she took good pains not to miss him, I notice. And that brings me to something that I have ever wondered about."

"For instance, honey?"

"Angie was under eighteen when she run off and got married, Jim."

"That's a fact, Arvay."

"It's always puzzled me how in the world she got a license to marry in Florida under age without neither one of us being there nor giving our consent."

Jim laid his folded paper in his lap and sat silent for a while. Then he braced himself and said evenly, "She wasn't by herself that day, Arvay. I was there." Jim waited a moment and

198

spoke again. "She didn't go without consent at all. I was there."

Arvay's eyes took on that remote and unknowable look like the eyes of a python in repose. She had retreated within herself to her temple of refuge. Why, she asked herself, should she be surprised at being ignored like this? It had always been that way as long as she could remember. She had never been counted or necessary. Coming to know that she was born to be like that, she had finally found a refuge for herself from the whole round world. Not a happy, laughing place, but it was safe from all hurt, harm and danger. And who had toled and tricked her out of her refuge? That Jim Meserve who had come grinning with his teeth down the Big Road, and now to treat her like this. Making such a serious move with her own and only daughter and just as good as telling her that she couldn't help herself. All of a sudden Arvay whirled on Jim with clenched fists.

"So you can brag about you was there, eh?" Arvay accused hotly. "You, you deceiving scoundrel-beast!"

The house shook when Arvay slammed the front door behind her. She did not go into their communal bedroom. She felt then that she would never enter it again. She went into Angie's room and went to bed with her Bible. She stretched on her back and looked up at the ceiling. She tried to read again, but turned restlessly on her side. She kept on opening the Bible, but never finished a single verse. What had been done to her was too tearing-down to bear. And the reason that she construed for it all was most hurting.

She didn't belong where she was, that was it. Jim was a Meserve. Angeline was a Meserve. Kenny was a Meserve, but so far as they were concerned, she was still a Henson. Sort of a handmaiden around the house. She had married a Meserve and borned Meserves, but she was not one of them. A handmaiden like Hagar, who had found favor in the master's sight. They didn't have to count her when anything important was to be done. Just go right ahead and ignore her. Took her for dumb and ignorant, and so narrow in her mind that she couldn't be expected to see that Hatton was a fine boy. Like she was ignorant and dumb enough to hold anything against the boy because he happened to be born up North! She could see as well as the next one that Yankees were like everybody else. She was as happy as the next one that Angie had married Hatton, and she would of freely give her consent if they had give her time to know the boy and get used to the idea. You couldn't find a nicer and more mannerable young man no-where in the world, nor a better husband for her daughter. Oh, she might of said a off-hand word or two about Hatton being a Yankee, but they ought to of give her credit for being too sensible than to take it serious-like.

So now she would wash her hands of the whole mess. She would take no more pride in the development. It was Jim's ideas and Hatton's carrying 'em through. Let 'em have it! She couldn't turn her back on her children, but so far as Jim Meserve was concerned, she was through with him for good and all. This time she meant it. Never would she go back to his bed again.

Then Arvay turned over on her stomach and buried her face in the pillow. Arvay sobbed and wept. Her resolutions against Jim Meserve were just like the lightning-bugs holding a con-vention. They met at night and made scorning speeches against the sun and swore to do away with it and light up the world themselves. But the sun came up the next morning and they all went under the leaves and owned up that the sun was boss-man in the world. Well, she would hold out until Jim came and carried her back across that hall by main force, which he did at midnight.

200

CHAPTER 19

S ince the fishing operations began, Jim was all new life
and energy. He was back and forth to the coast sometimes twice a week.

"What you got to be running back and forth so much for?"
Arvay asked petulantly. "You don't spend no time around
your home at all these days. Can't that expert of yours that you
place so much confidence in handle things?"

"Certainly! Alfredo don't fail to bring in the stuff if they can
be found at all, and he's as honest a man as I ever expect to
meet. I go up there as much just to be around boats and
fishermen as I do to look after my business. Arvay, I love the
sea!"

"I'm convinced that you must love something over there.
You break your neck out of here every chance you get."

"We'll soon be living on the coast regular, I hope. I'm just
hanging on at the packing-house till I get enough money
ahead to see Kenny through the University up there in
Gainesville, then I can afford to gamble just on my fishing. I
don't want to draw out what I put in Hatton's firm so that the
Meserve name can stay in there, and Kenny can have a share
when he gets out of college. Though, from the way he talks,
it might not be necessary at all. He claims that he's going to
make his living with his box."

"I hope that you ain't paying that no mind. I been hearing the darkies picking boxes ever since I been old enough to know anything, and I got my first time to see any of 'em make a living at it. Just something for fun. It's all right to humor Kenny to an extent, but who you reckon is going to pay good money to hear anybody pick a box?"

"That's Kenny's business. Maybe he knows what he's talking about. He keeps up with that kind of a thing, and claims that white bands up North and in different places like New Orleans are taking over darky music and making more money at it than the darkies used to. Singers and musicians and all. You do hear it over the radio at times, Arvay. Kenny claims that it is just a matter of time when white artists will take it all over. Getting to it's not considered just darky music and dancing nowadays. It's American, and belongs to everybody. Just like that swamp; so far they have slept over the darky way of picking a box. He aims to be the first one to make it something for the public, and he might be right for all we know. Anyhow, just in case he might be wrong, I mean to give him a good education so he can have something to fall back on. That done, I can give my whole time and thoughts to building me up a first-class fishing fleet. That's how I aim to make your living from now on. Angeline is already well-cared for."

"Think that you'll ever make it?

"Without a doubt, Arvay. The last four trips, Alfredo has come in with big-pay hauls. The last time, he took that boat out and sunk her!" Jim's eyes glowed light with excitement like a boy at a ball-game.

"My God, Jim! You mean that Alfredo done sunk your boat?"

Jim laughed gaily. "Naw, indeed. When a shrimper says that, he means that he come in loaded to the rails. From the load on board, the stern of the boat is riding low down to the water. Fishermen got their own way of saying things. Got their own way of talking by signs too and a whole lot of crazy things. You really ought to be along with me some times. They'd make you laugh yourself to death. That's the only real life to live, though my own folks would never have looked for a Meserve to take to a thing like that. As I reckon I told you, my father wanted me to take up law. If not that, the Army out of West Point. He never said where the money was coming from."

"They you broke off, took to knocking around, worked in teppentime, and married somebody like me."

"That's a fact. Seems like I had more sense [than] the rest of my crowd." Jim grabbed Arvay by both corners of her mouth and playfully stretched it across her face and kissed her in the middle of it.

"I had too much sense to follow their lead. While my old man was sitting around reading and taking notes trying to trace up who did what in the Civil War, and my two brothers were posing around waiting for the good old times that they had heard went on before the War to come back again, I shucked out to get in touch with the New South. So far, I don't think that I have made out so bad, do you?"

"Can't say as you have, Jim. Fact is, from where we started off, you've spied noble. That's why I can't see why you always want to be tackling something new. We got a mighty good home, and with what you bring in, we don't want for a thing."

Jim looked at Arvay wistfully for a moment and said, "Maybe you will see into my reasons some day, Arvay. It ain't for me to point out some things for your information. I'll sure feel fine though when you come to realize for yourself."

"Seeing that I don't catch on to what you mean, Jim, look like you would tell me," Arvay replied after a pause.

"Naw, Arvay. That way wouldn't do me no good. Just search around inside yourself and some day you will understand what I mean." Jim's eyes wandered to a pair of fishing-boots over in one corner of the room and went and picked them up and looked them over carefully. "Alfredo is doing so fine with that boat that I feel like some kind of a king, only bigger and better. I just dare him to make six more trips like the last one! Damned if I won't haul off, reach back, and take that last piece of change that I still got stuck away and buy me

203

another boat. That would make it the sooner for us to move to the coast for good."

"Get rid of our home?" Arvay asked in alarm.

"You ever known me to chunk money away like that?" Jim waved an arm towards the front of the house. "With the county paving a road south right in front of our door, and with all those new houses going up across the street there, that big development across the viaduct, this five acres is worth a young fortune now. It will be worth many times more a few years from now. I told you that I was saving it for Kenny. If he didn't have nothing else it would give him a good start in life. Give me one good year with my fishing and we won't need it for ourselves. We'll have the goddamn world by the tail with a down-hill pull."

"You really is set on moving to the coast, I see," Arvay murmured after a moment's thought. "How is Alfredo and all making out down there?" Arvay turned her head and looked away off as if she were not really concerned with the answer. Just asking for politeness.

"Just fine! His wife is a mighty fine cook, you know, and she's boarding some of the single men to help out, and they're coming along fine. I promised to bring you along with me sometime and have her fix us up a good sea-food dinner and generally have a grand time."

Arvay didn't say anything and Jim urged on. "When must I let 'em know?"

"I wouldn't want to put her to all that trouble, Jim."

"No trouble at all, honey. She would enjoy doing it and having you."

"I might be in your way."

"Aw, honey," Jim protested. "You never have been down there with me. Come on!"

"Naw."

"Well stay here then!" Jim shouted and slammed on out of the house and jumped into his car and drove off swiftly.

The shrimping fleet moved north for the summer and worked the Georgia and South Carolina coasts with Thunderbolt, Georgia, as a general base. Alfredo had gone up and Jim got regular reports, but was sorry that the distance was too great for him to make. That made him even more impatient to cut loose from his job and do nothing but fish. But when the fleet headed south in the fall, Alfredo brought him news of a good boat that he could get reasonable. The owner couldn't spare the time to fish it profitably by reason of women, whiskey and maybe too much whistling. Alfredo ran into the owner at just the right minute, and pledged Jim to buy the boat before anybody else found out that the man was willing to sell it so cheaply. It was really a bargain, and in better shape than the one Jim already had. More modern and all. Diesel powered and more icing-space.

Jim decided that this was too good a chance for him to miss, so he took the last two thousand dollars left over from his liquor venture, raked and scraped around otherwise, and laid the price of the boat on the line.

"You never got hold of such a bargain in your life, Boss, and you never will again in this world," Alfredo told him. "That damn fool sure did us a favor. He's gone crazy about some woman here in Savannah, and all he's after is some ready cash to satisfy her mind. No notion of work at all no more. Well, his loss is our gain."

"You said it, Alfredo," Jim replied. "But I owe this chance of luck to you. Once more and again you have shown yourself to be a true friend to me, and taking care of my interest. I couldn't find a better friend nowhere. Anything that I can do for you at anytime, the favor is in me."

Alfredo asked for nothing, and that made Jim feel even more obligated. Therefore, some weeks later when Jim was at Alfredo's house for a business talk and one of Mrs. Corregio's meals, he was moved to offer something that he found that they prized more than money.

The fifteen-year-old Felicia, who was, as Arvay complained, well developed for her age, was looking at a newspaper in a wishful way.

"Oh," she sighed, "look like folks enjoy themselves so

much at these football games. Gee, I wish I could go to one one time."

"Nothing to hinder you from going, is it?" Jim asked.

"You have to have different kind of clothes from what I got to go to a place like that, Mister Jim, and then, unless you belong to that college, you have to be asked to the social part, I mean. I don't have the clothes, and there's nobody to ask me to it."

Immediately Jim saw his chance. "Oh, I don't know about that, now Felicia. Kenny's up there at Gainesville, and almost like a brother to you. I don't have the least doubt that if he had any idea you wanted to go he would ask you."

"Oh, don't pay no attention to Felicia, Mister Jim," Mrs. Corregio hurried to say. "Some things is out of her reach and she might as well realize. She's been to her high school games and that ought to do her."

But Jim could see the wishfulness in the mother's eyes as well. She was merely afraid to ask anything of him.

"A person ought to do a few of the things they want to do in this world before they pass on, Felicia. You just leave it to your Uncle Jim, and he'll fix it for you."

"I was just talking, Mister Jim. Kenny wouldn't want to be bothered with nobody like me in a place like that."

"You don't know who Kenny wants to be bothered with. You let him talk his own chat."

Feeling that it was a very small thing that he could do for Alfredo, within twenty-four hours Jim had had a confidential talk with Angeline first, and then gotten off a letter to Kenny.

That was how it happened that Arvay saw Felicia at the football game. The Meserve family was bound to be there. Kenny was drum-major for the band, and they had to be there to see a thing like that at the big game on Thanksgiving Day. Kenny had reserved seats in a box for his family, and the number of friends whom Angeline specified. Prominent citizens of Citrabelle had the next box to gloat over their local boy.

They were all there early and in their places ahead of time

to watch the huge grandstand fill up and greet old friends from other towns who would be sure to be there too. Angeline and Hatton seemed to know everybody. Jim and Arvay were kept busy accepting introductions and shaking hands. Prosperous looking young folks out of families that Arvay had never expected to pull level with.

"Our children might not be the bell-cows, but if they ain't they's right up in the gang," Arvay made a proud aside to Jim. "They seem to be right in with the best they is."

"Naturally," Jim boasted. "They got good manners, they got something, and they look like something. That's the stuff that makes for friends."

Jim and his party and everybody else became conscious of a young couple who had entered at one end of the field, and were parading down the other side. Everybody was asking, "Who is that?"

"Why, that's Kenny, my boy." Jim spoke so that he could be heard for several boxes around.

"Who is that pretty girl he's got with him?"

That was what everybody wanted to know. The girl attracted a lot of attention first, because she had an unbelievable mass of curly black hair that poured and tumbled nearly to her waist, and glittered in the sun, in a company of almost universal bobbed heads. Men like hair and they looked. Then she was so fresh and tender-looking. They noted that she was really built from her neck on down. The men looked at that and the women took in her clothes. She was dressed in a white sweater suit, topped by a perky white tam over one eye, white buckskin oxfords, and a loose-fitting light-weight white coat. It was just the right thing for her dark hair and eyes. Brilliant big eyes, and a high natural pink in her cheeks. Kenny Meserve, ever the showman, was doing his stuff. He paraded along, pausing to make introductions, or when he was hailed by some yearning student who hoped for an introduction to his date. He had the eyes of the public, and he seemed to know it. It was a very eye-taking thing as he made his progress around three quarters of the grandstand, pretending to look for someone, till he arrived before the box where his party sat.

Arvay was not expecting, so she did not recognize Felicia until the couple was almost at the entrance to the box. She had no right to look for Felicia at a place like this, and certainly not in that kind of clothes. When she did make out who that was with Kenny, she was thunder-struck by lightning.

"Hey, folks!" Kenny hailed, and handled Felicia as proudly as if he had been escorting the Princess Royal. "Feliciana's here at last to use that seat I reserved in the family box." He went on to usher the smiling girl in to her seat. "Take care of her for me, kinfolks. I got to go. The band will parade in in a few minutes. Angie, I'm trusting you to look out after my interests. Feliciana is my date for the day. All of these college back-biters have had a look at her and their mouths are fairly drooling. Stand by me, Sis. Fight off the competition the best you can."

"We'll hold that line," Hatton promised.

"Satisfaction!" Kenny smiled and turned to go with a wave of his hand. "See you later and tell you straighter."

Arvay was entirely excused from keeping Felicia's company. Angeline's crowd took care of that. They made introductions, and kept up a great clatter until the teams marched in led by their respective bands. Kenny, now dressed in a showy uniform, and carrying a decorated baton, was the star of the piece. The Gators were on the home grounds, and the grandstand went wild when Kenny came prancing down the field. He shed more glory on his folks by saluting them as he passed the box in his tour around the field.

Kenny and the band brought up the drooping spirits of the students, alumni and fans at the half, when the visiting team had the Gators at 6-0. He ran over and spent some time in the box with them as the game took up again. Then he had to join the cheer-leaders and do his stuff. Jim was about to split his britches, but Arvay had no trouble at all in keeping quiet. She had never seen a football game before, anyway, so she could be excused for not going crazy when the Gators crushed across the enemy's goal line for a touchdown and then converted. In the last five minutes of the game, and on the third down, they did it again, and converted. It seemed to Arvay that over a million crazy people piled out onto the field and fell in behind the Gator band doing what they called the snake-dance. The bank president was a Gator grad, and he grabbed Jim and carried him out there too, and only the wives were left sitting there. The other women smiled indulgently, and Arvay acted it out as they did and chatted along, but she was going crazy in her own way.

Where and how did Felicia get those clothes that she had on? What was she doing here? Kenny had never mentioned Felicia in a single letter to her, so something underhand was going on. How much of Kenny's acting towards Felicia was put on and how much was real? Was Kenny bleeding them out of money that they could use otherwise to put clothes like that on that Felicia's back? Or was Jim crazy about something else in that Corregio home besides Alfredo's wife's cooking? Was it the mother or the daughter? Oh, that was too awful to think about. Laying around with the father and running after the son.

It turned out that Angeline and Hatton had good friends in Gainesville too. It was already arranged for Arvay and Jim to go to the home of one of these friends with them to dinner, and to rest and change their clothes.

The home was very good, and everything was done to make them comfortable, and Arvay tried to feel and act happy. She acted it out the best she could, but she couldn't feel that way. First and foremost, the presence of Felicia had her worried. She had no idea what it meant, but the rest of the family seemed to know. As in the case of Angie and Hatton, maybe Kenny would be married to this girl before she knew anything about it at all. That made her miserable. The very name of Corregio called up sorrow and suffering to her mind. Why did that girl have to show up on a day like this, and in company with her son?

In addition, Arvay felt so out of place. All that this day meant in college circles was strange to her. She felt awkward

209

and out of place. Listening to the people around her, she became terribly conscious of her way of speech. She hated to open her mouth for fear of making a balk, and putting her children to shame.

"Let's don't bother with the dance, Jim," Arvay suggested. "We got a long drive ahead of us, and it's getting late. Let's just say good-bye, thank the folks and go on home."

"But we can't do that, Arvay. Kenny is doing some special playing tonight at the dance, and he would feel mighty hurt if we wouldn't even wait to hear him."

Arvay found that she had to go. The family double-teened her and reluctantly she changed into a fresh dress and went to sit with Jim along the wall with a number of women who were chaperoning their daughters.

The sight that Arvay dreaded to see came before her eyes. Kenny came with his guitar around his neck and with Felicia on his arm. She created just as much excitement at the dance as she had at the game. She was dressed in a fluffy ruby-red tulle dress with a girdle of crushed cloth of gold. All of her decorations were gold. Gold kid slippers and a big gold flower in her flowing hair. She looked like the daughter of some foreign ruling-man. Almost instantly, she and Kenny were the center of things.

Angeline looked beautiful too. In a pale green something with silver-gilt touches, she and Felicia standing together had the floor. Angeline chummed up to Felicia and kept things looking like a pair of sisters.

Jim and the banker, who had stayed for the dance because his own niece was a guest, stood together near the wall chatting away when an important-looking man joined them and began to talk along. It turned out that he was the head of the Chamber of Commerce at Leesburg.

"Those are two really beautiful girls, yonder. The two standing together with that crowd of boys around them."

"Home town girls." The banker jumped in quickly and rocked back and forth on his heels. "Products of Citrabelle, prettiest little town in Florida, and grows nothing but pretty girls. Ain't that right, Jim?"

"Correct. Why, those two are about the ugliest in town. Fact is, they were run out of Citrabelle for the day so that the folks could enjoy their Thanksgiving dinner." The three men chuckled, and Jim went one better. "Just a couple of culls off of my place."

"I'll take your culls off of your hands and take 'em to Lees-burg to ugly up the place."

"Aw, naw you don't, neither!" the banker objected. "Don't try to steal our samples. Come on down to Citrabelle and pick you a pair out of stock. This is Mr. James Kenneth Meserve, one of our first citizens, and that red-head is his daughter, and that black-haired one is his son's date."

"Congratulations, Meserve. You got a good thing all the way around."

"Yeah, but you haven't seen the best as yet. Turn around here and meet my pretty wife."

There was plenty to smile over, if Arvay had been in any notion to smile. Her face got cramps for the next hour while she tried her best to carry off everything nice. The orchestra assembled and the dance began. The parents took the chairs ranged around the wall and watched the young folks dance. A waltz, a fox-trot, and then Arvay and Jim grew proud as the drums opened up on Kenny's specialty, *House That Jack Built.* The way they had heard it at home was nothing to what this band could do with it. It was really *something.* The students seemed to be familiar with the piece enough to jump in every time they got to that line, "That milked that cow with the crumpled horn"—they all shouted it out.

The hall was full of exciting activity. The young folks were doing the Lindy Hop, and it seemed to Arvay that everything that could be done with a shin-bone was being done. Hun-dreds of young healthy boys were hurling pretty well-dressed girls around. Arvay noted that there was not a homely girl in the place, and a high percentage ranged to real beauty, and her own daughter was right up there in the front ranks. She could not enjoy anything, however, for Felicia Corregio was there flashing around the room and stopping close to the band between every dance.

Jim and the rest insisted that the Corregios were as white as they were, but it made Arvay feel haunted to see any member of that family. Over the exciting rhythm of Kenny's composition Arvay could hear the mournful tolling of a bell. Pictures came before her eyes. Earl growling and hurling himself against the screen. Lucy Ann lying still and white and bleeding on the ground. The growling rumble of human men turned into a mob. Tolling, tolling, tolling sound of the bell. The siege in the swamp. Earl's quiet face in death. Tolling. Dead-and-gone. Dead-and-gone! The bell struck out with halting tongue.

Arvay struggled and tried to shake it off. Long ago she had brought herself to admit that the Corregios were not responsible for what happened, and as Jim said, Alfredo had acted a noble friend through it all. He had shown himself a faithful helper and friend since then, too. But the name called up that which she had tried hardest to forget. What human can desert his memories? The bell kept on tolling in her head. The heavy, slow-talking clapper seemed to be beating against her very skull. She waited and suffered between strokes. As the piece came to an end, Arvay leaped to her feet.

"Well, we done heard Kenny's special, Jim. It's time for us to go."

"Aw, what's the hurry, Arvay? I'd like to watch and hear some more of this thing."

"What for? This dance ain't for us. It's for these boys and girls."

"Yeah, but I want to watch and see. Looks like Kenny knows what he's talking about. Those white boys are playing that rag-time down to the bricks, and you saw that dancing, didn't you? I want to see as much as I can of it. You could almost think those were colored folks playing that music. I want to . . ."

Arvay was on her feet and had Jim by his arm. The band was

resting for a minute or two, and Hatton, Angeline and Felicia were over there talking and laughing with Kenny. Arvay looked and wanted to go.

"I done begged you and begged you," Arvay gritted out in a low tone. "I'm going, and I'm going this minute. You can take me if you want to, Jim. Suit yourself. If you don't come on this instant, I'm going anyhow. I'll go on out of here and grab the first thing smoking and go on home. You can stay here and gap at that Felicia until you get good and tired. I'm going!"

Jim backed the Buick out with a *zoosh,* wheeled around and headed through town in a hurry.

"You going too fast, Jim, with all these hundreds of cars on the streets. You're liable to hurt somebody."

Jim paid no attention. He cut through traffic like a razor and kept on going to the highway. No sooner did he hit it than he did what Angie and Kenny's crowd called washing his foot in the tank. That Buick squatted to the road and Arvay saw the needle moving up to fifty, sixty and beyond. She was terrified. She hated fast driving, and Jim so well knew it, but she was in no mind to ask him any favors. She gritted her teeth, held onto the door with one hand and put on brakes with her feet. East by south the car raced along with not one word being spoken between them.

Arvay was ever so glad when they approached Orlando. It was too big for Jim to dash through there, and this time of the year, Orange Avenue would be fairly working with northern cars. He would be slowed to a creep by the lights and traffic, and maybe by the time they got through there, Jim would have come to his sense.

But Arvay did not know the road. It was all strange to her coming from the direction they had. They came right into highway U.S. 17, which took them south without really entering the city. Also, there was that new three-lane stretch of twenty miles to Kissimmee. Jim stuck his foot in the tank and went from there. They were out on the Kissimmee Prairie, in the Florida cow-country, and little traffic. Arvay took one look

213

and saw the needle slip past seventy, and closed her eyes. Before she knew it, they were in Kissimmee and approaching the bridge leaving town.

"Jim! Jim! Jim! Look out for that bridge! Don't kill me about that gnatty-tail gal! Jim! Oh, Lord have mercy!"

Jim took the bridge just like he did the rest of the road, and they flashed on past ranches with the trees and fence-posts whirling in a mad dance past Arvay's eyes. Jim never said a word. "Wahooo!" the horn cried when Jim overtook a night-operating truck, and the wind yelled "whooo-ooom" as the Buick flashed past. Arvay screamed again when Jim passed a truck, and found another meeting him. He slashed between the two by a slight wiggle of the wheel almost rubbing hub-caps as he went with both. His hand was steady on the wheel, his face was grim and his foot was in the tank. Arvay screamed again as they entered Lakeland. The Buick dived down the slight hill to the ornamental lake, and for a second, it seemed to her that Jim would never be able to swerve to the right around the lake. It seemed as if it would plunge straight ahead into the water. Jim made the curve smoothly and kept on going. The car consumed on its way and Arvay screamed and cried. She had been sobbing and crying constantly for the last fifty miles when Jim pulled up into their drive with a sudden stop. Without a word, he reached across her, flung open the door on her side, and Arvay stumbled out crying very hard.

Jim made no effort to assist her up the steps as he usually did. He stomped up on the porch, unlocked the door, flung it open, switched on the hall light, and wheeled to go and put the car in the garage. Arvay staggered on into the bedroom, and sank down on the side of the bed in a lump, still shaking and crying.

Arvay would have felt better if Jim had stayed outside a while and given her a chance to collect herself, but he didn't. In no time, he came walking heavy over the floor. Hard-heeling and coming fast. He flung the bedroom door wide open and came and stood spraddle-legged in the middle of the floor. Instead of coming to her and trying to soothe her feelings, Jim just stood and looked down on her as if she were a chair. Arvay quit sobbing and leaped to her feet.

"Don't you stand there gapping at me, after you done done your best to kill me dead on that road! I got a good notion to take that gun and blow your infernal brains out!"

Jim went to taking off his clothes. He acted more like he had not heard what she said than anything else. Arvay stood there getting madder as he stripped and got into the pants of his pajamas.

"Oh, so you call yourself discounting me, do you?" Arvay screamed. "I think too much of myself to kill you like I ought to, but I'm through with you, Jim Meserve. I'm just as through with you as I is my baby-shirt."

She ran to the closet, snatched down her nightgown and headed for the door. Jim picked up the jacket of his pajamas, and let Arvay get as far as the door. Then he reached forward, caught her by the arm and flung her back into the room so forcibly that the back of her legs came up against the bed and she sat down without planning on it. Jim stood over her and glowered.

"Did I tell you that you could leave this room, Arvay?"

"N-n-no, Jim."

"Well, what did you start out of here for, then?"

"I-I thought that I had better go sleep—"

"You thought like Lit! Did I tell you to do any thinking?"

"No, Jim, you didn't."

"Well, don't let me hear none of your thinking unless I give you my command."

Jim stood and frowned down on the thoroughly frightened Arvay for a long time. She felt like a mouse under the paw of a cat. She looked up at him fearfully, caught his eyes on her, and then down quickly.

"Where I made my big mistake was in not starting you off with a good beating just as soon as I married you. I have never laid the weight of my hand on you in malice, and you done got beside yourself. What you mean by sitting there all drawed up into a winter knot? Get up from there and get out of those clothes."

Arvay got up timidly and Jim gave her a little shove towards the dresser, and Arvay's fighting blood got up. Besides, she was persuaded by now that Jim was not going to hit her. He never had so far. She whirled on him.

"Don't you dare to shove me, Jim Meserve! I'll wade knee deep in your blood. And I'm not a'going to take off . . . Jim! Jim! Don't hit me!"

Jim didn't hit her. He just grabbed the powder blue flat crêpe dress at the neck and ripped it off her, and flung the rags of it against the wall.

"Didn't I tell you to off with them rags? Off with 'em! Up with that petticoat and down with them pants before you make me hurt you. Move!"

Arvay, pulled at her underclothes in a desperate effort to get them off. Her slip stuck as she got it up to her shoulders, and she screamed as she felt Jim with a rough hand rip it off and hurl it away. She reached for her nightgown on the bed to cover herself, but Jim brought her up short.

"Did I command you to put on a gown, Madam? Leave it lay!"

Arvay stood with nothing on but her shoes and stockings, then remembered them and fairly clawed them off, and stood shivering with fright as naked as she had been born. She looked longingly at the closet door and took a step in that direction.

"Don't you move!" Jim bellowed harshly. "You're my damn property, and I want you right where you are, and I want you naked. Stand right there in your tracks until I tell you that you can move."

Arvay, her lips trembling to keep from crying, stood there with her legs close together and waited. Jim threw back the bed covers to the foot of the bed, then sat down in the little rocker, rested his hands on his thighs and looked Arvay over in a very cool way for awhile. Then he rested his face in his hands and sat silent and motionless for minutes. He was

216

moved by love and pity, but Arvay could not know this from the way he spoke when he suddenly lifted his head.

"All right now," Jim commanded. "I reckon that you can go to bed. But move in a hurry before I change my mind."

Arvay leaped in and began to scramble the covers up over her to her very neck. With a springing jump, Jim was at the bedside and grabbing the upper corners, flung all the covers back over the foot of the bed.

"Who the hell told you to pull up any covers?" Jim demanded sternly. "You're too damned fast and previous! I'll let you know when I want you covered up, Madam."

Arvay laid there among her fears. But her fear of loss was much greater than her physical fear. Felicia and all the Corregios fell off Arvay's shoulder like a loose garment in her anxiety for reconciliation with this man who stood like a statue of authority beside the bed. No bells tolled; no memories could find a place with her then. The hours of that morning before they had set out for Gainesville had seemed ordinary then. Looking back on that time from where she was now, they seemed to form a time of untellable bliss. If she could but have them back again! The most ordinary minute of peace with Jim in the past appeared like time spent in Paradise.

After what seemed like months to Arvay, Jim took his ample time and got in the bed with her. He stretched himself full length upon her, but in the same way that he might have laid himself down on a couch. After more years of suspense, Jim elevated himself from the shoulders up and looked down into Arvay's eyes.

"Hug my neck, Arvay," Jim said in the same way that he could have been telling her to pour him another cup of coffee.

Arvay flung her arms around Jim's neck with gladness. It could be that she had made her escape out of Hell. While she hugged and kissed her husband, Arvay prayed and promised God. Ah, but let these golden moments roll on a few years longer, please, God. She made vows and promises. If God would fix it so that she got over this greasy log, she would certainly sand the next one. That is, she would keep the Corregios out of her mouth and mind. Grant her this one favor of peace and agreement with Jim once more and again, and she would not bother God for no more favors. She would not even part her lips if the time should ever come when Kenny saw fit to court and marry Felicia, hard as the pill would be for her to swallow. By this time Arvay had hugged and hugged and kissed and kissed for what she decided was abundant and sufficient time. She lowered her arms and waited.

"Who told you to stop hugging my neck?" Jim demanded. "Get to hugging my neck and kiss me until I tell you it's time to knock off. I don't want no flabby kind of kissing neither. Go to work!"

Arvay hugged and she kissed and she kissed and she hugged.

"But Jim, you ain't acting mutual with me. That makes it hard work to do."

"You can't kiss me and talk at the same time, so hush talking."

Jim could feel Arvay's skin changing temperature, and the change in her breathing. The change became more and more pronounced. She kissed him violently and hungrily for a minute, then braced her hands against his shoulders and did all she could to shove him away from her.

"Go 'way from me, Jim, and leave me be!" Arvay began to scream and cry. "I can't stand this bondage you got me in. I can't endure no more! I can't never feel satisfied that I got you tied to me, and I can't leave you, and I can't kill you nor hurt you in no way at all. I'm tied and bound down in a burning Hell and no way out that I can see. I can't see never no peace of mind. It's a sure enough hard game when you got to die to beat it, but that's just what I aim to do—kill myself!"

Arvay ended on a high and agonizing scream of desperation.

Jim said nothing. Resting on his elbows, he took Arvay's face between his hands and looked down in her eyes which were running over with tears. Gradually, the features of her face relaxed and that calm Buddha mask that she always wore came over her face. But Jim was concentrating on her eyes. Once again he saw that greenish infusion creep in and mingle with the sky blue of her eyes. That peculiar thing about Arvay's eyes that he had a momentary glimpse of the first time that he had encountered her on the street at Sawley. He had seen it more fully when he had kissed her for the first time that Sunday at the table when they had become engaged. It had been daringly out in the open that flaming hour under the mulberry tree. It was an eternal and a compelling mystery how Arvay's face could stay as stiff as a false-face on Halloween while that something crept up like a tiger in the jungle peeping out through shielding leaves at its prey, and looked out through the eye-holes of the mask.

"No, I can't see no way out of my binding bondage but death, Jim. I aim to kill myself, so tomorrow I'll be dead and gone. I never is sure whether you love me or not, and I just can't endure no more."

For an answer, Jim kissed Arvay with a kind of happy arrogance, then snuggled his head down on her breast in that way he had that Arvay thought was so much like a helpless child, and went off into peaceful sleep.

Arvay buried her hand in his hair as she loved to do and stayed awake for awhile with her thoughts. And she had promised to escape this man by death tomorrow.

Tomorrow? When and what was that? Who ever has believed in the reality of death in the presence of vibrant life? It is a parable sometimes told by the old. Some man in a far country, whom you never knew, went off somewhere one time, and being a fool, laid down and died. But who, in love, ever paid any attention to a made-up tale like that?

CHAPTER 20

You really mean to take her out, Boss?" Alfredo asked and looked for an answer in Jim's face.

"Hell, yes! Just got my pilot's license, took a week off from my job to be here, and then not go?"

"Okay. It's a little windy out there, and you not being too experienced, I didn't know whether you felt to take the risk. Quite a few boats ain't going out today. But then some are going right on. Even if you hadn't decided to go, I was going. This little wind is going to die down before night anyhow. From the northwest, and it won't blow real strong."

"Sure, Eddie Halliard and several more of the best men are going out," the Mate chimed in. "A little wind is even a help in getting the net over the side. Let's go, My Captain."

"Damn! But that sounds good!" Jim beamed. "First time in my life. Captain Meserve of the *Angeline*. Say it again, Stumpy, and lemme hear you."

"Gimme an order so I can answer you right."

"Wait, Stumpy, lemme get in the pilot-house with my hands on the wheel and look important. You and my Third Man stand there on deck and look scared. Alfredo, you get ashore and get aboard your own command, so everything'll look natural. All right now, let's go through it right."

Jim struck a pose, frowned ferociously at his crew, cleared his throat and bellowed.

"You Third Man, have you got all necessary stores on board?"

"Yes, My Captain, we are well provisioned."

"Mate!"

"Yes, My Captain!"

"Everything ship-shape below?"

"Yes, My Captain. We can cast off and head for the inlet."

"Well, why the hell don't you do it then, and let's go?"

They all broke into a laugh. The lines were cast off, and Jim moved the *Angeline* out safely from the dock and stood out in the stream. The *Arvay Henson,* Alfredo in command, waited long enough for the *Angeline* to clear sufficiently, then came out to pair with the *Angeline,* and the two moved off, gaining speed gradually towards Mosquito Inlet.

When Jim had piloted his boat through the tricky inlet, and her bow slid out into the Atlantic, Jim waved at Alfredo gaily and said to Stumpy, who stood on deck by the pilot-house door: "Stumpy, Heaven can't be no treat to me after this. I got all the Heaven I want right now."

"It ought to feel fine to be captaining your own boat, but I don't ever expect to own one. I done swore on a stack of women so high that I was going to save up and own me a boat someday, but I knowed that I was lying when I said it. Too much good likker that needs drinking up, and everytime I see a pretty woman switching along, I got to stop and drop a flag on it."

They laughed, noted that the *Arvay Henson* had headed north, and swung that way. As the bow of the *Angeline* cut the choppy water, Jim looked to starboard over the seemingly limitless sea to the horizon where it curved away from sight in waving lines. He looked to port, at the dim line of the Florida coast, and forward at the three boats ahead, and was content.

"You're not afraid with a new captain like me, Stumpy?"

"No, indeed. You're doing just all right. I watched you how you brought her through the inlet. That was where the danger was. Anyhow, a fisherman got so many good chances to lose his life that if he stops to dwell on that, he'd be scared to death all the time. I ain't scared of a thing but old Bozo."

"Who in the hell is Bozo?"

"Nobody ain't told you who Bozo is as yet? Man, you ain't no real fisherman until you meet old Bozo and fight him."

"Who is he, and where can he be found, Stumpy?"

Stumpy laughed and summoned the Third Man from the galley.

"Come on up, Charlie. The Captain wants to locate Bozo. You fought him last, didn't you? Come on up and tell My Captain where Bozo can be found!"

The Third Man, who had been putting on breakfast, came up the steps, wiping his hand on a sugar sack towel, and put on a very serious face.

"I hate like everything that nobody never mentioned it to me while we was on the hill. We're way outside now, and you have to wait until we go ashore again. Still and all, I figger that I can give you some idea where Bozo lives, and how he can be found. Then you can go and challenge him to a fight anytime you want to."

Before the Third Man got through with his fantastic directions, Jim caught on that this was some joke. With the state of Florida as flat as a flounder, he was told that he had to cross the Lick-and-Spit Mountains just back of New Smyrna. Then he turned short to port and went through the land of the Mollymoes. A Mollymoe was a peculiar kind of a bird. He never relieved himself but once a year, and when he did, why, you could smell him for a mile or more. That was how he came to have his name. Come through that country and you were right at a big plantation. That was where Bozo lived. Yes, sir! Big house and everything. Bozo seemed to have a plenty. Rich and well-to-do. All you had to do then was to go right up and knock on the door, and when Bozo opened it, challenge him

222

to a fight. The man who whipped Bozo would be the king of the world.

"Did you whip him?" Jim asked to humor the joke.

"No, can't say as I did. Fact is, I never laid eyes on Bozo. Just like everybody else, all I ever saw was Bozo's cat."

"How was that, Charlie?"

"It was bad, Cap'n. As far as I seen it was mighty bad and more than I figgered that I could handle."

"Even being a fisherman?" Jim helped the story out.

"Even for a fisherman, and they can handle more'n anybody else in the world. You see, Cap'n, that cat was as big as a yearling calf to start off with. Then as things went along, when I seen that cat drink off a skillet full of hot boiling grease for coffee, and then take up a blazing li'dard knot out the fire and use it for toilet paper, I figgered that it was time for me to go! And man, I really went. I was running so fast till I had to turn sideways to keep from flying."

They laughed that off and then Jim asked, "So you never got a chance to see Bozo himself, eh?"

"What? Wait for Bozo? If his cat was that big and tough I didn't want to meet that Bozo riding nor walking. I went there feeling fit to fight, but my Mama always told me never to let my head start more than my behind could stand. If Bozo is any tougher than his cat, I don't admire to meet him."

"Same thing happened to me," Stumpy nodded solemnly. "All the fishermen'll tell you the same. Don't care how you meet him he's the privileged vessel and you better treat him that way."

"Much obliged for the information," Jim said. "And now that I know about Bozo, I take it that I'm initiated."

"Kee-rect, My Captain," the Third Man grinned. "Reckon I'd better go finish off breakfast. Old Bozo is liable to board us any time and we ought to be in shape to tackle him."

Jim sat on his stool at the wheel and contemplated the ocean of sea around him. The colors charmed and pleased him. There was the delicate green close at hand, and flipping inward toward the faint outline of the Florida coast. To starboard and infinity, it took on a blue-green, and where the sun rested on it, it seemed to be over-laid by a silvery veil. A line of porpoises dipped and dived in a solemn parade between ship and shore. Portuguese Men-of-War sailed in purple glory. That was another thing that fascinated Jim about the sea, the seemingly infinity of form. No matter how much you saw, the sea had still other marvels of shape and color. He would never, never tire of the sea.

Jim had his breakfast and returned to the wheel. The small fleet went on northward. Jim and his crew cracked jokes and contentedly followed until they noticed signs of slowing down of the vessels ahead.

"Alfredo's going to fish, I believe. Okay, boys, let's try along."

The Mate went to the smaller winch, Third Man took the try-net in his hands, and as the strong steel cable was played out and out the net, shaped something like a wind-sleeve at an airport, went overboard and down for sixty fathoms. Jim sent the engine ahead, and the boat made a large slow circle for half an hour.

"Let's get it!" Jim sang out, and his eyes were filled with eagerness as the net came over the port side, and was dumped on the deck. There were numerous kinds of deep sea life spilled on the deck when the net was emptied, but the men took little notice of it. The three of them were eagerly counting the shrimp.

"Nowhere near fifty there," Jim said in a flat voice when the count was over. "Not enough to be worth a drag."

The boat cruised for a half hour, then they tried again. As ever, the sea gulls appeared seeming from nowhere when a net was raised, and swarmed around, hungry for the rejected marine life that would be shovelled overboard when the shrimp was picked out. The men had not bothered to clear the deck before, but the try-net came up loaded this time. The birds were tired of waiting, and swarmed in.

"Near enough," Jim decided. "Let's go overboard."

The eager ritual was performed. Each man had a station and

hurried to it. Jim to his wheel in the pilot-house. The Mate to the big winch. The Third Man took the bag of the big net in his hand and stood at the starboard rail and waited.

The mast was amidship, immediately aft of the pilot-house. The boom, to which the big rig was attached by pulleys and strong steel cables, was drawn up at around a hundred and sixty degree angle against the mast with its loose end pointing almost skyward like a cannon at rest. Now the boom was slowly lowered by means of the winch, swung to starboard to let the big drag-net slide into the sea. First, the long, coarse-fringy chafing-gear touched the surface of the water, got wet and began to sink. Then the whole of the mesh sank down and down until the boards, used for weights, were lying flat on the ocean like two big doors afloat on either side of the net.

"Is she spreading right?" Jim asked.

"Yep, she's just all right," the Mate answered. Immediately, the Third Man dropped the big bag over, and Jim sent the boat ahead. The cable ran out and out from the big drum to the sixty fathom line and the big net with its protecting chafing-gear was sweeping the bottom of the ocean. The drag was on. The Third Man went forward, picked up the bamboo stick that had a huge round cork fixed to it about eighteen inches from the butt end. Below that it was weighted. On the other end was a small triangular pennant of dark blue. This was the flag. They dropped that overboard, and it stood up like a buoy with the little pennant flying. It was a marker so that the boat could stay over the shrimp, and drag back and forth through them.

The boat began the slow circling around that flag with the steel cable stretching out and down astern. The boat listed to port or to starboard from the weight of the big net sweeping the bottom according to the position of the boat in relation to the net. For two hours it would go on that way. Slow and easy around that flag.

As Alfredo had predicted, the wind was dying down. By the time the net was brought to the side, there was just enough sea to help lift the net over side. They had almost had bad luck.

225

The net was maneuvered around to port just in time to miss the stern and avoid fouling the propellers.

The bag was dumped on deck with its wealth of strange sea forms and the shrimp separated from the rest. The sea gulls miraculously appeared, as if spontaneously created out of the water and screamed to the crew to hurry.

"Not but eleven boxes," Jim said when the shrimp were measured up.

"Yeah," the Mate put in, "but that'll pay for ice and fuel. What we get after this will be gravy. We might sink her on the evening drag."

"Could be," Jim muttered. "Look, their feet are red. They're on the travel. Now if we just hit the right direction we might go in top boat."

"Let's make this a two-meal day and go over again, My Captain. I need some spending change. Anything I love is a big percentage."

"I'm more than ready, boys, if you don't mind the strain," Jim said and looked at the Third Man.

"Hell, yeah. Might be plenty nuggets at the bottom of this lake right under us. Let's go!"

They let the heading of what they had go until the drag was on again then the two men of the crew sat on the hatch cover and "cracked heads" and talked while the boat began again its slow circle.

"Wonder where do shrimp go when they disappear from the sea?" The Third asked. "Sometimes, don't care which way you go, they just can't be found."

"I believe that they get up under ledges close in shore, especially in bad weather."

"Well, we know that they travel down the coast in winter, go clean around the State of Florida and come into the Gulf. But where do they be when you can't find 'em at all?"

"You suppose that there's some underground, or undersea, passage across under Florida that connects the ocean and the Gulf and some of them know it and go that way?"

"Could be. Then, too, they travel at night sometimes. When

226

you see 'em with red feet, they been travelling at night."

The net was brought over the side again, and this time they had had better luck. Forty boxes, after being headed, went into the hold. Jim felt good. The men began to get gay and talk about what they were going to do on the hill. "The hill" meant being ashore. Fernandina, St. Augustine, New Smyrna, whichever port they went in, the ladies were going to have a very interesting time. Oh, but they were!

Jim's first trip as a captain lasted three days. They went up and down the coast, but no boat made a record catch. Eddie Halliard came in top boat with two hundred and six boxes. Jim had one hundred and eighty-six in his hold. He had beaten Alfredo by five boxes and felt very good indeed.

He was thrilled when the boats began signalling that they were leaving the fishing ground. A chance to stick his head in a crown could not have given him the pleasure that he got from receiving his first sign language and answering it.

With the *Arvay Henson* nearly a hundred feet off his starboard, he saw Alfredo leave his pilot-house and come on deck. Jim hurried to do the same and looked across. Alfredo flung both his arms to his left about waist high, left palm facing out and right palm towards his body. With his hands and fingers out straight, he made the fluttering motion of fish tails swimming.

"Haul hips," Jim interpreted. Leaving the fishing ground. Jim did the same to indicate that he had the message.

Alfredo made a loose fist of his right hand as if he grasped a round cylinder, threw his head back, and placed the fist to his mouth.

"And going to have plenty to drink," Jim read the flash and returned it.

With the same right hand, held this time slightly to the right of his body on a level with his chest, Alfredo made the motion of winding a clock in a strenuous way.

"Going home to sleep with my wife." Winding the clock being the last thing before going to bed. Jim replied and the three signs were in. The boats were going into port.

They turned their bows south, paired off, and were under way. It was important for each boat to have a partner to afford assistance in case of trouble, and trouble can come swiftly and disastrously on the sea.

Proudly, after a five hours' run, Jim brought the *Angeline* through the inlet, and laid her dead beside the dock. Alfredo tied the *Arvay Henson* alongside when he got in a half hour later. According to arrangement, he sold his shrimp through Toomer, a "factory" with a fleet of seven boats, paid off his two crews and everybody headed uptown.

Jim jubilated from place to place for two or three hours, then stepped into a Jook that was very popular with the fishermen. The Jook organ was blaring out popular records, some few couples danced off and on, and the bar was crowded. Jim was congratulated and treated and he stood for drinks in return. Young women who were pretty, and some who merely had pretty intentions, were being very fond of the men with plentiful percentages. Five and ten dollar bills were laid down for two-bit drinks, and the ladies were allowed to keep the change. What kind of a fisherman was that who grabbed up change?

Stumpy was in there up against the bar with a girl with a moderately good-looking face and a shape like a partridge. He was treating and she was pocketing change. When Jim sat down at a table, Stumpy saw him and came over.

"My girl has got a friend who wants to meet you."

"Well, I'm not going to run from her. Might even drop a flag on it if it suits."

Stumpy, with the two girls, joined Jim at the table and he promptly stood treats. He played the game according to the rules up to a certain point, but he was gambling with his stuff out the window. Jim fancied pretty women, the kind that gave him a tussle to get. This one was not ugly, just usual-looking, and was there to pick up change. But the girl didn't have to know what he was thinking, and she didn't.

"Who eats your white chicken?" Jim asked her. The girl bridled and looked flattered and took hope.

"Nobody, Captain Meserve. Haven't found nobody that I cares for."

"Then maybe there's a chance for me." His change came, and he put it in his pocket. The girl looked pained.

"Oh, you just ought to see the pretty new bed-spread that I bought yesterday. It's a dream!"

"I bet it is, too. Tell me how it looks." The girl thought that he was very dumb. She cuddled closer and began to try to put that thing on him. Jim petted and patted and looked impressed. "Go on and describe it to me. I'll bet it's got pretty flowers on it."

"Tell you what. You come on to my room and I'll let you see it."

"I'd just love to. But look at Stumpy over at the bar getting into a spending-duel with the Third Man from the *Savannah*. Let's watch him."

"Aw, yeah?" Stumpy was retorting. "We brought in plenty on the *Angeline*. I know that I can beat you spending."

"Aw, is that so? Well, make me know it. I don't believe nothing until I see it. I don't believe that the old sow had pigs. I don't even believe that lard is greasy."

Both called up their lady friends, bought rounds and let the girls pick up the change. They kept on until both of them were stony.

"Still I aim to beat you," Stumpy said. "I got my owner right here with me. Brought him along because I suspicioned some piker like you was going to get up in my face. Hell, it's plenty more shrimp out there in the ocean, and we sure know how to find 'em. Lemme have ten dollars, Boss, until the next trip."

Jim didn't grab at his pocket at all.

"Look, Stumpy, it ain't that I'm scared that you won't pay me back. But why do away with ten dollars you haven't even made yet? I paid you nearly a hundred dollars about six o'clock this evening."

"That's right, but it's all gone now."

229

"How about knocking off, and beginning to put something away for a rainy day?"

"Because that ain't no sensible way for a fisherman to do, Boss. I might get washed overboard crossing the bar the very next trip. A shark may get me before the next week is over. What do I need to put away money for somebody else to spend? I knowed a fisherman once who cut a caper like that and it brought him all kinds of bad luck. I knowed him mighty well. He was a good friend of mine."

Stumpy, high as a Georgia pine, made a gesture with his arm to call witnesses to his tale.

"Practically everybody in here knows who George Kemp was."

There was almost unanimous agreement. Those who did not know him personally, knew about him. One of those good fishermen who had fallen from grace. Good-hearted as he could be. A good boy, but a poor boy. Jim just had to hear George's pitiful story as a warning if nothing more.

George had been a regular fisherman, then all of a sudden something got the matter with him and he started to saving money. Stay out six, seven, ten days and never felt right unless he sunk his boat. Made a heap of money for his owner, a Portuguese factory outfit, and money for himself. Saved it all up and finally bought himself a boat of his own. Then he got to making himself some big money, but the poor fool didn't learn no better. Kept right on dodging good likker and hiding away from loving women and saving up money for hard times.

"So look what happened to the back-slider. A fly gal out to do herself some good gigged poor George on down to the courthouse and married him. And neither did she lose any time letting George know just what she married him for. I been told that love ain't nothing but the easy-going heart disease, but that she-eel made it quick. Had George working so hard till he soon come down with heart trouble. Doctor give him up for dead.

"You know, My Captain, lying is lying and joking is joking, but to stick a crooked stick like that up a straight man's behind

230

is really too provoking. Knowing that he wouldn't be here long, George got to thinking. He admired to leave that eel just like he found her, which was down and out. So he calls all of us who was his friends to his house, gives away every cent he had, drinks up all the likker that he can hold, makes the three leaving-the-fishing-ground signs, and lays down on his bed and dies."

Jim doubted the story mightily, but practically every man there swore it was so. It was added that George found that he had two thin dimes on the back of his dresser, so he tossed them in his mouth and swallowed them with a drink of water. George had won the big pot after all. You just can't beat a fisherman.

"And what lesson do we learn from that?" Stumpy parodied a Sunday school teacher to the amusement of the crowd. "What do the Bible teach and tell a fisherman to do?"

"Spend it just like you make it!" came back in a roar from the crowd. "Don't leave a thing on the hill when you go to sea! Fatten no frogs for snakes!"

"Kee-reck!" Stumpy cried out, and looked at Jim in triumph. Jim laughed, reached in his pocket and handed Stumpy the ten.

Stumpy, who had been given his name for being tall, yelled for drinkers to treat, and to cheer him in his victory over his opponent. The ten-spot vanished in a blow.

Then in honor of the triumph of his crew-man, and of his new life, Jim stood the next round of drinks. For some time Jim had been yearning to feel his own deck under him, and that was his good-bye gift. Leaving Stumpy still "specifying," Jim drove back across the bridge to the shrimping docks and stood for a long time watching the life of the river, whose surface looked oily under the light of a cloudy moon. There was the fleet of boats tied up, two and three abreast; the shrimp factories, the swift life and death circle in the water traced out by phosphorescent streaks.

If he just didn't have to ever go back and be bothered with

231

the packing-house! Kenny had two more years in college, and that seemed like an eternity to Jim now. Just thinking about the long wait got Jim so impatient that the spirit of profanity descended upon him. Leaning on the starboard rail Jim spoke in tongues and double-cussed all the way.

CHAPTER 21

Time came when Arvay had a new addition to her house. It was a spacy and pretty sleeping-porch added onto the south side of the home. What had once been the [side] window of the living-room was now a pair of glass doors opening out onto the new porch.

Arvay was stunned by the newness of the idea, but she made no objections. She had seen that kind of porches attached to houses of people, but of a class of folks whom she thought of as too high-toned for her to compare with. For the used-to-be Arvay Henson, that kind of a thing was a mighty high kick for a low cow.

So Arvay was much relieved when Angie took charge of the empty new porch, forbidding any of the old porch chairs to be moved in. No, Angie declared, there had to be brand new things, and things meant especially for a porch like that. Things built for coolness, and bright and reclining-like. Angie selected wicker furniture with cretonne cushions and covers, a chaise longue for that corner to the right of the door. A pair of daybeds with good mattresses and bright covers and pillows fitted into spaces against the house wall for lounging by day and for sleeping on hot nights, with shaded lamps handy to read by. When Angie got through Arvay thought that the porch was prettier than anything that she had ever seen in her life. It put her in mind of an inside flower garden.

Arvay tried not to let on, but to save her soul she could not take up on that porch at first. She felt highly privileged to have it under her care, but she could not feel that she had any right to be there. She swept and dusted and petted and patted pillows and tended to the plants that Angie had spotted around in there for looks to make up for her uncomfortable feeling. A kind of outside show of ownership. She never sat down unless Jim insisted, and then she did not lean back in the deep, comfortable chairs. Arvay made excuses about the damp night air to keep from mussing up those day-beds until Jim declared that he would be damned if he was going to foot bills for a sleeping porch and good beds and then stick in the same old room on warm nights. He was going to sleep out there. Arvay followed Jim meekly and found that she managed to sleep all right. It got easier every time that she tried it. After a week of that, Arvay took her mending out there one afternoon, and after a few minutes of trial, sat all the way back in a chair. She had not been settled like that very long before Hatton's mother called her on the phone, and in well-covered pride, Arvay invited her over to sit awhile and share a pitcher of cold lemonade with her.

Mrs. Howland made much over the porch, and over the lemonade. They chatted pleasantly, and afterwards Arvay decided that she had never passed a more agreeable afternoon. The porch belonged to her after that. She had noted a difference in Mrs. Howland's manner with her, she thought. She took to inviting other women friends to drop in and they all expressed envy of her porch. It built Arvay up and made her feel more inside of things. It was a kind of throne room, and out there, Arvay felt that she could measure arms and cope. Just looking around her gave her courage. Out there, Arvay had the courage to visit the graveyard of years and dig up dates and examine them cheerfully. It was a long, long way from the turpentine woods to her sleeping-porch.

Arvay's unsureness went away when she stepped out there. She had bright ideas and thought up things to say in answer to people. Arvay joked and laughed with Jim and they had a great deal of fun these days.

Every evening, as soon as supper was over, Arvay led the way out there to lounge around and wait for an event of her day. For the last year or so, she had been a little too bound for her usual good health. So her doctor had given her a routine to overcome this. He was a young new doctor that Angie had thrust upon her. He was against laxatives and the castor oil mixed with turpentine that Arvay had been raised to. Seven in the morning and eight at night had come to be Arvay's hours for her vigil. That gave her a good two hours after supper on the porch to enjoy the place with Jim.

Arvay had no fault to find with her routine. It was funny, she reflected more than once, how things could change around. Once upon a time, she would not have given what she was doing a second thought. But now she had to restrain the impulse to make a victorious announcement and put herself in the way to receive compliments.

This particular evening was soon before Easter, but other-wise it was a good deal like others that Arvay already knew about. The differences were that Arvay heard the first whip-wills-widow of the year from somewhere outside in the dark. Then a bull alligator bellowed in rumbling thunder from a lake off towards the south. Jim lowered his newspaper and gloated.

"Spring is here!" He laid the paper down and lit his pipe. "When you hear a bull gator bellow and a whip-poor-will call, spring is here for sure. The weather man can't fool a gator."

"Sure sign," Arvay agreed. "Umm Jim! Just smell that night-blooming jessamine that Hatton and Kenny set out for me last Fall! Ain't it sweet?"

"Mighty, mighty nice. Mighty nice." Jim picked up his paper again.

"You mentioning the gators and spring and all puts me in the mind that Kenny and his foolishness will come loping up here before long."

"No more'n three more months now," Jim conceded cheerfully.

"With the house rammed and crammed with his cronies a'whooping and a'hollering and banging on that pianner and everything else they can get their hands on and eating up everything just as fast as I can get it cooked for 'em," Arvay complained happily. "Wonder how they's all making out over in New Orleans right now."

"That's right." Jim said. "You remember that Kenny mentioned in that last letter that they—the Gator band, I mean—was going to New Orleans to play at some kind of music-festival at that college up there. . . ."

"Tulane University," Arvay supplied with a touch of pride. "I declare to my rest, I never knowed that there was so many of these colleges in the world until Kenny got mixed up in one. Every time I turn around he's teaching me another name."

Jim yanked the hunting-case gold watch from his fob and snapped it open.

"That final concert was from three to six today, wasn't it? Yeah, they're all through playing now and on the way to Gainesville, I reckon by now. Though the professor might let 'em stay over tonight and head back for Gainesville tomorrow sometime."

"What time is it now, Jim, near about eight?"

"Two minutes of."

"Then I reckon I better go." Arvay put her hands on the arms of the chair and got up. "I don't know what kind of a caper it is that Kenny cuts that makes folks act so crazy over his playing, but it sure is something or other."

Arvay moved leisurely towards the door into the house. As she went, the perfume from the flowers surged around her. The moon was rising, and some mocking-birds in a tangerine tree began to trill sleepily. The whip-poor-will was still sending out his lonesome call. Arvay paused in the door and looked back on the softly lighted porch. It was to her the most beautiful and perfect scene in all the world. She was as near to complete happiness as she had ever been in her life. The porch told her that she belonged. Slowly she turned away and went on to the bath.

Just then the telephone in the hall began to yell in long pulls. She heard Jim's solid tread down the hall, and the instrument rattle.

"Hello! Hello! Yeah, that's right . . . Yes, it is . . . Speaking."

Sounds like somebody sort of strange, Arvay decided.

"Long distance? . . . Did you say New Orleans?"

"Jim!" Arvay yelled through the closed door. "Didn't they say New Orleans? Do, My Maker! What's done happened to Kenny?"

"Just a minute, honey," Jim said quickly and impatiently through the door. "Oh, hello! Hello, Kenny boy! . . . Sure, I know your voice. Glad to listen to it any old time. What you got to say?"

Arvay leaned back, but she did not relax. Kenny couldn't be too bad off if he was able to come to the phone.

"Oh, he did, eh? That's just fine. How did you make out? . . . Gee, I'm proud to hear that. . . . You don't say! Oh, I knew all along that you could do it. Sure. . . . Oh, you did? . . . Well, if you've done put your name down on it, I don't see that's anything more to be said. Naturally, me and your mother will feel sort of disappointed for you not to go ahead and finish school. Wait just a second, and I'll get her to the phone. . . ."

There was really no need for Jim to call Arvay. She had heard him through the door and was both eager and anxious to get to the phone, but found herself too seriously involved.

"Tell him to hold on for just a minute, Jim, then I'll be there."

Arvay heard Jim give her message over the wire.

"You got to catch the New York train in three minutes? Too bad. I'll tell her what you say. She says to give you her love. Wire us the minute you get there, and back it right up with a letter so that we'll know where to reach you. If you

237

need anything, don't feel bashful about letting me know. I'm with you, son. Good-bye."

Arvay tried desperately to make it, but the click of the receiver found her scrambling to a standing position with her clothes up around her waist. Jim waited in silence until she came out of the door and told her.

A famous leader of a famous New York band had been playing an engagement at a celebrated New Orleans hotel. The engagement ended the very day that the Gator band had arrived at Tulane, but the bandleader had sent his men on ahead, and waited to scout the Gator band. He was there to hear Kenny play for three sessions. He liked Kenny's piece a lot. It was a rhumba and it went over swell. As soon as the concert was over that evening, he had managed to get Kenny to one side and make him an offer. Fifty dollars a week to start with, and double that in ninety days if Kenny took with the public in New York. So much for the exclusive use of Kenny's piece besides, and when it was published, Kenny would get something from that too. Kenny thought that it was a great opportunity, and he had grabbed it. The band was going into a famous nightclub in New York in two weeks.

A coldness as from outer space crept over Arvay as she listened. It stiffened her tongue and choked her throat so that it was a long time before she could speak.

"And you stood there and let him go?" Arvay managed to say at last.

"What else could I do, honey? He had done passed his word and signed the contract. He couldn't go back on that. And then again as he said, he never has had any notion of doing nothing else but playing music for a living. It don't matter too much whether he finishes school or not. He figured on two or three years after he finished school to get to the very place that he got today. Looking at it from that standpoint, he's five or six years ahead of schedule. And if he don't make out up there in New York, he can come on back to school, can't he? I don't see no reason for you to feel so bad."

"I reckon you don't, Jim. I feel and believe that you'se

238

telling the truth from your very heart. But just the same, I hope that you and nobody else don't never feel like I do right now. You never is known the feeling I got right now. All the little family I done got together is gone and done left me in one way or another."

Arvay sobbed and cried and leaned her head against the wall and shook. Jim reached out and warm-armed her up tight against his chest.

"You're ever so wrong, honey baby." Jim petted and tried to soothe. "You still got your children as much as ever. And even if you didn't, you still got me, ain't you?"

Arvay freed herself and pushed past Jim and towards the front of the house. Through the width of the living-room she could see the enchantment of the porch, but she saw it as from afar and in a vision. Like John on the island of Patmos. A golden land of refuge where all would be peace, but from which she was now expelled. Her power seemed broken. She stood looking, and new tears crept out from her eyes. Tears without sound that nevertheless flowed freely.

"Just like I always thought and feared . . . they all done turned from me and gone. . . . Why couldn't I have been setting quiet-like on my porch when my baby come to me and told me that he aimed to go off and leave me? So then I could of handled my feelings."

Arvay turned into her old bedroom and fell across the bed on her face. She was conscious that she had left Jim standing very still and looking after her with a heavy expression on his face. Behind the closed door of the room, she went forth to face the demon of waste and desert places and take him for her company.

CHAPTER 22

Arvay had no idea how long it had been since she had left Jim standing open-armed in the hall. Lying on her face, she heard him enter the room and switch on the light. Out of the cracks of her eyes she saw him quietly changing into his night clothes. She began to charge him with not caring how she felt. He had loosed Kenny to leave home regardless of her feelings. Now, with her crying her heart out, he was going on out on the porch to sleep and leaving her to her misery and lonesomeness. But no, Jim came to the side of the bed and pulled her to a sitting position. Arvay did not help him, but she did nothing to resist him either. She let herself be hauled to her feet and hugged.

Without a sound Jim began to unloose her clothes and to handle her like she was a little child. Arvay was warmed and began to help out. In her nightgown, she stood looking diffidently at Jim for a while, then made the first step.

"Wouldn't you ruther us to go out on the porch to sleep, Jim? It feels kind of hot inside here to me. Come on."

Timidly, she took Jim's hand and led the way. Jim gripped her hand hard and followed her with lighter movements than he had used in the bedroom. Arvay believed in her porch again. Jim was still willing to be with her there. No sooner did

240

she step through the French doors than she felt strong again, and went on to bed.

In the gentle darkness with the spring perfume drifting through, and the voices of nightbirds charming her ears, Jim near at hand on the other bed, and the comfort of her body, Arvay could hunt and find her way back to light and warmth.

Of course Kenny was a good and loving son to her. He would not have gone off sudden like that unless he had a reason. Kenny meant to be loving and kind. What was his reason then? Arvay searched and searched for a sacrifice and could find none unless she put it on the Corregios. She could not risk accusing them to Jim, but she could use and handle them as she pleased if she didn't talk out loud. She was free to controverse all she wanted to in her mind. Kenny had jumped out and gone up North to be his own man.

That Felicia, no doubt put up to it and prompted by her mother, who would naturally want her to luck up on a good, nice white boy to marry to. And naturally she would go her length to tie up somebody like Kenny. Sure she would. Her Mama would make her see that she couldn't get to Kenny and handle him like she wanted to as long as he was under the influence of his Mama. So the first thing she had to do was to talk him into leaving school and going away off somewhere on his own. Handle his own money and do as he pleased. Then they could turn and twist his poor young mind any which a'way they pleased, which was to skull-drag him into marrying Felicia and letting her handle all his money. Oh, it was as plain as day!

Lying there in the dark on her day-bed, Arvay resolved to deal with Felicia and her mother and handle them anyway she pleased. In order to hate deeply and completely, one must have an image stripped of everything but that which lends itself to scorn and hate. Arvay had thought of herself since childhood as a soldier in the army of her Lord. A soldier of the Cross, and a follower of the Meek and Lowly Lamb, never once, in all these years, and hearing the expression as often as

241

she had, [noticing] the contradiction in the term. Who was the enemy to be assaulted without mercy and exterminated? Who else but the folks who did not accept the Prince of Peace and Him Crucified?

Felicia and her mother were nothing but heathen idolaters, and not to be treated white. Arvay proceeded to set up images of them among the African savages and heathen Chinee. They were not fellow-humans, nothing of the kind. She stripped them bald-naked and mocked at them. They were as stark-naked as a jay-bird in whistling time, and Christianity was the gospel of sufficient clothes.

She ought to know. She had heard the accounts of the foreign missionaries often and again, and she was one who had paid strict attention. She had sympathized with these martyrs for God who suffered themselves to be sent far, far away from a well-cladded Christian country to those heathen countries, where, for not knowing Christ in the pardon of their sins, folks went brazenly around with all kinds of things right out in the open.

The poor suffering missionaries had not come right out with certain words, but they made it plain enough for anybody to understand that their sad duty was mostly in looking conditions over, praying over conditions, and then telling the benighted heathens for Christ's sake, to cover conditions up. Every letter that the missionary society got from the missionaries had a plea in it for more covers.

And right here, in these United States, a Bible land, and a praying and gospel country, were these two naked huzzy-heathens trying to pass themselves off as folks, white folks at that, and doing their level best to tole her son off from her. They were no different from that awful Herodias and her daughter Salome who had got John the Baptist killed for nothing. They had been put in the Bible to warn folks against just such sluts as Felicia and her Mama. Babylonian females with no God in their hearts, and no weapon against evil in their hands. Just out to bring ruin and destruction on widows and orphan-children. That back-sliding Corregio woman was no doubt right at this minute getting ready to drag her low-down self and her trashy daughter up to New York running after Kenny. Maybe the poor boy went off like that to get away from them. No telling. And go up there, like that Salome, dressed in nothing but veils to tempt the poor boy with her body. Arvay shuddered at the picture, for her interpretation of a veil was a skimpy piece of utterly transparent stuff pinned on a hat. And she wouldn't put it past Felicia to go dancing and prancing before Kenny and even chunk the scrap of veil away. A'jumping and a'wringing and a'twisting herself with her naked legs flinging every which a'way. You could be bound that they wouldn't be crossed at all. And no responsible person around to lay a halting-hand upon her. And his Mama not on hand to lead the poor boy away.

Arvay shook and shuddered at her home-made picture. It was horrifying to her, but strangely brought her comfort. She could reconcile. Her baby hadn't gone off from her of his own will and was distant from her only in the flesh. Furthermore, the wickedness of those Corregio females was too awful. God didn't like ugly, and neither did God eat okra. You could get too slick for God to stomach you. Therefore, He was bound to take her part against wicked evil. He just wouldn't put up with a thing like that. Felicia and her Maw would catch it and catch it good! No doubt about it. Kenny would soon need his mother's care again and be back home. She could see him right now lounging around on her porch with his long-legged, good-looking and joking self.

Sure of her victory, Arvay felt better right away. She did not even hate the Corregios anymore. Foreseeing their sorrowful fate, she was inclined to feel sorry for them. They didn't count as her enemies anymore. To complete the banishment, Arvay reached up and turned on the light over her head and took a pleased look all around the porch. Hearing Jim stir a little from the influence of the light, Arvay cut it off quickly and went peacefully off to sleep.

CHAPTER 23

Arvay woke up that morning in August feeling sluggish
and irritated. She felt irritated because she felt empty-
handed and sluggish. She had been feeling that way
off and on ever since Kenny had gone up North. Arvay had
no arrangements for spending idle time. She did not read
things, and was not even given to fancy-work. Her life had
been patterned to serve and now there was nobody for her to
wait on and do for. Her impulses were balked and it made her
sluggish in her mind. That called to her mind that she was not
as young as she used to be.

Jim was up and out of doors a good half hour ahead of her.
Even before she put her feet to the rag rug, she could hear Jim
and Jeff Kelsey, Joe's third son, laughing boisterously out
around the back door and it irritated her. The contrast to her
own feelings this morning was painful.

What in the world did they find to skin back their gums and
sniggle over to all of that, Arvay wondered, as she got into
her underclothes. Giggle! Sniggle! Skin back their gums!
Cackle! Must of found a mare's nest and couldn't count the
eggs.

As she flung on her housedress, she made up her mind to
go out in the kitchen, and by the way she acted, put a damper
on all that. She hurried herself to get to it. Then she caught

herself and walked slow. It would be better if she let on that they themselves had got her out of humor by the foolishness they were carrying on. She would go about her business of fixing breakfast just as usual, then wait till somebody said or did something that she could take exception to, and turn their dampers down for 'em good and proper.

Jim and Jeff were outside the kitchen door under the tree just as she had thought. Instead of going to the door and passing the time of day as she ordinarily would have, she made a great clatter of putting fresh water in the kettle, lighting the stove under it, and measuring out the cup of grits to cook.

"Mawning, Miss Arvay," Jeff ventured with a hesitant smile as Arvay came near the door. "You looking fine as silk."

Arvay more grunted than spoke, and Jim looked up at her in surprise. "What's the matter, honey?" Jim asked with some concern. "Don't look like you're feeling so good this morning."

"How can I when I get woke up with a whole lot of whooping and hollering around my back door?"

"Oh, that's too bad, Little-Bits. It wasn't intended. Fact of the matter, I had the idea that you was woke before I was, and was just laying there sort of resting. Jeff ain't been here but a very few minutes. But I'm ever so sorry if we woke you up."

Jeff said nothing. He looked uneasy, and fumbled around with the pruning tools that had been brought from the shed. He began to bunch them together to go away from the door. The laughter that had lit up his face faded from the hair-line and died out finally under his chin.

"Oh, then I'm a liar!" Arvay snapped. "I reckon that I ought to know whether I was asleep or not. Tell me!"

Jeff grabbed up the tools and went on away from there. As he neared the line of the grove, he cast a look over his chunky shoulders at Jim that said, "I ain't deserting you, Boss, but you know how things is. Around that back door ain't no place for me right at present."

"Hold on there, a minute, Jeff!" Jim called after him, and

Jeff halted at the line of the grove and waited. "I ain't through telling you what I want done."

Jim joined the husky young Negro and after a moment of embarrassment on both sides, they began to laugh.

"Look like Ole Miss got up on the wrong side of the bed this mawning. Whew! I'm due to be scarce around your house today."

"Her feathers seem to be ruffled about something, though I ain't got the least idea what it is. But she'll be all right in a minute or so."

"Good mawning, Boss!" It came in a well-known baritone voice from behind, and Jim turned to see Joe inside the side gate and approaching in a good-humored roll.

"Come on over here, you trashy rascal, you! I got you fair and square this time, and I aim to put you to work. Haul it on over here."

The men disappeared down in the grove somewhere. Arvay placed the bucket of fresh eggs handy, but before she broke any in the skillet of hot ham grease, she went to the door and called. She had got in her lick and she felt better already. She was fixing enough so that Joe and Jeff could have something too.

In a few minutes, Jim and Joe appeared at the door. Jim came straight on in, scraping his feet on the steps before he stepped into the kitchen. He pulled her ear playfully as he passed her and fled into the bathroom from her pretended lunge at him.

"Look out for yourself, Joe, the best way you can!" He yelled back in mock alarm over his shoulder. "It's a bear-cat aloose in there."

He returned in a few minutes with his hands washed and his hair combed a little, and took his place at the table. Arvay saw Jim and Joe exchange winks, then Joe's hat came scaling into the kitchen and landed under the table.

"If it don't get throwed back at me, I know that it's safe to hang around."

"Aw, come on in here and set down, Joe, and quit your

246

foolishness!" Arvay scolded. "What become of Jeff? Don't he want nothing to eat today?"

"I'll go let him know," Joe said smilingly. "Jeff sure would feel hurted if I didn't. He ever favors his guts."

Jeff and Joe came back together after a while, and settled out under the camphor tree. Jim felt devilish and began to tease Joe again about working in the grove that day.

" 'Course I don't expect to get a lick of work out of you." Jim kept it up. "You ain't hit a lick of work since we closed down the still, and you don't want to see no work, nor even hear-smell of none."

"Well, you know, Mister Jim, I'm a business man, and keeps my arrangements in my hand."

"Naw!" Jim feigned great surprise and interest for the sake of the play. He glimpsed a faint grin running around the edges of Joe's aging face and was prepared to be amused. "Back your crap."

"Well, you recollect when we first shut down the still, always being more of a business man than anything else, I opened me up a grocery store to sell things."

"Before you start that lie, Joe," Arvay broke in, "you and Jeff come on inside and get yourselves a plate of breakfast. It'll be kind of cool there in the doorway."

The plates piled high with soft grits, fried ham and eggs, and the coffee pot on the floor by the door, and nothing more to eat in sight, Joe protested to Arvay that that was enough. Please don't offer them anything more. Jeff took his to the bench outside under the tree, but Joe sat down in the door. Taking whole fried eggs at a bite, and ramming them with chunks of grits, Joe smiled through his charge, set down his plate and went back to his narrative.

"Yeah, I remember when you opened that store," Jim pushed the tale along. "But if I remember correctly, it didn't last you very long."

"That sure is the evermore truth, you'se telling, Mist' Jim. What with folks trading in them big stores downtown, and me crediting so many that did buy from me, and my big family

247

eating out of the store, I used that place up in no time at all."

"What you didn't swap off for coon-dick," Jeff flung in from the outside. "Case of canned tomatoes or corn for a gallon of moonshine. It couldn't last long that a'way, Paw."

"Hush up! You got that talk from your Maw. That's what Dessie claims, but I know better. I never done nothing like that at all . . . not more'n eight or nine times."

"So what finally become of your grocery-store, Joe?" Jim asked with exaggerated interest.

"Oh, well, when things got pretty low on the shelves, and with Dessie 'buking and dogging me all the time, when a Crack—I mean a white man from back in the woods over towards Davenport come along one day and offered to trade me a half a dozen shoats able to crack corn for what I had in the store. I swapped him, lock stock and barrel and he had the store and I had me some hogs. So then I was out of the store business and into the hog business, and figgered that I had done beat him outa some fine hogs, and could make me a independent living out of raising hogs."

"And that's a mighty good business, Joe, if it's handled right. You make much on your meat?"

"Funny thing, though, Mister Jim. Them hogs must of been crossed with hound-dog or gator once. Man, they could eat! I mean they could do a mean piece of biting, but look like they never put on no meat. 'Course, I found out that hog-shorts was kind of high, and I couldn't see my way to laying in too much at a time with the money that I was handling along in then. Them crossed-up hogs didn't gain none, but they lost a'plenty. They got to walking kind of lap-legged and squealing so till I couldn't get my night rest. First, they reared up and squealed. Then they stood still and squealed, then they took to laying down and squealing right on. Got me sick and tired of hearing them take on like that. So when a widow-'oman cross the railroad tracks but sort of on the outskirts, come over one day and offered to swap me a dozen fat chickens for a half a dozen poor hogs, I took her right up on it. Look like she didn't mind paying out money to pour shorts into them hound dogs on hog frames. So she had the hogs and I had the chickens. I was out of the hog business and right into the chicken business."

Jim threw back his head and laughed and laughed. Not a grin out of Joe though. He was acting out a drama of misfortune, and he had masked his face to fit the part. Until the curtain fell he was a modern Job, and suffering many things.

"So how did you make out with your chickens, Joe?" Jim asked it very seriously.

"Well, suh, look I must be born for bad luck. Here I was figgering on taking them twelve chickens and running 'em into a big chicken business. When them hens laid, I would set them eggs and hatch off a whole heap more and then from them hatch off still some more and really be in the business in a great big way. But first off, it seems like them devilish chickens was in a moult and wouldn't be laying no eggs for quite some time. Then somebody looked 'em over and told me that them white narrow-made chickens didn't have no habit of setting. All they did was lay eggs; that is, if they ever got around to doing some of it. They didn't had no feathers on 'em right then to amount to nothing, and they wasn't laying a frazzling egg, but they sure had they appetites along with 'em. By the time I found out how I had been beat out of my hogs, them greedy-gut devils had done et up all the feed I had on hand. They was eating up more feed than I could afford with the money I was handling just then."

Joe remembered to feed himself heartily for a minute or so, then went on. Arvay was surprised how entertained she had become in a tale that she knew was not more than half so.

"So what become of those poor chickens?" she asked eagerly.

"Them chickens et like mules, Miss Arvay, but I say this for 'em, they had mighty good manners and nice behavior. Smart and sensible in they heads, too. You could make 'em understand. Without me even mentioning it to 'em, they seen that I was doing the very best I could to help 'em out. When I come across a nice green patch of grass out in the country like, I always went right home and took 'em out there and give 'em a chance to crap a nice mess of fresh grass. They could catch all the grasshoppers and worms around like some meat to go along with they greens. They seen that I was willing to divide with 'em what I had. It got so, that all I had to do was to go out in the yard, and they would lay down and cross they legs, making it convenient for me to tie 'em up and carry 'em to where I had done found something for 'em."

"Hush, Joe, hush!" Arvay commanded in all good nature. "I done heard a gracious plenty about you and your business head. You ain't going to hit a lick of work your ownself, so shut up and let Jeff do something."

Joe laughed and cleaned his plate, and poured himself another cup of coffee.

"No'm, I don't speck I will do much long in these dog days. I wouldn't exactly say that me and work had words, but we'se sort of at variance, you might say. Then too, I'm knocking along in years. I'm near abouts old enough for your daddy, Miss Arvay. Anyhow, I done raised Kenny and trained him to make a good living. I done done my share."

Arvay felt the same painful twist that she had felt years ago about Joe and Kenny. Then she took hold of herself. It wasn't right to feel jealous that way. She saw now why she had been so set against the music. It gave Joe a hold over her boy that made her feel excluded.

"Between me and you, Miss Arvie, we sure pulled that boy through, didn't us?"

Arvay shook her head slowly. "You mean you did, Joe. You learnt Kenny all that your ownself. I don't know the first pick on a box."

"That's where you'se ever so wrong, Miss Arvay. 'Tain't everybody that can learn music like that. Kenny took to it because he brought that talent in the world with him. He got that part from you. He just naturally worried and pestered me to death to teach him. I knowed that he couldn't help hisself. What's bred in the bones'll be bound to come out in the flesh. Yeah, that boy come here full of music from you."

"I always thought about Kenny as taking after Jim," Arvay said as if she were talking to herself. Joe looked at Jim and gave a great guffaw.

"Mister Jim? Why, Mister Jim couldn't even tote a tune if you put it in a basket for him. Looks, yeah, but that music part he takes right after you."

Arvay thought a minute, then her face lightened. "You could be right at that, Joe. I ever loved to hear and to play music. I took to it just like Kenny did when I was a chap of a child. And just like you say, Larraine never could learn none. Only different from Kenny, I had small chance to learn much of it. I ever wanted to learn more though. I know that I could of learnt a lot more than I know if I had of had a chance." Arvay sat quietly for a minute and her face lighted timidly. "Yeah, I guess, I hope, that Kenny did take his music after me."

"Couldn't be nobody else, Miss Arvay," Joe said positively. "And it sure is a noble gift to have. I learnt what I know by the hardest, but you and Kenny is just gifted to that. It's a shame and a pity that you didn't have more chance."

"I thank you, Joe," and Arvay smiled diffidently. "And I want you to know that I'm ever so proud about the way Kenny is making out. I'm glad too that he appreciates you and what you have done for him enough to send for you to be with him up North there. Kenny would look for you to come looking nice and clean, and I would want you to go that way too, Joe. How you fixed for something to put on up North? Jim's got a shirt or two that he could spare, and I reckon we could see to it that you get a new suit of clothes."

"Thank you so much, Miss Arvie. You'se mighty kind and thoughtable like. I is sort of low on changing-clothes, since you make mention of it."

Jim snatched out his watch and brought the meeting to a close.

"Quarter to eight. You all through eating, Jeff?"

"Them few little mouthfuls *been* gone too long to talk about," Jeff laughed. "I'm ready for the question. Let's go!"

"You come on too, Joe. Come on and keep us company some. You ain't no good for nothing else."

"You gwan and leave Joe here with me. I got a few things to give him, and I got to hunt 'em up."

Arvay wasted no time. She was concerned about her son. Joe was to see to it that Kenny behaved. As she charged Joe to keep a stiff hand over Kenny, she moved around briskly searching through Jim's things and coming back with an accumulation of shirts, ties and underwear for Joe.

"You better take these, Joe. Jim's got more than he can wear out anyhow. And Joe, you being one in the family and knowing how I tried to raise my chillun, and how I want 'em to behave, maybe it would be better for Kenny if you was to stay up there with him until he takes the notion to come on home. See to it that he behaves himself and walks in the right way just like I would do, hear Joe?"

"Yes Ma'am. I'll sure hold his feet to the fire and keep him straight. Without a doubt, Miss Arvay. You know that Kenny ever would mind me. It'll be just like you was there."

Arvay made a slight dissenting movement of her body. It was not that she doubted Joe, but nobody and nothing could be the same as a mother's care.

"He's still a baby, Joe, and more particular, my baby-child. He ain't no hard grown man to be off by hisself like that. Don't care what he say, you go with him and stand by him, Joe, and prop him up on every leaning side. Don't allow him to forget his principles and his raising. And if he should mention anything about returning back home, you encourage him to it, Joe, will you please?"

"Sure will, Miss Arvay. It wouldn't do for him to be up there among strangers and out of work. Don't you worry none. We Meserves'll look after one another."

Arvay was comforted to think that "Uncle Joe" would be there with Kenny. She knew so well how much Joe loved her boy. Still and all, it was not the same as Kenny being where she could do for him herself. However comfortably Kenny might be making out up there, her arms were still empty and

252

her hands had nothing to do. With Earl dead, Angeline married off and needing nothing, Kenny up there doing so well and not calling on her for a thing, Jim off from home so much with his boats, there was little for her serving hands to do. She felt like a dammed-up creek. Green scum was covering her over.

Thinking like that, the lift that Joe had given her was all but dissipated even before he left the house. She felt unnecessary. To take up the slack, Arvay decided to make a big potato pone for Jim. He ever loved it, and it took up a lot of time and called for work. She got out a big baking-pan, washed off a mound of sweet potatoes and started to grate them. The food-chopper would have done it easier and in a third of the time, but she wanted the feeling of doing. She peeled and grated with great care, fighting against that sluggish and lonesome feeling.

That was what Arvay was doing when she heard Jim yelling for her around three o'clock.

"Arvay! Arvay! Run here quick! I got something to show you! Run!"

Arvay did not run, but she walked very fast. From Jim's voice, it sounded like some kind of alarm.

Following the direction of his voice, Arvay hurried south through the grove. About midway, she saw Jim standing alone with his back almost to her. He was fooling with something that she couldn't make out until she was in twenty or thirty feet of him. Then she saw and stopped dead in her tracks.

Jim had the biggest diamond-back by the neck that she had ever seen, and the snake was trying to get aloose. Jim was holding it out at arms' length from him and laughing. The snake was trying to coil itself around his arm. It was eight feet long if it was an inch, and being a rattler, thick according. Arvay had a deep-seated fear and dislike of snakes. Any kind of a snake. She shrank from worms even because they reminded her of snakes. She avoided touching the shed skin of a snake, even with her shoes.

"A snake! Jim! My God a'mighty, Jim! What you doing with that thing up in your hands?" Arvay screamed this out in

253

jerks. Her heart was thumping so that she felt stifled.

Jim looked at her fright and chuckled. "Going to put him in a box and . . ." Jim had to halt to struggle with the reptile to keep it from coiling about his arm. "Jeff . . . gone to the barn . . . to get me a box."

Successful for the moment, Jim turned a bragging, triumphant face on Arvay. She could tell that he was expecting her to admire what he was doing. Just like a little boy turning cartwheels in front of the house where his girl lived. But this was nothing to be fooling with. Supposing that thing got aloose. The thought of that possibility frightened Arvay so that she began to grow numb. She could see the lightning-like strike of the big head and feel in her own body the fiery pang from the long, curving fangs. And for a thing like that to happen to Jim. Oh, it was too horrifying! Then from her fear and pity, Arvay grew angry. Why would Jim do a thing like that, frightening her to death for nothing? It was all so unnecessary. If it happened, it would be her instant death. She could not bear to see it. Weak and trembling all over, she closed her eyes in dread.

But she could not refrain from looking, and she opened her eyes a moment later on a truly frightening scene. The writhing snake struck Jim's middle with the lower third of its body. Almost too quick to follow, it wrapped around and anchored. With horror Arvay saw more and more of the thick and powerful body ripple like water and crawl around Jim's waist. Two solid coils of awful beauty around Jim's middle, and Arvay, feeling faint, could see them tightening down.

With her mouth open and dry, Arvay's eyes flew to Jim's face to see what he was doing about it. Jim was no longer laughing. His lips began to slide back from his teeth. Arvay saw why. The tight coil about Jim's waist was terrible, but it was not the worst. The rattler was freeing its head, and Jim was grimly putting every ounce of the strength in his hands and arms to hold onto the neck of that snake. It was unbelievably powerful, and Arvay saw the big flat head being almost imperceptibly but surely withdrawn through Jim's two clutching fists. The tip of the mouth slid down and disappeared within the upper hand. With a steady rhythm, the body of the snake quivered around Jim's waist as it exerted all its power back-crawling and straining to free its imprisoned head.

Jim's face was a straining, gasping horror now to Arvay. Hair falling over his forehead, big veins standing up in his face and neck, eyes dilated with fear and pain, and sweat pouring down in great drops.

Arvay never knew what happened to her then. She saw the imminent danger to her husband, her great love, the source of all the happiness that she had ever known, the excuse for her existence. And in this terrible danger, she went into a kind of coma standing there. Fear surrounded her about. She saw as through a casing of glass. She heard Jim faintly.

"Ar . . . vay! Help . . . me." It was breathed out on agonizing gasps.

In her consciousness Arvay flew to Jim and slew that snake and held Jim in her arms like a baby. Actually, Arvay never moved. She could neither run to the rescue nor flee away from the sight of what she feared would happen.

Then, after an endless time, Arvay heard the thump of running feet and heard Jeff scream, "My God, Mister Jim!" and Jim's agonized answer: "Jeff! . . . Oh, Jeff!"

Jeff was there and the covered box discarded on the ground. And Jeff, his prominent behind setting far out, had grabbed the snake by the tail. His strong white teeth, bordered by blue gums were snarled back in fear and rage as he threw his strength into pulling and unwinding the coils by stepping rapidly backwards around Jim and destroying the purchase of the reptile. Maybe two or three seconds that seemed like years to Arvay, and Jeff breathing loudly through nose and opened mouth asked, "Got a safe hold on his head now, Mister Jim?"

"Yeah . . . Jeff."

"I'm going to fling him. Get ready to leave go the same time I do."

Jim, with the pressure removed from his body, took a second to fill his lungs with air. Then he whispered more steadily, "Ready."

A quick and violent movement of the arms and bodies of both men in concert, and the huge rattler sailed through the air and thumped to the right, a good twenty feet away. Arvay was sure that it would be killed by the fall. A stunned minute, then it went into battle position with a movement so smooth and quick that the eye could scarcely follow. The quivering tail was sending out that ominous sound.

In her relief, Arvay felt to run and fling herself upon Jim and hug and cry in relief and thanksgiving, but Jeff was ahead of her. He looked at Jim, waving on his feet, and flung a brawny arm across Jim's back and steadied him until he could well steady himself. Two or three minutes at the outside while Jim breathed deeply. Arvay found herself, too, in that time and took a step forward to satisfy her mind of the miracle. If she touched Jim, then she would know that he was really alive and saved.

But Jeff gave her a look that halted her where she was. The look forbade her to approach the person of Jim Meserve. It called her unworthy of such an honor and pleasure and privilege by reason of cowardice and treason and trashiness. The look held. Jeff wanted her to know that she had been judged. Then he turned back to hovering and fussing around Jim. Arvay saw that Jim was not even looking at her. In that moment Arvay realized what fear had done to her, and how she looked to those who knew about it.

Neither Jeff nor Jim asked for her aid or assistance in any way. Jim leaned on Jeff, and Jeff never even looked in her direction. He talked, but he did all his talking to Jim.

"I better see you to the house and covered up in the bed. You ought to lay down just as quick as you can, Mister Jim." Jeff hovered and guarded just as if Jim had been an infant child. Just the way Arvay wanted to do. "Lawd have mussy, Boss! It's a wonder you ain't dead. Sure proud I got to you in time."

Jim, supporting himself with one arm about Jeff's stout

shoulder, took a deep breath and patted Jeff feebly. "Don't believe that I could have held out another minute longer, Jeff. You're all that stood between me and Old Stony Lonesome. Never had any idea a snake was all that strong."

"Mighty deceiving thing, Boss. Strong as a mule. Lemme get you to bed in the house so I can come back and kill that snake."

Arvay saw Jim remember to be himself. He saw her standing there forlorn with Jeff spitting on her in his mind, and he went to making Jeff's ears and eyes out to be liars.

"My poor wife, Jeff, ain't it too bad that women folks makes such a poor out at running?"

Arvay felt whipped all over with thorns. Jim had not really told a lie with his mouth, but the way he said it and tried to smile it off to fool Jeff was too pitiful. But Arvay could see that Jeff was not swallowing it down. He was nice and polite with Jim, and stretched his mouth both ways towards his ears in a smileless gesture to let on that he agreed. But his prominent eyeballs with the fat top lids purposely kept away from Arvay. The men kept coming slowly to where she stood and farther away from the snake all the time. About ten feet away from her, Jim straightened himself and grinned the best he could.

"I believe that the old man can make it now, Jeff. You must be just about as wore out as I am. Don't you dare to hit another lick of work today. Don't never forget, Jeff, that I got you folded away in the hip-pocket of my heart. Gwan home and get in the bed and make things tough for your wife."

"Thank you, Boss, but first I got to go back there and kill that old snake."

"Don't bother, Jeff."

"Boss! That damn thing is ever so vi-grous! Dangerous as he can lay in his rusty hide. He come durned near taking your life. He's got to go way from this world."

"Naw, Jeff. Leave him be. It wasn't no fault of his. He didn't try to tackle me. I was the one that tackled him. He acted the perfect gentleman in every way. A gentleman, Jeff, puts up the best fight that he's got in him to defend his life and what

257

belongs to him. He spied noble in the fight. He put out the best he had, and it come mighty nigh being too damned much for me. Look back there! He ain't making the first move to run away. I tip my hat to a fighter like that and leave him be."

"But, Boss, that's a rattlesnake!"

"So I hear, Jeff." Jim laughed lightly as he came up to Arvay. "Let him alone, I tell you! He's a gentleman who never picks a fight, and never is known to run from one that anybody picks with him. And till the day he dies, he is one general that never loses a battle. I like that kind of a heart. I tried him fair, and he was the best. Let's don't take a cowardly advantage and double-teen him. I don't want him to die calling me a coward, and less of a man than he is. I don't know whether you get my meaning or not, but you leave him be."

Jeff was unhappy about the snake, and it showed in his face. Jim looked at Jeff and chuckled.

"Here, Jeff, take this five dollars and gwan home and make your wife wish that you had of worked hard all day. Light a shuck out of here! See you bright and soon tomorrow."

Jeff brightened considerably at Jim, but never once turned his face towards Arvay.

"You sure you can make it on to the house from here, Mister Jim?"

"Just as sure as you snore. If I see myself giving out, my wife will help me along somehow. Bye, Jeff."

Arvay did not *hear* Jeff snort. He thought too much of Jim for that, but Arvay, happening to be looking at Jeff's barrel-like chest, saw it. She saw the print of that snort just as plain as day. The scorn and despisement in it cut Arvay so that she felt like killing him dead on the spot. She wanted to scream out to Jim and tell him, and make him kill Jeff then and there. But what could she say to Jim? Lynch this man for scorning me because I was right there when you were in danger of death, and I didn't even move my hand to come to your assistance, and now you got to make him stop scorning at me for that? No, no, that would never do.

"So long, Boss. See you in the morning."

"Bye, Jeff."

Then Arvay was alone with Jim in the strangeness of the familiar grove, and they had to get back to the house some way or another, and then when they got there, they had to go inside, and be in there together.

Jim walked along all right. He didn't walk very fast, but he was steady on his feet. Jeff was gone now, and Jim was not smiling any more. They just walked along until they got to the house and went inside. Arvay halted in the kitchen. Jim never paused. He kept on through to the front of the house. Arvay stood around in the kitchen with her arms bent at the elbows, and her hands drooping off her wrists like damp clothes hanging from a nail. She took a few steps one way, and stood, and then after a while she took a step or so in some other direction and stood again. No use in trying to fool with the potato pudding anymore. She couldn't keep her mind on a thing long enough for that. She wanted to just go out on the porch and stretch out, but Jim was up there somewhere.

"Do, Jesus!" and Arvay moved herself a little. "Oh, my Maker! Do, Father!" and Arvay shifted a little here and there about the kitchen, for she didn't know how long. She baked off the potato pone in a mist of gloom. Maybe three times, but twice for sure, Arvay heard Jim at the telephone, but could not make out who he was talking with nor what he was saying. Maybe he was telling Angie what had happened. Maybe even talking to Kenny in New York. Then Jim got very quiet up there, and Arvay decided that he must be lying down.

Towards sundown, she took the fryer out of the ice-box that Jim had killed for her the day before, and put it on the stove to fry, and mixed up a mess of soda biscuits. She couldn't think of much to do, so she took some cold boiled sweet potatoes left over from the night before and sliced them and fried them brown in some bacon grease. Everything was all ready then. She had a good excuse to break a breath with Jim. In trembling fear she passed on through the narrow hall.

Arvay found Jim at last, across the bed in Angie's room. Oh, but it couldn't be so! She stood there in the open door and nothing was said. But Jim couldn't be asleep, because all the lights were on. For the very first time since she had known him, Jim was acting stiff and stout. She was on the point of backing off from the door when Jim sat up and looked straight at her.

"Jim," Arvay trembled out, and then she halted. That look that Jim was giving her, she couldn't make out. He wasn't mad, that she could easily see. One time it looked like he was hurt-ed deep inside, and then again it looked liked he was snurling at her. She tried for a minute, but for to save her ever-dying soul, she couldn't tell which it was. Anyhow, it was sharp. You could stab a breeze of wind with it and it would bleed. Arvay found herself breathing in those short quick breaths, that when dogs did it, the folks in west Florida said that they were "hassling." Arvay tried again. "Jim, I, maybe you . . ."

Jim cut her short. "Arvay, when folks have anything worth saying, they walks in noble and they talks bold." He had on his blue-striped pajamas, Arvay noted. He put his two hands down on the mattress on each side of him in a bracing way, and leaned forward ever so slightly and kept on eye-balling her and waiting.

"I—I just thought I better let you know that supper is on the table."

Jim looked at Arvay some more, and then he began to laugh in a slow, easy way. "All right, Arvay. You had the biggest chance in the world to make a great woman out of yourself. A Past Grand Noble chance. But you crapped out on it and lost the dice. So I reckon now that I will have to do the talking. Take a seat."

Arvay heard just what Jim said. It was not an invitation to rest her feet. It was a straight command. It was in the voice, in Jim's gray eyes, and Jim had rocks in his jaws. With her skirt wrapped tight about her legs, Arvay crooked timidly onto a chair by the wall and faced Jim. She saw that Jim's eyes, face and all over was so charged that involuntarily, she flung up her forearm to ward off a blow.

"Jim! Jim! You ought to give me a chance to say how sorry I is for what went on today. I'm sorry to my heart."

To Arvay's surprise, Jim made no move, and his voice was calm and low. But before he said anything, he gave a short laugh and rested his head in his hands.

"What happened today, Arvay?" And then he raised his head and looked at her and his eyes said that he bet she didn't know. That stung Arvay and she spoke according.

"You grabbing up that rattlesnake, and almost got snake-bit to death, and then just because I didn't know what steps to take . . ."

"See that, Arvay? That shows the difference between me and you. I see one thing and can understand ten. You see ten things and can't even understand one. A person can have very good eyesight, Arvay, and even wear glasses on top of that, but if they get in the habit of butting around with their eyes shut tight, they won't be able to see a thing."

"I was right there, Jim, and seen all that was there to see. Maybe now you aim to tell me that that wasn't no rattlesnake, and you never had him up in your hands. I maybe ain't got all the brains you carries, but I'm here to tell you that I'm not half as dumb as you all make me out to be."

"Naw, you ain't dumb, Arvay. You got plenty of sense if you would only use it. I guess you must be short on spirit in a way. Know what really took place today? No, so I'll have to tell you. Jim Meserve, the man that's been loving you so hard for twenty-odd years, thought that he saw a chance to do something big and brave and full of manhood, thinking maybe he might win admiration out of you and compliments and a big hug around his neck. He knowed all the time how dangerous it was, and that he had a chance to lose, but he was a man in love, so he took the chance. With Jeff around, Jim just barely broke even, that is, with the snake. He lost heavy otherwise. That was really what happened out there today, Arvay."

Arvay could not help from crying. "Jim, you have never

261

known me to make a oath, but I swear that I didn't want you to get hurt by that old snake."

"And I believe you, Arvay, but that only makes things worse. Maybe you couldn't of done one thing to help me, but you could of showed what you was made out of by trying. Even if it was only to show me that you understood my intentions towards you by saying a word or two. I would of felt better even if you had let me know that you saw what I was after, but you hated my guts and then pitched in and helped the rattlesnake out. Not understanding is the part that I don't like."

"Maybe you done got the idea that I don't love you and want you, Jim, but I declare I do. I don't know what come over me. . . ."

"I feel and believe that you do love me, Arvay, but I don't want that stand-still, hap-hazard kind of love. I'm just as hungry as a dog for a knowing and a doing love. You love like a coward. Don't take no steps at all. Just stand around and hope for things to happen out right. Unthankful and unknowing like a hog under a acorn tree. Eating and grunting with your ears hanging over your eyes, and never even looking up to see where the acorns are coming from. What satisfaction can I get out of that kind of a love, Arvay? Ain't you never stopped to consider at all?"

"A'plenty times. But all I could ever see was that the only holt I ever had on you was the way you craved after my body. Otherwise, I felt you looking down on me all the time."

"I heard that from you, Arvay, way back yonder, and it was a lie even when it was fresh. Look like you never have got over that old missionary distemper. Yes, I craved your body, and can't see a thing wrong with that. What the hell would I marry a woman for if I didn't want her like that? If it wasn't for that, I could just as well couple up with another man for a buddy."

"And you took the advantage of me that way, too. Keeping me ever feeling that way towards you, so you could handle me like you pleased. Yes you did!"

"You're a got-that-wrong, Arvay. You're a high-charged

woman and you was born that way. That was all the matter with you before I come along. But in place of looking things in the face, you took and blinded your eyes and took up with that old missionary foolishness to make believe that you was much too nice to feel natural. Like I said, you just ain't given to looking at things, and that is a pity and a shame. Fighting back and holding a grudge against me because I filled the bill in the finest part of our life. I was your man, that's all, just like you was my natural woman. It's a mighty good idea to let God run things. He ain't give nobody a thing He didn't expect 'em to use, your goddamned lap-legged missionaries to the contrary."

"Jim, you say you been loving me so, and I wouldn't understand, but now, you show me and tell me how I—"

"You want to expose yourself by asking me that, Arvay? I used to hope that it wouldn't never be necessary, but you done convinced me that it is, if you're ever to see and know."

Jim leaned forward and rested his elbows on his knees again. His forehead was in his hands, and his shock of black hair fell forward over his fingers.

"I didn't have a damn thing when I married you, did I, Arvay?"

"Well, nothing much to speak of, Jim."

"But with you to care for, and loving you like I did, I got off of that teppentime still just as quick as I could, so as to make a better life for you. I knew that that was all that you had ever been used to, Arvay, but I saw you as due a much higher place. So I got out from there and moved you up a notch by coming down here. It was hard scrambling, Arvay, and I didn't mind that so much. All I ever wanted to hear from you was that you realized that I was doing out of love, and thought of you so high, that I wanted to see you pomped away up there. I never have seen you as a teppentime Cracker like you have thrown in my face time and again. I saw you like a king's daughter out of a story-book with your long, soft golden hair. You were deserving, and noble, and all I ever wanted to do was to have the chance to do for you and protect you. But never one time have I heard you mention that you understood all that."

"Oh, Jim! Jim! I . . ."

"Naw, Arvay. You've had your time to talk and you didn't do it. Let me finish what I got to say.

"You saw me in the ham-scram buying this place and making things as nice and as comfortable for you and our children as I could. I went in with Joe stilling likker, and run a heavy risk of going on the chain-gang to get hold of enough money to put you up closer to where I felt that *my* woman ought to be. I tried to keep it from you, knowing how you felt about things like that, so you'd think high of me and feel that you had done pretty fair in marrying me. When you did find out, you never came to me and flung your arms around me and told me you appreciated the length I was willing to go for you. Naw, you got jealous of the time I had to spend with Joe."

Arvay crumpled and fluttered one hand against her chest, but Jim went right on.

"I did my level best to throw my long arm of protection around you to keep you from getting hurt about Earl. I could see what was on the way a long time before you did, but you wouldn't hear to a thing. It would of happened, even up there in west Florida, but that wouldn't have been near so bad as right there where you had to live, and I could see that. But no, you would let that be. Then when he was surrounded, I humbled myself among men to keep things from being worse than they turned out to save your feelings. But if you ever understood that, I never have been made wise of it. You have as good as accused me of helping to get him killed."

"Jim, oh, if . . ."

"And without saying anything to you, I took pains to tie Alfredo to me, so he wouldn't kick up no stink to fret and worry you more than you already was, but you couldn't even see through that. He stood by me like a major and kept down a whole lot of hard feelings and talk that would have been if he hadn't, and you been doing your damndest ever since to break things up. Yeah, I paid for that outfit that Felicia had on at Gainesville that time, and stood all expenses besides, and glad to do it. I was glad that Kenny had sense enough to ask her up there. I wouldn't have no shrimping business right now if it hadn't been for Alfredo being so faithful and pushing things ahead just like everything was his own. But it was all for your benefit that I was getting it done. You've never turned him nor his family a bit of thanks, and you never have had the feeling to even go down and see what I was doing, or trying to do, and you never have said once that you realized that I was scuffling like that to place you higher up."

"How could I, when you never let me know?"

"Some folks, Arvay, would have been awake enough to glimpse and see. And so far as that swamp is concerned, for twenty years it hung over my heart. I saw that it worried you, and I kept on working as hard as I could to get to the place where I could get it cleaned off for you. So when Hatton married Angie, and I seen how bad you felt over it, I put in to make them children pay you back. Hatton's made big money out of the deal, as I knew he was bound to do, but that wasn't my main reason for sicking him on it. That was done as a honor and a comfort to you, but you soon let me see that you hadn't the least notion why. I had just done something else to fret you. Same way with Angie getting married. Same way with Kenny stepping out on his own. I could see that your glory would be added to, but you haven't give me one bit of credit for love."

There was a shapeless silence crowding around in the room. It was smothering Arvay, and she wanted to say something, do something to push and drive it away, and let her find some way to creep closer to Jim again. Finally, she said what she had said before.

"Jim, I love you. If I don't, I hope God will kill me right now."

For answer, Jim stood erect, flung wide his bath-robe and his body was bare to the line of his pelvis. Arvay screamed. From his short-ribs to his pelvis, was a band of raw-red abraded flesh. The crawling mechanics of the snake applied with such tremendous muscular tension had scoured Jim raw.

265

Arvay saw Jim's lean belly trembling as he breathed.

"Your kind of love, Arvay, don't seem to be the right thing for me. My feelings inside is just how I look outside. Naw, Arvay. I done got my mind made up. I'm leaving you in the morning."

"Naw, Jim, naw! You know I love you, Jim. So why you got to quit me like this?"

"Because I'm sick and tired of hauling and dragging you along. I'm tired of excusing you because you don't understand. I'm tired of waiting for you to meet me on some high place and locking arms with me and going my way. I'm tired of hunting you, and trying to free your soul. I'm tired."

"You mean to turn me loose to scuffle for myself after I done had children for you, and been with you all these years, and . . ."

"I didn't say that I was tired of taking care of you, Arvay. I'm leaving, yes, but this house, just like it stands, is yours to do with as you will or may. I'll send you something to live on every single week. You don't need to worry over that. I'm pushing fifty now, Arvay, and no use in me hoping no more. I ever loved married life, but since I've missed it so far, no use in me hoping no further."

"Married life? Good gracious, Jim, ain't we been married all this time?"

"Oh, we got the proper papers all right, and without a doubt, the folks around the court-house are more than satisfied. But to come right down to the fact of the matter, you and me have never been really married. Our bonds have never been consecrated. Two people ain't never married until they come to the same point of view. That we don't seem to be able to do, so I'm moving over to the coast tomorrow for good. My arrangements are done made. You can consider that me and you are parted, Arvay."

"Well," Arvay murmured out at last, "what you been pointing out about not loving me ought not to take me by surprise. I never is believed that you really loved me, Jim, so your saying it now ought not to hurt me so, but it do."

"I never said that I didn't love you. I told you just as plain as ever I could that I'm through and done with filling in where you choose to be insufficient. I eat high on the hog or nothing. I don't have no notion of breaking into my arrangements to leave here tomorrow morning, but if I ever see any signs of you coming to be the woman I married you for, why then I'll be only too glad and willing to try it again."

"So, if I'm ever to be with you again, I got to make the first move."

"My meaning exactly, that is, providing you make it inside of one year from this day. If it takes you any longer than that, I won't be expecting you at all. I'm gone like a turkey through the corn."

Somehow, Arvay got out on the porch, where she crumpled on her bed.

CHAPTER 24

There is always room in oblivion. That is one place that is never full. Since Jim had left her, Arvay sometimes felt herself lost in the edges of the wastes. Her days had nothing in them now but hours. Hours that somebody else had gotten all the light and service out of and chunked them away. Old, worn-out, lifeless marks on time. Like raw, bony, homeless dogs, they took to hanging around her doorway. They were there when she got up in the morning, and still whimpering and whining of their emptiness when she went to bed at night.

Only one day out of her week had any significance. Every Monday she received an envelope addressed in Jim's handwriting. It held a money order for fifteen dollars folded in a sheet of blank paper. The fall and the winter had about passed over, but not one word of writing had appeared on that sheet of paper as yet. She tore open the envelope and looked eagerly, but never any writing appeared.

So Arvay began to fear that her life with Jim was over. He had made no move towards her, and for the life of her, she could not seek out and discover what Jim expected of her. There was some hidden key to re-open the door of her happiness, but where and what it was, she could not discover it in spite of her torture.

God and the Devil can relieve their melancholy by the exercise of power. Men, therefore, feel themselves more or less god-like to the extent to which they can create happiness, tears and terror among their fellowmen.

Arvay felt now that she had this vanity stripped from among the nourishments of her life. Her living children were on their own. She had no control over either now. She could neither confer nor deny. Jim had made himself absent so that no act of hers did anything to his days. The day of his departure, he had moved Jeff and his wife, Janie, on the place to look after things, but Jeff let no opportunity pass to have it understood that he was working for *Mister* Meserve and taking orders only from him. This was not the Jeff Kelsey, with the face like a cherub that had been built onto, when he was a child on this place. Since the day of the snake, Jeff seemed to have little use for her at all.

She went to sleep one afternoon out on the sleeping porch with her face turned towards the wall. When she somehow woke up suddenly and turned her face over her shoulders, there was Jeff standing with a "lazy boy" in one of his big brawny hands, the other hand on his hip, and his face pressed against the screen wire, staring at her. His face was pressed so hard against the screening that his nose was flattened, and his lips were distorted into purple blobs. His eyes were fixed on her and unmoving. Neither did he jump away when he saw her see him.

Traditionally, Arvay immediately thought of rape and murder. That look was so powerful and intense. But as she studied Jeff's face and eyes she got another shock. Jeff was not longing after her body. It was anger and dislike. If only he had his hands on her, he would tear her to little bitty pieces like a rag-doll.

When Jeff turned away it was with a savage abruptness. He walked a few steps and began to slash at the weeds viciously with the lazy boy. With her looking right at him, and Jeff knowing it, he slashed off the tops of some of her verbenas.

"Why, the impudent scoundrel-beast!" Arvay muttered

from between pressed lips and jumped up from the day-bed and hurried into the house. "I don't aim to take his sass at all. I'll march right out there and run him off this place!"

But with her hand on the knob of the front door, Arvay halted. Jeff was going to give her a whole lot of back-talk and remind her that *Mister* Jim had put him on the place, paid his wages and gave him his orders. Every Monday, just as regular as pig-tracks, Jeff got a letter from Jim. On three different occasions Jeff had knocked off on Friday and gone to the coast, and Arvay had sense enough to know that it was at Jim's commands. She couldn't fire Jeff—nothing of the kind—and Jeff knew it. In his absence, Jim wouldn't just trust any and everybody on the place. She could only move Jeff by appealing to Jim, and Jeff had the place in the best shape that it had ever been. He took such good care of the grove that Arvay would not have been surprised to catch Jeff out there with a curry comb dressing down the leaves. She had heard Jim what he told Jeff out there the day of the snake. No, no use in her flying out there. Jim was not going to get rid of Jeff at all.

"Jim's done quit me, and I don't believe that he wants me no more at all. If he did, he would tell me what it is he wants me to do so that we could go back together. That was just his way of doing things. So what am I doing hanging around here for? Just to get something to eat from a man that's done throwed me down? That don't make me out to be nothing. If I looked upon myself in the right way, I would pack my few things and go on back to west Florida where I reckon I belong."

But that was too drastic for Arvay's feelings. Any day, maybe tomorrow, Jim would come driving up and take her to the coast with him. Jim had left her in this house. She wanted to be where she would be easy to find when he came. He might not put himself to the trouble to proag all the way to west Florida. By her leaving, he might not consider it worth his while to even write a letter.

Arvay wished and wished from one point to the other every day. She would follow her pride and go back home to her mother. No, Jim was her husband and she would stay right where he put her. Back and forth. Light and cloud, and always wondering what Jim wanted her to do.

The door bell rang hard before she could hardly take her seat again, and Arvay went back to the door. A tall, skinny, pimply-faced boy had her signing for a message.

Arvay held the yellow envelope as if she was holding a snail. She was afraid that an enemy, a bad enemy, had gotten to her in that envelope. Jim was telling her not to bother. He was in love with another woman and wanted his divorce. No, Kenny was hurt or in some kind of trouble up North. It could be that Jim was sick or hurt and wanted her to come look after him. Lord have mercy! Lord have mercy! Arvay began to open the envelope with fumbling hands. Her relief made her whimper when she read the message:

MAMA SICK IN THE BED. LARRAINE MIDDLETON.

Arvay read it over several times. It seemed a funny kind of a message to her. It told her so little. It didn't say whether her mother was just poorly or ill-sick in the bed. It didn't tell how long Maria had been ailing, nor from what. It didn't say come or nothing. Not even whether Maria was in need of more money. Arvay sat down on the porch and pondered for some time. She wondered if she should wire or write for more information from Larraine. If she wired right back, in a day or so she would know better what to do.

Then Arvay decided. God worked in mysterious ways His wonders to perform. He planted His footsteps on the seas and rode upon the storms. Or so the old hymn said, and Arvay believed what she had heard sung in a church. God was taking a hand in her troubles. He was directing her ways. The answer was plain. He meant for her to go back home. This was His way of showing her what to do. The Bible said, "Everything after its own kind," and her kind was up there in the piney woods around Sawley. Her family, and the folks she used to know before she fooled herself and linked up with a man who

271

was not her kind. Arvay tossed her head defiantly and rhymed out that she was a Cracker bred and a Cracker born, and when she was dead there'd be a Cracker gone. Jim's and even her own children's ways were not her ways. She had tried and tried but she did not fit in. Let Jim and them have their ways. She would go back and let Jim strain with his house and his impudent, biggity niggers his ownself.

Arvay was conscious at that moment that she had not really been trying to find the answer that Jim expected of her. As always, she had been trying to defend her background and justify it so that Jim could accept it and her along with it. She had been on the defensive ever since her marriage. The corroding poverty of her childhood became a glowing virtue, and a state to be desired. Arvay scorned off learning as a source of evil knowledge and thought fondly of ignorance as the foundation of good-heartedness and honesty. Peace, contentment and virtue hung like a rainbow over turpentine shacks and shanties. There love and free-giving abided and not on decorated sun-porches. Even Larraine and her family stood glorified in this distant light. Arvay felt eager to get back in the atmosphere of her humble beginnings. God was showing favor to His handmaiden.

Arvay got brisk and phoned in a telegram to Kenny. Then she called Angeline and told her, and asked her to please let Jim know. Then she went excitedly about her packing. She was going *home!* Home to the good old times and simple, honest things, where greed after money and power had no place.

Arvay had gotten so used to ease and even a certain amount of luxury, that she took things for granted. She hauled out the luggage that Kenny had sent her as a present and began to pack her things in happy anticipation. Her wardrobe bag, over-night case and combination hat- and shoe-box were of dark-blue leather with her initials on every piece in raised silver. The trade-mark in the rich linings said *Mark Cross.* It did not occur to Arvay that the people she was raised with didn't even know about things like these. At the moment it did not enter her mind that this assembly of luggage had cost Kenny more than a turpentine worker ever handled in a year. That the people whom she was now gilding up had not the means to produce a son like Kenny. That the kind of father that they had had something to do with her children's good looks, and that beauty that everybody gave Angeline credit for was enhanced and made evident by her self-confidence which arose out of assurance brought on by means which Jim had provided. That her natural means had been pointed up by care, clothes and surroundings. Arvay was not analyzing. She was packing frantically to flee away, and to be gone from her married life for good. God was giving her another chance.

Nor did Arvay see the inconsistency in her exclamations when she got a taxi at the station. While the driver was loading her luggage, she stood on the sidewalk and admired around.

"Oh, I see several good changes since I been gone! What's that new building down the street there?"

"Our new and modern hotel, the Stephen Foster. We got two self-service grocery stores now, too, and with this national highway right through here, we even got some tourists camps. One coming into town from the east and one on the west."

"Oh, that's just fine and noble!"

"Sure is. The lumber is all cut out, and no more saw-mills here now. The teppentime woods is all worked out too, and if you ask me, it's a demned good thing. The folks, white and colored, that follows that kind of work don't have the kind of money to spend to make good business. I'm glad to see 'em gone from here."

"Oh," Arvay said on a less happier note. "How do folks make they living around here now?"

"Well, new ways of using peanuts has been found, and peanuts is a big money crop around here now. They're raising tobacco in a better way and more of it, and a lots of folks are getting well-off at it. Then this new paved highway through here brings in a lot of business for the hotels and the eating places and rooming houses and taxis. We handle much more money than we used to."

"That's nice," Arvay mumbled.

"Certainly it is!" The taxi man was almost belligerent about it. "We got a Junior Chamber of Commerce now, and it's out to bring more business and more prosperity to Sawley. Why, we even got a daily paper now, and it's doing well. Since the Old Gentleman died and Young Brad Cary took hold of things, some good changes have been made, but a lot of these old fogies and dumb peckerwoods don't like it."

Arvay took sides with the peckerwoods in a timid way.

"Still and all, in the good old days, the folks in Sawley was good and kind and neighborly. I'd hate to see all that done away with."

"Lady! You must not know this town too good. I moved in here fifteen years ago and I done summered and wintered with these folks. I hauled the mud to make some of 'em, and know 'em inside and out. I ain't seen no more goodness and kind-heartedness here than nowhere else. Such another back-biting and carrying on you never seen. They hate like sin to take a forward step. Just like they was took out their cradles, they'll be screwed down in their coffins."

The taxi got under way and proceeded eastward and out of Sawley to where used to be the gate of her old home.

The taxi stopped, and one look at the place, and Arvay began to draw back from old times right away. With her own modest but modern home as a yard-stick, the Henson place was too awful to contemplate. And people who held to old ideas shocked her most unpleasantly in the person of her own sister, whom she identified in that ton of coarse-looking flesh sitting on the dilapidated old steps in a faded cheap cotton dress and dirty white cotton stockings.

Larraine was taking a dip of snuff as the taxi drove up, a habit that Arvay abominated, and which she had not seen for years. Larraine lowered her snuff-box, looked the taxi up and down and from end to end with a kind of distaste, and did not seem to recognize the passenger. Larraine just looked with sullen eyes. Her gray hair was bobbed and untidy. Her eyes said that there was nothing in the taxi that she wanted to see at all.

Arvay stood on the ground beside the taxi and revealed herself.

"Why, hello there, Larraine! Look like you don't know me."

Even so, Larraine did not greet Arvay directly. She turned her head off to the right and said, "Carl, Arvie done come. That's her."

A soiled, heavy-set man jerked his head out from under the hood of an unbelievably battered old Model T and flung his heavy features towards Arvay, standing beside the taxi. No! This drab creature could not be the once neat and self-assured Carl Middleton. His face marred and his body shaped by making too many humble motions. His face showed that he was not glad to see her for a moment, then was re-arranged to suit his words.

"Why, hello, little sister! So you did get here, eh?"

Arvay replied in kind, but she was thinking, "If that chuckle-head of yours was a hog head, I'd be willing to work for it for a solid year. Good God! I wonder if I have changed as bad as they have!"

"You want your things put off *here?*" the taxi-man asked and looked at the house and the people.

"Why, yes. Would you be so good and kind as to place 'em on the porch for me?"

Neither Carl nor Larraine said one word of encouragement. There was a loaded and waiting silence as their eyes watched the transfer of the luggage from the car to the dilapidated porch. Larraine did not move out of the way, except to slide a trifle to one side. The man had to scrouge past her.

Arvay had to do the same. Larraine looked upwards at her as she passed. Arvay went on into the narrow hallway, and stood looking in through the open door of the parlor when she heard shuffling steps back of her, and turned to see the shapeless mass and bulk of her sister coming heavily up the steps behind her, followed closely by Carl.

Arvay noted the museum-like arrangement of the parlor in the brief pause before she went on into her mother's room across the hall. She could see and recognize most of the things that she and her husband had sent Maria Henson in the last few years, arranged for display. The strange quiet made her fear that her mother was already dead, and that they hated to tell her. As she turned from the parlor door, she glimpsed two female faces peering at her from the back porch. Those would be Larraine's two daughters. They were mule-faced and ugly enough, Arvay decided as she stepped across the sill of her mother's room. Even in a croker-sack, Angeline would look like their mistress.

The room was very dim and still even in the bright light of early afternoon. Arvay could hear two things: the rattle of cook-pots in the kitchen, and the squeak and patter of rats in the walls. What was worse, she could smell the strong odor of rat-urine over everything. She flew a little angry that Larraine and all those grown children she had, had let things get into such a shape. Her mother was a yellowed picture of skull and skin sunk down in a deep feather pillow in the middle of the bed. She seemed to be asleep or dead. Arvay could detect no movement of any kind. She tipped to the head of the bed and leaned over.

"Mama!"

Instantly the old eyes flew open. One claw-like old hand came from under the cover. The face turned a little towards Arvay, and the old eyes peered.

"Arvie," came over eagerly, but unwilling to believe.

"It's me, Mama. Don't you know me?"

Just then, Larraine and Carl entered and took up positions at the foot of the bed. The old woman seemed not to see them, as she concentrated on the face bending over her. Then recognition, or rather assurance, came into her eyes. The old hand caught Arvay's lower arm, and the old head sank back on the pillow with a blissful smile.

"I winned! I winned!" Maria said weakly. "I lasted out until my baby child got to me. I begged my God to spare me, and

276

He did. But every occasionally, I was skeered I wouldn't make it."

"Mama, you're mighty sick," Arvay exclaimed in alarm, looking down into the face intently. One hand felt the old forehead for fever. "How long you been sick like this?"

"Going on nearly a month, now, Arvie. I was took down awful sick."

"How come you didn't let me know before now, Mama?"

The old eyes looked towards the foot of the bed and then closed.

"I thought that you knowed all the time, and just couldn't see your way clear to come. I didn't feel no ways slighted about it, Arvie. You done took care of me so good ever since your Paw died, till I knowed it wasn't that you didn't care, you just couldn't spare no time to come."

"Why, I just got the wire yesterday evening, Mama, and caught that mid-night train. I'd of been here too long to talk about if I had of known you was sick and needed me."

"Them telegraph folks must be acting mighty loose and careless these days." Carl jumped in very quickly. "I sent you word over three weeks ago. Don't see how it could of missed you like that."

"Never mind," Maria muttered and closed her eyes again. "My baby is here with me now, and you and Larraine will kindly excuse yourselves so I can be with Arvie a spell. I'll call you if I need anything."

Larraine went out slowly, and Carl let her pass him, then followed sullenly, stretching the room door back to the wall as he left.

"Close to that door!" Maria ordered in the strongest voice that she had used so far. "I hates for folks to be standing around eavesdropping me."

Arvay closed the door and came back to the bed.

"I left a paper with Bradford Cary to place in your hands, Arvie, in case I might be gone when you got here."

"A paper?"

"Yeah, a paper fixing things so you could come into this

277

place all by yourself without no trouble of any kind. Mr. Cary fixed it up for me as tight as bees-wax, and it's in his hands until it passes into yourn. He's sure been nice and kind."

"Bradford Cary?" Arvay's face and voice showed her surprise. "How on earth did he come to be helping you out so?"

"Now, 'tain't a thing stuck-up about Bradford Cary, Arvie. Just as easy to get along with as poor folks. Drove out to see me soon's he got back from New O'leans where Kenny played so good and told me all about it. His youngest boy was playing in that same band, and he went over there to hear it and come back bragging on Kenny. Set right down in my parlor and talked with me. Every time he seen anything in the paper about Kenny, he come out and read it to me, and talked with me."

"Well!" Arvay breathed out. "I never would of thought it of Bradford Cary, but I sure think it was mighty white of him to do it. I got to see him and thank him."

"Do that. And when he seen how Carl and Larraine was using me, hanging around just like turkey buzzards to get out of me any little change that I might git hold of, which was what you and Jim was sending me by the month, and then didn't do nothing for me, and I told him that I wanted you to have the place when I was gone, he took and fixed me up that paper so that they couldn't git hold of a thing. You go straight to him and git it when I'm gone."

"Thank you, Mama, that is, if I should happen to be the longest-liver. You might be the one to close my dying eyes."

"Naw, baby, I ain't here for long. All I could do to hold out till you could come. I know so well them limbs of Satan never sent you no word to come. They was laying round here waiting for me to die so they could move in here and take everything. Carl ain't made nothing worth mentioning for ever so many years. Long time ago folks let him know that they didn't want to hear him preach, and he won't do no kind of work, and so his family is terrible absent of things. Just living off of me, all they was able. Disfurnishing me of the little money you sent me, and piling in here and destroying up the groceries I buy to carry me along from one time to the next one. That's all they's fitten for. Stuff they trashy guts and lay 'round like gators in the sun."

"I can't say that I feel good towards them for doing you like that, Mama. But if they's as hard up as all that, you can make over this place to Larraine if you want to. I can't say that I'm in any pressing need."

"Naw I ain't going to do it nothing of the kind. I wouldn't even give 'em air if they was stopped up in a jug, the no-manners way that they have treated me. Me here old and sick, and ain't able to do nothing for myself, and them with they hands out all the time to take from me. Larraine is done had more than her share. Naw."

"All right then, Mama, have your way. I sure can't feel good towards them for not letting me know."

The old woman tried to speak, hiccoughed several times instead, and nodded her head. When she was able to speak again, she beckoned Arvay to hold closer.

"Feel right here under this bed-tick, baby. Git it out and take it with you."

Arvay felt between the feather tick and the supporting shuck mattress, and drew out a large Manila envelope. She drew out first, two large, slick-printed unmounted photographs. One was of Kenny with his guitar in his hand standing beside a microphone. It was signed, *From Kenny to his darling Grandmother.* The other was a picture of Kenny with his guitar in a playing-position standing in front of the New York band. In both cases, he had that smile on his face. Dressed in a fine-fitting tuxedo and looking very rich. There was a blue rectangle of paper in there too. A money-order for twenty-five dollars made out to Maria Henson and signed by Kenny Meserve.

"This is noble of Kenny, Mama."

"Wasn't it though? Never forgot his old Grandma at all, up there with all them rich folks."

"When did you get it, Mama?"

"The day before I took down sick. No chance to do nothing

279

with it. And I didn't want them gluttonous varmints to git they hands on it, so I stuck it under me here in the bed. You take it and do what you see fit."

"All right, Mama."

"And he sent all that without me even asking him for a thing. All I done was to write him a loving letter. Mr. Cary wrote it off to Kenny for me, and he upped and done all that. Your chillun's got plenty soul and heart in 'em, Arvie. Look how Angie sends me things every Christmas, and fine things too. You and Jim sure is raised your chaps to be nice and kind. 'Tain't that a'way with Larraine nor none of her whelps."

The old woman gulped and hiccoughed again, and caught Arvay's arm and tried to pull herself into a sitting position, peering pleadingly into Arvay's eyes.

"Arvay, you been ever nice and good to me, but I got to beg one more favor of you whilst I'm still on pleading terms with mercy. I hope that you can see your way clear to grant it."

"If it's in my poor weak power, Mama, it's already granted. Tell me, and if I can do it, I sure will."

"Arvie, I know that I don't amount to much. Just one of them nothing kind of human things stumbling around 'mongst the toes of God. Ain't seldom had, nor neither done what I desired. It wasn't for me to have and to do. My footprints'll be erased off before my head is hardly cold. But, don't care for that, Arvay. I would dearly love to be put away nice, with a heap of flowers on my coffin and a church full of folks marching around to say me 'farewell.' I know that they won't care one way or another, baby, but I sure would love to die knowing that they'd be there just the same. To make pretend-like I'm mighty missed. And please, Arvie, baby, don't take me right from this house to the graveyard and finish with me. Take me to the church and pass me around."

"I'll do it, Mama, just like you say, that is, if I'm the longest-liver. You can put your dying dependence in me."

"Thankee, baby. It's four whole days till Sunday come next, and that's a mighty long time to hold anybody over. But working folks don't have no time during the week days to be at leisure. . . ."

"Don't care what day of the week you might die, Mama dear, you'll be held over and put away on a Sunday. I'll have big services held over you on a Sunday so everybody that wills can come."

With Arvay perched by one hip beside the pillow and stroking her hand, Maria sank back down in the depths of her pillows with a look of utter rapture on her sunken face. Her toothless mouth had caved in so deeply that the nose and chin seemed about to meet. Arvay saw the thin lips work as if they tasted some delicious morsel as Maria closed her old eyes. There was a look of great triumph, as if the shabby old woman had vanquished life after all.

After a time the old woman stirred, and the second time she seemed to be trying to say something. Unable to understand the faint mumblings, Arvay tried to interpret for her mother.

"Want me to call Larraine for you, Mama?" And Arvay got up quickly to go, but the thin bony old hand clung to hers and held her back. Arvay sensed that it was some satisfaction at her presence that Maria was still trying to express. The muttering and gurgling went on for some minutes, then Maria belched, worked her lips for a moment and was very quiet. Stroking the old hand for a while, Arvay finally looked down and began to look for signs.

Arvay saw that the spark of life was gone, and quickly tipped to the door and called in Larraine. By the time that Larraine, Carl, and the three grown children who were with her assembled in the room of death, Arvay had solemnly folded her mother's tired arms, and was fishing two pennies out of her change purse to close the eyes. She sobbed as she leaned over and performed the rite, not for the passing of the old woman who was old and tired, but that the eyes she was closing forever had looked upon so little that had been joyful. Maria had passed a lonesome visit to this world.

Larraine joined in the crying and dropped down heavily on the foot of the bed, then got up hurriedly either from the

281

thought of sacrilege or fear of the dead, and sat on the big wooden box that held Maria's quilts. Belatedly, her children joined in the keening. "Poor Double-Maw! Poor Grandmaw! Dead and gone! Done left us here behind! Dead and gone! Dead and gone!"

It was a measured mourning like the slow strokes of a tolling bell for death, and without sing, like the slack head of a drum. It was the traditional chant.

Arvay began to straighten out the covers on the bed a little more and said in a kind of a whisper, "Next thing, we got to see about putting Mama away." The sobbing cut off instantly as if on signal, and they all moved slowly towards the door, as if afraid of being overheard by the shell of life on the bed with the two coppers holding down the eyelids. Arvay, being near the head of the bed, was the last to leave the room. She literally pursued the others outside in the backyard near the wash-pot where they had halted as around a family hearth.

Larraine began to cry hard and deep, and Arvay was touched to her heart. She ran towards 'Raine with open arms, and Larraine met her half way. They clung tight to each other and cried and patted each other with fondness.

"Don't cry so, 'Raine," Arvay consoled. "Mama lived out her time, and she's just gone to her rest. Don't cry after her so hard."

" 'Tain't that so much, Arvie, you child. It's the fix I'm in. I ain't got a thing to bury Maw with. Oh, Arvie, honey, you don't know what I been through! I ain't hardly got changing clothes. Not a dust of meal nor flour in the barrel. Out there in them scrub-oaks where we live ain't hardly fitten for a dog! But I didn't mean to leave Maw lay there and let the rats eat her whilst we went round begging up enough money to put her away. We might git hold of a few boards, and I could git Carl to knock together some kind of a box to bury Maw in. Make her a grave down there in the back of the place like."

"Aw, my God!" Arvay shuddered at the picture. "Don't fret about that part no more, 'Raine. I'm putting Mama away and putting her away very nice. You don't have to bother yourself at all."

"It sure is a help-out, Arvie. Things have been mighty hard with me."

Arvay remembered the mention of groceries, and went for the bill-fold tucked away in the slot in her hand-bag. Fired with sisterly concern and pity, Arvay opened the bill-fold, riffled through until she came to some smaller bills and impulsively handed Larraine a ten. From little economies, from Jim, from Kenny, from Angeline and Hatton, Arvay had over a thousand dollars in her pocket-book. This was her stake for life when she had boarded the train in Citrabelle.

"Buy yourself some groceries with that, 'Raine. I reckon that'll be sufficient to carry you over the funeral. Then we can talk things over and figger out some better way for you."

Arvay smoothed down the pack of paper money to replace it. She paid no attention to the hungry way that Carl had stared at it, and the two or three steps that he had taken nearer her for a better look.

"Well then, Arvie, since you going to take care of all the expenses, you have the man to make you out a bill, and when Carl gets to pastoring another sizeable charge, we'll be only too glad to pay you back our part."

"We ain't got no part to pay, 'Raine. Your Mama saw fit not to leave you nothing, but to make over this whole place to your sister, so naturally it's her place to put her away. I ain't got nothing to do with the mess."

Arvay turned towards Carl "I haven't asked 'Raine nor you to spend one cent on putting Mama away. I promised her that I would do it, and I'm not a'going to back out on my word. I'd rather to give 'Raine than to take from her."

"I hope that you don't call that little piece of change that you handed 'Raine money, not with all you got to do with. The more some folks gets their hands on, the more grasping and mean they gets. Naw, I'm clean out of this burial business and I aim to stay out of it. 'Raine, you can act with no sense at all. Give your sister leave to run into town and run up a bill

283

for maybe over a hundred dollars, then look for me to pay half of it and more, when she's got vast money, and then this place on top of that. You take my name right out of it, and leave it out."

"Who asked you to go into any debt to bury Mama?" Arvay snapped. "I'm positive-certain I didn't, because I know so well that you ain't got nothing to do it with. I come prepared to do whatever was necessary to be done. I got a *husband!* He covers the ground he stands on. He ain't never let me know what a hard day means."

Arvay was halted by something that leaped up into Carl's brown eyes. Before, he had merely been peevish and surly. Now he looked insulted and fiery mad.

"As my sister's husband, all I thought of asking for you to do would be to drive in town and notify the funeral home to come and get Mama and prepare her for the burial. If you'll kindly do that, I won't ask nothing more of you."

"Then let that rich and noblefied husband of yours run into town for you. I sure ain't a'going to do it. And my wife ain't a'going and none of my children neither. We got to come under humble submission to you and take your orders I reckon. Put your foot in the road and walk if you want any messages toted."

Arvay stood wordless and amazed at the way things had turned out, and the fierce behavior of Carl. She looked from one to the other of the group to try and find the answer. Did she glimpse a quiet gloating look on Larraine's face? For a second she thought that Larraine looked ever so glad about the falling-out.

"I don't see no need for all this carrying on over nothing." Arvay spoke with calm out of her puzzlement. "I didn't come here to run the hog over nobody, and to hurt nobody's feelings. If I have, I didn't mean to, and I'm sorry to my heart."

"That's what I say," Larraine exclaimed heartily, and crossed to Carl and flung one arm about his shoulders. "With Mama laying in there on her cooling-board, you all ought not to be fussing and carrying on."

284

Arvay noted that 'Raine did not urge Carl to go to town, however. Instead, she began to drag him off towards the kitchen. Arvay felt too that her way of pacifying Carl exaggerated things. "Come on in here, sweet dumpling, and lemme fix you a cup of coffee and a little snack to eat. You know better than to let yourself get all fretted up like that! Don't care what nobody else do to you, you know that I'm always with you."

The exasperated Arvay stood and looked behind the two ungainly figures as they reached the back porch and creaked across the boards and disappeared into the kitchen.

"Well, people!" Arvay sighed as she looked around at the slyly grinning faces of her nephew and two nieces and felt her face getting hot. When she passed stomping through the back to get her hat, she saw 'Raine through the kitchen door with her arm about Carl's shoulders giving him pity. Carl was weighing down an old kitchen chair with the back gone, and just taking it. Just like an image being made over. 'Raine acted as if she did not see or hear Arvay when she passed the door. But Carl seemed unable to ignore Arvay's nearness.

"Arvay!" Carl loosed his head from Larraine's fat arm and looked towards the door.

"What is it, Carl?" Arvay halted.

"When you get so that you can speak to me like you ought to, and not like I was some old throwed-away dog, and quit trying to throw up all Jim got in my face, I'll do what you ask me to do. If not, I ain't doing nothing at all."

"You shock my modesty, Carl Middleton, carrying on so ignorant like that, and your wife's Mama laying dead in the house and needing quick attention. Don't do me no favors at all. I can walk to town, and I want you to know that I don't mind doing it, neither. And you keep my husband's name right out of your mouth. Jim ain't got *you* to study about. So far as he thinks about you, you can kiss his high-toned, independent, money-making foot!"

If the look that Carl gave her then had been a bullet, it would have worked her three times before it killed her and

five times after. Arvay whirled on off and went into the bedroom where Maria's body lay on the bed looking so peaceful
in the face.

But the house was not peaceful around her. There was a
mighty kind of scampering, rustling, pattering and gnawing in
the walls and seeming from every direction around converg-
ing on the room. Placing on her hat, Arvay was struck with
such horror that she started to run back to the kitchen and call
on Larraine and them for help. Somebody to stand on the
watchwall and guard until she could get back with the undertaker. But she checked herself and began to consider what she
could do to protect her mother's face and hands from mutila-
tion while she was gone. Arvay pulled up the sheets, the three
heavy quilts and the counterpane over Maria's head and
tucked them all around under her body tightly and snugly
until the corpse looked like a mummy in its wrappings.

Arvay took up her pocket-book and went on out to the gate
with the creeping, jubilant noises in the wall behind her.

A long-nosed, black Cadillac sedan made an almost silent
stop at the gap just as she reached it.

"Hello there, Arvay!" A quiet cultivated voice expressed
sudden pleasure. After a minute, Arvay recognized that Bradford Cary II was greeting her like that.

"Oh, oh, howdey do, Banker Cary."

"Very glad to know that you're back in town. Thought that
was you I saw in the taxi coming out this way, so I asked the
driver and he told me. I have been in the habit of dropping
out here now and then to see your mother, and as soon as I
could get away after I heard that you were here, why I thought
I'd make two visits in one."

Arvay thanked him shyly, and also for his past goodness to
her mother. Then she told him the news, and of her destination. She was conscious too that by now, all the Middletons
were up around the front of the house where they could look
and listen.

"No need for you to put yourself to all that trouble, Arvay.
We have known each other all *your* life, and we are friends,

286

I'm sure. You just let me take all this bother off your hands. I'll make all the necessary arrangements and give you a chance to rest and settle your nerves. But for God's sake quit calling me Banker Cary like all these Crackers around here. I'm Brad to you, Arvay."

"Okay, Brad." Arvay smiled diffidently. "I leave everything in your able hands, and I thank you all I know how."

"And I know that you have no intention of spending a night in such an awful place as this, Arvay." Cary was looking her clothes and her accessories up and down. "Tell you what you do. I'm going to see the undertaker and make all other arrangements. But first thing, I'm sending that taxi out here to pick you up with your things. I'll speak for a suite at the Stephen Foster for you, and you can walk right in, have a nice hot bath and go to bed. My wife and I will get in touch with you this evening in some way or another. Now, just do as I tell you, and everything will be all right."

The Cadillac moved off smoothly but fast. It almost vanished by the time Arvay looked over her shoulder and back again. In the low voice that Brad used, it would have been next to impossible for any of them to have heard what had been said, but Arvay knew so well that all of them had been looking as hard as they could. She went lightly up the steps and into the house. She looked in on the well-wrapped body, then across to the parlor where her luggage was piled.

Arvay was sad when she looked around the room in there. Her poor mother had been so proud of the presents that she, Jim, and her children had sent from time to time, that they had never been used. They were all there on display—that blue-worked chenille spread with the peacock in the center, the set of dishes that she had asked Jim for six years ago—rowed out on the mantelpiece, table and what-not to the most showy advantage. The bath-robe and bed-room slippers from Angeline. The set of plated silverware that she had sent in Kenny's name two years before because her mother had hinted that she had never owned a piece. House-dresses, tablecloths, bath towels, and things like that. As much as her mother made patch-work quilts, the sewing box with all its fixings had never been touched. The various photographs of the Meserves at different ages were arranged on top of the dilapidated old organ, and around the lamp on the center table.

There was only one object on display which Arvay did not recognize. It was a cheap celluloid soap dish on the lower shelf of the what-not. 'Raine or some of her family must have given Maria that.

Arvay was called from her mood of pity by the honking of the taxi at the door. She ran into the bedroom and retrieved the Manila envelope from Kenny to Maria from where she had hidden it and ran to the front door and asked the taxi-driver to take care of her luggage.

As Arvay was stepping into the taxi, the undertaker's conveyance arrived and Arvay took time to lead the two men into the bedroom and see Maria's body unwrapped and deposited in the basket. The owner of the funeral home was along himself, and most deferential.

"I won't hold you up for but just a minute, Mrs. Meserve. But if you would give us her birth date and such little information, we won't have to trouble you again. Banker and Mrs. Cary said that you were not to be put to no more disturbance than was necessary."

When Arvay had given the dates of birth, marriage and death, full name, maiden and married, the director was satisfied. He asked nothing about Maria's children at all. He acted as if he did not see the Middletons hovering around the front yard.

But suddenly Carl came forward to the edge of the yard.

"I ain't ordering no caskets and no coffins neither!" he announced in a most positive and an accusing way. "Don't be sticking my name on none of your bills. Let the folks pay for 'em that's doing all the flourishing around and talking."

"That they will! And the one that's making *this* bill can evermore do his paying. I don't reckon that Banker Cary will feel it necessary to call on you for no help, Reverend Middleton."

Arvay was astonished, but the sight of all the Middletons coming out from their listening posts at one time took her attention so that she couldn't find a word before Carl burst out.

"Mr. Banker Bradford Cary? I seen him here just a while ago talking with my wife's sister, but what's he got to do with it?"

The undertaker fairly reared back. "Banker Cary is a public-spirited citizen. The late Maria Henson is one of Sawley's oldest and one of its most *respected* citizens. He feels that her passing is more than a family affair. She is an honored and public citizen. Things will be carried out that way."

Arvay waved her sister good-bye and the taxi whirled her away. She had that last look of 'Raine looking wistfully after her, with one fat hand which had been lifted suddenly and spontaneously, being sort of arrested in the air and hanging there. Standing there in the weed-grown yard in her shabby dress, starting to be warm and friendly, then withdrawing herself.

Arvay felt grateful towards her sister as she flash[ed] away. But for 'Raine's intervention, she might have been married to Carl. Been the mother of those awful-looking young men and women that he had fathered. Had to get in the bed with something like that! Do, Jesus! Arvay had no wish to go back out there and run any risk of another run-in with Carl. For some strange reason, he was very mean and bitter against her. But 'Raine had heard where she would be until after the funeral. 'Raine would find some excuse to make it to the hotel. Then they would talk about old times, put hard feelings behind them and be sweet sisters together. Now that they were the only Hensons left, they ought to draw closer together.

But it was Carl whom Arvay saw next day at the hotel.

"Send him on up to my room," Arvay told the bell-hop.

"No Ma'am, Mrs. Meserve. I wouldn't risk that if I was you."

"How come? He's just my sister's husband."

"Yes Ma'am, I know, but he come in here acting and talking so funny that the Boss sent me ahead to bring you a message in private. He says that you better come on down in the lobby so you can have some kind of protection. Mrs. Banker Cary called up lessen an hour ago and said that you was to be looked after real careful and get the best of attention. The Boss don't aim to take no chances on nothing happening to you."

Arvay freshened up and went down and took a seat not far from the desk. She saw Carl rise to his feet from over near the front door. This was a Carl, shabby, but fairly neat. His thinning hair was brushed and laid down with water. Something of the old prideful Carl of nearly thirty years ago was about him. He came towards Arvay with the suspicion of a timid smile on his face.

"Hello, Arvay, I thought that I'd better take this chance of having a talk with you."

"About what?" Arvay asked coldly, the memory of the day before sharply in her mind.

She could see Carl's face change instantly. It got hard, and he sat down abruptly in a chair close by. The manager fiddled with a pen and paid attention.

Carl took a long time to answer. His forearms rested on the chair and his head was thrust forward in deep thought. Finally Carl seemed to whip himself up to a point and said, "I come here in the spirit of good will and compromise, but since you feel to be scornful, I'll let you have it raw. I want that thousand dollars you owe me."

"For what?" Arvay asked astounded. "I hope you don't think that I aim to give you no thousand dollars to compromise on the place. It's mine to do with as I will or may, and I don't have to compromise."

"Oh, it's your place all right, and that's how come you're responsible in a case like this."

"Like what? I don't know what you're talking about."

"Me getting hurt so serious on your place last night."

"You hurt? How did it happen, Carl, and in what way can I be responsible. I wasn't even there."

290

"Matters a difference where you was. You're the owner just the same. I was walking across that old rottened-down back porch of yours that you neglected to fix and a board broke under me and I fell through and got crippled up pretty bad. Your own sister said that I ought to get double that, but I thought that I would come myself and make things easy on you. I'm ready and willing to compromise the thing for a thousand."

"A thousand?" Arvay sat there dumbfounded.

"A thousand hard dollars, and mighty reasonable at that. That ought not to be nothing for your high-toned rich husband to raise."

The manager cleared his throat to attract Arvay's attention, rustled some papers and shook his head for her to say nothing.

"Oh, er, Mrs. Meserve, not that I want to butt into your business, but as a hotel man I know something about liabilities. Now, for instance, is Middleton renting your place?"

"No."

"Is he a tenant, that is, working for you and living on your place?"

"No."

"Well, did he come there to visit at your invitation?"

"Naw indeed!" Arvay looked at Carl through narrow eyes. "From what I can learn, he and his family just come there and bunked on Mama."

"Then you don't have to worry about any claims that he might make at all. In fact, he's liable for trespassing on your premises. Turn the matter over to Banker Cary and let him handle things."

Arvay turned a very grateful face to the manager and smiled. "I thank you ever so much for your information." She tensed her body to rise, but the sympathy for the defeated overcame her. Then there was the memory of the neat, virile, vigorous and confident young man that Carl Middleton had been when she first knew him set against the picture of him now. Arvay was full of pity, and fumbled for some way to make him the gift of a small sum. Say fifty dollars, maybe. She nodded her gratitude again at the desk and turned to Carl.

"You say that you're hurt powerful bad, Carl?" And Arvay began to look him over for the signs.

"I said so and I am." Carl snapped.

"I must say that you don't look it to me." Arvay became slightly tart.

"Naturally," Carl retorted sarcastically. "I been *trying* to treat you like a lady. Where I'm hurt at ain't to be exposed in public."

"Oh! I'm mighty sorry to hear that. But still you don't get around like you was hurt too bad nowhere. For me to take any steps at all I would have to know exactly."

"Well, if you'se determined for me to get common with you," Carl sneered and got to his feet, "it's my behind, and could be inside injuries besides for all I know." He took a step towards Arvay. "I guess now you want me to show it to you."

Arvay did not wilt as Carl seemed to expect of her. "Nope," she answered in a matter-of-fact voice. "My Mama always told me not to look on backlands. I'd rather you went to a doctor and let him tell me what is your condition."

"I been trying all I could to save you extra expense."

The manager snorted at that and the two bell-hops sniggered. That enraged Carl more and he glared around the lobby and announced, "I got me a good lawyer who says I don't have to go to all that rigmarole."

"Well then, Carl, you can just go back and tell that lawyer you got that I'm not giving you no thousand dollars, and he can law me for it all he wants to. I'm in no way responsible, but if you're in as bad a fix as you say, I can tell you something mighty good for a case like that. Get hold of some mutton tallow, then melt it and mix it together with some teppentime and grease yourself good back there."

The manager, the bell-hops and three male guests who were seated in the lobby sniggered.

"Teppentime and mutton-grease!" Carl exploded. "I come . . ."

"Yeah, it's mighty healing and dependable," Arvay confirmed earnestly and calmly. "Can't be beat in a case like that. Now, if it was a burn, you would need some baking soda and mix it good with some wet Octagon soap, and you take. . . ."

The laughter was more public this time. Nobody was pretending to hide it. Carl's anger and chagrin and Arvay's earnest manner made it twice as funny. Also it was plain that Arvay did not know that it was funny. She looked at Carl and all around her and went on.

"But I ain't joking. It really is mighty healing. Takes the soreness right out. I keep it on hand all the time. My husband and my . . ." The howls of laughter drowned her out and Carl's angry voice prevented Arvay's taking up again.

"You, you, female hypocrite you! I come here to get satisfaction for being mortal hurt on your rotten property! I didn't come here for you to teach and tell me how to grease my behind!"

"That'll do, Middleton!" the manager said sternly. A quick look passed between him and the burly porter who had been ostentatiously polishing the brass plates on the swinging doors that led into the dining-room. The porter straightened up and made ready to move forward. The bell-hops went on the alert. The manager came out from behind the desk and took a commanding stand. "I said *that will do!* You have got beside yourself, entirely. Mrs. Meserve is much too important to be handled carelessly, and anyhow, this hotel does not allow loose talk in front of ladies. You have worn out your welcome, and we'd much rather have your space than your company."

Carl glared and frowned at the manager and looked as if he felt to fight, but he went on out without another word. Arvay thought that Carl looked whipped and pitiful as he shuffled out through the big doors. She saw him walking slowly and with his head down as he passed the wide window. The manager stood like a victorious champion of protection until Carl was good and gone, then comforted Arvay.

"You don't need to fret about being sued, Mrs. Meserve. You sued by him! That's a joke. When Banker Cary got through with him it would be manners and behavior. Ha!"

"I can't see what made him come here and carry on like that. To save my soul, I can't make him out," Arvay said in genuine confusion.

"Oh, the fool is stuck on you, Mrs. Meserve. Sweet on you and cutting the fool."

"Sweet on me?" Arvay looked around in astonishment. "He sure got a funny way of showing it."

"Oh, he just thought up that mention of money after you treated him so cold. Started to blabbing soon as he got in here about how he courted you when he first came to town."

"Courted *me?* Why, this is my first time even hearing of such a thing."

"Oh, nobody's paying his talk any mind, but that's what he claims. Said that you were so young that you might not understand and he tried to court you through your sister, but you sent word back and turned him down."

Arvay gave a gasp. "I sent word? Why, he's raving crazy." But the phrase said something to Arvay.

"He could be lying, or you never got the message one," the manager said off-hand. "Anyhow he claims that he lost interest in being a big man when he missed you, and lost interest in everything when you married. Makes out that he would have amounted to a whole lot if he could have married you." The manager's lips twisted in scorn and disbelief. "Oh, he ain't just started this whining about you. I've been told that he's been whispering it around for ever so many years. Must have made his poor wife feel mighty fine to hear a thing like that."

Arvay flushed to her hairline. "Never heard nothing as crazy as that in all my born days. Married to my own sister and acting like that. His feelings may be serving him all right, but his common sense must be gone astray."

"Crazy as a bed-bug," the manager agreed sympathetically. "So you see why I couldn't let him up to your suite and you be in there with him by yourself. No telling what the fool might try to do. I figure him out to be plumb crazy."

"I help you to say," Arvay chimed in with a nervous laugh and hurried off to her room.

Arvay fell on her face across the bed and laughed hysterically. It was too funny. Weak as she was, Carl believing that she could prop him up. Wanting to lean on her small strength! Larraine whom she had always looked upon as so self-satisfied feeling so frail of her chances that she needed to steal herself a husband from Arvay. Then both Carl and Larraine felt themselves less than she was. Maybe there were a lot of weak-feeling folks in the world. Weak as she herself was, it was strange to know that people had been depending on her. They must believe that she could hover them.

Still on her stomach across the bed, Arvay reached for a pillow and snuggled it under her head. So Carl claimed that he had sent her a message about marriage. Even if it was true, Arvay had no resentment nor felt any loss. Poor Larraine! No need at all for Carl to ever know the difference, but it was a pitiful thing. Now, he comes hunting her after all these years for a consolation and all she has on hand to give him is some teppentime and mutton-tallow to grease his behind. Teppentime and tallow. If Carl had loved her sure enough all these years as he said, it was a curious end to a long-time love affair. However, poor, poor Larraine! Poor Carl too. Life had funny ways.

CHAPTER 25

"N"othing left for me to wish for except that I wish poor Mama could see how she's being put away."

Arvay looked at the glass-sided hearse, the lavender casket inside that opened out like a couch and the smother of floral pieces. And all the people that old Maria could have wished for were there to pass around and say her a last farewell.

Bradford Cary had really made a big thing of putting Maria Henson away. Arvay was touched and pleased. Her mother's dying wish had been realized. With wet eyes, Arvay went through the funeral with satisfaction and gratitude in her heart. She could not fathom the kindness and goodness of it all, but she was not probing and asking questions of herself nor anybody else. It was so, and that was enough for her. Arvay did not know that the urge to hold public office had been growing in Bradford Cary for the last two years. But he had to look like a man of the people and he was too well known as a monied aristocrat. The association of his youngest son with Kenny in the University band had given Cary an idea, and he had followed it up by cultivating Maria Henson. Months before her death it had spread around Sawley and the county in general of Cary's kindness to her and his attachment for her. Her grandson, Kenny, was assumed to be his product and protégé. Poor people began to think mighty well of Bradford Cary II. He was a big man who made himself one of them. That was ever so much better than one of them trying to make a big man of himself. They began to say that a man like that ought to be in office and looking after their affairs. Cary let on that he was surprised at such a thought and lingered back. Many people began to push and shove him forward.

Maria's death gave him his opportunity and he took it. The local paper gave great publicity to her passing as an old and worthy citizen. The kind of citizen who was the foundation and backbone of our great nation. Clean-living, plain, honest and a devoted Christian. The common people saw themselves glorified in Maria and they loved it. That Bradford Cary was standing the expenses of the big funeral was spread by mouth. It went faster when it was understood that Cary had refused to let it be put in the paper. He was a good-hearted man who wanted no credit for what he had done.

But even if Arvay had known about the skillful manipulation, she would not have cared any more than Maria would have. Everything had been done in a fine and handsome way. Bradford Cary II had spread his prestige like a gold-worked coverlet over Maria Henson and sent her to rest as she had wished and more. Arvay was moved to her foundations and satisfied. If only her mother could see the hundreds of cars, the casket, the flowers, and the long, long line of people passing around her casket and looking down in her face!

Arvay felt sad at her mother's death, but she returned from the cemetery with happy satisfaction. A sacred promise had been kept. A dying plea had been granted. Maria, who had lived on scraps and crumbs all her life had been put away like a queen. It was some payment for all that she had missed. Bradford Cary, who had never noticed her when she was growing up, now chose to be her friend. The proof was all around her. Introductions to big and important people, dinners and taking all care and worry off her hands. Then putting her mother away the way he did. No, Arvay would not have welcomed any pulling-down whispers about the Bradford Carys.

And with her the feeling lasted. Nearly a year later she read of his entry in the gubernatorial race with great pride and pleasure. When he won, she looked upon it as a personal triumph. She had no idea what a part she had played in Florida politics. She did not realize that she had helped to make a governor of the state.

One thing she did know, however. She came away from her mother's funeral changed inside. Big, book-learnt people had seemed glad to know her and had treated her very nice. They said praising things to her and made her ever so welcome. They complimented her on being a fine wife and mother and seemed to find nothing wrong with her. Maybe she was not as bad off as she had thought she was. It made her feel to hold up her head and to look upon herself.

What put her ahead of Larraine and the other girls who had come along with her? Seemed like it was Jim Meserve. She had caught the choicest man of them all. How had she managed to do it? The only thing that she could see was her face and her body, and maybe Jim liked her ways too. Then it could be that she wasn't too ugly after all, and her difference from the girls she used to envy was not a mistake as she had thought. Perhaps Jim's hankering after her was not such a burden to bear when she looked around at the lives of her old friends. Certainly the afternoon of her life was more pleasant than the morning had been.

CHAPTER 26

onday had been in town many hours when Arvay
opened her eyes. She saw that it was ten o'clock by
her watch. Arvay had had a good sleep and sat up in
bed at peace and agreement with the world. She was full of
resolution. She was willing to take the blame for any variance
with Larraine and Carl and shoulder the job of straightening
things out.

With a breakfast of broiled country-cured ham, fried eggs,
hot soda biscuits with country butter, and coffee inside her,
Arvay set out to make a move. The tasty ham put her in the
mind of something. She would make 'Raine the present of a
big ham along with a pile of other groceries. Enough to do the
family for a whole month and then slip her sister twenty-five
dollars for spending change. No sense in two sisters not being
thick friends and depending on one another. Arvay considered that she would be wrong to hold anything against 'Raine
and Carl. Not having, and never having things made people
do things and act in ways that they wouldn't if they ever had
anything that they wanted. If she could make it up with Jim,
maybe it would be a good thing to talk him into sending for
the family and finding Carl and his two sons something to do.
Why, they could live in the house in the grove! The very
thing.

Arvay felt a happy giving off as she went into the store. She bought a large ham for Larraine and pictured 'Raine's face when she drove up with the load of good groceries that Arvay was taking to her. It was on a second thought that Arvay ordered three more hams to be shipped to her at Citrabelle. She explained to the clerk that you couldn't cure country meat down where she lived. Too warm all the year round. She ordered a bag of paper shell pecans as a present for Jeff and Janie. Let them know that she appreciated them too. Maybe Jeff was not snappy for just nothing. He was not that way with Jim and the children. The fault could be in her. She would show him that she meant him well. Then she ordered one packed for 'Raine and two more shipped to her home. On top of the cases of canned goods and staples that she ordered delivered to 'Raine, Arvay bought a fat hen for chicken dumplings and a lot of fresh stuff to go along with it. She and 'Raine would fix a good dinner and they would all eat together for the first time in many years and have a good time together. Then Arvay remembered how they used to love fried round steak for Sunday morning breakfast and turned back and bought five pounds of top of the round to take with her.

A pleasant picture from her childhood came up before her. The Henson kitchen of a Sunday morning. A pot of soft grits on the back of the stove all ready and waiting. Big pan of biscuits made out and ready to shove into the bake-oven at the last minute. Quart bottle of molasses on the table and the dish of country butter. Big black iron skillet with grease in it waiting for Maria to get through pounding the steak with the hammer. The steak salted, sprinkled over with heavy black pepper and beat and beat until it was tender, then doused in flour and dropped into the hot pan to fry. Thick brown steak gravy with onions in it to go with the grits. Yes, they would have a good old-fashioned Sunday breakfast together. Then after that, she would make 'Raine come into town with her and pick out a couple of decent dresses, and a few other things to wear. 'Raine was bound to feel a lot better when she had silk stockings and got fixed up to look like something.

With the box of groceries loaded in the taxi, Arvay rode along the road happily noting the scene of things. The woods had not the lush, exotic look of south Florida, but there was a sturdy green fullness that was pleasing. Nowhere in the world, Arvay considered, did oak trees grow so fine. The dogwood that she missed in south Florida, the crêpe myrtle and rambler roses before a door. They didn't do well down south and she wished that they would.

"If you will be so kind as to set that box of groceries on the porch for me," Arvay told the driver at the gate, "you needn't never mind waiting for me." Arvay paid the man and tipped him. "I'm mighty much obliged to you."

The taxi drove off and left Arvay standing in the shabby yard and beaming towards the door.

Arvay waited for a sign of life, and seeing none decided that the place looked mighty quiet, and that everything was closed up so. Carl's wreck of a car was nowhere to be seen, and no smoke coming out of the chimney. They must have run into town for something. She might as well go on in and start the cooking.

The door was closed, but it was not locked. There had been no key to it in Arvay's memory. She turned the door-knob and went inside. The first thing that she noticed was that the old sewing machine was gone out of the hall, and the hat-rack was missing. That made Arvay jerk her head around to look inside the parlor, and she could hardly believe her eyes.

There was nothing in there except that relic of an organ, which had been nothing for years but a rat's nest. Yes, there was something else, but it hurt Arvay's heart to see it. All the pictures of the Meserves were there, mutilated, and trompled on the floor.

The scene was the same in every room. The house had been cleaned out of everything. Even the backless chair in the kitchen was gone. One old fork with the tines bent was lying against the wall, probably overlooked.

The back porch was just a framework. All the sound boards had been ripped off and hauled away. Only the three or four

301

rotten boards were left. The wash-pot was gone out of the backyard, and the three wooden wash-tubs from the wash-place.

In deep anguish, Arvay moved about, stumbling through the brittle dead weeds of the past summer, and suffering without words and without tears. Her soul was sunk in defeat. Her sense of accomplishment was gone. Both she and her dead mother had been robbed and defeated. All that fine funeral was in vain. Perhaps her mother had not got off in her high journey after all. Held back from her flight by such low-lifeted doings. No doubt Maria would get to creeping into 'Raine's shabby shack between midnight and day to frighten the fatal life out of the rascals. Arvay hoped that it would happen. Then no, she didn't. She didn't hope any such thing. She wanted her mother to be at rest at last. She had had enough of dirty, poverty-paralyzed places. Immortal Glory was where she ought to be, and setting down.

Arvay stumbled around, farther and farther away from the house crying, "Mama! Mama! Please don't fault me. I done the best that I know how." Then tears began to run from her eyes. She came to the pear tree that was the farthest to the west and looked down. There was trash piled up around it. She went to the other one, and the big fig tree and looked. They were all the same.

"They're gone, but they aim to come back, I see, and set these trees on fire."

Arvay was scattering the trash away from the trees when her neighbor to the east waved a hand at her and came through the fence. She was a woman about ten years younger than Arvay's mother, and had always been there next to them. She spoke to Arvay very warmly, and there was something peculiar in her eyes.

"You expecting to see your sister and her fambly, I reckon, ain't you?"

"Well, I sort of was."

"I reckon then that you didn't know that they moved out last Thursday. Sort of soon in the morning like. Got some man

302

that raises hogs across the river to come with his truck and carry the things off for 'em. Bright and soon in the morning, it was."

With her hands propping up her lean shoulders by resting on her pelvic bones, the gray eyes bored at Arvay and told her that she understood things. Arvay didn't open up so the neighbor could talk, so she dropped another feeler.

"I was in to see your Maw pretty occasionally after she took down sick in the bed, fetching along a mouthful of chicken soup, and a few soft things that I figgered her stomach could handle. Every time she would be expecting you, and wishing for you to come. I was mighty glad when I seen that you was here."

"And I would of been here long time before if I had of been notified. I got the message that she was sick, and caught the train that very night."

The woman looked at Arvay with belief and pity, then glanced down at the pear tree.

"Look like somebody was getting ready to burn you out in case that you stayed around here and moved in." She wound up the gray ball of hair at the back of her head. "But I don't reckon that it would happen if you was to go on home. They would treasure them pears and them figs after they was living on the place."

"But they'll never live here, Miss Hessie. Mama didn't want it, and she must of had her reasons, and I don't intend to allow it."

"Them was your Maw's wishes all right. I know it to be a fact. She loosed 'Raine and her fambly, long time before she took down sick. You wouldn't be doing the right thing to whip around and go against her wishes."

"Don't you worry, Miss Hessie. It'll never come to pass. I'll fix it so that even when I die they won't go over Mama's wishes like they please. I don't know just exactly how to go about it, but if any way can be found, they'll never make it."

"With the right kind of folks on this place, it could come to be real pretty, but not wishing to hurt your feelings about

303

your folk . . . Oh, I can readily see that you'se different from them all the way. Don't seem like you was ever born in the same fambly. I hope and trust that they didn't take off Sister Maria's memory-things. She wanted so for them not to come nigh 'em. I know that they wasn't brash enough to take *them* outa that house."

Arvay nodded her head miserably without speaking, and Miss Hessie's eyes flew wide open. "Naw, Arvay, naw! You don't mean to tell me! I can't believe that unlessen I go see it with my own eyes."

Without a word, Arvay turned and led the way to the house. Miss Hessie groaned when she saw the back porch. She grunted and grunted as they went around the house and entered by the front door.

"This looks like groceries you fetched along, too. Umph! Umph! Umph! All that good eatings for folks to do you like that."

Miss Hessie was utterly outraged when she stood in the empty parlor.

"If it was me, nothing would do me but to call the high Sheriff and stuff they rusty hides in jail! That's good enough for 'em, and just what I would do, too."

"Oh, Miss Hessie, I feel so outdone I don't know exactly what I aim to do. Come on back outside. I hate to look at it no more'n I can help. Poor, poor Mama! Her life-time memories being wallowed and dogged out in a hog-pen!"

"Send the high Sheriff to get 'em back. That's what I sure would do."

"But what would be the use, Miss Hessie? By now, I'll bet they ain't fitten to look at. Slums like them would just as soon scour the floor with Mama's tablecloths as not. It's just like my husband says. He says folks makes a bad mistake when they call places slums. He says folks are the slums instead of the places they live in. Places don't get nasty and dirty and low-down unlessen some folks make 'em like that. Place some folks in what is called slums and they'll soon make things look like a mansion. Place a slum in a mansion and he'll soon have it looking just as bad as he do. It ain't right to blame it on the place. Leave land alone by itself, and it'll grow up into trees and flowers. It don't grow up into slouchy people."

"You sure is telling the truth there, Arvay. Much as 'Raine and Carl and all them big grown children was around here, just look at this place! And it looks even worse now with this big highway passing right by here. This shackly old house tore down, and a little care, and your place could be made to look mighty pretty."

They were out on the porch again, and Miss Hessie stood over the box of groceries and looked down.

"You got fresh meat in here, ain't you, Arvay? I know that you was expecting for it to be used right away, but you got disappointed in them not being here. I better take it on over home with me and fix it for you. By the time you get through messing around over here, you might have a good appetite."

"That's a fine idea, Miss Hessie. Make use of everything except that ham and them pecans. I'll take them down home with me. I'll come and eat with you all, if you don't mind."

"You know so well that we'll be only too glad to have you. My grand-boy, Orrie is home right now. I'll send him to tote that box over for me."

Arvay liked Miss Hessie fine, but right at this time, she was glad for her to go and leave her alone to herself. She tore out immediately for the mulberry tree far down over the brown grass and dead weeds in the back. It was late February, and the huge limbs and limber branches were nude of leaves. They made a pattern of dark lacings against the tepid sky. But soon now, three weeks at the most, tender green leaves would push out of those tight little brown bumps; badges that the tree put on every spring to show that it was in the service of the sun. Fuzzy little green knots would appear. These would turn out to be juicy, sweet, purple berries before the first of May. But most of all, this tree would become a great, graceful green canopy rolling its majesty against the summer sky. Here had been her dreams since early girlhood. Here, in violent ecstasy, had begun her real life.

Like her Mama's keep-sakes, this mulberry tree was her memory-thing. It brought back to her the happiest and most consecrated moments of her lifetime. As with other mortals, life is full of compromises and defeats with few clear victories to show. Here, Arvay, the woman, had triumphed, and with nothing more than her humble self, had won her a vivid way of life with love. This tree was a sacred symbol. She wished that she could use it like a badge and pin it like a bouquet over her heart.

Arvay flung a challenging look towards the highway. There was the world in shining cars; flying and flashing past. The nation crossing and re-crossing before her tree.

But between the tree and the world there stood that house. Now Arvay looked at it with a scrutiny, and darkened. Seeing it from the meaning of the tree it was no house at all. It was an evil, ill-deformed monstropolous accumulation of time and scum. It had soaked in so much of doing-without, of soul-starvation, of brutish vacancy of aim, of absent dreams, envy of trifles, ambitions for littleness, smothered cries and trampled love, that it was a sanctuary of tiny and sanctioned vices. Its walls were smoked over with the vapors from dead souls like smoky kerosene lamps.

By a lucky chance, she had been carried away from it at a fairly young age, but still, its fumes and vapors had stuck to her sufficiently to scar Jim and bruise her children. There was no getting away from it. It was a fact in truth. If it could still hurt and disease her at that distance and for so long a time, how then could she hold things against Larraine who had never been away? Look what it had done to her and to Carl and to their children, and here was another crop about to come off from them. The house had caught a distemper from the people who had lived in it, and had then diseased up people. No, it was no longer just a building. It had caught a soul of its own now. It caught people and twisted the limbs of their minds. What was in its craw gave off a bad breath. It stood between her sign of light and the seeing world. It had just about stifled what the tree had given her. The tree, the servant of the sun, was being made out to be nothing by that ill-deformed brute of a thing. How much had it blinded her from seeing and feeling through the years!

Arvay got to her feet with great deliberation. She stood and looked up through the bare limbs of the tree once and then strode with purpose towards the house. Starting at the back, Arvay walked around it slowly and warily like a battler looking for an opening to charge in for the kill. She circled the place three times. Now and again she could hear frantic squealings and pattering as the dismal and disappointed denizens scurried around seeking something for their hunger. Arvay thought that the sounds just suited the place. It was the voice of the dark, the creeping, the gnawing and destroying. The old house was singing its song.

That determined and answered Arvay. She flung the back door wide with a clang and went inside. From room to room Arvay went gathering up and piling together the trash and rags that had been left behind. There was plenty everywhere. Then she went out in the yard and collected and shoved the masses under the sides of the house, particularly under Maria's old bedroom. Back in the house she started in Maria's bedroom and began to light fires. From room to room she went, and when she saw that they burned clear and swiftly, she ran out and set the piles underneath the house and watched them take on greedily with grim satisfaction. By the time that cars began to halt at a safe distance, and people collect on the highway to watch the fire, Arvay was seated under the mulberry tree. Looking at the conflagration, exultation swept over her followed by a peaceful calm. It was the first time in her life that she was conscious of feeling that way. She had always felt like an imperfect ball restlessly bumping and rolling and rolling and bumping. Now she felt that she had come to a dead and absolute rest.

The dry old house burned furiously, and as Arvay watched the roaring and ascending flames, she picked herself over inside and recognized why she felt as she did now. She was no longer divided in her mind. The tearing and ripping and

307

useless rending was finished and done. She had made a peace and was in harmony with her life. The physical sign of her disturbance was consuming down in flames, and she was under her tree of life. Arvay felt a piercing pain when she thought about her present terms with her husband. It could be that she had stumbled and fumbled around until it was too late to take in the slack. If that was the case, she would never be really happy in her lifetime. But even so, she knew her way now and could see things as they were. That was some consolation.

Arvay sat on and pictured images in the soaring flames. Evil, witchy-looking things formed, growling and twisting in agony, then perished in the cleansing fire and their thin remains were carried off by the smoke. The roof of their old den crashed in with a great roar and the victorious hosts of flames leaped and howled. After a while there was nothing but coals of embers lying low to the ground and panting out gusts of heat. Not a flicker of flame left at last.

Then Arvay got up and walked resolutely over to her neighbor's home. Miss Hessie looked at her for a moment and then told her in an off-hand voice, "Good you got here. Dinner's all ready and done."

"And I'm ready to eat it," Arvay answered and laid her hat and hand-bag on the bench on the back porch.

In the conspiracy of silence, Miss Hessie poured warm water in the wash-basin and handed Arvay a clean towel, then she turned away and put the dinner on the table. The grandson made a pitcher of ice water without asking a word about the fire. The three sat down to the table and helped their plates generously. Arvay shook her head with conviction after the first mouthful and accused Miss Hessie of being a fine cook. Miss Hessie challenged Arvay to try her and see if she was guilty. They all ate hungrily for a while.

"Appears like we had a fire in this vicinity," Miss Hessie remarked casually and helped herself to some water-melon pickle.

"I reckon that I can stand the loss, though," Arvay answered just as off-hand.

"Without a doubt. When you planning to re-build?"

"Re-build? Never to my knowing, Miss Hessie. I can't see that I belong here no more."

"That's right. What would you need a house for here with your husband and your family otherwise. Be much more sensible to sell."

"Don't know as I want to be bothered with that either, Miss Hessie. Take up too much of my time."

"Just leave it lay there and eat you up in taxes?"

"No'm. It sort of come to me to make of it a better use. Brad Cary's got the welfare of this community at heart. . . ."

"He is that. Things have took on and bloomed since he put his shoulder to the wheel here recent. A honest and sincere man. Always looking out for Sawley's advancement. But what did you have in mind?"

"Him and Evelyn, his wife you know, was talking it over with me and some others last night about this town needing a play and a pleasure park, mostly for the young'uns. It come to me since I been setting here that Mama would feel glad to know that the place was all given over to pretty flowers and somewhere for folks to set down and rest. Believe I'll turn it over to Brad and them for what they want to do for a park."

"That would really be a great improvement for Sawley, Arvay. I can't help from wishing, though, that my grand-boy here was old enough to buy it in and handle it. So you cutting loose from Sawley, eh? Never expect to live here again?"

Arvay sat erect and looked Miss Hessie in the eyes.

"Miss Hessie, my husband come along and took me off from that place and planned and fixed bigger things for me to enjoy. Look like I ought to have sense enough to appreciate what he's done, and still trying to do for me, and not be always pulling back here. You've known me ever since I was a baby in my mother's arms. You know all about us. What would I be hanging on to that old place for?"

"Not a blessed thing that I can see, Arvay. Nothing ever was there for a girl like you. And from what I can learn, you have really been blessed. But as I said to Maria over and again,

309

no more than I expected, and no more than you deserve. No use at all in you pulling back here for that little piece of land."

"Oh, I won't, Miss Hessie, except for a visit with friends. Don't you worry about me hanging onto nothing here, more especially since Mama's gone. My last string has done been loosed. It would be a turning back on my travels."

"Yes indeed it would."

"Brad has been noble with me as a friend, and then putting poor Mama away like he did. So I aim to give this place to help out what he's trying to do. Only thing I ask and require is for them to save that mulberry tree and give it every care. I feel sure they'll grant me that."

"Without a doubt. You know I'm along with your Ma, Arvay. If I never see you no more after you leave here this time, I'll remember you in my prayers."

"Do that, Miss Hessie, and I'll do all in my power to take care of things my ownself. No need of wearing God out."

CHAPTER 27

It was late in the afternoon when Arvay arrived home. She stood on the front porch and looked everything over with pleasure. Then she knew what she wanted to do first. Without taking off her hat or considering her luggage piled on the porch, she hurried straight down to the house in the grove. As she neared the house, she recalled the last time that she had been here. It was the night that she had seen Lucy Ann lying on the ground between the house and the privy. But it gave her no painful turn as she had always thought that it would do. Now it was just part of the life that had passed. A storm that she had weathered through. So she did not hesitate and halt. She hailed Jeff and Janie cheerfully as she ran.

They had been taking their comfort and came to the door in their bare feet and stood side by side. They looked at Arvay as she came and then at each other in puzzlement.

"Yeah it's me!" Arvay answered their looks with laughter. "Hello there, Jeff, you old rascal, you! Hi there, Janie!"

Arvay came to the steps and stood there looking up at them and smiling like a child. "You all look like new money in town to me. I sure am glad to see you."

Jeff was defrosted like lightning. He stammered from the rapid change of climate, but his face showed pleasure. "Why, Miss Arvay! We'se real glad to see you back." Jeff could hold out no longer and went all the way. "I was just telling Janie how I wished that you would come on back home."

"Sure was," Janie backed Jeff up, but Arvay could see the lie in Janie's eyes. But she could also see that they were both sincere now in saying that they were glad to see her. To see this kind of Miss Arvay home again.

Arvay braced her hands on her hips and looked up at them. "Well, you no-manners thing! I so well know that Dessie never taught you no kind of manners like that, Jeff. I know Dessie too well for that. You haven't had manners enough about you to ask me in, and if you don't make room in that door, I ain't going to give you what I brought you."

Loving play-acting, they made a great show of making way for Arvay to enter. She stepped in, laughing, shoved Jeff, smacked Janie on her hips and sat down near the door. They were eager to know all about the burial and what all had gone on up there.

Arvay gave them an animated account of the funeral, but left out what she did not wish to remember, that was about how Larraine and Carl had behaved towards her. She dwelt more on the visits and the meals and other entertainments which the Carys had furnished. They were extremely interested, but suddenly Jeff cut her off.

"Who lifted your things inside for you, Miss Arvay?"

"Why, come to think about it, Jeff, nobody did. They're still out on the front porch."

"Oh Lawd, Miss Arvay! Maybe somebody done took 'em already."

"Do, Jesus! I sure hope not, Jeff. Kenny's present to me. You reckon anybody would bother 'em?"

"Sure would. Things ain't like they used to be around here, Miss Arvay. Never no more. Folks passing and re-passing all the time now. I have to watch this grove like a hawk now. Several attempts been made to steal fruit."

"Naw! You don't mean it, Jeff."

"Yes, Ma'am! Only day before yistiddy, three men together was in there just helping theyselves, and to my King oranges

312

at that. With that new settlement right here at us, and that club and all them folks across the bridge, I got my hands full these days. You better gimme the keys to the house and I'll run and see about your things. Be right back."

Arvay was so embarrassed that she had not left the keys with Jeff when she went off, that she hung her head and colored.

"I was so worried about Mama's condition that I clean forgot to hand 'em to you before I went off," Arvay dissembled.

"I thought you must of," Jeff conceded cheerfully. "I had sense enough to know that you wasn't locking up against us, because us Meserves don't mistrust one another. I made mention of it to Janie."

All of the turmoil and uncertainty that Arvay had felt before she went away visited her swiftly for a moment. Jeff hurried off through the sunset, and Arvay sat and fiddled with the edge of the tablecloth for a minute or so before she came to herself and began to describe her mother's casket and the flowers, all of which Janie was more than eager to hear about. Jeff was back very shortly, but Arvay had command of herself by then.

"Jeff, why do you want to make things hard on yourself? You could just as easy have brought the present that I fetched you while you were coming."

"It clear slipped my mind, Miss Arvay. I was too worried about your things and glad to see that they was still there. I put 'em in your bedroom for you. Then again, I didn't know what it was that you wanted us to have."

Then Arvay took an attitude that she would have died before adopting before she went away.

"My dumbness, Jeff. Common sense would of told me that you couldn't read my mind." Arvay stood up gaily. "Come on, you all. Let's all got up to the house and I'll show you what I brought you. I can finish off about the funeral up there."

Arvay watched with a glow while Jeff and Janie made great admiration over the ham and the bag of pecans. Janie was a good-looking brown girl. She turned large soft eyes on Arvay with deep emotions.

313

"I declare, Miss Arvay, but you sure is folks."

"Sure is," Jeff added sincerely. "Just like Mister Jim, ain't she, Janie? And everybody knows that Mister Jim is quality first-class. Knows how to carry hisself, and then how to treat everybody. Miss Arvay's done come to be just like him."

The reflection upon her past condition escaped Arvay in the shine and the gleaming of the present. Her face flushed, and tears came to her eyes.

"Jeff, Janie!" Arvay turned her eyes away to try and hide her feelings. "Why, that's just about the nicest thing that I ever heard in all my born days! It is! I thank you so much for telling me that."

"But it's the living truth," Jeff confirmed with feeling. "You felt for us and remembered us. Made us feel like we amount to something with you. We feel proud and glad to work around you. You'se quality all the way."

Arvay was touched and sat down abruptly in one of the wicker chairs. She looked all around the porch and her throat worked painfully. She was glad that she had had Jeff to bring the box out on the porch to open it. After a long wait, she spoke.

"You all, going back up there in Sawley learnt me more than I'm able to tell you about. I done seen and felt things that I don't want to never see and to feel no more. I don't want to find it in me, and I don't want to find it nowhere around me. If I got any narrow-hearted littleness in me, I hope to God to cut myself and let it run out."

Arvay did not use many words, but she told them that she had burned the house, and turned her back on what it stood for for good and all. She had found that she did not belong there after all. Without realizing, she had come to prefer Jim's way of handling things.

There was a feeling silence. Arvay took in the pleasure of her porch, and a long look southward through the grove. This was her life and she loved everything about it. Jim had said that she loved like a coward and he had been telling the truth. If ever she was to be with him again, it was her move. She

314

stiffened herself internally and said casually, "And Jeff, as soon as I rest up for a day or two, I'm going to the coast and spend a few days with my husband."

"That's ever so fine and nice, Miss Arvay. I'm proud and glad to hear you say it. You just say what day you aim to go, and I'll have the car here and all ready for you."

"The car, Jeff? Why, Jim's got it on the coast with him, ain't he?"

"That one, yes, Ma'am." Jeff fumbled around nervously. "But it's another one—I mean that I can get hold of one for your convenience."

"You bought yourself a car since I been gone, Jeff?"

"No'm."

"Then I can just get on the train, Jeff."

"No, Ma'am. You ain't to—no, I mean it's too much trouble for you to be fooling with the train. Have to go up to Palatka and lay over, and then take another train to get to the coast. Then you have to change at St. Augustine to get to New Smyrna. No'm, I can have the car here at the door any day you see fit to make the trip. You had much better go by car."

Arvay sat there and looked at Jeff and thought. There was a bug under this chip. Jeff was as good as giving her an order not to go by train. This was a roundabout order from Jim Meserve and nobody else. The faithful Jeff was carrying out an order. The thought gave Arvay some hope. Maybe he had not forgotten her then.

"All right, Jeff. If you think that that is the best way for me to go, then I place myself in your hands. I got a few dirty clothes on hand that need to be done up. Some of those pieces I would like to take with me. I would love to be there day after tomorrow, but getting those things done up . . . ."

"Oh, that's no trouble, Miss Arvay," Janie spunked up. "Gather up all you feel you need, and I can suds 'em out first thing in the morning and they'll be dry in no time. I can have 'em all pressed off by dinner time. I can go in there with you right now, and whilst I'm helping you to unpack your things, you can pick out what you want freshened up."

"Why, Janie, I would thank you from the bottom of my heart if you was to help me out like that. I'll thank you until you're better paid."

Arvay woke up next morning with hope and determination. Nothing beats trial but a failure, Arvay decided. She might not win Jim back, but she meant to give it a poor man's trial. That is the best that she could do. If she failed, it was not going to be because she never tried.

The place felt like Dessie's best days all that day. Good will and cheerful willingness all around her. Janie was in the kitchen ironing by eleven o'clock. Arvay had volunteered to cook enough lunch for everybody.

"I'll bet that old east coast is something to see," Janie said wistfully as she shoved the iron back and forth busily. "And boats. I never is seen nothing like that myself, but Jeff claims that it's something wonderful to see."

Arvay looked quickly at Janie and understood. She had not thought about Janie going along before, but now, why not?

"Why, ain't you going along with me tomorrow? Jeff told me that it was a nice big sedan car that he was getting. I thought that it was understood that you would be going with us."

"Oh, Miss Arvay! Oh, Miss Arvay! I'm so glad and happy. 'Tain't nothing that I wouldn't do for you. You'se so nice and kind."

"You still got to use your influence on Jeff, Janie, to get him to kill and pick us some frying-size chickens to fix and take along with us. I think that it would be much nicer if we fixed us up something to eat to take along. See can't you talk Jeff into killing and cleaning four chickens for us. We got plenty turning round to do. While he's doing that, you and I can be stirring up a tater pone to take along. We got plenty here to eat, no need in us going off empty-handed and depending on eating hot dogs along the road, now is it?"

"No ma'am!"

"And then there's my husband. Jim ever favors his stomach, and he just dotes on my tater pone."

The two women did a lot of turning and fixing for the trip. Arvay kept herself so busy that she had no time to fear the outcome of her journey. She steeled herself and refused to anticipate. Let tomorrow speak for itself. She got out an old cheap suitcase and lined it with white paper to hold the lunch. She and Janie laughed at the amount that they were taking. There was the big potato pone, four fried chickens, buttered biscuits, two dozen hard-boiled eggs, potato salad, and the gallon thermos jug full of hot coffee with cream and sugar in it.

Jeff, bathed and soaped so till the skin of his face looked tight and stretched and dressed in his Sunday suit of blue serge, had the car at the door at six o'clock the next morning. With his change of clothes went a formal manner. Jeff stood stiffly as he held the back door for Arvay to get in. He carefully stowed the lunch and Arvay's over-night case in the back with her. Janie, looking as if she had wallowed in a rainbow, beamed and gleamed as she leaped into the front seat beside Jeff, and the car rolled off. Arvay's hands were cold and moist in the palms as the car turned into the highway, but no one could have told it from her face.

At first, Arvay kept her mind off her mission by studying Janie and Jeff. That innocent-looking face that Jeff had, with a surprising earnestness and dependability behind it. He had never failed Jim in any particular, and in spite of all the laughing and talking that he was doing with Janie up there, was never likely to do so. He seemed never to forget the slightest thing around the place, and never neglected to take care of it.

Janie now, that mixture of colors that she had on. Nothing that Angeline would have thought about picking out to wear at all. But strangely, they did not look funny on Janie. That cheap silk dress became her looks very well indeed. Her short hair was as straight as anybody's today and the way she had it fixed, it improved her looks. Janie was a pretty colored girl and good-hearted. Jeff had made a very lucky pick. If she did not move to the coast, they would be mighty comfortable to have around. How did colored people get their hair straight-

317

ened? There were no kinky-haired women these days.

As the car turned into U. S. Highway 1 and sped north towards Melbourne, Arvay began to look at the scenery. This was a different Florida than she had known. This Indian River was a beautiful thing. The groves of leaning palms that bordered it, the beautiful homes scattered along its western bank, the arrangements of the flower yards, and the signs of free-spending wealth impressed her. So many kinds of palms, flowers, pleasure boats out on the river with happy-looking people in them, and fish leaping up and splashing back. And cars, cars, cars, flashing past heading south, and cars behind and in front of them going north. And they all were "really trotting" as Jeff said. Many of them passed Arvay as Jeff never went over forty-five. Arvay smiled because she knew that must have come from Jim. He knew that she was nervous at fast driving.

That thought was encouraging, and then again it was not. Jim was the kind who would take care of her whether he wanted her again or not. Her great trial was still before her.

The car began to slow, and Jeff pointed out the ancient Turtle Mounds, kitchen middens of a people who had disappeared ages before the coming of the Spaniards; rusting old iron pots left over from the indigo industry of the Minorcans; foundations of an old fort left by the Spaniards. Jeff was very proud of his information, but Arvay was not paying him as much attention as she seemed. She was straining forward, drawing back from what was before her. Then before she knew it, Jeff was swinging the car across a high wooden bridge. The Halifax River was before them. This was the waterfront of New Smyrna. They were there.

A short drive down a narrow road seaward, and Jeff swung the car off, and parked in a wide, grassy space before a big shed-looking building that had its backside in the river.

"Here we is, Miss Arvay. We'se at the shrimping docks."

Arvay sat looking at the structure and the activities around it. Several cars and trucks were parked around. On the river Side she saw many boats berthed single, double and triple alongside the warehouses and open docks. Her feet felt heavy and cold, but Arvay decided that it was too late to run now. She had come thus far and she might as well wade on in. She lifted one hand to the handle of the door.

"Just keep your seat, Miss Arvay. I'll jump out and run in and ask if our boats is in," Jeff volunteered importantly.

"Well, all right, Jeff," Arvay murmured wearily, "but I reckon I ought to get on out and stretch my legs."

Janie jumped out behind Jeff and went with him into the dusky interior of the building marked with the name of a shrimping "factory." There were four more big dark doors with other names beside them, but Jeff headed into the one that had Toomer on it. In a very few minutes, he was out again.

"I asked for Captain Jim, Miss Arvay. Miss Mary Toomer, that takes care of all the business in the office, says that our boats is really in, and that Captain Meserve's done sold his shrimp and set led up, and drove off uptown. Want me to go hunt him up?"

"No, Jeff. He'll be back sometime or nother. Yeah, I reckon you better. No telling what time he might come. Tell him, tell him, oh, you can just tell him that I'm waiting here."

Arvay made to get out of the car. She did not want to meet Jim with Jeff or anybody else present. She would rather get out of the car and walk around by herself and wait. As she made to alight, a smiling, middle-aged white woman came out of the door and introduced herself. She was Mrs. Toomer, and said that Arvay's chauffeur had told her that Captain Meserve's madam was present. She knew that Captain Meserve would want to be told as soon as possible that his wife had come. One of the fishermen was going uptown. If Arvay wished, she would send him along with Jeff to locate Captain Jim. While they were gone, she would be pleased if Mrs. Meserve would step inside the office and have a seat.

Arvay went inside and smiled and answered something back when Miss Mary said something. Miss Mary was nice and pleasant, and Arvay was sure that she would like her fine, only she was too tense right now to say and do the right thing in company. Fearing that she might be acting dumb and saying the wrong things, Arvay said that she would love to look around the place and excused herself. Out of the office, Arvay walked up and down the dock, looked off over the woods and around, but saw nothing at all with her eyes.

Then Arvay saw Jim coming. He was driving his usual fast but certain way as he swung expertly into the parking space. He was parked and striding towards the building before the car with Jeff and Janie came trailing in and stopped.

"Oh, hello, Jim!" Arvay tried to be brisk and off-handed, but flushed and faltered. Her eyes could not stay where she wanted them to.

"Hello, Arvay," Jim said casually, but looked her over boldly.

"Oh, I got so much to tell you about, Jim," Arvay chattered in nervous haste. "I know you'll want to hear how everything went off in Sawley." Arvay saw Jeff and Janie hovering around, obviously waiting for orders. They must be gotten rid of. If Jim turned her down, how could she ever go back to the house in Citrabelle if Jeff and Janie had witnessed her downfall? She turned to Jeff.

"I reckon that you want show Janie over the town, don't you, Jeff? It's all new to her, and she wanted to come see it so bad. Tell you what to do. We'll whack up the lunch. You and Janie take all you want, and leave some for me to eat. Then you won't have to hurry back."

"Hold on a minute, there," Jim interrupted. "Just what is in this lunch you're talking about?"

Glad for a chance for conversation, Arvay told Jim. Jim started at once for the borrowed car, and went into the lunch. He grabbed up a chicken wing and ate it with appreciation. Then he partitioned it out himself, and transferred the suitcases to his own car.

"That's enough for Jeff and Janie. They're going straight back home where there's plenty more. Give a man that needs it a chance. Me for instance. And potato pone, too. My favorite groceries."

320

Arvay was pleased that Jim wanted her cooking. She opened her eyes wide and asked, "Oh, you want Jeff to take the car on back?"

"He better get away from here. Who's going to look after things while he's off fooling around? Hit the grit, Jeff, and get on back home. Give that road a cold fever."

With the lunch on the seat between them, and eating as they pulled off, Jeff really tore out and left Arvay standing before Jim and feeling weak. Her easy retreat was cut off. She would have to deal with things one way or another, and she didn't know where nor how to start. They stood there in silence until the car was long out of sight, then Arvay looked up at Jim and said diffidently, "I'm just dying to see the boats."

"You haven't seen 'em yet?" Jim asked in surprise.

"Why, no, Jim. That is, I would rather for you to show 'em to me yourself."

"Oh, so that's the way it is, eh? Well, come ahead. Wait a minute till I grab that lunch box. I'm hungry as a dog for some of that tater pone."

With Jim lugging the suitcase, Arvay followed him through the shed and out on the river side of the building. Jim walked ahead a piece and stopped. Arvay could tell that he meant for her to look around and she did.

"Oh, Jim! You got three boats already! And, my goodness! You got one named after me."

"That was my very first one, Arvay. The *Angeline* was next. That trashy Kenny scraped up the money for that last one, so I named it after him. I aim for the next one to be the *Hatton Howland.* The fifth one will be named after that baby that Angeline is about to have. Next one after that will be named the *Big Jim,* meaning me."

"Oh, Jim, but you are doing well. Can we go on board now and look around? This is my first time to even see a boat as big as this."

With his pride well shuttered, Jim helped Arvay aboard the *Arvay Henson,* and they inspected the others too. He stuck to showing and explaining the boats. Nothing personal at all.

When Arvay was tired of climbing around, they went back to the *Arvay Henson* and sat down in the cabin.

"Let's eat!" was all the encouragement that Arvay got out of Jim. If there was any talking coming off, Arvay saw that she would have to do it herself. As they ate, Arvay fenced by telling Jim what had happened in Sawley. With him, however, she did not leave out the part about Larraine and Carl. She did not damn them, though. She surprised Jim by making allowances and excuses. They were really not to be blamed. But Jim's jaws got grim.

"Did Carl cut a caper like that because he had some idea that you had no kind of protection?"

"No. That is, I don't see how he could of got a notion like that."

"Oh," Jim said and waited some time before he spoke again. "I wouldn't quit my business to go hunt up that toadfish, but he'd better have sense enough not to never come in my sight. I hope that you didn't back off because you felt helpless at all."

"No, it wasn't that way, Jim. I just felt that they were so far back that I was sorry for 'em."

"Well, then that's okay. Say, it's some mighty nice boats tied up here, Arvay. I'd take you on board and let you see 'em and introduce you around, but you ain't dressed for nothing like that. Them high heels and that narrow skirt ain't suitable."

Arvay flashed out with light and leaned forward. "But I really want to do that, Jim. Where can I get something to put on so that I can go along?"

Jim looked at her for a minute, thrust his hands deep into his pockets and finally said as if he were talking to himself, "It would be a kind of waste of money to buy a outfit just for that. It wouldn't be needed any further, and—"

"But why can't I go out on the trip with you, Jim? I'm so proud and pleased with how you have done, that I want to go along with you and see you handle things if you'll let me."

"You really mean that, Arvay?" Jim asked after a pause.

"Jim, I'm so proud, I'm so pleased, that just a little bit more and I'd bust wide open right here. All I wish is that I had of been here with you all along and helping you out like Miss Mary does for her husband. I know that I got the smartest husband in the world, so why wouldn't I feel proud?"

Jim didn't kiss her. He just took hold of her arm very firmly and led her across the deck to the rail.

"Come on then, honey, and let's go uptown and fix you up with something to put on. But mind you now, it's tough out there. Well, you can go along this time anyhow."

Jim bought a pair of the blue jeans that the fishermen wore, two blue shirts, and the tall rubber sea-boots, and Arvay changed into them in the back of the store. Jim told her that the Third Man bought the stores for the gallery, but Arvay would go into a grocery and come out with several things that a wife would naturally buy. Jams, and jellies, salad dressing, lettuce and tomatoes, in fact several dollars worth of extras for the galley which she kept on calling the kitchen and Jim kept on correcting her. Then they crossed the bridge again and pulled up in front of the shrimping docks.

That night they visited several boats and Arvay was introduced around. Alfredo was captain of the *Angeline,* and a husky Negro around twenty-five was in command of the *Kenny M.* Arvay was surprised at that, but soon learned that it was a common thing. There were as many if not more colored captains than white. It was who could go out there and come back with the shrimp. And nobody thought anything about it. White and Negro captains were friendly together and compared notes. Some boats had mixed crews. They all talked about the same things, and they all cursed out the owners. Everything that went wrong on a boat was named after the owner. Did the fuel pump on the engine go bad? It was a Toomer, Meserve or whatever the owner's name so-and-so of a bastard! It was that way about everything. Arvay found that Jim knew all about it, as did the other owners and laughed it off.

"The men got to have some outlet for their feelings. They don't mean a bit of harm. They run the risk of their lives out there, and they got a right to some fun. Cussing the boss out behind his back is a lot of pleasure. I forget that I'm the owner and cuss my ownself out at times. I heard the captain of the *Kenny M.* cussing the winch to every kind of a Meserve so-and-so that he could lay his tongue to this morning when we were berthing. I just let on I didn't hear him."

Jim laughed and Arvay joined in with him. They made the rounds of the Jooks and it was the same way about getting their heads bad. Jim watched Arvay closely as he explained that life was mighty uncertain on a shrimping boat. So many ways that a man could go. Get swept overboard in rough weather; go overboard to cut the net loose when it got fouled in the propeller and a shark happen along; get a bad case of fish-poisoning, and other chances to lose his life. A man had to enjoy himself while he could. The very next trip might be his last. So if they bought likker and love recklessly, what of it? Arvay noted that he relaxed when she agreed that they had a point there. Even though most of them spent their money right away, and depended on going out there and getting more. If they never came back, how could they enjoy money in the bank anyway?

To point this up, they ran into Captain Dutch Smith of the *Savannah.* Last trip, he had lost a man going over the St. Augustine Bar and Dutch was very sad about it. The bar was always risky, and this time it was extra rough, and somehow the man had gone on deck without a line around his waist and had been swept overboard by a big sea.

"He must have been death-struck," somebody consoled Dutch. "I can't imagine what he was thinking about to have done like that. He sure knew better."

But Dutch just wouldn't be consoled. "I sure hate to lose a man," he kept on saying over and over.

"Well, Dutch," Jim put in, "he'll come to beach pretty soon and get a decent burial. That is, unless he met up with a shark. They all come to the beach sooner or later. We all do, I mean. Every man comes to the beach at last. Even if it's a shark, that's your beach, ain't it?"

324

All the fishermen agreed. Everybody comes rolling home to the beach some old day. No telling when you might come rolling in.

Arvay slept on board the *Arvay Henson* that night in Jim's narrow cabin. Jim saw her comfortable, then went below. Neither Mate nor Third Man slept on board that night. The Negro had a wife to go to, and the Mate had found love for the night.

They ate and had visitors all the morning. Fishermen dropping in to meet Jim's wife, or just dropping in to pass off time. Stripped to the waist, Jim went over his Diesel engine and got it to running the way he wanted it. That afternoon, Jim took on fuel and ice. Arvay was thrilled watching the five tons of crushed ice cascading down into the hold. There was laughing and talking as other boats drew up one by one and took on ice. The *Ramos,* with Fritz Toomer, son of the owner, in command, the *Savannah,* the *Thunderbolt,* the *Rosalie I,* which was called the *Rosalie Eye* with Sapelo, a popular Negro, as captain. They all seemed to like Sapelo, which was not his real name; he had got it from the island off the Georgia coast where he hailed from.

They were all getting set to cross the bar on the first tide which would cover the treacherous New Smyrna Bar around six o'clock the next morning. Jim was in the notion of heading for the Cape, that is Carnaveral, where he had done mighty well this last trip. But some of the captains talked north, off St. Augustine or Fernandina. The *Kenny M.* was going that way. Alfredo was undecided.

The rest of the day was spent very pleasantly, but it was a form of torture to Arvay, because she did not know whether she was merely a guest on board and still parted from her husband, or whether she was part of the thing.

She was awakened about five o'clock in the morning by the throbbing of the engine beneath her. She got up and peeped down and saw that Jim was the first man up. He was warming up his engine and seeing to everything. Then the other two men began to stir around down there. There was activity all around her now as engines warmed up, men moved about on the decks of other vessels and there was a general bustle, and a calling back and forth from boat to boat.

Somebody came aboard cursing. The Third Man had gotten his head so bad that he had neglected to buy canned milk. A couple of cans were borrowed, and the man hurried on off.

A gray mist was sheeting the water when the lines were cast off and the *Arvay Henson* eased slowly off from the dock. She had not moved many lengths before the *Savannah* paired with her and they throbbed outwards towards the bar. Arvay hurriedly dressed and went out on deck. She saw boats pairing and falling in line behind the *Arvay Henson,* though none were very close. The Mate explained to her that there would not be enough water over the bar for nearly an hour yet. They were slowing along to cross it at its best, which was none too good at that. The *Arvay Henson* would get there ahead of time, but would anchor and wait for a while. Be in the first boat over, no doubt, but wait till it was safe.

"Want me to fix you some breakfast?" Arvay asked Jim, who was at the wheel inside the pilothouse just in front of the door to the cabin where she had slept.

"Nope. We'll wait for that until we get outside."

The boat roved on down the river gracefully enough. Arvay saw for the first time the forests of mangrove swamps that lined the water on each side. Flocks of white herons perched among them like great white blooms among the dark leaves. She pointed at the swarms of sea gulls moving overhead.

"They fly pretty, Jim, but from what I heard so far, they got mighty poor voices for singing."

Jim laughed. "Eating fish must be against good singing. None of these birds that live around the water got any voices for singing worth talking about."

"But look at them big-mouthed things, Jim!"

"Pelicans."

"Ain't they crazy, though? Look how they lights on the water! Stick out their feet and land on their heels!"

"He's putting on brakes to skid to a stop."

"And look at his head, Jim! Shaped like a pair of big sewing scissors, got a grin running all the way around that long bill from one side to the other. Oh, I like to look at 'em. They're crazy as they can be, but cute!"

Away off somewhere ahead, Arvay began to detect a thunder and a growling roar. It got plainer all the time. The Mate who was standing on deck in front of the door to the pilot-house looked at Jim a time or two, but Jim had his eyes straight ahead. Something was the matter, Arvay knew from the way the Mate kept looking at Jim. The thunder and roar kept getting closer and louder all the time.

Looking over Jim's shoulder through the glass of the housing, Arvay made out the dim shape of a boat coming to meet them. The sun was not up yet, and the boat was a dark mass against the grayness of the mist. The approaching vessel cut a white pompadour with its bow as it came ahead. When its bow was abreast of the bow of the *Arvay Henson,* the captain, a chestnut-colored Negro, stepped out of his pilot-house and stood on deck looking over at the *Arvay Henson.* Jim left his wheel at once and stepped on deck. The two boats were probably fifty feet apart. Jim made some mysterious motions with his hands, and the captain of the other boat doubled his two black fists, and struck one on top of the other rapidly several times. They smiled and waved at each other, and both went back to their wheels.

"Everything fast above and below?" Jim called out, and Mate and Third Man began looking around hastily for a check-up, on deck and below. Two low stools and a pail were brought in and carried below. Jim got up off the high stool that he had been sitting on to steer and shoved it into the cabin. There was a rope fixed to the bulkhead near the floor, and Jim secured the stool to the bulkhead by passing the line tightly around the legs of the stool and tying it securely. He closed the four windows in the cabin and looked around to see that nothing was left that could shift. Then he went back and stood at the wheel and peered straight ahead of him. The Mate was standing on deck in front of the door, and gave Jim a hard questioning look over his shoulder, then fixed his eyes ahead. Arvay could see that he was not pleased about something.

The grumbling thunder ahead increased in power, and the Mate turned and spoke.

"He said that it was pounding on the bar."

Jim seemed not to hear. He kept his eyes straight ahead, and the boat held on her course.

"He said that he turned back to wait until there was more water over that bar."

For all the attention that Jim paid, the Mate might as well have saved his breath. Now amid the rumbling and roaring ahead, Arvay could distinguish a sound like a whale letting out its breath. *Shhhaaaaow!* It came now and then and mingled in with the tumult and the roar.

Now a misty moisture began to cloud the windows of the pilot-house. Jim spoke over his shoulder.

"You better get inside there, Arvay. Lay down in the berth so you won't get flung off your feet and maybe get hurt."

Jim acted calm, but Arvay could feel the excitement in him just the same. Standing in the cabin door, whose level was a good foot higher than the decking of the pilot-house, she looked ahead over Jim's shoulder and her eyes stared out in sudden fear. Perhaps ten boat lengths ahead was a colossal boiling and tumbling, grumbling and rumbling of the sea that sent a white spray mounting like somebody shaking a world-sized veil. Havoc was there with her mouth wide open.

The Mate came in from the deck, fastened the door securely after him, gave Jim a sullen look and stumbled on down the stairs. Arvay closed her door to shut out the sight ahead, and lay down in the bunk.

Suddenly, the *Arvay Henson* reared up and then stumbled. The shock was so violent that Arvay leaped to her feet in fright. Through the forward window she saw waves, gray-headed from their birth, leap up around the boat, and come storming over her bow. A hand, powerful enough to have formed creation, grabbed the boat and flung her halfway around to port. She listed way over, and for a second it seemed

328

that she would pitch-pole over. Arvay was hurled back against the berth, but scrambled up and peered out to see about Jim. His face was set and his jaw muscles bunched. With his feet braced far apart, Jim was fighting a battle with the wheel. Twisting his body halfway to the floor on the right, he brought the bow around and dead on course again.

The Mate came plunging up from below. "Captain! My Captain! You gone crazy? Turn back! This bar is too rough to cross right now. Oh, Captain!"

Jim never turned his head nor even seemed to hear the terrified shouts of his Mate. The boat shuddered and swung violently to starboard.

"Captain! Goddammit, you're going to lose the boat and kill us all! Captain! Captain!"

The frightened Mate, a stocky, butt-end of a man, noting that Jim paid no attention, fell on his knees and wrapped his arms about Jim's left leg, and begged Jim with his eyes. In this struggle where Jim was fighting for the life of his boat and all on board, he tried to shift his leg, but was held fast by the Mate. Arvay saw and acted almost instinctively. She flung the door open, leaped upon the Mate and grabbed him by his hair to pull him away from Jim's leg.

"Let go my husband's leg!" She pounded the man about the face with her fists then yanked and pulled again. "You want to make him wreck his boat? Turn loose!"

In the struggle, Jim was able to kick the hysterical man loose and brace his body and fight the elements.

The Mate, in a lump against the outside door, began to cry and pray. Jim twisted his body slightly to the left and lashed him with his tongue.

"Don't you be praying on my damn boat, you bastard you! Get up off of your damn rusty knees!"

But the Mate mumbled and prayed incoherently. Jim paid him no more attention for a minute or so. Arvay, standing behind Jim, fierce with anger at the Mate who had done such a senseless and dangerous thing, was like a she-bear in her rage. Jim seemed not to know that she was there. His body

329

strained, contorted, with his eyes ahead and his jaw-muscles showing. Arvay thought that the going was getting a little easier. Anyhow, with both hands gripped on the wheel, Jim whirled his body around to face the Mate.

"Pray, you goddamned white-livered bastard, you! Pray! I'm crossing this bar if I land you slap in Hell! Pray! Oh, you can pray on my damn boat, eh? Why you didn't pray last night while you were crawling that barrel of whores? Why you didn't pray while you was guzzling rotgut likker? You didn't have time to pray then, did you? All right now, pray your damn prayer now! Pray, goddamn you, pray!"

The boat shook and shuddered once more, and the Mate's voice was lifted again. Jim whirled on him again.

"Don't you pray another lick on this damn boat, you puking-drunk, seven-sided son of a so-and-so! Get below!"

The Mate looked at Jim's face and fairly tumbled down. Jim kept his furious face straight ahead, and the boat held her course. He said nothing to Arvay, and she said nothing to him. She stood just back of him and looked fearfully over his shoulder. She had never been so frightened in her life as she was now. The boat gave another shudder and then a leap, and glided out onto the calm waters of the Atlantic.

The contrast was utterly startling. No waves, just an undulating motion that made the distant horizon seem to go up and down slowly and gently. The sun was not up yet, but he had sent his messengers on ahead. A diffused pinkness lit up the sky to the east, then suddenly the rim of the great ball rushed up from the east of the ocean, and laid a red sword westward across the swaying water. Arvay was enchanted.

"Oh, Jim! I never have seen the ocean before. Oh, it's just too pretty for anything. Look how it's changing colors from gray to blue! I'm so proud you brought me with you."

"I thought you might like it, Arvay. Biggest thing that God ever made. It's pretty like you say, and then it can be ugly. It's good and it's bad. It's something of everything on earth."

"Oh, but it is!" Arvay looked and gasped in awe and admiration. The sea vastness, the unobstructed glory of the rising sun, the delicate and forming colors on horizon and sea made new sensations for Arvay. She felt herself stretching and extending with her surroundings. Her eyesight seemed better, and her hearing more keen. The fear that she had experienced while crossing the bar was like a birth-pain. It was already forgotten and gone. In this mood a happy suspicion visited Arvay. She moved so that she could study Jim's profile and asked diffidently, "Jim, it would have been a whole lot easier for you to have crossed the bar later on, wouldn't it?"

Jim looked at Arvay and his eyes were set for battle.

"Maybe so, Arvay. What do you want to know for?"

"Well," and Arvay spoke in a soft maiden voice. "Because the notion just come to me that you took that awful chance so that I could see the sunrise out here on my first sight of the ocean. That right?"

"Yes." Jim bit it off shortly.

"Then, Jim, you're the boldest and the noblest man that ever forked a pair of pants. You'se a monny-ark, Jim, and that's something like a king, only bigger and better. I'm proud enough to die."

"If it reached from me to you, Arvay, I'm glad." He looked ahead for a long minute, then turned his head to the left and yelled down below.

"Cup-Cake!"

"Yes, my Captain!"

"Shake your rusty-dusty down there! I'm hungry as hell."

"It's on the fire and your name's done called. You don't come now you needn't to come at all."

"Copasetty! I'm rearing to go. You and the Mate hurry up and eat so he can come take the wheel for a while so my wife and I can come eat."

"I heard you, my Captain!" The Negro yelled back up.

Fifteen minutes later, the Mate, now calm but shame-faced, came up and took the wheel.

"Take it easy." Jim spoke as if nothing had happened between them. "We're headed for the Cape, but give some of the other boats a chance to catch up with us."

331

"Okay, my Captain," the Mate said cheerfully, and Jim and Arvay went below.

Cup-Cake, the Third Man, had done himself proud. Hotcakes, bacon and eggs, syrup and butter on the table and hot coffee in plenty. He beamed and smiled as Arvay downed a heavy breakfast.

"Something about this ocean must bring on a big appetite," she excused herself for eating so heartily. "Or else it's Cup-Cake's cooking one. Look like I can't hardly get enough."

A half second later she knew that she had said just the right thing. Jim smiled and opened his eyes wide and looked at her with pleasure. Cup-Cake grinned all over himself.

"You just wait till I pitch you a dinner," he said. "I never do feel right to do when we'se tied up. But outside now, I can be myself in a galley. Ain't I telling it right, my Captain?"

"Oh, you'll do in a rush, Cup-Cake. I hope that my wife don't take and spoil you too rotten, bragging on your cooking. You got to be useful on deck, you know."

Cup-Cake laughed that off and rinsed out a big pot, dropped a ham hock in it, and put it on the fire. He brought out the big bundle of turnip greens from the ice box and began to pick them over.

"Sure glad you bought these, Mrs. Captain. Lay a good poultice of these, seasoned down with ham, against a man's ribs, and it'll just about cure him of whatever might ail him. Make a dead man set up on the cooling-board."

When they came top-side again, a dozen or more boats were in the offing, and more approaching from the west. The sun had become a light yolk yellow and was walking with red legs across the sky. Jim stood out on deck and made sign language back and forth from boat to boat. Now and then at Arvay's insistence, he translated for her. She made great admiration over their being able to talk to each other like that.

Finally, the *Arvay Henson* paired off with the *Rosalie I,* and put on power for the seven-hour run down to the Cape. Now and then they slowed and tried along. Finding nothing, they held on towards the Cape.

It was late when the fleet anchored off Cape Carnavarel, and none of the boats were disposed to begin operations that day. They would eat, have a good rest, and get set for two drags the next day, a three-meal day. A drag right after breakfast, one right after dinner and head and ice shrimp after supper.

Arvay and Jim sat out on deck on the hatch for a long time that night. The talk was too impersonal for her happiness, but she put on a happy face.

"Jim, I just can't get over the ocean. It's too big for me to even imagine. And night or day, it's something wonderful to look at. I feel like I never want to go away from it no more. Seems like I been off somewhere on a journey and just got home."

"Funny, Arvay, but I ever had that feeling. That's why I was bent and bound to go back to fishing. Once I had seen and been on the sea, it got inside me, and I ever longed for it like a drop of water."

"Like a drop of water, Jim?"

"Sure, Arvay. Don't you realize that the sea is the home of water? All water is off on a journey unlessen it's in the sea, and it's homesick, and bound to make its way home some day."

"Oh, I never thought about a thing like that, Jim."

"You ought to, though. You can't kill it. Mix it up in anything, and in anyway that you will or may, but sooner or later it separates itself out and heads back home to the sea. Falls on the ground, soaks down, gets to a tiny branch maybe, and that heads into a creek that runs into a river that maybe runs into a bigger river and all that millions-times multiplied drops of water marches like an army back to the sea. Some gets soaked way down in the ground in rivers and pools so far down in the rocks that folks walking along don't even know that it's there under 'em. Maybe it might get stopped up in a place like that for thousands and thousands of years, but the water never gives up. It gnaws and gnaws at them rocks till they finally gives way, and then the water gets loose and runs as fast as it can back home to the sea. Maybe, in an hour after it gets home, the sun and wind might draw it up again in a cloud and the cloud travels out over the land, and that drop is on another journey, but don't worry, it will arrive back home again. The very same water that you see out there was right here when the world was formed. Changed places and forms too many thousands of times for you to imagine, been off from home and come back just that many times. It'll always be water, though, and always come back home. It's a million times stronger and more durable than anything that ever lived in it nor passed over it. I look at it and think about it, and I never get tired of looking and thinking."

"That's something to think about, Jim. It's never entered my mind before. Maybe it's like that with everything and everybody. If it's in there, it will return to its real self at last."

"That's well-spoken, Arvay. If it's there, it'll come out some old day. Like the water in the underground cave like Silver Springs. Underground for nobody knows how many hundreds of miles, and for nobody knows how many centuries of years, to break through in that crystal clear spring at last. That's the way life is, when you come to think about it. Some folks are surface water and are easily seen and known about. Others get caught underground, and have to cut and gnaw their way out if they ever get seen by human eyes."

That was as near as they came to anything personal, and right after that Jim stretched himself and stood up.

"We ain't doing nothing but rocking and rolling out tonight, but tomorrow we got to get them nuggets off the bottom and on ice. No, I wouldn't trust you to set out here after I'm gone in. Rail too low. Once you start to falling off of a boat you can't stop. Motion of the boat will pitch you on the way it's going. Come on in and stay in the cabin till you hear somebody stirring in the morning."

Soon the next morning things were astir. The engine was pulsing when she woke up. There was a great to-do with nets and winches on the after deck. Right after breakfast the fishing was to begin. The excitement invaded the galley, and the minute that it was over, the men left her below and went top-side. By the time that Arvay had washed up the dishes, and reached the deck, they were going over with the try-net. Jim at the wheel sang out, "All right, boys, let's try along!"

The sleeve-like net, operated from the smaller winch, went over the side, and Jim sent the boat slowly ahead. A half hour later it was reeled up, and lifted over the side, and the contents dumped on the deck. A lot of curious-looking strange things were in it, but only twenty-odd shrimp. Jim tried to look casual, but Arvay could see that he was disappointed.

"Don't seem to be many, but let's go overboard anyhow."

The Mate went to the big winch. Cup-Cake got the big bag of the net in his hands and stood to the starboard rail to drop it overside after the big net went over and was spreading right.

"All right, let's go overboard!" Jim called out from his place at the wheel. Down came the boom, swung to starboard, and the big net went sinking down and down. The Mate watched closely to see if it was spreading evenly and right. When the boards disappeared under the water, the Third Man dropped the bag overboard, and Jim sent the boat ahead. It went round and round in a big circle slowly, listing to port or starboard from the pull of the heavy net sixty fathoms down on the bottom of the ocean. The steel cable attached to the mast made a straight line to the net below, and moved back and forth like a slow pendulum across the stern as the boat circled and circled. Things got quiet on board as the two-hour drag went on.

"All right, let's get it!" Jim called at last, and the Mate and the Third Man ran to take up their positions. Finally, the big net was brought to the side and lifted by the winch to the deck.

A cloud of gulls and pelicans appeared from nowhere, making their dissonant call-cries, and hovered for prey. They swooped and swirled as the bag was emptied on deck.

Turtles, numerous kinds of fish, a leopard shark, strange unimaginable-shaped things from the bottom of the sea cascaded out on the deck. Things in shells, soft-looking queer-shaped things; four octopi, about four feet across, bent their arms like swastikas and rolled about the deck trying to find their way back to the water. Jim stood with his hands on his hips looking down gloomily on the mass. Plenty of stuff, but few shrimp in all that mass. Arvay saw several things that looked to her like living pin-cushions and thought to get one to save and take home with her. As she stooped to pick it up, everybody yelled at her at the same time to leave it alone.

"That's a damn whore's-egg!" Jim cautioned. "Ruin you if only one spine of it gets into your hand." Arvay jumped back from the sea-nettle and stood far off to the side.

The men went in killing things. First that astonishingly limber-bodied shark. It could whip its body around as if it hadn't a bone in it. With shovels and the axe, they fell upon it cursing the whole shark family as improperly born cutters of nets, and hefted it overside, where it was immediately fallen upon by other sharks and disappeared in a few minutes down their under-slung, saw-toothed mouths.

"A basket and a half of shrimp in all that mess," Jim said in deep disappointment, and the men were just as gloomy.

"If this kind of luck keeps up, no percentage for nobody worth mentioning," the Mate said in a heavy voice. Cup-Cake said nothing, but he did not smile as usual.

"All right, clean up the deck," Jim muttered, and went back in the pilot-house.

With shovels, the men scooped up the mass of strange life on deck, and tossed it back into the water. The sea birds screamed and swooped, picking up the dead, and catching the weakened creatures before they could dive out of reach. Turtles, sea-nettles and things with shells had nothing to worry about. Few soft-bodied things had a chance. Arvay watched the slaughter with pity. As Jim had said, the sea was good and it was cruel too. It was thing eat thing out here. She turned her head away until the struggle was over.

Arvay thought that Jim avoided her after that. He had little to say at the dinner table, and got busy down in the hold somewhere back of the engine. She went and stretched out in the cabin, but she could hear him below being surly and snappish with the men.

"It's me," Arvay wept up there in the cabin alone. "He don't want me here nohow, and now, he's blaming me for a

Jonah. I know that he wishes that I was dead and off his hands, and I wish so too."

There was an old coverless *Adventure* magazine on the table beside the head of the bunk, and Arvay picked it up and tried to read it some. All she did was to turn pages from front to back and then the other way. She looked out of first one window and then another, at the peaceful, waving horizon, at the distant boats circling and circling around flags. She could tell when the nets were taken on board by the swarms of birds and their hungry, unmusical cries.

Arvay felt even worse when Jim came and stood on deck just outside the pilot-house and she heard him mutter, "It certainly is funny. Everybody catching something but me."

Half an hour later, she heard him say in a lifeless way, "Supposing we try again, men." He took his place at the wheel, and finally gave the order to "get it." Arvay didn't bother to follow him on deck when the try-net came over the side. The kind of silence that prevailed out there told her enough. Only the hungry birds had anything to make noise about. The shovels scraped on the decks in a dispirited way. Then buckets of sea water sloshed over the deck and ran off chortling through the scuppers. Jim came nowhere near her to say nor to do a thing.

An hour later, though, she heard him swearing out there like anything. At the end of the long catalogue of damns and other trimmings, he shouted, "We're going over without a try. There's shrimp in this goddamned ocean and we got to get 'em."

Jim sat unsmiling at the wheel, never once turning his head to look at Arvay shrinking like a Portuguese man o' war on the beach, for the entire two hours. He kept looking at his watch towards the end, and finally yelled, "Goddamn it, let's get it!"

Before the net came over the side Arvay knew that the luck had changed. It was something like three savage warriors out there on the deck shouting, jumping, swearing and working the machinery.

"The stuff is here!" The Mate screamed.

"We're going to sink her!" Jim crowed.

"Going in high boat!" Cup-Cake bellowed.

"You're damn tooting!" Jim added, "or report to Hell the reason why."

There was furious action out there, and Arvay raised herself to peer out of the window over the bunk that gave on the after deck.

"The bailing-net!" Jim shouted. "We got to bail before we can bring her over the side. Look at the goddamned sharks grabbing at the fish gilled in the net and cutting my goddamned net to pieces!" Arvay had always known that Jim was a cursing man, but she had never heard him to this extent as he called the sharks every kind of low, unprincipled thing that he could lay his tongue to, and plenty seemed to be available. He played the dozens with them and went way back in their ancestry. Never had a shark's mother been married or begot a shark in a decent bed. And as for their pappies, they were thus-and-sos. "Liable to cut up this net so that all our catch gets away!"

But the furious and quick work saved the day. Very little got away. However, a huge silver-grey man-killing shark was inside the net and was dumped on the deck. With shouts of vengeful joy the three men fell upon it with the axe, shovel and gig. Its head was a bloody mess in no time, and it lay like dead. The men were stooping to pick up the carcass and dump it overboard by means of the winch and cables, when the limber thing whipped around all of a sudden and almost got Jim's right foot. The shark actually did take off the heel of his boot. Arvay, watching through the window, involuntarily let out a scream. There was more blaspheming the honor of female sharks, and the men fell upon the monster again. When it lay still again, they hacked through the tough hide and ripped open the belly. Arvay ran outside to see what they were looking at with so much interest. There were little live sharks inside inclosed in transparent sacs.

"Let's heave the whole she-bang over the side and let the little bastards drown!" Jim cursed.

The cables were hooked on and the huge sea-beast splashed bloodily overboard, but the men were put out to see the baby sharks free themselves of their envelopes and swim off. The men expressed the shame and the pity that they had gotten away, and Arvay thought, carried on like little boys.

They turned back to the huge mass of sea life piled on the deck and began to separate the shrimp out with zeal.

"Over two tons, I'd say," Jim estimated with satisfaction. "This gives us the start to sink her tomorrow and go in high boat."

"Just look at the money piled up there!" The Mate gloated. He sat down on a stool to look and admire some more. "I can see myself on the hill soon as we get in making some fool fisherman go broke trying to beat me spending money."

"Okay," Jim muttered, "we got 'em, let's fall to cracking heads."

"Yes, my Captain!" the crew answered and sat down to heading shrimp. No matter how late it might be, there would be no sleeping aboard until all the shrimp were headed and on ice. Good humor prevailed. The men remembered funny stories and told them to each other.

Arvay felt glad about the haul herself. She could not be looked upon as a Jonah, and Jim was in such good humor now. But then again, a winning Jim might easily be farther away from her grasp than a losing Jim. She turned around and leaned her back against the rail and looked at the three men working away. Jim was sitting on the hatch cover and looking as male as a coconut tree. What woman wouldn't be glad to get hold of a man like that? The tiny lines from the outside corners of his eyes, and around his mouth took nothing away from his looks and appeal in Arvay's eyes. Naturally, all the other females on earth were bound to see his wonders. They could not help themselves. Arvay sankled around and reached a spot close to Jim and stood and looked on for a few minutes.

"Could I give you all any help in any way?"

Jim looked up at Arvay sharply and the look flustered her.

"Maybe I could cook some supper for you, or . . ." Arvay added in a desperate hurry lest Jim tell her that there was nothing that she could do for him.

"Now that's a fine idea, Arvay. A most grand noble notion. Of course, I know that old Cup-Cake don't want to hear the news. Nothing would suit him better than to sneak off down there into the galley and pass an easy time ruining up groceries while me and Titty-Nipple squat up here heading shrimp, and getting our hands all stuck up on their horns. Now, with you being so cool and kind as get us some supper, we got old Cup-Cake's trashy hide dead in the works."

Arvay laughed from happiness and fluttered her eyelids up and down.

"What you all reckon you want me to fix for you to eat, boys?"

"You eat them few stone crabs that I picked out and laid aside for you," Jim helped out. "Fix them for your ownself. I want a great big mess of these shrimp fried to a turn with fried potatoes, and, oh, just anything more that you feel to fix. You ought to know how to feed me by now. You sure know how to cook, so suit yourself."

They all wanted the same. Whatever Mrs. Captain took a notion to fix. Fried shrimp, however, was the preference.

Then a great grin spread clear across Cup-Cake's face. "I'll have to leave you all heading by yourself for awhile. I got to hull them shrimp for Mrs. Captain. That's too hard a work for her to do."

Jim, in mock fury jumped up, and grabbed up a stool as if he meant to haul off and lam Cup over the head with it.

"What did I tell you, Titty?" Jim shouted triumphantly. "That sooner's too slick and slippery to handle. Naturally the shrimp ought to be cleaned first, but I'll show the hammerhead that I'm just as slick as he is greasy. We all will shuck shrimp for cooking, and rush that no-count jar-head back to heading shrimp."

Jim jumped up and filled a pail with the fresh, grey-green

340

shrimp and beckoning to the crew, headed for the galley on the lope. Cup and Titty followed him laughing. By the time that Arvay descended to the galley, they were laughing and cleaning the shrimp, and indulging in horse-play. Arvay looked on and noted how like little boys they acted. Didn't men ever get grown? Arvay asked herself indulgently. It was nice to see how they could play like that. It made her feel good and like taking care of them.

She fixed the dinner in a warm family atmosphere and was glad when they all praised her and said how good it was. They ate so Arvay could believe them, and it made her feel very good. She shooed them on back to their heading and cleaned up the galley as she would her own kitchen.

With nothing more to occupy her hands, Arvay went back to her personal probing. She could not rest easy. What she had come to do was still ahead.

Arvay could hear the three men laughing and joking over their work on the after deck as she came up from the galley. She stood in the pilot-house for several minutes listening. They sounded so happy and free of care together. It made her wonder if Jim was thinking seriously as she was. How was she to get out what she wanted to tell him? The sea was calm and nice. She decided to go out on the forward deck and feel the breeze and think.

Numerous were the eyes of the night. Clear and bright before the rise of the moon. She took a seat on a coil of anchor rope and began to [go] back over things. She went back over her life from the day she had first met Jim up until the day of the snake. Frankly and with truth she counted up and put values on things. Jim was right. She had pulled back and halted, and must have tried his patience something awful at times. And what made her halting and doubting so bad—Jim had given her no cause to doubt him. Her case was not the same as many women that she knew. So far as she knew, Jim had never messed around with another woman. She had never had to put on a play like some she knew had to do. They flashed around what their husbands had given them to cover up the fact that they had fine clothes and rings and things, but couldn't lay their hands on their husbands after dark most of the time. Jim gave her too, and then he was present in her bed. Why then had she doubted herself? What more did she want than she had already received?

She had been a good mother, that she could swear to. She had taken good care of Jim in every way. What more then would he be expecting out of her? What had he demanded? Not whom she had descended from. Jim had never said a word along that line. He knew her folks, and if he was satisfied, what had she been whining over? Then in a flash it came back to Arvay what Jim had said to her that Sunday when they had got engaged to marry. He had told her exactly what he wanted in a wife. She had clean forgotten about it and had made herself touchy and miserable all this time for nothing. Love and be sweet to him. She had done that to the best of her ability. Certainly she had loved Jim all that she was able to love anybody. Her whole heart and mind was his and had always been so. Have him children. She had done that too. Look pretty. She had certainly kept herself looking the best that she knew how. Whether she was pretty or not was according to Jim's own eyes. He had told her often and again that she was pretty, so he must have been satisfied.

So much for the foundations and the past. What could she learn from that to help her out right now? Jim could have made up his mind to do without her.

Arvay thought some more and took a stand. According to Jim's own words, he had a good right to take her back and give her a chance to show that she had changed. She had been weak and cowardly in the past, never realizing what he had done for her, and making not anything of being his wife. But then on the other hand, she had suffered about everything that a woman could suffer through loving and clinging to Jim. From where she had come from, Jim could never realize what it had cost her to scramble and struggle along to keep alongside of him the way he travelled in life. The battle had been awful, but she had fought down the things that had made the difference between them. She had suffered a sad birth and a sadder death from her love. Now, after all the pressing pain of the journey and winning against herself in order to stand beside him, she certainly ought to be allowed to receive her crown of victory. Since she had rejoined Jim, she had tried to show him the change in her by signs, but so far he hadn't seemed to take a bit of notice. Maybe since they had parted that day in August, some other woman had come in between.

At that thought, more fighting blood than Arvay thought she had in her rushed to her heart. Her temples throbbed and her ears felt hot.

No, she told herself. It was not going to be that way at all if she could help herself. She did not aim to step aside and let no other woman take her place with Jim Meserve. She was going to have her husband back or die in the attempt. Whatever it took to bring it about she was going to do it. And she did not mean next year sometime either. She meant right here and now.

Arvay felt so intense that she could not keep her seat. She stood erect and her hands were clinched.

She was going to deal with things. Oh, yes she was! And she was not going to fool around with a try-net. She was going overboard with the drag and sweep the very bottom.

Arvay was eager to rush in and settle her fate, but she could hear the men still talking and laughing over their work. She would have to wait until that was over with.

The white, white, Florida moon rose up and began to gild the ocean. The calm surface rose and fell like the breast of a sleeping woman. Other boats twinkled off in the distance to right and left of her. A school of fish flashed silver sides as they broke surface and hurled themselves in the air to fall back, and flash again and again. Arvay saw what they were fleeing, when the fin of a huge shark rushed along in their wake. The shark too disappeared under when a school of porpoises came ploughing and diving and re-appearing on the route of the shark. The moonlight lit up her pale gold hair coiled in thick braids around her head.

Arvay let the scene swamp her. She felt privileged to be there. It was like being taken into a new lodge. The fellowship of beauty-seers. Jim had made all this. Well, anyhow, he had provided this ocean-sea for her to look at. Well, to bring it down a little more, she would never have known anything about such as this [except] by hearsay if it wasn't for Jim.

So was some other woman to receive such things from Jim? Would she stand on the front of Jim's boat and see and feel what she now saw and felt? The thought was not to be put up with. Maybe she would be young and ever so pretty, and of high family and learned in books and ways. Arvay crimped her mouth and accepted the challenge. Be she who and what she would be or may, Arvay grimmed herself to go up against her. That woman would have to beat what she could do and be, and that was going to be a gracious plenty. If and when she got hold of Jim, it was not going to be as a gracious gift from Arvay. Not because she had backed off from her. Her scars would always keep her in mind that she had been in a battle. Win or lose, Arvay was determined to trot out the best horse she had in her stable, to never turn her back on the enemy, and if she lost, not to go off crying.

A great freedom and calm came to Arvay with her determination. Nothing ahead of her but war, and she was ready and eager for it to start. She sat down again on the coil of rope and pleasured herself with the night. She sat and fed her senses with the light, the movement of the sea and the march of the stars across the sky. This was all hers until death if only she had the courage and the strength to hold it, and that she meant to do. Finally, it came to her just how to begin with Jim. Now, there was Isaac and Rebecca at the well and smiling lovingly at each other. No, that wouldn't do. They had already done that part years ago. She and Jim were a married couple, even if at variance. What Ruth said to Naomi fitted things more better, but put into words that fitted just her and Jim.

"Jim, your loving Arvay has throwed off every hindering weight so as to follow you along in an easy way. Whither thou

344

goest, I will go along too. Thy kind of people shall be my kind of people, and thy God, my God."

Reciting this over and over so as not to forget it, Arvay went in the cabin and went to bed. The men were still working outside, but they were not chattering so much now. Their words were few and sounded tired to Arvay. They ought to be near about through. That being the case, her time was close at hand.

But how was she to get Jim off to himself to talk in private? The shrimp headed and put on ice down in the hold, Jim would go below with the crew as usual. He would pass close to the door of the cabin it was true, but not halt his steps.

Why not change what she had been doing since she had been on board and leave the door open? Jim would notice that. Well, she could attract his notice more easily anyway.

Arvay heard the movements of finishing off out on the after deck and she tensed herself and found that her limbs were trembling. She became conscious of how she was dressed. She had no silk female things on board to adorn herself with. Nothing to sleep in but one of the blue work shirts that Jim had bought her. It stopped half way between her hips and her knees. With the sound of the men dragging and scuffling baskets of shrimp as they carried them below, Arvay got up and brushed her hair and fixed her face. That was all that she could do for her looks. She opened the door about a third of the way and lay down again to wait in agitation. Now that the action was at hand, she found herself tense and trembling.

Arvay traced every movement outside with her ears. The men got through icing. She heard the hatch cover close finally, and the crew going below with tired steps, mumbling a little as they went. But she missed the well-known steps of Jim Meserve. All was quiet below when she heard Jim enter the pilot-house. She could hear him moving back and forth softly out there, and glimpse his form each time that he passed the open door. Jim did not turn on the light out there. He seemed to be fumbling back and forth as if he were searching for something. Arvay got so that she could not stand the suspense

345

any longer. She closed her eyes and called out softly, "Jim?"

"Yeah, Arvay," Jim answered wearily, and stood in the crack of the door.

"Come here, Jim. I got something to tell you."

Quickly, Jim pushed the opening a little wider and stuck his head inside the cabin. Lying there on top of the covers, Arvay felt shamefaced about her clothes. Jim was looking at her very hard from her head to her feet. Most particularly from where her shirt-tail stopped on down.

"What is it, Arvay?" Jim asked after a long time, Arvay thought.

Arvay gritted her teeth and plunged on.

"You can't go down below to sleep tonight, Jim, that is, not until I have a talk with you nohow. You can't go . . ."

"Who says I can't?"

"I say so, Jim. You're not going down there and crawl into no bunk, not until I get through with what I want with you."

Jim's face went very tense, and his eyes narrowed down. Boldly, he stepped inside the cabin and closed the door firmly behind him. He leaned his back against it and folded his hands behind him. Not a word was exchanged between them for a minute or so. Arvay's eye-lids had lowered while Jim just stood looking at her.

"You called me, Arvay, so here I am." He looked at Arvay for a long and a searching time with his eyes still narrowed down. Only Arvay thought that his head drooped a little bit.

Arvay realized that she had the floor, and it threw her into a vast panic. That chance that she had yearned for through long terrible months was in her hand. But her speech of explanations and review had flown out of her presence and was blowing off somewhere over the big ocean. She didn't have any ideas. She didn't even have any words. She was on the point of crying.

"You can't go below," Arvay stumbled out. "You got to . . ."

"Arvay, do you realize that you are giving orders to the captain of a ship? And on the high seas at that? That's mutiny, which is a high crime punishable by death, and instant death if I feel like it. And then on top of that, it's pretty damned biggity and imposing."

"Captain or no captain, Jim, you're my husband, ain't you?"

"Even so, all that cheek and brass that you're acting with, you must think that you've found some weapon to your hand since I seen you last."

Arvay's blue eyes flew wide open at that. If she sounded biggity to Jim, then he didn't realize how scared she was. She mounted to the pulpit and took her text from that.

"Do I need any more weapon than I already got? Did I ever need any different?" Arvay shot an impudent and challenging look at Jim. "Maybe the reason you never see no bear-cat with hip-pockets is because he don't have no need to tote no pistol with him. I was born with all I ever needed to handle your case."

Jim's eyes now flew wide open. His body gave a jerk.

"There now! The mule done kicked Rucker!" Jim exploded, and Arvay caught him eye-balling her in a new way. "You're mighty plague-goned impudent and sassy these days." He gave Arvay a strong under-eye look. "Who's been pomping you up so? Who's been telling you that you're pretty?"

"Jim Meserve, that's who."

"Oh, is *that* the case? When did I tell you all that, Arvay?"

"Every since I knowed you . . . in one way or another. Aw, I ain't near so dumb as I used to be. I can read your writing. Actions speak louder than words."

Arvay had every intention to keep on talking and acting flip until she got out all that was in her to say, but her eyelids fluttered and drooped before that look that Jim was giving her. She just couldn't help herself. But a sound of movement made them fly open again. There was Jim coming towards the bunk like he was stalking a prey. Involuntarily, Arvay flinched.

"Don't you holler!" Jim growled. "Putting me on the linger like you did! I ought to take my belt to you and run your backside crazy!" All of a sudden, Jim stood over Arvay on the

347

bunk and offed with his jacket and flung it from him without looking to see which way it went. He tore at the buttons of his shirt frantically and threw it as if it had done something to him. "Holler if you dare! You had better not even cheep!"

It was a moment of great revelation for Arvay. She got a glimpse of something which she would never have believed possible before. Jim, Jim Meserve, Lord, had his doubts about holding her as she had hers about him. She was not the only one who had trembled. All these years and time, Jim had been feeling his way towards her and grasping at her as she had been towards him. This was a wonderful and powerful thing to know, but she must not let him know what she had perceived. Arvay trembled visibly and looked up innocently afraid and scared at Jim. But one time in her life, she wanted to fully express herself in words and let Jim know how she had improved and changed.

"Just lemme tell you one thing more, Jim. You—I want you to overlook how dumb I used to be. But, Jim, I just wasn't wise of things. Like Mama used to say, being dumb never kilt nobody. All it did was to make you sweat, and Jim, since I've been with you, I done sweated mightily."

"Aw, hush up!" Jim hurled his shoes, one after the other against the forward bulkhead. "No need for any long explanations. I can read your writing, Arvay." He stood up and shucked his pants. "You took long enough to stumble round the tea-cup to get to the handle." Jim dropped suddenly down on the side of the bunk and snatched off his socks. "And don't try to get cute and resist me, neither." He fairly flung himself at full length on the bunk, grabbed Arvay by her ears and shook her head fretfully. "Kiss me, Arvay!"

Arvay really kissed him. Jim took her face between his hands and looked into her eyes for some time.

"You had a damned good chance to be rid of me, Arvay. Me *and* my habits for good and all. Just live off apart from me with full support, but you didn't have sense enough to make good of it. And that's your hard luck, baby."

"Why, Jim?"

"Why? Because you'll damn sure never get a chance like that again. Never no more in this world, nor even in Georgia, will I act the goddamn fool for your benefit like that again. If being with me don't suit you, you got nobody but your own-self to blame. You brought this on yourself. You could have stayed away from me, but you didn't. So you're planted here now forever. You're going to do just what I say do, and you had better not let me hear you part your lips in a grumble. Do you hear me, Arvay?"

"Yes, Jim, I hear you."

The sweetness of the moment swept over Arvay so that she almost lost consciousness. Jim shook her roughly and growled.

"Well, hell! You don't act like it. What the hell you think I got a neck for if it ain't for you to be hugging?"

Arvay's arms went up in a languorous curve and clasped tightly around Jim's neck, and without being urged, she kissed him fondly time and again. Jim was gripping her shoulders so hard until it hurt her, and trembling all over his body like a child trying to keep from crying. Like a little boy who had fled in out of the dark to the comfort of his mother. After a while, Jim sighed deeply, and his head slid down and snuggled on her breast. From long habit, Arvay's fingers began to play through his hair in a gentle way. Almost immediately, Jim sighed and went off into a deep and peaceful sleep.

The *Arvay Henson* rode gently on the bosom of the Atlantic. It lifted and bowed in harmony with the wind and the sea. It was acting in submission to the infinite, and Arvay felt its peace. For the first time in her life, she acknowledged that that was the only way. She shifted her body sufficiently to lie on her right side, and with her arms still about the sleeping Jim, snuggled him more comfortably in the narrow bunk and held and hovered him as if he had been her little boy.

The movement of the boat was soothing and drowsy-like, but Arvay could not sleep. A great exaltation had come upon her, and her mind spoke in voices to her. She heard them as plain as day.

All that had happened to her, good or bad, was a part of her

349

own self and had come out of her. Within her own flesh were many mysteries. She lifted her left hand before her eyes and studied it in every detail with wonder. With wonder and deep awe like Moses before his burning bush. What all, Arvay asked of herself, was buried and hidden in human flesh? You toted it around with you all your life time, but you couldn't know. If you just could know, it would be all the religion that anybody needed. And what was in you was bound to come out and stand.

Earl was in her and had to come out some way or another. Arvay looked back and shuddered. Then a new feeling came. Yes, Earl had been bred in her before she was even born, but his birth had purged her flesh. He was born first. It was meant to be that way. Somebody had to pay off the debt so that the rest of the pages could be clean. God must have thought that she was the one who could shoulder the load and bear it. He had not trusted it to her mother, nor yet to Larraine. God had made her a mother to give peace and comfort around. Earl had served his purpose and was happily removed from his sufferings. It was pitiful that she had not seen things in the right way from his birth. She had been purged out, and the way was cleared for better things.

Then it was like the Resurrection. The good that was in her flesh had taken form. Angeline, female beauty, had come out of her, and Kenny, as handsome a boy as you would find anywhere. Kenny had come bringing the music part inside her that she had never had a chance to show herself. It had to be there or it could never have come out as it did. He represented those beautiful sounds that she used to hear from nowhere as she played around with her doll under the mulberry tree. But give credit where credit was due. Jim was the other part. Joined together, they had made these wonders. Human flesh was full of mysteries and a wonderful and unknown thing.

Arvay bent her neck and kissed Jim tenderly on top of his head. Jim Meserve was her man and her care. Naturally, children would grow up and seek for partners just as she had done. It was the thing to do. It was meant to be that way.

350

Arvay hoped fervently that her two children would find the same kind of fullness that she had found. Angeline seemed to have it already. She hoped and prayed that Kenny would find the same. It was not for her to worry about how and with whom they found what she had found. Jim was her business. Arvay bent and kissed his hair again. It was funny that she had never known Jim in full until this night. Jim was not the over-powering general that she had took him for. Oh, he had that way with other folks and things. No matter of doubt about it. From a teppentime shack to his own fleet on the ocean was a long, long road to travel. But that was the outside Jim. Inside he was nothing but a little boy to take care of, and he hungered for her hovering. Look at him now! Snuggled down and clutching onto her like Kenny when he wore diapers. Arvay felt such a swelling to protect and comfort Jim that tears came up in her eyes. So helpless sleeping there in her arms and trusting himself to her.

And just like she had not known Jim, she had known her own self even less. What she had considered her cross, she now saw as her glory. Her father and Larraine had taken from her because they felt that she had something to take from and to give out of her fullness. Her mother had looked to her for dependence. Her children, and Jim and all. Her job was mothering. What more could any woman want and need? No matter how much money they had or learning, or high family, they couldn't do a bit more mothering and hovering than she could. Holy Mary, who had been blessed to mother Jesus, had been no better off than she was. She had been poor and unlearnt too. Even poor Carl had felt her need and care. Maybe as he said, he would have come to more than he had if he had had her beside him.

Thinking and feeling that way, Arvay could not sleep. The few hours left of the darkness passed away with Jim held in her arms. Jim was hers and it was her privilege to serve him. To keep on like that in happiness and peace until they died together, giving Jim the hovering that he needed.

A breeze of dawn sprang up, and the boat rocked gently

with it. The slightly increased motion made Arvay look out upon the sea. She saw that the sun was rising. It seemed to her that the big globe of light leaped up from a bed fixed on the eastern horizon and mounted, trailing the red covers of his bed behind him. Arvay pictured that he looked and saw the *Arvay Henson* with her and Jim on board and laid that rosy path across the crinkling water straight to it to look and see if she was carrying out her work. The sunlight rose higher, climbed the rail and came on board. Arvay sat up as best she could without disturbing Jim and switched off the artificial light overhead, and met the look of the sun with confidence. Yes, she was doing what the big light had told her to do. She was serving and meant to serve. She made the sun welcome to come on in, then snuggled down again beside her husband.

AFTERWORD

ZORA NEALE HURSTON: "A NEGRO WAY OF SAYING"

I.

The Reverend Harry Middleton Hyatt, and Episcopal priest whose five-volume classic collection, *Hoodoo, Conjuration, Witchcraft, and Rootwork,* more than amply returned an investment of forty years' research, once asked me during an interview in 1977 what had become of another eccentric collector whom he admired. "I met her in the field in the thirties. I think," he reflected for a few seconds, "that her first name was Zora." It was an innocent question, made reasonable by the body of confused and often contradictory rumors that make Zora Neale Hurston's own legend as richly curious and as dense as are the black myths she did so much to preserve in her classic anthropological works, *Mules and Men* and *Tell My Horse,* and in her fiction.

A graduate of Barnard, where she studied under Franz Boas, Zora Neale Hurston published seven books—four novels, two books of folklore, and an autobiography—and more than fifty shorter works between the middle of the Harlem Renaissance and the end of the Korean War, when she was the dominant black woman writer in the United States. The dark obscurity into which her career then lapsed reflects her staunchly independent political stances rather than any deficiency of craft or vision. Virtually ignored after the early fifties, even by the Black Arts movement in the sixties, an otherwise noisy and intense spell of black image- and myth-making that rescued so many black writers from remaindered oblivion, Hurston embodied a more or less harmonious but nevertheless problematic unity of opposites. It is this complexity that refuses to lend itself to the glib categories of "radical" or "conservative," "black" or "Negro," "revolutionary" or "Uncle Tom"—categories of little use in literary criticism. It is this same complexity, embodied in her fiction, that, until Alice Walker published her important essay ("In Search of Zora Neale Hurston") in *Ms.* magazine in 1975, had made Hurston's place in black literary history an ambiguous one at best.

The rediscovery of Afro-American writers has usually turned on larger political criteria, of which the writer's work is supposedly a mere reflection. The deeply satisfying aspect of the rediscovery of Zora Neale Hurston is that black women generated it primarily to establish a maternal literary ancestry. Alice Walker's moving essay recounts her attempts to find Hurston's unmarked grave in the Garden of the Heavenly Rest, a segregated cemetery in Fort Pierce, Florida. Hurston became a metaphor for the black woman writer's search for tradition. The craft of Alice Walker, Gayl Jones, Gloria Naylor, and Toni Cade Bambara bears, in markedly different ways, strong affinities with Hurston's. Their attention to Hurston signifies a novel sophistication in black literature: they read Hurston not only for the spiritual kinship inherent in such relations but because she used black vernacular speech and rituals, in ways subtle and various, to chart the coming to consciousness of black women, so glaringly absent in other black fiction. This use of the vernacular became the fundamental framework for all but one of her novels and is particularly effective in her classic work *Their Eyes Were Watching God,* published in 1937, which is more closely related to Henry James's *The Portrait of a Lady* and Jean Toomer's *Cane* than to Langston Hughes's and Richard Wright's the proletarian literature, so popular in the Depression.

The charting of Janie Crawford's fulfillment as an autonomous imagination, *Their Eyes* is a lyrical novel that correlates the need of her first two husbands for ownership of progressively larger physical space (and the gaudy accoutrements of upward mobility) with the suppression of self-awareness in their wife. Only with her third and last lover, a roustabout called Tea Cake whose unstructured frolics center around and about the Florida swamps, does Janie at last bloom, as does the large pear tree that stands beside her grandmother's tiny log cabin.

> She saw a dust bearing bee sink into the sanctum of a bloom; the thousand sister calyxes arch to meet the love embrace and the ecstatic shiver of the tree from root to tiniest branch creaming in every blossom and frothing with delight. So this was a marriage!

To plot Janie's journey from object to subject, the narrative of the novel shifts from third to a blend of first and third person (known as "free indirect discourse"), signifying this awareness of self in Janie. *Their Eyes* is a bold feminist novel, the first to be explicitly so in the Afro-American tradition. Yet in its concern with the project of finding a voice, with language as an instrument of injury and salvation, of selfhood and empowerment, it suggests many of the themes that inspirit Hurston's oeuvre as a whole.

II.

One of the most moving passages in American literature is Zora Neale Hurston's account of her last encounter with her dying mother, found in a chapter entitled "Wandering" in her autobiography, *Dust Tracks on a Road* (1942):

As I crowded in, they lifted up the bed and turned it around so that Mama's eyes would face east. I thought that she looked at me as the head of the bed reversed. Her mouth was slightly open, but her breathing took up so much of her strength that she could not talk. But she looked to me, or so I felt, to speak for her. She depended on me for a voice.

We can begin to understand the rhetorical distance that separated Hurston from her contemporaries if we compare this passage with a similar scene published just three years later in *Black Boy* by Richard Wright, Hurston's dominant black male contemporary and rival: "Once, in the night, my mother called me to her bed and told me that she could not endure the pain, and she wanted to die. I held her hand and begged her to be quiet. That night I ceased to react to my mother; my feelings were frozen." If Hurston represents her final moments with her mother in terms of the search for voice, then Wright attributes to a similar experience a certain "somberness of spirit that I was never to lose," which "grew into a symbol in my mind, gathering to itself . . . the poverty, the ignorance, the helplessness. . . ." Few authors in the black tradition have less in common than Zora Neale Hurston and Richard Wright. And whereas Wright would reign through the forties as our predominant author, Hurston's fame reached its zenith in 1943 with a *Saturday Review* cover story honoring the success of *Dust Tracks.* Seven years later, she would be serving as a maid in Rivo Alto, Florida; ten years after that she would die in the County Welfare Home in Fort Pierce, Florida.

How could the recipient of two Guggenheims and the author of four novels, a dozen short stories, two musicals, two books on black mythology, dozens of essays, and a prizewinning autobiography virtually "disappear" from her readership for three full decades? There are no easy answers to this quandary, despite the concerted attempts of scholars to resolve it. It is clear, however, that the loving, diverse, and enthusiastic responses that Hurston's work engenders today were not shared by several of her influential black male contemporaries. The reasons for this are complex and stem largely from what we might think of as their "racial ideologies."

Part of Hurston's received heritage—and perhaps the paramount received notion that links the novel of manners in the Harlem Renaissance, the social realism of the thirties, and the cultural nationalism of the Black Arts movement—was the idea that racism had reduced black people to mere ciphers, to beings who only react to an omnipresent racial oppression, whose culture is "deprived" where different, and whose psyches are in the main "pathological." Albert Murray, the writer and social critic, calls this "the Social Science Fiction Monster." Socialists, separatists, and civil rights advocates alike have been devoured by this beast.

Hurston thought this idea degrading, its propagation a trap, and railed against it. It was, she said, upheld by "the sobbing school of Negrohood who hold that nature somehow has given them a dirty deal." Unlike Hughes and Wright, Hurston chose deliberately to ignore this "false picture that distorted. . . ." Freedom, she wrote in *Moses, Man of the Mountain,* "was something internal. . . . The man himself must make his own emancipation." And she declared her first novel a manifesto against the "arrogance" of whites assuming that "black lives are only defensive reactions to white actions." Her strategy was not calculated to please.

What we might think of as Hurston's mythic realism, lush and dense within a lyrical black idiom, seemed politically retrograde to the proponents of a social or critical realism. If Wright, Ellison, Brown, and Hurston were engaged in a battle over ideal fictional models with which to represent the Negro, clearly Hurston lost the battle.

But not the war.

After Hurston and her choice of style for the black novel were silenced for nearly three decades, what we have witnessed since is clearly a marvelous instance of the return of the repressed. For Zora Neale Hurston has been "rediscovered"

357

in a manner unprecedented in the black tradition: several black women writers, among whom are some of the most accomplished writers in America today, have openly turned to her works as sources of narrative strategies, to be repeated, imitated, and revised, in acts of textual bonding. Responding to Wright's critique, Hurston claimed that she had wanted at long last to write a black novel, and "not a treatise on sociology." It is this urge that resonates in Toni Morrison's *Song of Solomon* and *Beloved,* and in Walker's depiction of Hurston as our prime symbol of "racial health—a sense of black people as complete, complex, *undiminished* human beings, a sense that is lacking in so much black writing and literature." In a tradition in which male authors have ardently denied black literary paternity, this is a major development, one that heralds the refinement of our notion of tradition: Zora and her daughters are a tradition-within-the-tradition, a black woman's voice.

The resurgence of popular and academic readerships of Hurston's works signifies her multiple canonization in the black, the American, and the feminist traditions. Within the critical establishment, scholars of every stripe have found in Hurston texts for all seasons. More people have read Hurston's works since 1975 than did between that date and the publication of her first novel, in 1934.

III.

Rereading Hurston, I am always struck by the density of intimate experiences she cloaked in richly elaborated imagery. It is this concern for the figurative capacity of black language, for what a character in *Mules and Men* calls "a hidden meaning, jus' like de Bible . . . de inside meanin' of words," that unites Hurston's anthropological studies with her fiction. For the folklore Hurston collected so meticulously as Franz Boas's student at Barnard became metaphors, allegories, and performances in her novels, the traditional recurring canonical metaphors of black culture. Always more of a novelist than a social scientist, even Hurston's academic collections center on the quality of imagination that makes these lives whole and splendid. But it is in the novel that Hurston's use of the black idiom realizes its fullest effect. In *Jonah's Gourd Vine,* her first novel, for instance, the errant preacher, John, as described by Robert Hemenway "is a poet who graces his world with language but cannot find the words to secure his own personal grace." This concern for language and for the "natural" poets who "bring barbaric splendor of word and song into the very camp of the mockers" not only connects her two disciplines but also makes of "the suspended linguistic moment" a thing to behold indeed. Invariably, Hurston's writing depends for its strength on the text, not the context, as does John's climactic sermon, a *tour de force* of black image and metaphor. Image and metaphor define John's world; his failure to interpret himself leads finally to his self-destruction. As Robert Hemenway, Hurston's biographer, concludes, "Such passages eventually add up to a theory of language and behavior."

Using "the spy-glass of Anthropology," her work celebrates rather than moralizes; it shows rather than tells, such that "both behavior and art become self-evident as the tale texts and hoodoo rituals accrete during the reading." As author, she functions as "a midwife participating in the birth of a body of folklore, . . . the first wondering contacts with natural law." The myths she describes so accurately are in fact "alternative modes for perceiving reality," and never just condescending depictions of the quaint. Hurston sees "the Dozens," for example, that age-old black ritual of graceful insult, as, among other things, a verbal defense of the sanctity of the family, conjured through ingenious plays on words. Though attacked by Wright and virtually ignored by his literary heirs, Hurston's ideas about language and craft undergrid many of the most successful contributions to Afro-American literature that followed.

IV.

We can understand Hurston's complex and contradictory legacy more fully if we examine *Dust Tracks on a Road,* her own controversial account of her life. Hurston did make significant parts of herself up, like a masquerader putting on a disguise for the ball, like a character in her fictions. In this way, Hurston *wrote* herself, and sought in her works to rewrite the "self" of "the race," in its several private and public guises, largely for ideological reasons. That which she chooses to reveal is the life of her imagination, as it sought to mold and interpret her environment. That which she silences or deletes, similarly, is all that her readership would draw upon to delimit or pigeonhole her life as a synecdoche of "the race problem," an exceptional part standing for the debased whole.

Hurston's achievement in *Dust Tracks* is twofold. First, she gives us a *writer's* life, rather than an account, as she says, of "the Negro problem." So many events in this text are figured in terms of Hurston's growing awareness and mastery of books and language, language and linguistic rituals as spoken and written both by masters of the Western tradition and by ordinary members of the black community. These two "speech communities," as it were, are Hurston's great sources of inspiration not only in her novels but also in her autobiography.

The representation of her sources of language seems to be her principal concern, as she constantly shifts back and forth between her "literate" narrator's voice and a highly idiomatic black voice found in wonderful passages of free indirect discourse. Hurston moves in and out of these distinct voices effortlessly, seamlessly, just as she does in *Their Eyes* to chart Janie's coming to consciousness. It is this usage of a *divided* voice, a double voice unreconciled, that strikes me as her great achievement, a verbal analogue of her double experiences as a woman in a male-dominated world and as a black person in a nonblack world, a woman writer's revision of W. E. B. Du

Bois's metaphor of "double-consciousness" for the hyphenated African-American.

Her language, variegated by the twin voices that intertwine throughout the text, retains the power to unsettle.

There is something about poverty that smells like death.
Dead dreams dropping off the heart like leaves in a dry
season and rotting around the feet; impulses smothered too
long in the fetid air of underground caves. The soul lives
in a sickly air. People can be slave-ships in shoes.

Elsewhere she analyzes black "idioms" used by a culture "raised on simile and invective. They know how to call names," she concludes, then lists some, such as 'gator-mouthed, box-ankled, puzzle-gutted, shovel-footed: "Eyes looking like skint-ginny nuts, and mouth looking like a dish-pan full of broke-up crockery!"

Immediately following the passage about her mother's death, she writes:

The Master-Maker in His making had made Old Death.
Made him with big, soft feet and square toes. Made him
with a face that reflects the face of all things, but neither
changes itself, nor is mirrored anywhere. Made the body of
death out of infinite hunger. Made a weapon of his hand to
satisfy his needs. This was the morning of the day of the
beginning of things.

Language, in these passages, is not merely "adornment," as Hurston described a key black linguistic practice; rather, manner and meaning are perfectly in tune: she says the thing in the most meaningful manner. Nor is she being "cute," or pandering to a condescending white readership. She is "naming" emotions, as she says, in a language both deeply personal and culturally specific.

The second reason that *Dust Tracks* succeeds as literature arises from the first: Hurston's unresolved tension between

361

her double voices signifies her full understanding of modernism. Hurston uses the two voices in her text to celebrate the psychological fragmentation both of modernity and of the black American. As Barbara Johnson has written, hers is a rhetoric of division, rather than a fiction of psychological or cultural unity. Zora Neale Hurston, the "real" Zora Neale Hurston that we long to locate in this text, dwells in the silence that separates these two voices: she is both, and neither; bilingual, and mute. This strategy helps to explain her attraction to so many contemporary critics and writers, who can turn to her works again and again only to be startled at her remarkable artistry.

But the life that Hurston could write was not the life she could live. In fact, Hurston's life, so much more readily than does the standard sociological rendering, reveals how economic limits determine our choices even more than does violence or love. Put simply, Hurston wrote well when she was comfortable, wrote poorly when she was not. Financial problems—book sales, grants, and fellowships too few and too paltry, ignorant editors and a smothering patron—produced the sort of dependence that affects, if not determines, her style, a relation she explored somewhat ironically in "What White Publishers Won't Print." We cannot oversimplify the relation between Hurston's art and her life; nor can we reduce the complexity of her postwar politics, which, rooted in her distaste for the pathological image of blacks, were markedly conservative and Republican.

Nor can we sentimentalize her disastrous final decade, when she found herself working as a maid on the very day the *Saturday Evening Post* published her short story "Conscience of the Court" and often found herself without money, surviving after 1957 on unemployment benefits, substitute teaching, and welfare checks. "In her last days," Hemenway concludes dispassionately, "Zora lived in a difficult life—alone, proud, ill, obsessed with a book she could not finish."

The excavation of her buried life helped a new generation read Hurston again. But ultimately we must find Hurston's

362

legacy in her art, where she "ploughed up some literacy and laid by some alphabets." Her importance rests with the legacy of fiction and lore she constructed so cannily. As Hurston herself noted, "Roll your eyes in ecstasy and ape his every move, but until we have placed something upon his street corner that is our own, we are right back where we were when they filed our iron collar off." If, as a friend eulogized, "She didn't come to you empty," then she does not leave black literature empty. If her earlier obscurity and neglect today seem inconceivable, perhaps now, as she wrote of Moses, she has "crossed over."

HENRY LOUIS GATES, JR.

SELECTED BIBLIOGRAPHY

WORKS BY ZORA NEALE HURSTON

Jonah's Gourd Vine. Philadelphia: J. B. Lippincott, 1934.

Mules and Men. Philadelphia: J. B. Lippincott, 1935.

Their Eyes Were Watching God. Philadelphia: J. B. Lippincott, 1937.

Tell My Horse. Philadelphia: J. B. Lippincott, 1938.

Moses, Man of the Mountain. Philadelphia: J. B. Lippincott, 1939.

Dust Tracks on a Road. Philadelphia: J. B. Lippincott, 1942.

Seraph on the Suwanee. New York: Charles Scribner's Sons, 1948.

I Love Myself When I Am Laughing . . . & Then Again When I Am Looking Mean and Impressive: A Zora Neale Hurston Reader. Edited by Alice Walker. Old Westbury, N.Y.: The Feminist Press, 1979.

The Sanctified Church. Edited by Toni Cade Bambara. Berkeley: Turtle Island, 1981.

Spunk: The Selected Short Stories of Zora Neale Hurston. Berkeley: Turtle Island, 1985.

WORKS ABOUT ZORA NEALE HURSTON

Baker, Houston, A., Jr., *Blues, Ideology, and Afro-American Literature: A Vernacular Theory,* pp. 15–63. Chicago: University of Chicago Press, 1984.

Bloom, Harold, ed. *Zora Neale Hurston.* New York: Chelsea House, 1986.

————, ed. *Zora Neale Hurston's "Their Eyes Were Watching God."* New York: Chelsea House, 1987.

Byrd, James W. "Zora Neale Hurston: A Novel Folklorist." *Tennessee Folklore Society Bulletin* 21 (1955): 37–41.

Cooke, Michael G. "Solitude: The Beginnings of Self-Realization in Zora Neale Hurston, Richard Wright, and Ralph Ellison." In Michael G. Cooke, *Afro-American Literature in the Twentieth Century,* pp. 71–110. New Haven: Yale University Press, 1984.

Dance, Daryl C. "Zora Neale Hurston." In *American Women Writers: Bibliographical Essays,* edited by Maurice Duke, et al. Westport, Conn.: Greenwood Press, 1983.

Gates, Henry Louis, Jr. "The Speakerly Text." In Henry Louis Gates, Jr., *The Signifying Monkey,* pp. 170–217. New York: Oxford University Press, 1988.

Giles, James R. "The Significance of Time in Zora Neale Hurston's *Their Eyes Were Watching God."* *Negro American Literature Forum* 6 (Summer 1972): 52–53, 60.

Hemenway, Robert E. *Zora Neale Hurston: A Literary Biography.* Chicago: University of Illinois Press, 1977.

Holloway, Karla. *The Character of the Word: The Texts of Zora Neale Hurston.* Westport, Conn.: Greenwood Press, 1987.

Holt, Elvin. "Zora Neale Hurston." In *Fifty Southern Writers After 1900,* edited by Joseph M. Flura and Robert Bain, pp. 259–69. Westport, Conn.: Greenwood Press, 1987.

Howard, Lillie Pearl. *Zora Neale Hurston.* Boston: Twayne, 1980.

————. "Zora Neale Hurston." In *Dictionary of Literary Biography,* vol. 51, edited by Trudier Harris, pp. 133–45. Detroit: Gale, 1987.

Jackson, Blyden. "Some Negroes in the Land of Goshen." *Tennessee Folklore Society Bulletin* 19 (4) (December 1953): 103–7.

Johnson, Barbara. "Metaphor, Metonymy, and Voice in *Their Eyes."* In *Black Literature and Literary Theory,* edited by Henry Louis Gates, Jr., pp. 205–21. New York: Methuen, 1984.

————. "Thresholds of Difference: Structures of Address in Zora Neale Hurston." In *"Race," Writing and Difference,* edited by Henry Lewis Gates, Jr. Chicago: University of Chicago Press, 1986.

Jordan, June. "On Richard Wright and Zora Neale Hurston." *Black World* 23 (10) (August 1974): 4–8.

Kubitschek, Missy Dehn. " 'Tuh de Horizon and Back': The Female Quest in *Their Eyes." Black American Literature Forum* 17 (3) (Fall 1983): 109–15.

Lionnet, Françoise. "Autoethnography: The Anarchic Style of *Dust Tracks on a Road.*" In Françoise Lionnet, *Autobiographical Voices: Race, Gender, Self-Portraiture,* pp. 97–130. Ithaca: Cornell University Press, 1989.

Lupton, Mary Jane. "Zora Neale Hurston and the Survival of the Female." *Southern Literary Journal* 15 (Fall 1982): 45–54.

Meese, Elizabeth. "Orality and Textuality in Zora Neale Hurston's *Their Eyes.*" In Elizabeth Meese, *Crossing the Double Cross: The Practice of Feminist Criticism,* pp. 39–55. Chapel Hill: University of North Carolina Press, 1986.

Newson, Adele S. *Zora Neale Hurston: A Reference Guide.* Boston: G. K. Hall, 1987.

Rayson, Ann. "*Dust Tracks on a Road:* Zora Neale Hurston and the Form of Black Autobiography." *Negro American Literature Forum* 7 (Summer 1973): 42–44.

Sheffey, Ruthe T., ed. *A Rainbow Round Her Shoulder: The Zora Neale Hurston Symposium Papers.* Baltimore: Morgan State University Press, 1982.

Smith, Barbara. "Sexual Politics and the Fiction of Zora Neale Hurston." *Radical Teacher* 8 (May 1978): 26–30.

Stepto, Robert B. *From Behind the Veil.* Urbana: University of Illinois Press, 1979.

Walker, Alice. "In Search of Zora Neale Hurston." *Ms.,* March 1975, pp. 74–79, 85–89.

Wall, Cheryl A. "Zora Neale Hurston: Changing Her Own Words." In *American Novelists Revisited: Essays in Feminist Criticism,* edited by Fritz Fleischmann, pp. 370–93. Boston: G. K. Hall, 1982.

Washington, Mary Helen. "Zora Neale Hurston: A Woman Half in Shadow." Introduction to *I Love Myself When I Am Laughing,* edited by Alice Walker. Old Westbury, N.Y.: Feminist Press. 1979.

———." 'I Love the Way Janie Crawford Left Her Husbands': Zora Neale Hurston's Emergent Female Hero." In Mary Helen Washington, *Invented Lives: Narratives of Black Women, 1860–1960.* New York: Anchor Press, 1987.

Willis, Miriam. "Folklore and the Creative Artist: Lydia Cabrera and Zora Neale Hurston." *CLA Journal* 27 (September 1983): 81–90.

Wolff, Maria Tai. "Listening and Living: Reading and Experience in *Their Eyes.*" *BALF* 16 (1) (Spring 1982): 29–33.

CHRONOLOGY

January 7, 1891   Born in Eatonville, Florida, the fifth of eight children, to John Hurston, a carpenter and Baptist preacher, and Lucy Potts Hurston, a former schoolteacher.

September 1917–
June 1918   Attends Morgan Academy in Baltimore, completing the high school requirements.

Summer 1918   Works as a waitress in a nightclub and a manicurist in a black-owned barbershop that serves only whites.

1918–19   Attends Howard Prep School, Washington, D.C.

1919–24   Attends Howard University; receives an associate degree in 1920.

1921   Publishes her first story, "John Redding Goes to Sea," in the *Stylus,* the campus literary society's magazine.

December 1924   Publishes "Drenched in Light," a short story, in *Opportunity.*

1925   Submits a story, "Spunk," and a play, *Color Struck,* to *Opportunity's* literary contest. Both win second-place awards; publishes "Spunk" in the June number.

1925–27   Attends Barnard College, studying anthropology with Franz Boas.

1926   Begins field work for Boas in Harlem.

January 1926	Publishes "John Redding Goes to Sea" in *Opportunity*.
Summer 1926	Organizes *Fire!* with Langston Hughes and Wallace Thurman; they publish only one issue, in November 1926. The issue includes Hurston's "Sweat."
August 1926	Publishes "Muttsy" in *Opportunity*.
September 1926	Publishes "Possum or Pig" in the *Forum*.
September–November 1926	Publishes "The Eatonville Anthology" in the *Messenger*.
1927	Publishes *The First One,* a play, in Charles S. Johnson's *Ebony and Topaz*.
February 1927	Goes to Florida to collect folklore.
May 19, 1927	Marries Herbert Sheen.
September 1927	First visits Mrs. Rufus Osgood Mason, seeking patronage.
October 1927	Publishes an account of the black settlement at St. Augustine, Florida, in the *Journal of Negro History;* also in this issue: "Cudjo's Own Story of the Last African Slaver."
December 1927	Signs a contract with Mason, enabling her to return to the South to collect folklore.
1928	Satirized as "Sweetie Mae Carr" in Wallace Thurman's novel about the Harlem Renaissance *Infants of the Spring;* receives a bachelor of arts degree from Barnard.
January 1928	Relations with Sheen break off.
May 1928	Publishes "How It Feels to Be Colored Me" in the *World Tomorrow*.
1930–32	Organizes the field notes that become *Mules and Men*.
May–June 1930	Works on the play *Mule Bone* with Langston Hughes.
1931	Publishes "Hoodoo in America" in the *Journal of American Folklore*.
February 1931	Breaks with Langston Hughes over the authorship of *Mule Bone*.
July 7, 1931	Divorces Sheen.

September 1931	Writes for a theatrical revue called *Fast and Furious*.
January 1932	Writes and stages a theatrical revue called *The Great Day,* first performed on January 10 on Broadway at the John Golden Theatre; works with the creative literature department of Rollins College, Winter Park, Florida, to produce a concert program of Negro music.
1933	Writes "The Fiery Chariot."
January 1933	Stages *From Sun to Sun* (a version of *Great Day*) at Rollins College.
August 1933	Publishes "The Gilded Six-Bits" in *Story.*
1934	Publishes six essays in Nancy Cunard's anthology, *Negro.*
January 1934	Goes to Bethune-Cookman College to establish a school of dramatic arts "based on pure Negro expression."
May 1934	Publishes *Jonah's Gourd Vine,* originally titled *Big Nigger;* it is a Book-of-the-Month Club selection.
September 1934	Publishes "The Fire and the Cloud" in the *Challenge.*
November 1934	*Singing Steel* (a version of *Great Day*) performed in Chicago.
January 1935	Makes an abortive attempt to study for a Ph.D in anthropology at Columbia University on a fellowship from the Rosenwald Foundation. In fact, she seldom attends classes.
August 1935	Joins the WPA Federal Theatre Project as a "dramatic coach."
October 1935	*Mules and Men* published.
March 1936	Awarded a Guggenheim Fellowship to study West Indian Obeah practices.
April–September 1936	In Jamaica.
September–March 1937	In Haiti; writes *Their Eyes Were Watching God* in seven weeks.
May 1937	Returns to Haiti on a renewed Guggenheim.
September 1937	Returns to the United States; *Their Eyes Were Watching God* published, September 18.

February– March 1938	Writes *Tell My Horse;* it is published the same year.
April 1938	Joins the Federal Writers Project in Florida to work on *The Florida Negro.*
1939	Publishes "Now Take Noses" in *Cordially Yours.*
June 1939	Receives an honorary Doctor of Letters degree from Morgan State College.
June 27, 1939	Marries Albert Price III in Florida.
Summer 1939	Hired as a drama instructor by North Carolina College for Negroes at Durham; meets Paul Green, professor of drama, at the University of North Carolina.
November 1939	*Moses, Man of the Mountain* published.
February 1940	Files for divorce from Price, though the two are reconciled briefly.
Summer 1940	Makes a folklore-collecting trip to South Carolina.
Spring– July 1941	Writes *Dust Tracks on a Road.*
July 1941	Publishes "Cock Robin, Beale Street" in the *Southern Literary Messenger.*
October 1941– January 1942	Works as a story consultant at Paramount Pictures.
July 1942	Publishes "Story in Harlem Slang" in the *American Mercury.*
September 5, 1942	Publishes a profile of Lawrence Silas in the *Saturday Evening Post.*
November 1942	*Dust Tracks on a Road* published.
February 1943	Awarded the Anisfield-Wolf Book Award in Race Relations for *Dust Tracks;* on the cover of the *Saturday Review.*
March 1943	Receives Howard University's Distinguished Alumni Award.
May 1943	Publishes "The 'Pet Negro' Syndrome" in the *American Mercury.*
November 1943	Divorce from Price granted.
June 1944	Publishes "My Most Humiliating Jim Crow Experience" in the *Negro Digest.*
1945	Writes *Mrs. Doctor;* it is rejected by Lippincott.

March 1945	Publishes "The Rise of the Begging Joints" in the *American Mercury.*
December 1945	Publishes "Crazy for This Democracy" in the *Negro Digest.*
1947	Publishes a review of Robert Tallant's *Voodoo in New Orleans* in the *Journal of American Folklore.*
May 1947	Goes to British Honduras to research black communities in Central America; writes *Seraph on the Suwanee;* stays in Honduras until March 1948.
September 1948	Falsely accused of molesting a ten-year-old boy and arrested; case finally dismissed in March 1949.
October 1948	*Seraph on the Suwanee* published.
March 1950	Publishes "Conscience of the Court" in the *Saturday Evening Post,* while working as a maid in Rivo Island, Florida.
April 1950	Publishes "What White Publishers Won't Print" in the *Saturday Evening Post.*
November 1950	Publishes "I Saw Negro Votes Peddled" in the *American Legion* magazine.
Winter 1950–51	Moves to Belle Glade, Florida.
June 1951	Publishes "Why the Negro Won't Buy Communism" in the *American Legion* magazine.
December 8, 1951	Publishes "A Negro Voter Sizes Up Taft" in the *Saturday Evening Post.*
1952	Hired by the *Pittsburgh Courier* to cover the Ruby McCollum case.
May 1956	Receives an award for "education and human relations" at Bethune-Cookman College.
June 1956	Works as a librarian at Patrick Air Force Base in Florida; fired in 1957.
1957–59	Writes a column on "Hoodoo and Black Magic" for the *Fort Pierce Chronicle.*
1958	Works as a substitute teacher at Lincoln Park Academy, Fort Pierce.
Early 1959	Suffers a stroke.
October 1959	Forced to enter the St. Lucie County Welfare Home.

January 28, 1960	Dies in the St. Lucie County Welfare Home of "hypertensive heart disease"; buried in an unmarked grave in the Garden of Heavenly Rest, Fort Pierce.
August 1973	Alice Walker discovers and marks Hurston's grave.
March 1975	Walker publishes "In Search of Zora Neale Hurston," in *Ms.,* launching a Hurston revival.

About the author

About the book

Read on

Insights,
Interviews
& More . . .

She *Was* the Party

by Valerie Boyd

ZORA NEALE HURSTON knew how to make an entrance. On May 1, 1925, at a literary awards dinner sponsored by *Opportunity* magazine, the earthy Harlem newcomer turned heads and raised eyebrows as she claimed four awards: a second-place fiction prize for her short story "Spunk," a second-place award in drama for her play *Color Struck*, and two honorable mentions.

The names of the writers who beat out Hurston for first place that night would soon be forgotten. But the name of the second-place winner buzzed on tongues all night, and for days and years to come.

Lest anyone forget her, Hurston made a wholly memorable entrance at a party following the awards dinner. She strode into the room— jammed with writers and arts patrons, black and white—and flung a long, richly colored scarf around her neck with dramatic flourish as she bellowed a reminder of the title of her winning play: *"Colooooooor Struuckkkk!"* Her exultant entrance literally stopped the party for a moment, just as she had intended. In this way, Hurston made it known that a bright and powerful presence had arrived.

Author photograph by Carl Van Vechten, courtesy of the Van Vechten Trust

By all accounts, Zora Neale Hurston could walk into a roomful of strangers and, a few minutes and a few stories later, leave them so completely charmed that they often found themselves offering to help her in any way they could.

Gamely accepting such offers—and employing her own talent and scrappiness—Hurston became the most successful and most significant black woman writer of the first half of the twentieth century. Over a career that spanned more than thirty years, she published four novels, two books of folklore, an autobiography, numerous short stories, and several essays, articles, and plays.

Born on January 7, 1891, in Notasulga, Alabama, Hurston moved with her family to Eatonville, Florida, when she was still a toddler. Her writings reveal no recollection of her Alabama beginnings. For Hurston, Eatonville was always home.

Established in 1887, the rural community near Orlando was the nation's first incorporated black township. It was, as Hurston described it, "a city of five lakes, three croquet courts, three hundred brown skins, three hundred good swimmers, plenty guavas, two schools, and no jailhouse."

In Eatonville, Zora was never indoctrinated in inferiority, and she could see the evidence of black ▶

> In Eatonville, Zora was never indoctrinated in inferiority, and she could see the evidence of black achievement all around her.

achievement all around her. She could look to town hall and see black men, including her father, John Hurston, formulating the laws that governed Eatonville. She could look to the Sunday schools of the town's two churches and see black women, including her mother, Lucy Potts Hurston, directing the Christian curricula. She could look to the porch of the village store and see black men and women passing worlds through their mouths in the form of colorful, engaging stories.

Growing up in this culturally affirming setting in an eight-room house on five acres of land, Zora had a relatively happy childhood, despite frequent clashes with her preacher-father, who sometimes sought to "squinch" her rambunctious spirit, she recalled. Her mother, on the other hand, urged young Zora and her seven siblings to "jump at de sun." Hurston explained, "We might not land on the sun, but at least we would get off the ground."

Hurston's idyllic childhood came to an abrupt end, though, when her mother died in 1904. Zora was only thirteen years old. "That hour began my wanderings," she later wrote. "Not so much in geography, but in time. Then not so much in time as in spirit."

> 66 Zora had a relatively happy childhood, despite frequent clashes with her preacher-father, who sometimes sought to 'squinch' her rambunctious spirit. 99

After Lucy Hurston's death, Zora's father remarried quickly—to a young woman whom the hotheaded Zora almost killed in a fistfight—and seemed to have little time or money for his children. "Bare and bony of comfort and love," Zora worked a series of menial jobs over the ensuing years, struggled to finish her schooling, and eventually joined a Gilbert & Sullivan traveling troupe as a maid to the lead singer. In 1917, she turned up in Baltimore; by then, she was twenty-six years old and still hadn't finished high school. Needing to present herself as a teenager to qualify for free public schooling, she lopped ten years off her life—giving her year of birth as 1901. Once gone, those years were never restored: from that moment forward, Hurston would always present herself as at least ten years younger than she actually was.

Apparently, she had the looks to pull it off. Photographs reveal that she was a handsome, big-boned woman with playful yet penetrating eyes, high cheekbones, and a full, graceful mouth that was never without expression.

Zora also had a fiery intellect, an infectious sense of humor, and "the gift," as one friend put it, "of walking into hearts." Zora used these talents— and dozens more—to elbow her ▶

way into the Harlem Renaissance of the 1920s, befriending such luminaries as poet Langston Hughes and popular singer-actress Ethel Waters.

Though Hurston rarely drank, fellow writer Sterling Brown recalled, "When Zora was there, she *was* the party." Another friend remembered Hurston's apartment— furnished by donations she solicited from friends—as a spirited "open house" for artists. All this socializing didn't keep Hurston from her work, though. She would sometimes write in her bedroom while the party went on in the living room.

By 1935, Hurston—who'd graduated from Barnard College in 1928—had published several short stories and articles, as well as a novel, *Jonah's Gourd Vine*, and a well-received collection of black Southern folklore, *Mules and Men*. But the late thirties and early forties marked the real zenith of her career. She published her masterwork, *Their Eyes Were Watching God*, in 1937; *Tell My Horse*, her study of Haitian Voodoo practices and Caribbean culture, in 1938; and another masterful novel, *Moses, Man of the Mountain*, in 1939. When her autobiography, *Dust Tracks on a Road*, was published in 1942, Hurston finally received the well-

66 'When Zora was there, she *was* the party.' 99

earned acclaim that had long eluded her. That year, she was profiled in *Who's Who in America, Current Biography*, and *Twentieth Century Authors*. She went on to publish another novel, *Seraph on the Suwanee*, in 1948.

Still, Hurston never received the financial rewards she deserved. (The largest royalty she ever earned from any of her books was $943.75.) So, when she died on January 28, 1960—at age sixty-nine, after suffering a stroke—her neighbors in Fort Pierce, Florida, had to take up a collection for her February 7 funeral. The collection didn't yield enough to pay for a headstone, however, and Hurston was buried in a grave that remained unmarked until 1973.

That summer, a young writer named Alice Walker traveled to Fort Pierce to place a marker on the grave of the author who had so inspired her own work. Walker found the Garden of Heavenly Rest, a segregated cemetery at the dead end of North Seventeenth Street, abandoned and overgrown with yellow-flowered weeds.

Back in 1945, Hurston had foreseen the possibility of dying without money—and she'd proposed a solution that would have benefited ▶

66 Hurston was buried in a grave that remained unmarked until 1973. 99

7

her and countless others. Writing to W. E. B. Du Bois, whom she called the "Dean of American Negro Artists," Hurston suggested "a cemetery for the illustrious Negro dead" on one hundred acres of land in Florida. "Let no Negro celebrity, no matter what financial condition they might be in at death, lie in inconspicuous forgetfulness," she urged. "We must assume the responsibility of their graves being known and honored." Du Bois, citing practical complications, wrote a curt reply discounting her argument.

As if impelled by Hurston's words, Walker bravely entered the snake-infested cemetery where the writer's remains had been laid to rest. Wading through waist-high weeds, she soon stumbled upon a sunken rectangular patch of ground that she determined to be Hurston's grave. Unable to afford the marker she wanted—a tall, majestic black stone called "Ebony Mist"—Walker chose a plain gray headstone instead. Borrowing from a Jean Toomer poem, she dressed the marker up with a fitting epitaph: "Zora Neale Hurston: A Genius of the South." ❧

> 66 Wading through waist-high weeds, Alice Walker stumbled upon a sunken rectangular patch of ground that she determined to be Hurston's grave. 99

Valerie Boyd is the author of the award-winning Wrapped in Rainbows: The Life of Zora Neale Hurston. *Formerly the arts editor at the* Atlanta Journal-Constitution, *she is a professor at the University of Georgia's Grady College of Journalism and Mass Communication.*

A True Picture of the South

by Hazel V. Carby

ON APRIL 15, 1947, Zora Neale Hurston signed a contract with the publishing house of Charles Scribner & Sons for a novel concerned with life in Florida and titled *The Sign of the Sun*. She had finally decided to leave J. B. Lippincott, the publisher of all her previous books, because the company had firmly dismissed her last two projects. Hurston had become disillusioned after Lippincott turned down her proposal for a novel about the black middle class, and she was openly depressed when it subsequently rejected a manuscript set in Eatonville, the town in which Hurston had grown up and which had provided such rich source material for the writing of *Mules and Men* and *Their Eyes Were Watching God*. Hurston felt that the new contract promised a new beginning. The obvious enthusiasm of the Scribner editors for her new novel about a Southern white family renewed her confidence in herself, and the $500 advance enabled Hurston, at last, to finance the trip to Honduras that she had been planning for two years. She left in May and settled into the Hotel

Cosenza, in Puerto Cortés on the north coast of Honduras, to write her novel and to plan an expedition into the mountains. As Hurston described this expedition to her editor at Scribner, Burroughs Mitchell, she hoped "to find a lost city . . . which travellers have heard about for two hundred years, but has not as yet been seen."[1] Hurston wanted her novel to be "good" so she could finance the journey that she felt was "burning [her] soul to attack."[2]

Between May and November, Hurston wrote and revised the novel for which, at various times, she had a number of titles, including *Sang the Suwanee in the Spring*, *The Queen of the Golden Hand*, *Angel in the Bed*, *Lady Angel with Her Man*, *Seraph with a Man on Hand*, *So Said the Sea*, *Good Morning Sun*, and *Seraph on the Suwanee River*. In January 1948, after three months of editorial hesitation, Scribner finally decided to go ahead with the book and asked Hurston to come to New York to work on more revisions. Her dreams of the lost city were left behind when she returned to a cold New York in February 1948. Worried that she had "been in the bush so many months," Hurston warned Burroughs Mitchell "you might have to run me down and catch me and sort of tie me up in the shed until I get house-broke again."[3]

Hurston aimed to make *Seraph* ▶

on the Suwanee "a true picture of the South." She was delighted that Burroughs Mitchell was impressed with her use of Southern vernacular and idiom. In her previous novels and in the collection of folklore, *Mules and Men*, Hurston had established a reputation for her representation of black language and rhythms of speech. Though contemporary critics of Hurston's work have granted her a privileged position in the African American literary canon because of her sensitive delineation of black folk culture and black folk consciousness, particularly through language, Hurston's own views are more complex and controversial. In writing about *Seraph on the Suwanee*, Hurston repudiated theories of the uniqueness of black linguistic structures.

> I think that it should be pointed out that what is known as Negro dialect in the South is no such thing. Bear in mind that the South is the purest English section of the United States. . . . What is actually the truth is that the South, up until the 1930s, was a relic of England. . . . And you find the retention of old English beliefs and customs, songs and ballads and

Elizabethan figures of speech.
They go for the simile and
especially the metaphor. As
in the bloom of Elizabethan
literature, they love speech
for the sake of speech. This is
common to white and black.
The invective is practiced as a
folk art from earliest childhood.
You have observed that
when a southern Senator or
Representative gets the floor,
no Yankee can stand up to him
so far as compelling language
goes. . . . They did *not* get it
from the Negroes. The Africans
coming to America got it from
them. If it were African, then
why is it not in evidence among
all Negroes in the western
world? No, the agrarian system
stabilized in the South by slavery
slowed down change . . . and
so the tendency to colorful
language that characterized
Shakespeare and his
contemporaries and made
possible the beautiful and
poetic language of the King
James Bible got left over to an
extent in the rural South.[4]

Hurston's opinions of the formative
influences acting on the linguistic
structures of the black folk may ▶

cause some discomfort to critics who valorize Hurston for preserving and reproducing in her work cultural forms that they argue are essentially and uniquely black. In *Seraph on the Suwanee*, there are many phrases and sentences that evoke the language of Hurston's black figures in her previous work. Occasionally, the language is identical—whole phrases are lifted from the mouth of a black character in an earlier novel and inserted into the mouth of a member of the white Meserve family. The rhythm and syntax of Hurston's black folk haunt the reader throughout the novel.

Moreover, Hurston was concerned with establishing more than linguistic similarities between white and black in the South; she was actively trying to demonstrate her ideas of cultural influence and fusion in her novel. Kenny Meserve, the second son of Jim and Arvay Meserve, is trained as a musician by black Joe Kelsey. Hurston wrote a chapter, which the publisher later removed, on Kenny's success in New York, to explain this cultural exchange:

> I felt I had to add a chapter on Kenny in New York to explain his success. Though no one to my knowledge has come right

out and said it yet, we have had a revolution in national expression in music that is equivalent to Chaucer's use of the native idiom in England. Gershwin's *Porgy and Bess* brought to a head that which had been in the making for at least a decade. There is no more Negro music in the U.S. It has been fused and merged and become the national expression, and displaced the worship of European expression. In fact, it is now denied, (and with some truth) that it never was pure Negro music, but an adaptation of white music. . . . But the fact remains that what has evolved here is something American.[5]

As a white musician playing black music, Kenny was intended to represent Hurston's conviction that black music was no longer an expression of black culture but had become a form of national expression.

However, *Seraph on the Suwanee* is not just a vehicle for Hurston's theories of the relation between black and white culture. The novel was also an attempt to realize two ambitions that she had been working toward throughout the forties. Hurston ▶

wanted to sell a novel to Hollywood and to see her fiction transformed into film. In 1942, she felt optimistic. "I have a tiny wedge in Hollywood," she wrote with excitement in a letter to Carl Van Vechten, a patron of black art and black artists; she went on to tell him that she had joined the Paramount writing staff. But in 1947, Scribner tried and failed to interest Metro-Goldwyn-Mayer Pictures in the novel.

Hurston's second ambition involved a challenge to the literary conventions of the apartheid American society in which Hurston lived—conventions she felt dictated that black writers and artists should be concerned only with representing black subjects. In the same letter, she described how she had "hopes of breaking that old silly rule about Negroes not writing about white people."[6] In the postwar 1940s, Hurston was not the only black artist to confront the question of whether a racial art was also a segregated art, an art confined permanently within the limits of differences. For all black people, the Second World War embodied the acute contradictions in mobilizing against the ideology of fascism abroad, on the one hand, and, on the other, living with the fascist practices of racism and segregation at home. For many it was an unresolved question of whether being an American and being a Negro were compatible or incompatible categories. For intellectuals, making a decision "whether it was better to be a 'Negro Artist' and develop a racial art or to be an American artist who was a Negro" was complex and contradictory.[7] In literature, these tensions are present in the conscious decisions made by some black writers to write for white magazines or to create white subjects in their fiction.

In the nine years between the publication of *Moses, Man of the Mountain* in 1939 and *Seraph on the Suwanee,* Hurston concentrated her energies on writing nonfiction for white audiences. Her autobiography, *Dust Tracks on a Road*, was published in 1942 and won the Ainsfield-Wolf Award, sponsored by the *Saturday Review*, for its contribution to "the field of race relations." Throughout the forties, Hurston was a regular contributor of essays and reviews to magazines with a predominantly white readership. Of course she ran the risk of being positioned by these magazines as a "representative Negro" expressing "representative opinions," and she also invited, and received, ▶

heavy criticism from other black intellectuals for ignoring serious aspects of black life in order to pander to a white readership. But despite the risks and the controversy that her articles generated, Hurston seems to have sought and enjoyed her position as a conservative black spokesperson.[8]

However, it is important to remember that Hurston was not alone in her direct engagement with a white readership. Some magazines, like the *Saturday Evening Post*, regularly published work from a variety of black writers, and a significant number of black novelists, including Hurston, eventually published postwar novels about white characters. In 1947, Ann Petry published *Country Place* and Willard Motley published *Knock on Any Door*. Between 1946 and 1950, Frank Yerby published five novels aimed at a mass-market audience: *The Foxes of Harrow*, *The Golden Hawk*, *The Vixens*, *Pride's Castle*, and *Floodtide*. In 1954, Richard Wright published his controversial novel *Savage Holiday*.[9] White reviewers and critics often condemned black novels about black subjects for being narrowly conceived, for being overly political, and for being didactic. The term *protest fiction* was frequently used to describe novels by and about black people in order to suggest that somehow the practice of art had been compromised, if not contaminated, by the presence of political and ideological issues. The phrase *protest fiction* implied that fiction that was uncritical of the racialized structures of subordination at work in society somehow expressed universal, not partisan, values. When black authors created white characters in novels that were apparently not about racism or the suffering that resulted from a racist society, reviewers indirectly expressed their relief. A reviewer of *Country Place* in the *Atlantic Monthly* was glad that the novel "preaches no sermons, [and] waves no flags."[10] In the paperback edition of Petry's novel, the publishers inserted a page titled "About This Book" that explained that taking "the folksy, nostalgic front off 'Our Town'" was "a much more difficult task" than dealing with "the life of the Negro in our big Northern cities," the subject of Petry's first novel, *The Street*. Potential readers could safely retain their political illusions about the existence of democracy, for they were assured that Ann Petry was "a powerful American writer, unhampered by any one theme or hobby horse."[11] Writing about ▶

white people was thought by many white critics, reviewers, and publishers to require more literary skill, and more talent, than writing about black characters. In addition, being an author of a white novel could apparently resolve the contradiction of being both black and American.

Seraph on the Suwanee, a novel of a poor white family in Florida that gradually achieves upward economic and class mobility, was published in October 1948. Reviews on the whole were favorable if not overly enthusiastic, but Scribner was unable to interest any book clubs in the novel's distribution. The initial sales of *Seraph on the Suwanee* were good, about three thousand in the first few weeks of publication, and because of the favorable reviews, Scribner ordered another two thousand to be printed. But the events that created controversy around the novel and shattered Hurston's optimism had nothing to do with the fact that Hurston was black and her characters white. On September 13, Hurston had been arrested on charges rising from allegations of sexual misconduct with a ten-year-old boy. She emphatically denied all charges, using her passport as evidence that she had been in Honduras at the time the immoral acts were supposed to have taken place. It must have absolutely astounded Hurston that *Seraph on the Suwanee* could become a tool in the publicity that was eventually generated from the allegations against her. On October 23, the national edition of the Baltimore *Afro-American* published a distorted and inaccurate version of the original allegations (allegations that were eventually proved to be totally false) under the banner headlines "Did She Want 'Knowing and Doing' Kind of Love?" and "Boys, 10, Accuse Zora." Above the article itself ran the two headlines "Novelist Arrested on Morals Charge," "Reviewer of Author's Latest Book Notes Character Is 'Hungry for Love.'" The story was salacious: It suggested that *Seraph on the Suwanee* advocated sexual aggressiveness in women and then used selected sentences from the novel as if they provided evidence of the author's immorality. Hurston's exploration of the sexual expectations and repressions of the novel's protagonists became, in the hands of the Baltimore *Afro-American*, the means for crucifying her. She was literally tried and found guilty in the widely syndicated story and in a subsequent editorial, which appeared in the November 6 *Afro-American*, ▶

in which the paper defended itself against criticism of the front-page publicity granted to the case by arguing that "a hush-hush attitude about perversion has permitted this menace to increase." [12]

Charges against Hurston were not dismissed until March 14, 1949, and by then, as Robert Hemenway has argued, "the damage had been done." [13] Hurston felt betrayed by a fellow black person, a court reporter who had originally leaked the story to the press, and by a black newspaper that she referred to as "the *Afro-American* sluice of filth." This sense of betrayal led Hurston to contemplate and threaten suicide in a letter that she wrote to Carl and Fania Van Vechten:

> All that I have ever tried to do has proved useless. All that I have believed in has failed me. I have resolved to die. It will take a few days for me to set my affairs in order, and then I will go. . . . No acquittal will persuade some people that I am innocent. I feel hurled down a filthy privy hole. [14]

The letter seems to have been written as much from a feeling of hope that it could generate the assurance and support from friends that she needed as it was from a feeling of fear and despair that no one believed in her innocence. Hurston must have received the assurance that she sought, for she did not kill herself, and she gradually recovered her enthusiasm for living and for writing. But, presumably because of the negative publicity generated by the Baltimore *Afro-American*, Hurston seems to have done little to publicly promote her novel herself. In many ways, *Seraph on the Suwanee* was Hurston's most ambitious and most experimental novel to date. But while she regained her confidence and recovered her ambitions for her fiction in the manuscripts of three more novels, *Seraph on the Suwanee* was the last of her novels to be accepted for publication by any publishing house.

The relation between the themes of Petry's *Country Place* and Hurston's *Seraph on the Suwanee* are striking— both concentrate on complex questions of female sexuality and the sometimes violent conflict between men and women that arises from the existence of incompatible and gender-specific desires. Arvay Meserve grows up in a poor family in the turpentine town of Sawley at the turn of the twentieth century. As a young ▶

woman, she is convinced that she isn't important to anyone, and she develops a secret fantasy life in which she feels that she lives in mental adultery with her sister's husband. At twenty-one, Arvay turns her back on the "sins of the world," and uses religious devotion as a mask, an escape from the pressures of "spinsterhood" into a space that represents the only legitimate, autonomous existence for a woman. Arvay successfully gets rid of all unwanted suitors by throwing so-called fits until Jim Meserve arrives and refuses to be so easily dismissed. In the first part of the novel, Jim establishes his power over Arvay through two acts of violence. He "cures" her fits by dropping turpentine in her eye and subsequently rapes her under the mulberry tree, a tree that is symbolic of Arvay's innocent childhood. As the novel progresses, the successful gendering of each protagonist is dependent on the other. Arvay becomes "a slave" to her husband, Jim, while Jim measures and defines his masculinity entirely in relation to the extent to which he can take care of a woman. To Jim Meserve, all women are incapable of taking care of themselves, and, as they have no brains, a man, in order to become a true man, has to think for all women in his care. Readers of *Their Eyes Were Watching God* will be reminded of the pompous second husband of Janie, Jody Starks, who asserted that "Somebody got to think for women and chillun and cows," because they couldn't think for themselves.[15] The difficulty for a feminist reading of *Seraph on the Suwanee* is that Jim Meserve, unlike Jody Starks, does not conveniently die so that his wife can get on with her life. In *Seraph* it is Arvay's expectations and desires that must be transformed to accommodate the demands of her husband.

Nevertheless, the sexual politics of *Seraph on the Suwanee* cannot be easily dismissed. The sexual ambiguity of Jim and Arvay's roles is, at times, intriguing. It is clear from Hurston's letters to her editor when she was writing about Arvay's doubts, fears, and lack of confidence that she was thinking about the men she had met who had been intimidated in their relationship with a woman who was a success in her own right. In response to her editor's unsympathetic response to the character of Arvay, Hurston admitted that, at times, she got sick of her herself, and then she asked: ▶

Have you ever been tied in close contact with a person who had a strong sense of inferiority? I have and it is hell. . . . I took this man I cared for down to Carl Van Vechten's one night so that he could meet some of my literary friends, since he had complained that I was always off with them, and ignoring him. . . . What happened? He sat off in a corner and gloomed and uglied away, and we were hardly out on the street before he was accusing me of having dragged him down there to show off what a big shot I was and how far I was above him.[16]

Reviewers also became confused about whether Jim or Arvay was the seraph of the title—who exactly was the guardian angel, and who was the angel looking after? Frank G. Slaughter, in the *New York Times Book Review*, was convinced that Arvay set out to be the *Webster's* definition of a seraph: "One of an order of celestial beings conceived as fiery and purifying ministers of Jehovah." Herschel Brickell, in the *Saturday Review*, argued that it was "the hero, Jim Meserve," who played "the part of a 'fiery and purifying minister of Jehovah,' with sufficient success to make him seraphic."[17]

Arvay's discovery that she needs to be a mother to her husband long after her own children have grown is a vision of female fulfillment that is very different from, and more controversial than, the vision of female autonomy that Hurston created in *Their Eyes Were Watching God*. But it is the very complexity and depth of Arvay's frustrated and unsatisfied desires that make *Seraph on the Suwanee* a very modern text, a text that speaks as eloquently to the contradictions and conflict of trying to live our lives as gendered beings in the 1990s as it did in 1948. ∾

Notes

1. Zora Neale Hurston to Burroughs Mitchell, September 3, 1947, Charles Scribner's Sons Archives, Author's File 3, Department of Rare Books and Special Collections, Princeton University Libraries. I would like to thank Princeton University Libraries for permission to quote from the unpublished correspondence in this collection and to thank the library staff for their invaluable assistance.

2. Zora Neale Hurston to Burroughs Mitchell, July 31, 1947, ibid.

3. Zora Neale Hurston to Burroughs Mitchell, February 14 [1948], ibid. ▶

4. Zora Neale Hurston to Burroughs Mitchell, October 2, 1947, ibid.

5. Zora Neale Hurston to Burroughs Mitchell, October, "Something Late," 1947, ibid.

6. Zora Neale Hurston to Carl Van Vechten, November 2, 1942, Carl Van Vechten Papers, James Weldon Johnson Memorial Collection, Beinecke Rare Book and Manuscript Library, Yale University. I would like to thank the Beinecke Library for permission to quote from personal correspondence and to acknowledge the invaluable assistance of the library staff.

7. See Ann Gibson, "Norman Lewis in the Forties," in *Norman Lewis: From the Harlem Renaissance to Abstraction*, May 10, 1989–June 25, 1989 (New York: Kenkeleba Gallery, 1989), pp. 9–23. Gibson argues, convincingly, that a number of black artists in the forties, including Romare Bearden, Harlan Jackson, Ronald Joseph, Norman Lewis, and Hale Woodruff, "decided it was better to be an American artist who was a Negro."

8. Robert E. Hemenway, "Ambiguities of Self, Politics of Race," in *Zora Neale Hurston: A Literary Biography* (Urbana: University of Illinois Press, 1977), chap. 11, particularly pp. 288–89.

9. Willard Motley, *Knock on Any Door* (New York: D. Appleton-Century Company, 1947); Ann Petry, *Country*

Place (New York: Houghton Mifflin, 1947); Frank Yerby, *The Foxes of Harrow* (New York: Dial Press, 1946), *The Golden Hawk* (New York: Dial Press, 1947), *The Vixens* (New York: Dial Press, 1948), *Pride's Castle* (New York: Dial Press, 1949), and *Floodtide* (New York: Dial Press, 1950); Richard Wright, *Savage Holiday* (New York: Avon, 1954).

10. John Caswell Smith, Jr., review of *Country Place, Atlantic Monthly*, November 1947: 178, 180.

11. "About This Book," in Ann Petry, *Country Place* (New York: New American Library, 1949).

12. Press clippings from the *Afro-American* (Baltimore), October 23 and November 6, 1948; the *Iowa Bystander* (Des Moines), dated October 21, 1948; and the *Ohio State News* (Columbus), October 23, 1948. The clippings are in the Charles Scribner's Sons Archives, Author's File 3.

13. Hemenway, *Zora Neale Hurston*, p. 320.

14. Zora Neale Hurston to Carl and Fania Van Vechten, n.d., as quoted in Hemenway, *Zora Neale Hurston*, pp. 321–22.

15. Zora Neale Hurston, *Their Eyes Were Watching God* (New York: Harper & Row, 1990), pp. 66–67.

16. Zora Neale Hurston to Burroughs Mitchell, October 2, 1947, ▶

A True Picture of the South *(continued)*

Charles Scribner's Sons Archives, Author's File 3.

    17. Frank G. Slaughter, "Freud in Turpentine," *New York Times Book Review*, October 31, 1948: 48; Herschel Brickell, "A Woman Saved," *Saturday Review*, November 6, 1948: 19.

Grateful acknowledgment is made to Princeton University Libraries, Charles Scribner's Sons Archives.

Have You Read?
More by Zora Neale Hurston

JONAH'S GOURD VINE

Zora Neale Hurston's first novel tells the story of John Buddy Pearson, a young minister who loves too many women for his own good even though he is married to Lucy, his one true love. In this sympathetic portrait of a man and his community, Hurston shows that faith, tolerance, and good intentions cannot resolve the tension between the spiritual and the physical.

THEIR EYES WERE WATCHING GOD

The epic tale of Janie Crawford, whose quest for identity takes her on a journey during which she learns what love is, experiences life's joys and sorrows, and comes home to herself in peace. Her passionate story prompted Alice Walker to say, "There is no book more important to me than this one."

MULES AND MEN

The fruit of Hurston's labors as a folklorist and anthropologist, this celebrated treasury of black American folklore includes stories, "big old lies," songs, Voodoo customs, superstitions—all the humor and wisdom that is the matchless heritage of American blacks.

THE COMPLETE STORIES

This landmark gathering of Zora Neale Hurston's short fiction—most of which appeared only in literary magazines during her lifetime and some of which has never before been published—reveals the evolution of one of the most important African American writers. Spanning her career from 1921 to 1955, these stories attest to Hurston's tremendous range and establish themes that recur in her longer fiction. The stories in this collection map, in rich language and imagery, Hurston's development and concerns as a writer and provide an invaluable reflection of the mind and imagination of the author of the acclaimed novel *Their Eyes Were Watching God*.

TELL MY HORSE

This firsthand account of the mysteries of Voodoo is based on Hurston's personal experiences in Haiti and Jamaica, where she participated as an initiate and not just an observer of Voodoo practices in the 1930s. Of great cultural interest, her travelogue paints a vividly authentic picture of ceremonies, customs, and superstitions.

MOSES, MAN OF THE MOUNTAIN

Based on the familiar story of the Exodus, Hurston blends the Moses of the Old Testament with the Moses of black folklore and song to create a compelling allegory of power, redemption, and faith.

DUST TRACKS ON THE ROAD

First published in 1942 at the crest of her popularity as a writer, this is Hurston's imaginative and exuberant account of her rise from childhood poverty in the rural South to a prominent place among the leading artists and intellectuals of the Harlem Renaissance. It is a book full of the wit and wisdom of a proud and spirited woman who started off low and climbed high.

MULE BONE

Mule Bone is the only collaboration between Zora Neale Hurston and Langston Hughes, two stars of the Harlem Renaissance, and it holds an unparalleled place in the annals of African American theater. Set in Eatonville, Florida—Hurston's hometown and the inspiration for much of her fiction—this energetic and often farcical play centers on Jim and Dave, a two-man song-and-dance team, and Daisy, the woman who comes between them. Overcome by jealousy, Jim hits Dave with a mule bone and hilarity follows chaos as the town splits into two factions: the Methodists, who want to pardon Jim; and the Baptists, who wish to banish him for his crime.

African American folklore was Zora Neale Hurston's first love. Collected in the late 1920s, these hilarious, bittersweet, often saucy folktales—some of which date back to the Civil War—provide a fascinating, verdant slice of African American life in the rural South at the turn of the twentieth century. Arranged according to subject—from God Tales, Preacher Tales, and Devil Tales to Heaven Tales, White-Folk Tales, and Mistaken Identity Tales—they reveal attitudes about slavery, faith, race relations, family, and romance that have been passed on for generations. They capture the heart and soul of the vital, independent, and creative community that so inspired Zora Neale Hurston.

Don't miss the next book by your favorite author. Sign up now for AuthorTracker by visiting www.AuthorTracker.com.